Also by A.F. Brady

The Blind

For the unforgiven

"He who fights with *monsters* should see to it that he himself does not become a monster."

Friedrich Nietzsche, *Beyond Good and Evil*, Aphorism 146

NOW

Claire and I are sitting in the back of a black car, each looking out our separate windows. I see in the window's reflection that Claire has her hands clasped nervously in her lap, the strap of her handbag wrapped around her wrist. I methodically clench and unclench my fists. Claire reaches over my lap to lay her hand on my thigh, and I feel her looking at me with her sympathetic eyes, hoping I will offer her comfort. I readjust my sunglasses and fluff my pocket square.

As the driver turns onto Madison Avenue, a line of similar black cars appears with curbside doors swung open, and Manhattan's elite filing out onto the sidewalk. The burgundy awning offers little solace beneath the heavy afternoon sun, and sweaty husbands usher their second and third wives inside the building. I hear Claire whisper, "You ready for this?" as I open the door and hold a steady hand for her to take when she steps out of the car. I can't respond.

We are walking quickly down the carpeted aisle of the funeral home, nearly hip checking acquaintances out of the way. I don't want to talk to anyone. I haven't said a word since we left the house; there's nothing I know how to say. Claire is much more gracious than I am, and she's looking back over her shoulder to coo hellos and whisper apologies.

As we get to the first pew, I pull Claire by the wrist to enter the row before me, brusquely guiding her by the lower back as she shimmies down to the middle of the bench. She skids to a seat and I remain standing to her right. I don't need Claire right now, and I would rather she stay discreetly seated. I tighten my tie and survey my surroundings. I know everyone here, and everyone knows me. I can't remember most of their names, but they know who I am and they know what I've done.

I'm not looking at the coffin because I don't want to look at it and imagine its contents. Claire seems fixated on it. I glance quickly to see that it's tiny. It's tiny and white and lacquered. Juliette must have been five-nine or five-ten when she was alive; it doesn't look like she could possibly fit in there. On top of the coffin, white roses and orchids flow abundantly in a huge cascade. Just like Juliette to make everything perfect. Even her death is beautiful.

I scan the room, forced to lock eyes with people and nod politely, looking for someone in particular. Harrison Doyle, the New York County district attorney, walks through the door and gives me an inappropriately large wave. Harrison has been trying to get me to join him on his side of the law, but I'll never be anything other than a criminal defense attorney. He's afraid of me, and he should be. But right now, Harrison is not who I am looking for.

Even I can feel it when something in the air suddenly changes, and the mourners terminate their hushed conversations and slip into their seats. I watch as everyone around me sits, and finally I lay eyes on the person I've been waiting for. Jamie is walking through the doors with his chin to his chest, supported by Juliette's mother, Katherine.

Jamie looks up expectantly as he clumsily plops down next to me in the front pew. Satisfied that he has decided to sit with me, I take my seat and lay my arm over my son's shoulder. I think I feel Jamie's muscles tighten slightly underneath the weight of my arm. I imagine he must be uncomfortable, everyone looking to see how he's handling his mother's funeral, and he's not used to affection from his father. Claire reaches her hand over me to tenderly pat Jamie's knee. She knows how to do this better than I do.

"You okay, honey?" she whispers. Jamie nods, and a fat tear splashes Claire's hand. I watch the way they look at each other and make a mental note of what real sympathy looks like.

Some priest or minister or whatever he is begins the service and my mind wanders back to the time when Juliette and I were dating before we got married. She was vibrant then, jubilant. Before I broke her, she had all the life in the world.

I think of the first charity benefit we went to together. She had been planning it for months. I picked her up in a Rolls-Royce and brought her a wrist corsage that matched the rose in my lapel. She laughed her brilliant laugh and wore it proudly for the entire event, gazing at it, and me, while she was onstage, thanking the benefactors for their donations.

I remember the way the light left her eyes when she finally realized I would never change, despite her best efforts.

I'm pulled back into the present as the music stalls and Jamie rises from his seat. He takes a deep breath, sending shudders through his broad shoulders. The priest pats his back as Jamie places his notes down on the lectern in front of him and clears his throat to speak.

"Thank you for coming… My mother would have been so happy to see all of you here, continuing to show your support for her. Although today's event is not benefiting a war-torn nation, underprivileged children or endangered animals, we are here to honor a woman whose life and legacy are just as deserving of our admiration and protection."

I'm impressed with Jamie's words—I hadn't expected such eloquence from a kid not yet sixteen. But the discomfort is rising in my throat as I worry what he may have in store for his speech.

"I grew up in a single-parent home, but you would never have guessed that because Mom played both the role of father and mother to me for as long as I can remember. After Peter left, she picked up some typical male hobbies and took me to sports games, so I wouldn't feel deprived of a male influence."

This is exactly what I was afraid of, Jamie bringing up my absence and adding insult to injury by calling me by my first name. All the sympathy I had been getting from the crowd drains as they remember how I abandoned my wife and child. I tune out the rest of his speech and concentrate on appearing remorseful.

As Jamie continues his tribute to his mother, I imagine fond memories creeping into the minds of the mourners around me, and I turn to study the expressions on their faces. I've caught the eye of my ex-mother-in-law, Katherine. Katherine hates me, but despite our troubled history, she offers me a sympathetic nod. I mimic the nod back and robotically clasp Claire's hand.

When Jamie breaks down talking about how quickly his mother turned for the worse, I carefully observe the reactions from the crowd. I file these looks away in my brain for reference in the future. I wouldn't have to pay such close attention if only I could still conjure these emotions naturally.

But I haven't felt remorse, I haven't felt sympathy and I haven't shed a genuine tear in as long as I can remember.

The other two speeches are delivered by two of Juliette's childhood friends. I listen to the adulation and respect in the stories they tell; I laugh when the crowd laughs and bow my head when the crowd cries, just like I'm supposed to. When the pallbearers lift Juliette's coffin and Louis Armstrong plays, I pull out of Claire's grasp and escort my son down the aisle, closely following his mother's body. Juliette wasn't the first to die, and she wouldn't be the last.

"Jamie," I call when he finally exits the funeral home, "why don't you walk with us?"

Jamie extracts himself politely from a stranger's embrace and shuffles quickly to my side like a good obedient son. He is almost exactly my height, with the same thick, dark brown hair, mine developing dignified silver at the temples. Most of his good genes come from me.

Seeing a group approaching to offer condolences, I feel immediately exhausted and turn south on Madison Avenue, hurrying Jamie and Claire along. I don't have the energy to fake it with these people. Several teenagers, must be Jamie's friends from school, are huddled together smoking cigarettes on the southwest corner of Eightieth Street. One of them reaches out a fist as we walk by, saying, "Sorry, bro." Jamie fist-bumps him and nods with a tight-lipped smile as I pull him closer to me.

Claire fishes out a Kleenex from her handbag and dabs at the sweat beading on her upper lip. The heat doesn't bother me, and I rarely sweat. I think she looks sloppy using tissues, so I hand her the pocket square from my jacket. As we walk east on Seventy-Eighth Street toward Park Avenue, I see a taxi pull up in front of our destination, and I watch Katherine slither out with her third husband.

I stop walking, stalling our group—I can't bear the idea of sharing the elevator ride to the penthouse with my ex-mother-in-law and her shiny, replacement husband. Claire takes this opportunity to wrap Jamie in a kindhearted embrace. As soon as she pulls away, I follow suit and squeeze my son into my chest. I scan my surroundings for witnesses, but unfortunately, no one saw the hug. Disappointed that my shows of affection garnered no attention, I release Jamie and we walk the rest of the block to Katherine's apartment in silence.

I elongate my stride, leaving the other two behind, and quickly walk to Katherine's to get this charade over with. Claire and Jamie watch as I kiss both her cheeks. I hold her waist and look through her. If you didn't know me, you would call me sympathetic. Genial. Honest. Katherine revels in the attention, playing the part of mourning mother to perfection. I feed off this, and it helps me fall into the performance we put on in public.

Swarms of funeral-goers enter the palatial apartment, marching through the required rounds, commiserating with Juliette's family and close friends. Although we've been divorced for a decade, Juliette never remarried, so the crowd treats me as a grieving widower, and they all lavish me with hollow gestures of comfort. I delight in the attention from their frivolous posturing, wondering if all the kindness could lead me to have real feelings about Juliette's death.

Claire is keeping to herself near the bar, plucking bobby pins from her hair and arranging them in patterns on a mother-of-pearl coaster. Surprised by my approach, she stammers to attention, yanking the last pin from her hair, causing it to cascade down her shoulders.

"Have you seen Harrison?" I ask, not quite looking at her.

"He walked in a few minutes ago with Ethan and Elizabeth. I think he's still talking to Katherine." Claire is affectionately stroking my forearm, looking for some trace of loss or bereavement in my face.

"Charlie wasn't with them?" I muse hopefully.

"No, I didn't see Charlotte," Claire responds with disappointment. "It would be pretty inappropriate for her to be at Juliette's wake, don't you think?"

"Hmm." I swallow hard, momentarily picturing Charlotte in a lacy black bra. I shake the image out of my head and move toward Harrison, leaving Claire alone with her champagne and stack of bobby pins.

Harrison's fat, ruddy face lights up when I approach him, and he promptly puts down his cocktail, freeing his hands to pull me in for an awkward embrace. I hate it when he does this.

"Peter! How the hell are ya? So sorry to see you under these circumstances. Juliette was such a lovely girl. Beautiful. Just beautiful. Shame. Shame to see her go so young." Harrison keeps a sweaty palm on my shoulder and shakes his head. I shrug off his hand and crack the bones of my neck. I stand nearly six foot two, and Harrison is the only man in the room taller than I am.

"Thank you, Harry. And thank you for coming," I say, not caring at all. "I see you brought Elizabeth and Ethan. Charlie's not here?"

"No." Harrison shakes his head. "My daughter is in Phoenix doing some charity thing with kids over there. Something noble and important, as usual."

"Right, out there doing God's work, like Juliette used to do." I'm not listening to Harrison. Instead I'm looking at

Claire and Jamie and watching how their interaction seems a little too familiar, a little too comfortable.

"Seriously, now, you all right?" He seems to be attempting genuine sympathy. "Everything working out with the custody stuff?"

"Custody shouldn't hit any snags. There are details to work out with Juliette's estate but all that is tied up in trusts..." I begin moving away from him, terminating the conversation. I approach Claire and Jamie to investigate whatever's going on with them.

I watch several times as Claire stops herself from leaning over to pet Jamie's hair like a mother would. Jamie has Juliette's narrow angular features positioned on my strong-chinned, high-cheekboned face. Like his hair, his eyes are mine, a striking hazel-green, with emerald rings rimming the iris and gold flecks scattered inside. Good genes.

"Hey, kiddo," I say, mimicking the family sitcoms I feel I should emulate in this situation, "how's it going?"

"It's fine," Jamie responds, dropping his head to his chest. "I'm okay."

"You need any help getting ready to move into my place?" But I'm not listening to Jamie's response. And I'm not listening when Claire tells me to stop touching her ass in public. I would like to listen and attend to my family, but I just can't bring myself to care.

THEN

We met while I was working for a prestigious law firm. I had graduated first in my class from Columbia Law and was offered ludicrous starting salaries and promises of professional distinction at many firms across the city. I was quickly bored with the work; the courtroom wins came easily to me, and I didn't feel the clientele was bringing me the sort of challenge or notoriety I was looking for.

I was working toward a better future for myself and was open to exploring all avenues, so I accepted an invitation to a talk and reception given by Eileen Cutler, one of the foremost environmental lawyers in New York. As it turned out, Juliette had wrangled a ticket to the event, having spent years following Eileen's work as she fought against dirty corporations.

The reception was held at the Lotos Club, and as soon as I caught my first glimpse of Juliette, I was drawn to her. She listened intently to Eileen regaling us with stories of fighting the establishment, and I could plainly see that Juliette was passionate about just the sorts of things I cared nothing about. She was an environmentalist, a humanitarian, a woman obsessed with saving.

I was singularly focused on getting away from my upbringing, making a name for myself and never again feeling the way I felt growing up. I wasn't getting any of that from the law firm I worked at, and I had come to the event that night to see if I could find some people who could help me achieve my dreams of getting to the top. I was seeking wealth, respect, and above all else, I wanted to be unforgettable. Juliette seemed clearly on her way to just such a destiny, and I wanted her beside me.

"You seem enthralled," I said, startling her with my approach as I sidled up behind her.

"Oh. Yes, I've been a big fan of Eileen's for years. Such important work. Are you a fan, as well?" She was bold and shy at the same time.

"Becoming a fan. This is my first time hearing her speak. I'm not very familiar with her work." I stretched out my hand to her. "Peter Caine," I introduced myself, trying to create a more personal nature for the conversation.

"Juliette." She smiled and shook my hand. She didn't tell me her last name. I couldn't have known who her father would turn out to be.

As luck would have it, she didn't have plans after the talk, so I offered to take her out for something to eat. Still high from the encounter with her idol, she agreed, and we wandered east toward a hole-in-the-wall dumpling place she suggested. We sat side by side at the tiny bar, and she ordered for both of us.

"So, you're a defense attorney, you're twenty-eight years old and you're *not* from New York." She summarized our discussion, smiled and delicately popped a dumpling in her mouth.

"What makes you think I'm not from New York?" I asked.

"You stopped at every light and didn't jaywalk once. New Yorkers don't stop at lights."

"It's that obvious, huh? No, I'm *not* from New York." I had been developing the story of my past since before I started college, spending much of my time testing out details about my family before I settled on a suitable series of fabrications. "I'm kind of from all over the place," I told her.

"Army brat?" she asked, seeming genuinely interested.

"Not quite, no." I never went for the military-upbringing story. I feared it had too much of a blue-collar bent and it could alienate me from the influential people I was trying to fall in with. "My father was an art dealer, and we spent most of my childhood living in different countries in Europe."

"Oh, wow. That sounds interesting."

"It was." I tried to conjure up images of old European cities in my head. "What about you? Did you grow up in New York?" I steered the conversation back to her.

"Yes, born and raised in Manhattan." She turned her chair to face me. "Tell me what it was like living around Europe. Did you have a favorite place?" She seemed to want to keep the spotlight off her background just as much as I wanted to keep it off mine.

"I look back now and realize it was very glamorous when you think about it from an outside perspective, but it was hard for a kid." I'd practiced these lines. "I went to excellent schools, but I never stayed at the same one for more than a couple of years, didn't make lasting friendships and I was always somewhere I didn't know the language." These quick, heartstring-tugging snippets would provide just enough information for people to find me intriguing and sympathetic.

I took a dramatic pause and sipped from a green tea that Juliette had ordered for me.

"That's so lonely," she said with compassionate eyes. "Do you have any siblings?"

"No, it was just me and my parents. Definitely a lonely time." Although the story isn't true, the sentiments were. I *did* have a lonely upbringing, but it wasn't in Europe and it wasn't because I didn't have siblings.

The evening felt easy and natural, despite me telling her manufactured stories. She told me how she came to follow Eileen Cutler's career, and I told her of my dreams to be a high-powered defense attorney. I found her charming as she discussed her passion for helping others, and her work to open her own charitable organization. She seemed to imply family connections and money but kept the details guarded, and I didn't pry.

"Do you have any idols in your field?" she asked me, after gushing over Eileen. "Seems a difficult business to keep one's integrity."

"Maybe. But I find being a defense attorney quite honorable. The justice system hinges on the belief that lawyers are fighting for the rights of their clients, but often defense attorneys are underdogs in the fight." I turned my body to face her. "With my talents and abilities, I am simply serving to even the playing field. And yes, I do have an idol in my business."

"Tell me about him." She looked at me kindly. "I'm interested to hear your perspective."

"Ever since I wrapped my mind around going into criminal defense, there's one man whose career just blows everyone else's away. He's a legend in the business, and I met him at an event before I graduated." The excitement was rising in my voice. "It was Christmastime, and my cohort was invited to a big party hosted by different law firms. All the big names were there, as well as representatives from the pub-lic defenders' offices and the DA's office. I was first in my class, and I knew many of the lawyers were there to talk to me specifically."

Juliette seemed impressed, listening intently as she ate.

"This lawyer—my hero—was known and feared, having beaten many of the other lawyers who were there in court battles, and my classmates were practically starstruck when they noticed him standing by the entrance. He called my name—'Caine,' he said, and he didn't even look at me as he said it, he just lifted a glass of scotch in my direction."

Juliette's head bounced in a slow, methodical nod. "He knew your name?"

"Most of the lawyers did, yes." I suddenly felt reticent. I didn't want Juliette to get the impression that I was gloating. "They do their research before recruiting events."

"That must have been a thrill for you."

"Oh, absolutely. I was nervous and excited when I ap-proached him. He just handed me the scotch, picked up his martini glass and then turned and walked to a corner away from everyone. I followed him. I didn't really know what to do. I mean, I've been admiring this guy's career since col-lege, and I couldn't believe he was there to talk to *me*. Then he downed his whole drink in one sip and asked me if I was ready to give up all the bullshit."

"Gin?" Juliette asked.

"What?"

"Never mind. What was he talking about?" Her tone was deliberate, knowing.

"He pointed at the rest of the lawyers in the room and told me that they were all there to fawn over me, and if I was seri-ous about my career, I would call him instead. He asked me if I was ready to realize my talents and rise to the top." I re-

23

called the event with embarrassment. "All I had ever wanted to do was meet this guy and impress him, and when he was standing in front of me, I had no idea what to say."

"So, what *did* you say?"

"I told him I was willing to take any opportunity he was willing to give me. Looking back, now I see why he was immediately turned off. He told me that I was still soft, and I should call him when I toughened up. He put his card on the corner of a cocktail table and walked out without saying another word to me."

"Did you ever call him?" She had turned to face me and was studying my eyes.

"His card didn't even have a number on it. It was just his name. Like he was leaving me a challenge to go and find him, like that would prove that I was ready to take him up on his offer."

"And?" she asked excitedly.

"Well, truth be told—" I looked around us for eavesdroppers, then leaned in conspiratorially "—I tracked down his number months ago, and we're opening a firm together. I'm keeping it hush-hush for now, don't want to jinx myself before everything is finalized."

Juliette and I ordered a last round of drinks. She congratulated me and toasted the news that I was about to open my own firm with my professional hero. As I paid the bill, I found myself uncharacteristically drawn to her, and I didn't want the evening to end. I knew dragging it out beyond its natural conclusion would put a future encounter in jeopardy, so against my natural inclinations, I brought the evening to a close. She commended me again on my new business ventures and scooted her stool back.

"It has been a pleasure spending time with you, Miss Juliette, and I hope you will allow me to take you out again sometime." I stood and held my hand out to help her from her seat.

"Thank you, Mr. Caine." She bit her lower lip and smiled an unforgettable smile. As I guided her toward the door, she pulled a packet of matches from a bowl and scribbled her phone number inside. She raised her arm for a taxi on the corner and handed me the matchbook. "Call me," she said as a taxi pulled up in front of us. "I'd love to hear how the business turns out."

I watched the taxi heading uptown on Third Avenue until the rear lights blended in with the horizon. I called her the next day, and thus initiated the beginning of her end.

NOW

Everything feels status quo, not unlike any other day of my life, despite cremating my ex-wife and becoming the sole guardian to my estranged teenage son. But every person I pass looks at me a little closer, stays and chats a little longer, compassionately touches my shoulder, as if these changes were something drastic. Anna, my assistant, hands me my morning coffee as I pass her in the hallway, and a junior partner whose name I've forgotten blocks the path to my office.

"So sorry to hear about your wife, Peter," he says to me. "I hear she was a wonderful woman."

"Ex-wife," I correct as I push past him and continue down the hall. As a man known to not need sympathy, let alone accept it, I can't understand why my colleagues would still offer condolence for the loss of my ex-wife. I reach the door to my office, and I see Sinan walking toward me. I leave the door open for him to come in.

Sinan Khan, a Turkish lawyer from London, has been living in New York and making a killing as a defense attorney since the mid-1990s. Marcus brought him on to Rhodes & Caine almost as soon as we had formed. Sinan and I share the same moral flexibility, paired with a seemingly bottomless depth of knowledge of the law. He understands me.

"Got some stuff for you," Sinan declares in his baritone British voice, sidling up to my desk. "I have the case files from that custody thing I tried last year. I think you can use the same case as precedent in your kidnapping trial. It's a tiny loophole—I'm saying *ants* can't squeeze through it—but you should be able to sell it." He tosses the files onto my desk. "And Anna was about to walk in here with this stack of nonsense—" he flaps a bunch of envelopes in my face "—so I'll just leave them on your bookcase next to the Oban."

"Thanks. Sit, have a drink." I wave at a large leather chair in the corner of my office.

"Drink? It's 8:20 in the morning." Sinan oozes sophistication.

I look up at him and smile. "You Muslims and your prohibitions."

"Mmm," he sneers. "I have something else for you, as well." Sinan reclines in the leather chair and fiddles with a marble chessboard on the table next to him. "A blast from your past is on his way back out into the world."

"Back *out*? When did I ever have a client who went *in*?" I run my fingers through my hair, knowing full well to whom Sinan is referring.

"You should know *exactly* who I'm talking about, especially since he stands pretty much alone in your guilty column."

"Bogovian?" I blurt when Sinan substantiates my fears. "You're telling me Stu Bogovian is getting out? Has it been that long already?" Stu Bogovian was a New York congressman with a penchant for sexual assault. He came from an outrageously wealthy family who paid his victims for their silence, leaving Stu to never learn any self-control. I can't believe he could be released so soon. Seems like yesterday he went to prison, not the nearly twenty years it's really been.

"Yes, love. Stu Bogovian is getting paroled next Thursday. Mark your calendar!" Sinan holds up his hands and twinkles his fingers in mock celebration. "You think he still hates you after all this time?"

"Back off, Sinan." I feel the ugly anger rising in my stomach. "Who's representing him now?"

"Some Harvard prat. But don't fret, darling," Sinan teases, "no one remembers that *you* were the one who couldn't get Stu off, and from the trial transcripts, it sounds like Stu had no problem getting off!" Sinan laughs and knocks over the white marble queen with a thin black bishop shaped like an obelisk.

"He doesn't hate me—no one hates me." I swallow the acrid taste of defeat. "He hates Harrison Doyle. And he hates that ADA twerp who put him away, whatever his name was."

"You remember the assistant district attorney's name," Sinan sighs, knowing I wouldn't dare forget.

"Someone who *cared* would remember his name." I try to focus my attention on anything other than the Bogovian trial and the birth of my vendetta against Harrison Doyle. Sinan grins at me and emits a low grumbling laugh, amused to know I still get flustered. I draw in a deep breath and wrangle my irritation.

"Are you coming to this cocktail thing tonight?" Sinan probes, changing the subject. "I'm bringing a very beautiful young man from St. Louis."

"You don't even know where St. Louis *is*," I say. Sinan,

brilliant though he may be, is hopelessly elitist and thinks America is made up of Manhattan and Los Angeles.

"This is true. He's dead from the neck up, but gorgeous. You should come tonight and bring Claire. She's kind enough to talk to my beautiful St. Louis boy, so I won't have to." Sinan smiles and blinks his long eyelashes, trying to convince me.

"Sorry, my friend, I won't be able to get Claire to butter up your plaything for you. I'm not going to the party. I have drinks with Harrison tonight."

"Why do you continue to spend time with that terminally classless man?"

"He's useful," I say. "We should have him in our pocket." My nerves settle as I remind myself that I am in control, and Harrison's time at the top is limited. "And *you* should be facilitating these kinds of relationships, too." I wave a gold pen in Sinan's direction. "Not just lapping up the affections of impressionable Missourians."

"I bet he's going to rub the Bogovian thing right in your face tonight. Try not to lose your temper and knock him out."

THEN

Juliette and I went on four dates before I found out who her father was. Each time I picked her up at her apartment, she was already waiting for me in the lobby, so I never had to announce myself to her doorman and ask for her last name. It was over brunch at Union Square Cafe that I finally made the connection while I told Juliette of the first major case I was working on at my new firm.

"We were hired to represent Congressman Stuart Bogovian," I began. "It's just the kind of case we need to get noticed quickly." I explained to Juliette that since the firm was still new, having such a high-profile case right off the bat would get us the notoriety we were looking for. My partner, Marcus Rhodes, had been working for himself for decades, so he brought along a caseload as well as his reputation. I wasn't able to bring any of my clients from my previous firm, so when we were called about Bogovian, Marcus encouraged me to take on the case.

Bogovian was rich, slippery and completely unaffected by the expected behavior of decent society. Entitled to the degree that he viewed people as property, he never encountered a problem he couldn't pay his way out of. He had been charged with assault and attempted rape in the first degree. Allegedly, he pinned an intern between his desk and bookcase, tied her arms and stripped her of her clothes, intending to rape her, but she broke free and escaped.

I didn't want to share too much information about the case with Juliette, even though it was already in the news. I worried that she would get the wrong impression of me and the work I was doing if she saw the people I represented as monsters who didn't deserve freedom. I wanted her to see that they were people who required the best defense just like anyone else, and I was hired to uphold the law, plain and simple.

She already seemed to be getting uncomfortable when I talked about work; leaning away from me, responding with one-word answers and not really engaging. I wanted to assure her that I was one of the good guys, despite my profession's reputation.

"You're going to be the congressman's defense attorney?" she asked, not making eye contact.

"Yes," I said cheerfully. "Marcus and I agreed that I should take the lead on Mr. Bogovian's case."

"Your partner's name is Marcus?" She looked at me curiously, a forkful of salad balanced in front of her mouth.

"Yes, Marcus Rhodes. I'm sure you've heard of him."

Juliette let out a single burst of laughter. "Yes, I've heard of him," she snorted. "Marcus Rhodes is my *father*."

"Your father?" I balked. I should have known; her smile seemed so familiar. I was almost jealous. I looked up to Marcus, nearly regarding him as a father figure, much more so than my actual father. I almost felt that I wanted to keep him for myself and not share him with Juliette. "He didn't tell you he was starting a new partnership? You couldn't have thought it was a coincidence?"

"No, he doesn't involve me in his business life. I had no idea he was starting something new." She shook her head, seeming disconnected.

"I'm sure I've mentioned his name before today. Didn't you know I was talking about him?"

"Honestly, no. When you told me he left a card with no number, that sounded like a move my father would pull, but I didn't know for sure." She ate her salad as if this realization were no big deal, while I felt like the news was prodigious. I was working with Marcus Rhodes and dating his daughter. This was the world I was supposed to be in. Everything was beginning to feel right.

"I can't believe you're Marcus's daughter," I marveled. "What a serendipitous coincidence."

Still seeming a bit uneasy, she agreed, amazed that the world could be so small. "You're sure you know what you're doing getting involved in a case like this with my father?"

"Yes, absolutely. I've always wanted to have a mentor like your father, and I'm certainly ready to take on whatever Harrison Doyle throws at me."

Juliette held her glass up to me as if to toast my goals. I didn't think twice about her question as to whether or not I was prepared to take on the case. I felt unstoppable, and I was sure I could handle the DA.

Harrison Doyle was in his first term as district attorney, and he put a viper of an ADA on the Bogovian case, making sure he made a splash in the headlines right off the bat. That viper went by the name Eric Gordon, and he was intolerable. Both Gordon and Doyle seemed obsessed and pulled out all the stops, ethical and unethical, to ensure a win for the prosecution.

I allowed my professional ambitions to cloud my better judgment. Had I known what was going to happen, I never would have tried the Bogovian case, and I never would have developed the bad blood with Harrison Doyle.

NOW

Harrison is standing at the Four Seasons bar, waiting impatiently for me to arrive. Every time I see him, I have to actively suppress the memory of him humiliating me after the Stu Bogovian trial. I don't like Harrison, and I never have, but over the years, he has been hounding me to be his friend, even going so far as to offer me jobs with outrageous perks and benefits at the district attorney's office. He's not trying to make up for what he said after the Bogovian trial; he's trying to keep my mouth shut.

When I spot him at the bar, I see two empty glasses sitting in front of him while he works on his third drink. I cross the room, nodding hellos to men in suits at various tables. Some leggy supermodel-type stops me before I reach Harrison, kissing my cheeks three times. She must be one of the French ones. I grasp her by the waist and then release her, barely stopping to take the time.

Harrison pulls me in for a strong handshake.

"I'm having vodka. I think it's my third or fourth by now, not that anyone's counting. What are you gonna have, Pete?"

I recoil and wipe my hands on a handkerchief. Instead of allowing him to place my order, I lean behind him and ask for a single malt scotch from a bartender I know but whose name I have long forgotten.

The only reason I am here, as I tried to explain to Sinan earlier, is to remind Harrison that I have all the ammunition I need to take him down and ruin his reelection bid, and that it's in his best interest to stay in line. So, I play with him now and again. I know he'll get drunk and ask me to come to the DA's office, his typical move to try to settle the bad blood between us. He wants me in his pocket. With me as his underling, he would gain control, and I won't allow him to take away the power I have over him.

He thinks if he shows me affection and professional courtesy I'll forget what he did to me, and I'll forget the things I know. But I have no plans of joining the DA's office and becoming complicit in Harrison's dirty work.

I lean against the bar and look anywhere but at him and his droopy, drunken eyes. He is tuned into my every move, like a schoolgirl with a crush.

"Pete, Pete," Harrison is saying. I ignore him, not even bothering with one-word answers, sipping my drink and scanning the room for more interesting company.

"Nice work on that assault case last week, by the way. Didn't think you'd be able to pull that one off, not even *you*." He plies me with faux sincerity and compliments. I'm beginning to feel nauseous.

"Not even me?"

"I mean, the guy had the gun in his possession, right? With

her blood on the handle? You really have a way with overcoming physical evidence."

"Mmm-hmm." I swirl the ice cubes in my drink.

"Pete, I asked you here tonight because we've got to talk about my offer. I need you now more than I ever have."

Harrison is covering his ass, and I can see right through him. When he gets worried that I'll jeopardize his career ambitions, he invites me out and tries to entice me into submission, but he can't acknowledge this. If he admits that he's scared of what I know, he's essentially admitting he has something to hide. It's amusing for me sometimes, keeping up this cat-and-mouse game, watching him squirm.

"I've said it before, but clearly you don't listen, so I'll say it again." I don't even bother to look at him. "I am not, *ever*, going to work for you at the DA's office."

But again, he isn't listening. "Pete, I'm up for reelection. You know this. The campaign is strong, but I need someone like you—some soulless bastard like you—who can win cases without even getting out of bed in the morning. Use your talents to clean up the streets. Put the bad guys behind bars instead of defending them. Come on. What can I do to convince you?"

If I work at the DA's office, then I'll be complicit in his illicit dealings, and I won't have a leg to stand on if I want to roll over and expose the things I know.

I laugh right in his fat face. "Nothing, Harry. There's nothing you can do to convince me. If I were to go to your side, I would take your job. I'm not working under you or anyone else. We've been having this argument for years and I'm tired of it." Already sick of his drivel after just one drink, I throw my black card onto the bar behind Harrison's hulking form.

Harrison tries to steady himself on the corner of the bar and instead his elbow slips, and he barely catches himself on the seat of a barstool. "Jesus, Harry, you're in public." I quickly scan the room for onlookers, trying to ensure no one sees me with this classless mess. "People know me here. They know you, too. Pull yourself together."

As the bartender hands me back my card with the tab, I flick away the plastic Four Seasons pen and draw a Montblanc from my jacket pocket. I leave an enormous tip, hoping to keep the bartender's mouth shut when it comes time to gossip about drunken bigwigs.

"I need you, Peter. The ADAs have no fight in them, no spark. It's all perfunctory. No one grabs the bull by the horns like you do. I can guarantee you'll take my position when I retire. I only want one more term, make it five total." Harrison pulls my lapels. "Come on, Peter, whatever it takes."

His desperation is becoming revolting. "Get home and get some sleep, Harry. You're never going to get me away from criminal defense, and you're *never* going to get me to work under you." I gently slap his hands away from me and lead him down the stairs.

"I'll fix the Bogovian thing," Harrison proclaims. "Now that he's getting out, it'll be in the media again. I'll make amends publicly, righting whatever wrongs may have come to you, and then I can announce that you're coming to work for me. I mean *with* me."

I glare at Harrison with raised eyebrows. I knew he would offer me some kind of recompense to sweeten the deal, but I didn't think he would dare bring up Bogovian.

"No," I manage to growl.

Harrison sways and bobs and I reach a hand to his elbow to stabilize him. A man of his size should learn to handle his liquor.

"Charlotte." Harrison shakes a perceptive finger at me. "I know you have a thing for her." He pulls his arm away from me and stares me squarely in the face. "Come to the DA's office, and I'll give you Charlotte. What more could you possibly want?"

Both bemused and taken aback, I let a smile stretch across my face. His expression remains cold. "You'll *give* me your daughter? How could you possibly do that?" I laugh incredulously and walk down the wide steps in front of me.

"I'll give you my blessing, to—you know—sleep with my daughter." Harrison stays two steps above me, leaning against the banister, certain this offer will be what turns me.

"I didn't need your blessing, Harrison," I sneer through gritted teeth.

Harrison's face registers shock before sliding into understanding. Of course I'd already slept with his daughter.

With a laugh, I saunter down the steps. Still grinning when I reach the landing, I look back up to Harrison. He's walking back toward the bar, unruffled, appearing completely sober.

THEN

Marcus and I had rented office space for Rhodes & Caine, LLP, in downtown Manhattan on Church Street, just north of Leonard. I walked to work from my loft in Tribeca, and as I strolled to the office one morning when the trial preparations for the Bogovian case were just beginning, I thought back to home for the first time in a long time.

I had lied to Juliette about where and how I grew up, and although I didn't quite regret it, it was becoming clear to me that she was more than just a girlfriend and maybe she should know the truth. I had buried my past behind a curtain of carefully designed lies, and I never pulled back that curtain.

Juliette believed I spent my childhood moving from one European city to the next, but in reality, I grew up in Vermont. Not the only child of an art dealer father and sophisticated mother, as I told Juliette, I was raised by my uncle Tommy and his wife, Lee, amid the chaos of their already overstuffed home and family. Lee was pregnant with her fourth child when they reluctantly took custody of me. I was only eight months old. As my uncle frequently reminded me growing up, they took me in because he loved his sister, not because he loved or wanted me. My mother was deemed unfit by the courts to care for me, and she was never married to my biological father, who disappeared after I was born anyway. So, Tommy was my only option.

I have memories of my mother coming around the house sporadically, always looking for a handout, some compensation for what she considered to have been a raw deal in life. She would complain that the state had taken her only child, but as far as I could see, she never made an effort to clean herself up enough to win me back. The visits always ended in Lee demanding my mother take me back or help to support me, which would send her into a tailspin of self-pitying and hysterics.

While Tommy kept me fed and clothed, and implored his children to include me and treat me as a member of the family, they all saw me as an intruder. In their eyes, I was a thief stealing food from their mouths, taking up time and space that would have otherwise been theirs.

Tommy was never really a father to me and certainly not a role model. He was a man who just wanted to get by, to fly under the radar; living a simple life, hopefully ending in a simple death, leaving a simple body to become a simple ghost.

The apathy was thick, and I felt suffocated. My whole childhood, I felt I was living in a house with strangers I didn't know and who didn't know me. I didn't fit in with these people. They didn't have friends, they didn't have opinions and they didn't have ambitions. I, on the other hand, longed for success. I wanted greatness. To be noticed, to be known, to be respected. I was steeped in so much nothing in that house, that I yearned for *anything* to fill the void. No one asked anything of me, so I asked *everything* of myself.

To me, the point of life was to be the best. Not second best, not in the top ten: *the* best. I wanted to have the best house, the best life and be the best at my job. Nothing less would ever be enough for me. I wanted to be respected by *everyone*. This became the only thing that mattered to me. This was how I protected myself. Be the best at everything I do and be in control of everything else. Everyone would respect me and adore me if I were the best.

And Marcus was just the man to lead me to the promised land I was looking for.

Marcus was savage in his ruthlessness. His pursuit of excellence seemed impossible to contain, and he stopped at nothing to become the best. Not only was he the top defense attorney in New York, he also led a personal life that I idolized. He managed to keep himself head and shoulders above the reputation garnered by most lawyers in criminal defense and was counted among the high-society sect. He attended exclusive New York City social events and was a sought-after guest at major benefits and galas. He led a full and ambitious life and earned his prestigious standing. He was exactly the person I wanted to emulate.

I saw my reflection in the glass windows as I arrived at my office building, and I could see that I was poised to take my place at the top. If I could follow in Marcus's footsteps, I could be the son he never had, and he could be the father I always wanted. I would finally find the place where I fit, and I could leave my humiliating past behind me forever.

Once I arrived at work, Marcus invited me into his office to discuss the details of the Bogovian case. We had already had two meetings with Stu Bogovian to hear his side of the story and start working out what kind of tactics we would use.

"I'm glad you're going to be at the helm of this one," Marcus said to me. "It's the perfect high-profile case to get your name in the papers."

"I'm ready for him, but he's a scumbag, Marcus. Going to be hard to make him look good." I arranged my notes in front of me, ensuring everything was well organized.

"No one's arguing that he isn't a piece of shit, and neither will you. In fact, you're better off *acknowledging* that he's a piece of shit. All you need to do is show that the girl is lying. Out for a payday."

"But all the physical evidence clearly corroborates her story," I began, hesitant to go to trial for what seemed to be an unwinnable case. The intern had run directly to a precinct and told the cops what had happened. Bruises, bite marks, ligature marks on her wrists; it all fit with her story.

"It also fits a story about two people having some good old-fashioned kinky sex, Peter." Marcus looked at me with disappointment that I wasn't immediately willing to challenge the girl's story.

"You want me to say she's lying?"

"Of course you say she's lying." He leaned over the table and growled at me.

"But he's *guilty*. We should be working on damage control, a settlement, something out of criminal court."

"We don't settle, Peter. And if you tell me your conscience is getting the better of you, then I was wrong about you from the beginning. These aren't *people*, Peter. They're cases. Cases to be won, not to be settled out of court. How're you going to make a name for yourself if you let your conscience dictate?"

The last thing I wanted was for Marcus to have second thoughts about our partnership. I shook the notions of settlement and loss out of my head. I wanted to assure him that he had made the right decision by bringing me on as his partner, and my conscience was not going to be a problem. My professional standing was far from established, and now that I had had a taste of the life I wanted, I was willing to do almost anything to stay firmly on the right path. I had been dealt a disastrous hand with the Bogovian case, but I needed to impress Marcus and he wouldn't accept anything less than a win.

At first, I struggled with demolishing the accuser's credibility. She may have been a perfectly good girl, and a terrible thing happened to her. But Marcus reminded me again and again that our job was not to care about the alleged victims— that was for the psychiatrists. Our job was to know every minute detail of the law, inside and out. Ethics and personal principles didn't have anything to do with criminal defense. I had to suppress my better judgment. I had to develop a thicker skin. This was when my morals had to get flexible, when my natural charm took on a whole new application. Peter Caine wasn't really born until the Stu Bogovian case began.

It's not that I *changed* when I went to work with Marcus; it's more that I was shown that some of my natural proclivities would be more useful than others; inclinations toward behaving callously, with sarcasm and disregard for emotions. Kindness and sympathy had no place in the legal world we operated in, and Marcus helped me to squelch those tendencies before they interfered with my career.

This is why he invited me to open a partnership while I was so young and still impressionable. This is why he pulled me aside that night at the Columbia Law mixer. This is how he knew that I would be his prey.

NOW

After Claire had returned from work, she spent the evening running up and down the townhouse preparing for Jamie's arrival. She had gone to sleep past midnight, her hair wrapped in a polka-dot handkerchief like the ghost of Rosie the Riveter. I went to the office before she woke up but left her a note on a piece of Rhodes & Caine letterhead, something that I thought she might find special: *Now you get to be a mother.* I signed the bottom of the page with my favorite Montblanc pen. I knew using the word *mother* would have a deep effect on her.

Claire had always wanted to have children of her own. She looked after her three little sisters as if she were their mother when their own mother was no longer able to care for them. She used to put her sisters to bed, and then listen at the top of the stairs while her parents fought. She heard her father gaslighting her mother—convincing her that she was losing her mind, imagining the things she clearly saw. He destroyed her with his cheating and lies. When her father got angry, especially when he was caught in a lie or left evidence of another woman, he would turn completely cold. He wouldn't speak to Claire's mother, not even a word, for days at a time.

Claire invented stories for her sisters to help get through it—her only outlet to deal with what she was witnessing—and she would call the stories the Princess and the Ice Man. In the stories, the Princess always managed to escape the clutches of the Ice Man and lived happily ever after with her three little fairies.

In reality, Claire's mother found a different kind of escape; she jumped in front of a northbound R train.

Claire had begged me for years to have children, but I was finished. Jamie would be my only child, and I made it clear to Claire that if she wanted children of her own, it wouldn't be with me. In our arguments about having children, she told me she dreamed of having the chance to do it better. To be the kind of mother she never had. The kind who stands up to a philandering husband. The kind who won't allow herself to be destroyed.

Now that Juliette is gone and Jamie needs a mother, he is her opportunity to be the parent she always wanted to be. It's almost too perfect—Claire gets to be a mother, and I don't have to deal with a teenager I hardly know.

I can't be bothered to pick Jamie up and bring him to my house, so instead I send an embarrassingly large limousine. Katherine's staff will be sure to help him load his belongings into the limo. Of course, I'm hoping to not be home when he pulls up in front of the house on Twenty-First Street. I called home earlier and instructed the housekeeper to welcome Jamie and apologize that I won't be there. I told her to make up whatever story she wanted about my absence, forgetting that Claire would be home from client meetings by the time Jamie arrived. Claire could have managed a suitable lie with no problem.

As it turns out, I mistime my return home, and I see from the corner of Twenty-First Street that his limo is just pulling up as I'm making my way toward the townhouse. I duck behind a boxwood topiary in front of an apartment building and watch Jamie exit the car. The driver pulls his suitcases one by one from the trunk, arranges them on the curb and carries them up the steps with Jamie lumbering behind.

Claire answers the door almost immediately and embraces him as he stands at the top of the stoop, pinning his arms at his sides. They walk inside, and I decide to head to a bar I go to when I'm not ready to play house.

I never wanted to have children so playing the dad role is always a burden. Juliette had wanted to be a mother, as I find most women do, and she and her father pressured me into it.

It seemed my family-man role mediated my professional reputation; clients often told us that they admired my ability to create a work-life balance. Little did they know I balanced nothing. After Marcus died and Juliette and I got divorced, no one was around to insist I play daddy, and it's not like I couldn't afford the child support payments. Jamie existed, and so did I, and until today, I hardly had to know about him.

I check my watch—6:43 p.m. I throw a fifty on the bar and trudge east toward my house. On my way up to my bedroom, I find Jamie and Claire sitting in the living room together, a room I hardly ever go into. They both startle and jump to attention when they notice me in the doorway.

"Don't leap, I'm not a monster," I say, attempting to soothe their fright with a joke.

"Hi, honey," Claire squeals as she walks over to me. Jamie nervously tugs at the hem of his shirt, looking down at his sneakers, shifting his weight from foot to foot. Claire wraps her arm around my shoulders and kisses my cheek. This isn't normally how she greets me, and although I'm not sure why she's chosen to put on a show for Jamie, I'm all the more relieved that she'd rather fake it than face the awkwardness of the situation.

"Did you have a good ride over here?" I ask Jamie, not knowing what to say to him.

"Uh, yeah, thanks for sending the limo." Jamie peers up at me to respond, and then quickly returns his gaze to the floor.

"Sit down, Jamie. You can relax in my house. I mean, in *your* house."

"*Our* home," Claire corrects. "You should feel comfortable in our home." She returns to her seat and makes a display of taking off her shoes and kicking her feet up onto the couch. They both have twitchy, uneasy eyes. They're looking at me like children with their hands in the cookie jar, and I can't see any reason for either of them to behave like this.

"Is anything wrong?" I ask, although I couldn't care less about their responses.

"I thought you'd be home earlier," Claire softly confesses.

"Yes, so did I, but I got stuck at work. Had to go over a million depositions for this trial I have coming up," I lie.

Neither of them responds. As I stare hard at Jamie, I see his eyes dart up at me and a flush coming over his cheeks. He knows I'm lying. I look into his face, trying to feel something. Trying to see if the presence of my son in my home will stir up any emotions.

I once again can't reach down far enough inside myself to pull up anything more than insensitivity. Jamie knows I'm lying, and I just don't care.

THEN

Still early in our relationship, I met Juliette at the carousel in Central Park for an afternoon date. She said it reminded her of her childhood, and she would often come to listen to the music and watch the children playing. We sat together on a bench, just close enough to hear the carousel and bursts of laughter.

"How is everything going with the congressman's case?" Juliette asked, her voice tenuous.

"It's going well," I lied, still fearful that we were making the wrong decision going to trial. "Your father seems very confident that we will come out on top."

Juliette sighed heavily and intertwined her fingers in mine. "What do you think is going to happen? Are *you* confident you'll come out on top?" She squeezed my hand and looked at me with a genuine concern that I had never experienced before.

"Honestly? No. I can't get into details with you, confidentiality issues, but I'm not really convinced that we're making the right decision. But Marcus has been in the business far longer than I have. I trust him, and I know he wouldn't lead me astray."

"Peter." She pulled her hand away gently. "How well do you know my father, really?"

"He's my business partner. I think I know him quite well, why?"

"He's a very calculating man." She stalled and stopped herself before saying any more. "Just be careful, please."

"What do you mean?" I was immediately intrigued. Somehow, I had managed to go on four dates with Juliette before we realized that I was building a partnership with her father, and now she was making dodgy implications that I was in danger. "What do I need to be careful of?"

"I wasn't totally honest with you when I said I didn't know you were opening Rhodes & Caine," she confessed with an apologetic look.

"I figured as much. How could you not have known?"

"No, I didn't *know*, my father never told me anything. He really does keep me in the dark with his business dealings. I mean that I had suspected you were talking about my father when we were having dinner after the Eileen Cutler lecture."

"Why didn't you say anything?"

"You seemed so taken with him, so hell-bent on becoming like him—I didn't want to ruin your perceptions with the truth."

"Juliette, what are you saying? What's the truth?" I wanted to listen to her concerns, but I couldn't imagine that associating with Marcus could be anything less than advantageous for me.

"I'm sorry. I shouldn't have said anything. I know you're busy preparing for this case, and there's no reason for me to throw a wrench in it. I don't want to compromise what we have going on." She smiled warmly, clearly trying to shift her demeanor. "I'm really enjoying spending time with you." She grabbed my hand again, this time with both of hers.

"Tell me," I said. "Whatever goes on between me and your father has nothing to do with what goes on between you and me. They are very separate relationships, and it's important you know that." I kissed her knuckles. "I'm enjoying spending time with you, too."

She expelled an exaggerated sigh and flopped back against the park bench. "Please be careful with him. I know how charming he is. I know how successful he is. But he's a dangerous man, and he's capable of…" Again, she stopped midsentence and began wringing her hands, leaning forward toward the children at the carousel. "Our relationship… It's not good. We were close when I was a child and he was just getting a foothold in the legal world. But he changed. He became so…cold and—and I wouldn't want that kind of thing to happen to you."

"What makes you think it'll happen to me?" Her sentiment was kind, but I worried she was telling me this only to keep me away from the grueling hours of work, and maybe taking out some of her issues with her father on me.

"You remind me so much of him. The way he used to be. He was so attentive and charming, like you. And this job was what changed him. It's like he lost his humanity, lost all sympathy and compassion." Genuine concern warped her beautiful face—she wanted to be heard.

"Don't worry about me." I patted her thigh, almost dismissively. "I understand that defense attorneys don't have the best reputations, but we're not all bad. I know exactly what I'm doing."

We stood and began meandering slowly through the park

together. I looked at her warnings as a sign of her affections for me, and I swelled with pride and excitement that this woman who I found so desirable was showing such an interest in me. I didn't heed her advice against Marcus. I wasn't worried about him.

One evening early on in the Bogovian trial preparations, Marcus took me out to the Penthouse Executive Club. I felt completely out of place—I never liked strip clubs much—but I didn't want to disappoint him. He knew the doorman and we were escorted to an elevated VIP room, with an unobstructed view of the stage, two couches and our own small bar and bartender. Two beautiful women were waiting at the steps to usher us up.

"You ever been here before?" Marcus asked me as we sat together on one of the couches.

"Not to this one, but I've been to strip clubs before."

"You like strippers, don't you?" He held an emaciated blonde with enormous implants on his lap and pushed her face away from his.

I was never particularly interested in oiled-up women being paid to dance for me; I felt sorry for them. But I nodded anyhow.

"Of course you do. Who doesn't?"

I looked around the club—dark, smoky, everything lit in purple and blue—and began to feel a sickness crawling up my stomach. Women all around me writhed and bounced and although they were putting on a great show, I couldn't begin to believe that they felt anything more than degraded in there. I looked at their faces, wondering what they really dreamed of doing. Wondering what could have come of them if they didn't find themselves in this place.

"You want a dance, Peter?" Marcus asked me, roughly swaying the stripper on his lap back and forth.

"I think I'd prefer just to have some drinks and watch the show, thanks." I held up my cocktail and tried to focus on the stage.

"Suit yourself," he said, and I heard a squeak of pain come from the dancer. He wrapped his fingers around the back of her neck and pulled her down to the ground. She stumbled but complied, and her head flopped against the floor with her lower half still partially sitting on Marcus's lap. When he stepped on her cheek with his shiny black Oxfords, I jumped from my seat and reached out to help her.

"Marcus—Jesus Christ!" I blurted. He stared into my eyes with a stony cold look.

"You want me to stop?" he asked, with mock surprise in his voice.

"*Yes*, Marcus, please let her up." I extended my hand to help her to her feet, but Marcus held back my arm. I had never seen him like this. He was my hero, my mentor, he didn't behave like this; he was supposed to be a gentleman, noble, a man of the law. I shoved Marcus's arm away and took the hand of the stripper, getting down on my knee to help her up. I was ashamed. I didn't want to be associated with him in that moment.

"Let *go*, Peter," he snapped at me. Conflicted, aware that my career and future sat squarely in Marcus's hands, I let go of her arm.

"Marcus, this poor woman," I began, not yet stifling my instinct to protect her.

"This isn't a *woman*, Peter." He pulled her back up, and I could see her wince. "This isn't a person—that's what I'm trying to explain to you. This is an object. A *thing*. The sooner you can see that, the sooner you'll be a real criminal defense attorney. Until then, you're just another hotshot upstart. Her pain and humiliation mean *nothing* to me, and they should mean nothing to you." He roughly released her, and she scuttled quickly down the steps. My breath caught in my throat. I was disgusted.

Marcus wiped his hands on a napkin and gazed at the dancers onstage as if nothing had happened. I looked at my mentor, this legendary defense attorney, and finally saw exactly where his success came from.

Juliette was right, and I should have listened to her warning. It wasn't his gentlemanly behavior and legal wizardry that made him the most successful criminal defense attorney in New York. It was his inhumanity that allowed him to reach the top.

And just as Juliette warned, it was the same inhumanity *I* was expected to achieve if I wanted to reach Marcus's level.

NOW

I am supposed to be playing the role of father now that Jamie has moved in, and since I skipped out on dinner yesterday, Claire demanded that I stay home and interact with my son instead of heading to the office on a Sunday afternoon.

"His first night was incredibly awkward," she says, "and of course it was. He didn't even eat dinner. He just went up to his room like you did."

"Remind me how this is *my* fault, Claire?" I say, still getting ready to go to the office.

"You should have been here. You should have welcomed your son on his first night in your house. You didn't make any effort at all." Claire isn't looking at me. In fact, she hasn't made eye contact all morning.

"I have to work, Claire. How do you think I afford to provide all of this for him? Sometimes I won't join you for dinner. You've always understood that. He's just going to have to understand it, too."

"Oh, stop it, Peter. I know you weren't at work. I called the office while Jamie and I waited for you, and Anna told me you'd left hours ago. Don't feed me your lies."

Caught but unconcerned, I continued to focus on tying my tie.

"He didn't mention anything about his room. I tried so hard to make it welcoming for him. It's like I shouldn't have even bothered," Claire pouts. She's not talking to me anymore, just speaking her mind aloud and airing her frustrations into the mirror. I watch her shake the negativity off herself, still determined to make strangers into family.

"Peter, please at least have lunch with us today before you go into the office. For me. I got your note yesterday, the one that said I get to be a mother now? Well, you have to be a father now. It's Sunday. Please. Stay for lunch." She turns and rushes down the stairs.

I stand on the landing outside my bedroom and wait until I hear the murmur of chatter in the kitchen before I gently make my way down the steps to Jamie's room. I'm curious to see what it's like to have him in this house.

Jamie is impeccably tidy, and I am impressed with the way he's made his bed and folded his clothes in the closet. I walk around and look at the pictures sitting on the bookshelves, photos of me with bigwig CEOs on fishing trips, of me shaking the hands of politicians and criminals on the steps of courthouses. A photo I don't recognize is propped up against a frame; a picture of Juliette in a long yellow gown. As I lift it out of the way, I see it's obscuring a picture of me with my arm around John Gotti holding a giant fish. I lay the photo back in front of a different frame.

I sneak down the stairs to the parlor floor and hear Claire and Jamie chatting in the kitchen. I peek in through the slightly propped door.

"How have you been doing? It's only been a week since your mom passed." Claire doesn't look at him, busy shoving herbs and lemon peels into the cavity of a chicken.

I hear Jamie take a deep, ragged breath before responding. "It's weird. I mean I knew it was coming, you know? She was sick, but—I guess it still hasn't really hit me. I feel like I'm on vacation staying here. It doesn't feel like this is my house."

"Well, you just got here, sweetie. It's going to take a little while before you feel comfortable. Sometimes even *I* feel like I'm vacationing here." She peeks out from behind the carcass and grins warmly at Jamie.

I step into the doorway to make myself known before they can delve further into their irritating discomforts.

"Hello," I say, walking into the kitchen as if I hadn't been listening to them.

"Hi," they both respond at the same time. Claire's face flushes, and she busies herself with lunch instead of admitting to me that she's uncomfortable in my house. Jamie looks at me with the expectant eyes of a teenager. What could he possibly want from me?

"Jamie, welcome. I'm sorry I wasn't here to help you get settled yesterday. Big case I've been working on, I hope you understand."

He shrugs like he didn't even notice my disappearance.

"Good. I'm sure Claire took great care of you." I glare at her, silently letting her know her lecture was unwarranted.

"I'm making a feast for lunch here, Peter. Jamie didn't eat anything last night, and I don't want him to starve to death," she says lightly, obviously trying to change the subject.

"Fine," I say, using an authoritative voice I hardly recognize. "I've got some work to do, so I'll be in the parlor. Let me know when it's ready." I step through the threshold and sit down in front of the fireplace in the parlor. I pull some papers from my briefcase and open my laptop, but instead of working, I'm straining to hear what's happening in the kitchen.

Claire leaves the chicken to roast while Jamie tells her about his classes and friends at school. The details are boring, and I'm not hearing my name, so I tune out and focus my attention back on the computer.

After nearly an hour of mundane chatting, I hear the sounds of cupboards opening and closing and the clatter of plates and silverware. I focus back in on them to hear what they're saying.

"Do you like going to the movies?" Jamie asks her.

"I like watching movies at home—I haven't been to a movie theater in a long time. Ever since the bedbugs thing in New York, I got really grossed out by those places. There's a huge screen down in the basement with big leather chairs. It's really fun to watch down there. It's like being in a *clean* movie theater."

That's what I like to hear, something positive. At least I've provided a good place for movie watching.

"What kinds of movies do you like?" Jamie asks, classic teenage attempt to find common ground with a grown-up.

"I like everything. Action, comedies, romantic stuff that you probably hate. I like sports movies, too. My favorite is definitely *Field of Dreams*."

"I love that movie. Been watching a lot of the superhero stuff these days. Lots of Batman movies." Jamie's jovial tone turns pensive and my ears perk up. "I feel like Batman sometimes."

"You feel like a superhero?" I can hear the hopefulness in Claire's voice.

"No… I feel like an orphan."

"Oh, Jamie. I'm so sorry. You must miss your mom so much."

Now I'm getting agitated, and I don't know if I want to

listen anymore. I don't need to hear about Jamie's feelings of being orphaned. It's not *my* fault his mother is dead.

"Yeah, and I wish I knew my dad. It's like he doesn't really exist, you know? My friends tell stories about their dads coming to lacrosse games and taking them on vacations, and I can only tell them stories that my mom told me. And I know she made them up."

I stand and lean against the doorframe in the parlor to hear them, careful not to step on a creaking floorboard.

"What did your mom tell you?" Claire asks, and I hear the clattering of the oven door close.

"What a nice guy he is, and that person we saw on TV during big trials was just his professional persona. She said that he really loved me and wanted to stay with our family but that he didn't know how to. She told me about when they first met, and he would take her out on these fancy dates and plan these special surprises. She told me this one story about a scavenger hunt that he set up for her across New York City. She said he made her feel special. But *I* never saw him like that. He always ignored me."

I feel a twinge of defense brewing in my stomach as I listen to Jamie list my perceived shortcomings.

"One time he called me Charlie," Jamie adds. "Couldn't even remember my name."

Did I? I chalk it up to a Freudian slip.

"He's a good man, your dad." Claire begins her well-versed defense. "Just sometimes it gets lost under his...his armor. He doesn't mean to hurt anyone."

"Is he nice to you?" Jamie asks delicately.

I strain to hear how Claire responds. I know I'm not nice to her. At least not lately.

"Well, no, not all the time. But he can be. And when he

is, it makes all the other times worth it. When he's good, he's perfect, but when he's bad..."

Now I've had enough. I won't allow this conversation to continue. I loudly slap the laptop closed and make a point to rustle the papers as I shove them back into my briefcase.

"Does he even know how much he hurts people?" Jamie lays out a final question.

Before Claire can compose an excuse for my behavior, I walk through the parlor doors to join them in the kitchen. I can just see Claire quickly bring a finger to her lips and extend her pinky across the table. Jamie takes it in his pinkie and mimics her finger to his lips. I walk into the kitchen to see my newfound family sharing what they think are secrets behind my back. I don't tell them that I heard every word.

THEN

I left the club that night before Marcus did, sick to my stomach by his behavior with the dancer. Marcus's cruelty was deeply etched in his treatment of others, and as I walked home that night, I feared that Juliette's words were truer than I had given them credit for. I walked downtown, the air cool and fresh, my head filled with contradiction.

I had come to New York to become the next Marcus Rhodes. My ambitions were materializing before me, and I couldn't allow myself to be held back professionally because I took personal issue that my mentor turned out to be cruel and inhumane. I always knew I'd have to temper my soft side to succeed in this business, but I wouldn't allow myself to become like Marcus. He was just teaching me a lesson with the dancer, I told myself. A lesson I would be sure to learn sooner rather than later.

It took every ounce of my energy to dig up the dirt on the

Bogovian accuser. On the surface, she seemed picture-perfect. I asked around at her high school and her university down in North Carolina. I called everyone who might be willing to throw an old friend under the bus. A college roommate proved to be just the person I was looking for.

The case was making headlines well before we went to trial. Bogovian was portrayed horrifyingly, if accurately, in the press, and my job became harder as I was forced not only to deliver a case that would produce sufficient doubt, but also surmount the image the media had disseminated. Jury selection was a nightmare; everyone in New York had heard of Stu Bogovian and everyone had an opinion. Finding peers without preconceived notions proved incredibly difficult. I was meticulous in my preparations, acutely aware of Marcus's expectations of me.

The trial itself didn't take more than a couple of weeks. The alleged victim had a roommate in college who was willing to testify that she was into kinky sex. The roommate had told me a story about the girl being left tied to the bedpost in an encounter gone wrong, and she simply lay there, naked and spread-eagled, waiting for the roommate to find scissors to remove the binding. It started to seem plausible to me that this woman was nothing but a money-grubbing slut, like Marcus said she was, looking to extort a wealthy man. She had probably *asked* to be tied up, I told myself.

I brutalized the girl's reputation in court. I brought up every name, every story, every sexual encounter I could verify. After closing arguments, there was nothing to do but wait while the jury deliberated.

Marcus stood by me, reminding me to temper my sense of remorse for publicly destroying the intern's credibility. But mostly it felt like he was just trying to relieve me of human decency.

★ ★ ★

It took the jury four days of deliberation to come back with a verdict. When the jurors filed back into the courtroom and we all stood to listen to their decision, my confidence was so high, I had my celebratory cigar unwrapped and clipped in my jacket pocket. I had discredited the accuser. I had poked holes in the prosecution's timeline and evidence. Although I struggled with the moral depravity, I'd had to do what I'd done to get the win. I knew we would come out on top.

The foreman walked the paper to the judge, and as he read the verdict to himself, he looked directly at me. I could see the traces of a smile upturning the corners of his mouth. My confidence grew even more.

I stood up and pulled Stu's chair out for him. "Here we go," I whispered. Stu smiled and shook my hand.

The foreman returned to the bench, looked at the victim's lawyer as he spoke and refused to make eye contact with me or with Stu. "We, the jury, in the above entitled action, find the defendant Stuart Bogovian *guilty* of assault in the first degree." They went on to find him guilty of first-degree attempted rape.

The room suddenly felt warm and claustrophobic. I turned to look at Stu, who fell back into his seat and grasped his greasy hair with his sweaty palms. He tugged the bottom of my suit jacket and pleaded with me to do something. "What the fuck, Caine? I thought you said we had this in the bag?"

I couldn't choke out a word, watching Harrison and Eric Gordon explode with excitement as cheers rose from the crowd. My head felt stuffy and faraway, like I was watching the verdict on an old television through layers of static. Everything felt like it was moving quickly around me, but I was trapped in some slow-motion underwater world where I couldn't move or react.

The bailiff put Stu in handcuffs and court officers led him away while I stood, disoriented and confused, wondering if what was unfolding around me was really happening.

Stu struggled as the officers opened the door to exit the courtroom, and he screamed accusations and profanities my way. "You're a fucking fraud, Caine! You'll never succeed in this town, mark my words!" The door slammed behind him as Harrison and Eric walked across the aisle to gloat in my face, unable to contain their satisfaction.

Eric, smirking at me, extended his hand, clearly a faux-professional gesture.

"Can't win 'em all, eh, Peter?" He laughed.

I gathered up my papers and briefcase, nodded his way and muttered, "Well played."

Harrison, for his part, didn't even attempt to shake my hand or show any dignity. He just slapped his ADA on the back and led him away, looking at me with judgment plastered all over his face.

The reporters waiting outside the courthouse were merciless. Shoving cameras and microphones in my face, hollering questions as I shielded myself from their torments, walking quickly to the curb and jumping into the back of a cab.

Once home, my mind finally cleared, and the realization of what just happened began to sink in. The sickening taste of defeat didn't sit well with me. I poured myself two fingers of scotch to wash down the bitterness in my throat and turned on CNN to find Eric and Harrison on-screen. Harrison stood larger than life behind his ADA, and Eric took the microphone to speak. Before I could hear what he had to say, my phone rang, and I snatched it up immediately.

"Angry?" Marcus asked me from the other side of the line.

"Furious," I responded, though I was still more bewildered than angry.

"Good. That's the kind of fuel you need." He drew in a deep drag of his cigarette and I could almost hear him grin.

Just as I was about to respond, I suddenly understood what was happening. "You did this...you did this on *purpose*? You *knew* we would lose?"

"Of course we would lose, Peter. This was a completely unwinnable case. I've always known what you were capable of, and I'm not talking about legal skills." He sucked in another drag. "You needed to get your ego in check and you needed to access the useful parts of yourself."

"The useful parts?" A rapid succession of visuals passed through my head, and I remembered watching Marcus Rhodes, my legal hero, a god to my classmates in law school, gutting his opponents in courts without mercy or pity.

"The useful parts are the cold ones, Peter. The unsentimental, remorseless, brutal parts. That's what you need in your career. Put that sympathetic bullshit behind you and embrace the fury you feel right now." He was a monster, and I had sold my soul. Juliette's warning that afternoon in Central Park flashed like a neon sign in my head.

As Marcus instructed me to accept my spite and anger, I struggled to reconcile my thoughts. I couldn't accept that Marcus would set me up to fail and damage my pristine reputation, the one thing I wanted so badly to maintain. I looked up to him, and for me to learn from him and achieve his levels of success, I couldn't turn against him—I couldn't start to hate him.

"Why would you put me through this, Marcus? I did everything you asked of me. Why humiliate me like this?" I didn't want to whine or appear unappreciative, but I couldn't understand what we could possibly gain through failure.

"*I* didn't do this to you—Harrison Doyle did. Don't be mad at me, Peter. Get mad at *him*." I focused in on Harrison's pixelated face on the television. It wasn't Marcus who would be on the receiving end of my hate; it was Harrison Doyle.

I hung up the phone, in need of a distraction. I headed to Bull & Bear at the Waldorf, assured I was far enough uptown to avoid anyone involved in the Bogovian case. But, of course, with the luck I was having that day, Harrison was there, holding court at the bar. I dreaded speaking with him, though I wanted to hear exactly what he had to say. I craned my neck to listen.

"Peter Caine is an ineffective upstart, lacking the singular ability it takes to win cases—heart. Even his client called him a fraud."

Harrison went on to slander Stu Bogovian, spurred on by the gasps and guffaws of the rest of the lawyers. My ears filled with a burning heat, and the word *ineffective* blared in my head over and over again. Harrison Doyle said I was a feeble attorney, that I couldn't do my job. He trashed my reputation in front of colleagues and peers.

My humiliation turned to anger and was then replaced with a burning, malicious drive. Marcus was right—it was Harrison who put me in this position, not Marcus. Marcus was teaching me how to be the best, and I was going to get there. All I needed to do was follow Marcus's path, cold-hearted as it may be.

Ineffective? Never. I vowed to make Harrison regret those words. And oh, how the tables would turn.

NOW

This morning, Claire rises early, catching me as I put on my suit in my dressing room. It's rare that Claire and I wake up together, and even more infrequent that we share a morning coffee or breakfast. Even on the weekends, I always have something to do that takes me out of the house and away from her. She's used to living with a ghost; an indent in the other side of the bed, a whiff of aftershave as opposed to a real human being.

"Good morning," she calls, her voice foggy.

I pop my head through the doorway to look at her. "What are you doing up so early?" I cinch my tie tightly up to my throat.

"I wanted to make sure I was awake to send Jamie off to school before I go to work. Give him a nice breakfast." Claire yawns and stretches her thin limbs across the whole bed.

"That kid kept me up half the night traipsing around.

Floorboards creaking down there—it was deafening." I scrutinize my reflection.

"I didn't hear a thing. You're probably just imagining it." She takes a long sip of water and rubs the sleep from her eyes. "He's living here now. You have no more excuses to avoid developing a relationship with him. It's important—he's been through so much. He needs his father."

I don't respond. After their clandestine conversation yesterday, dancing on the edge of insulting me, I don't feel inclined to take parenting advice from someone who doesn't have faith in me.

Claire plods gently into her bathroom to brush her teeth. As soon as she shuts the water off, I close the bedroom door and quickly head down the stairs.

"What am I going to cook for this kid?" she says aloud when she walks into the kitchen. She's not speaking to me, instead posing her question to the inside of the fridge. I don't respond. She pulls out a package of bacon and starts laying strips in a frying pan. "All teenagers love bacon, right?" she asks into the pan.

The smell instantly fills the kitchen, and Claire inhales deeply while chopping vegetables for a quick frittata. She punches the button on the espresso machine and makes herself a coffee while she works. I keep my nose in the paper, making sure my presence stills her ability to return to a discussion about me once Jamie comes down.

Jamie appears in the doorway with his backpack slung over one shoulder.

"Morning," he says. He drops his bag on the ground and pulls up a seat at the round table.

"Good morning, Jamie." Claire smiles. "Did you sleep well?"

"Not really. I think I need to get used to my new room."

He looks nervously in my direction. "Sorry if I was loud. I was wandering around a bit."

"No problem," I lie.

"Bacon and eggs okay?"

"Great, thanks, Claire." Jamie stands and takes the plates from the cabinets and sets the table for breakfast. "It was good to talk to you yesterday," he begins but immediately stops himself.

"Yes," she agrees. She sips her coffee, and I think I see her shoot a wink his way.

"I walked around the house last night." Jamie fiddles with the knife by his plate, changing the subject from yesterday's conversation that I wasn't supposed to hear. "I couldn't fall asleep, so I went exploring."

"Where did you explore?" I ask, wondering if he'd been snooping in my things.

"Just around my floor and down here. There aren't any pictures of me in this house," Jamie says. "I mean, I don't want to be an egomaniac or anything, it's just there used to be so many pictures of me at home. And now I'm in a house with none. It's noticeable. There aren't any pictures of you, either," he says to Claire.

Claire frowns. Both of them look to me for explanation, but I've turned my attention back to the paper.

"No," she sighs. "No, there aren't. The framed photographs throughout the house were mostly gifts. Prints of Peter and whatever client he just successfully defended. He gets a lot of those as thank-you presents. It's just part of what he does for a living." She slices the cake-like frittata and brings Jamie two big pieces flanked by crispy strips of bacon.

Claire holds up the spatula in my direction and asks me if I would like a slice. She is looking at me as if she'd like me to leave. Like she has things to say to Jamie she doesn't want me to hear.

"No, thanks." I smile. "I've got to make a quick call in the other room before I head to the office." I hold up my cell phone and walk to the parlor again. I make a show of loudly speaking into the phone to no one and pacing the floor. Just as I expected, Jamie starts back in on the conversation, but I can't quite hear the beginning of what he says. I mumble a loud "mmm-hmm" into the phone and pull it away from my ear so I can listen to my son.

"Do you think he knows they're guilty?"

"I don't know if *all* of them are guilty," Claire responds, "but it certainly seems like they are. Peter once told me that it's not his job to care if they did it or not. It's his job to provide them with the best possible defense." I'm pleased to hear Claire defending me so beautifully.

"My mom told me about his cases sometimes—she wanted me to be proud that he was such a good lawyer. But then I would look up the cases online, see who he was defending and what they had done. The funny thing about all of Peter's cases—" Jamie chews a piece of bacon "—when his clients are found innocent, no one else ever gets arrested for the crime. So, it seems to me, his guy must have done it. But they still go free all the time."

Juliette seems to have spent quite a bit of time talking about me. I reflexively crack my neck in agitation.

"A person needs a proper defense. Our whole legal system is based on that notion. Innocent until proven guilty, right? And if the prosecution can't prove it, then it's the system's problem." Claire knows exactly what to say. I've trained her well.

"Do you ever talk to him about it?" Jamie's fork and knife clatter onto the plate.

"Not much anymore, but we used to. Peter compartmentalizes his life, and he keeps me separated from his business. I think it's easier for him to manage that way. He has to keep his emotions separate from work. It's just a by-product of the job. It doesn't make him a bad guy."

"And he keeps his emotions separate from me, too." Jamie lowers his voice, and I can hardly hear him over the grinding of my teeth. "I've never stayed in this house before. I've never even *been* here before."

Claire exhales heavily. "Give him a chance, Jamie. He can be a father to you, and I know under all this, he wants to. Please, try to give him some time to adjust." The faucet turns on as Claire begins washing up, and I can no longer hear their conversation.

I bark into my cell phone to keep up the facade that I've been on a call. As I walk back into the kitchen, I see the expression on Jamie's face, and for the first time, I realize how much we look alike.

THEN

The backlash from the loss came almost immediately. Harrison Doyle was eager to show the voters of New York that he had been the right choice for their district attorney and gloated to the media. I was at a café having breakfast, reading the paper days after the verdict was announced, and there were still stories about the trial because both Harrison and Stu Bogovian refused to let it die.

A *Post* headline read, "Invigorated DA Vows to Continue Success, Convict All of Manhattan's Criminals." Inside the article, Harrison was quoted as saying, "Ex-Congressman Bogovian was practically a career criminal, and until he was found guilty last week, he was getting away with countless heinous acts. His attorney, Peter Caine of Rhodes & Caine, LLP, had the reputation for being unbeatable, but clearly, he has met his match. In this new administration, we refuse to allow anyone to bully the courts, and justice will be done."

I felt assailed from all angles. It seemed no matter where I looked, I was being reminded of my first loss. In a television interview, I watched Stu rewrite the history of the trial.

"If I had an attorney worth his salt, I wouldn't be in this godforsaken place, wearing this hideous jumpsuit, trying to clear my good name." He sat inside an interview room at Rikers Island, inviting as many journalists as he could to come publicize his side of the story. "Of course I'm going to appeal the court's decision. And once the verdict is overturned, which it surely will be—" he nodded his fat, sweaty head "—then I will probably sue my former attorney, Peter Caine. He shouldn't be in this business if he is unable to properly represent his clients."

I spent those days and weeks learning what it felt like to seethe. I was enraged, livid, and I couldn't do anything about it. I had partnered with a man who was practically a celebrity and the face we put on in public and all the actions we took were scrutinized and dissected. My hands were tied, and I had to sit back and take it.

"You're breathing awfully heavily over there," Marcus said to me when I got to the office.

"I'm trying to keep from killing anyone."

He flashed a grin that filled his whole face and pointed to his bottom drawer. "Bottle of gin down there if you need it."

"I hate gin, never drink the stuff."

"It's good that you're feeling this way. You *should* feel this way. You've never lost before, and you're never going to want to lose again now that you know it doesn't suit you."

"You should have let me plead him out, Marcus. I don't need to go through *this* to know I don't like losing."

"No. I don't plead out. I don't settle," he growled. "You win and sometimes you lose, but you don't play it safe. You'll never get to my level playing it safe. I asked you to join me because I knew you had what it took, and this is just part of the learning process. Don't you *dare* make me regret bringing you on." He spoke to me the way I feared he would if I lost a case. But he wasn't angry at me for losing, I told myself; he was just teaching me a lesson.

Marcus told me he was going to limit the cases I worked on for a while after the media coverage died down. He wanted me to focus on other endeavors. "I'm going to keep you under the radar for a while. You're going to need to keep working, because I don't want you hiding under the covers like a scared little bunny rabbit, but I want you out of the media for a while," he said. "Get your bachelor pad in order, buy some suits, spend some time with Juliette. Spend some *money*, for crying out loud. You've earned it. But don't say a word to the press, and keep up appearances like you don't even know who the fuck Harrison Doyle is, you hear me? If he gets under your skin and anyone knows it, you're done. Show them all that nothing can get to you. Learn to wear the disguise, Peter."

"I don't want to step off the main stage and get lost in the background, Marcus. I didn't build this firm to be your number two. We are partners—equals."

He glared at me with his head cocked to the left and stood up from behind his desk. "We are partners, but we are *not* equals. Until you get into the headspace you need to get into, you're going to be number two, understand?"

"No, I don't understand, Marcus. You want me to be your partner, you put my name next to yours, you're encouraging me to take your daughter out, but still you don't seem to think I'm ready. I don't understand."

My frustration was overwhelming. Before I partnered with Marcus, I'd been undefeated in court at my old firm, I'd been swimming in money and living the high life. In law school,

I'd been at the top of my class, everyone had looked up to me, and now I was being made to lose cases, suffer indignity and public humiliation, and I was being told I was number two? This was supposed to be my ascent, not my downfall.

"You haven't *seen* success yet," Marcus said. "You think it felt good to win before? Just wait and see how it feels once we're 'equals,' as you say. Once you're up at my level and you know how to work this system, you'll be so high, nothing will ever bring you down. I know you're pissed now, and I know you don't want to have to go through this schooling, but if you want to get to the top, you'll do exactly what I say."

Once I acquiesced to temporarily stepping out of the spotlight at Rhodes & Caine, I found, with Marcus's help, it was easier than I thought to focus on life outside of work. He brought me to tailors who crafted me the highest quality bespoke suits and sent me to John Lobb to have shoes made. He introduced me to owners, maître d's and managers at all the important restaurants, and soon I became a regular, as well. I became more confident bringing Juliette out—I knew just where to take her and just how to behave. While a deep hate for Harrison Doyle and the feeling of humiliation still festered inside of me, I was able to distract myself with Juliette.

Juliette had just launched the Rhodes Foundation, a charitable organization she put together with the society and old-money connections she had through her parents and their friends. Juliette would personally research the plight of various unfortunate peoples, figure out their individual needs and throw massive fund-raisers benefiting the cause du jour. She was able to gracefully straddle the line between privileged child of high society and salt of the earth humanitarian.

I took her to Restaurant Daniel one night, excited to show

off the new connections I had made. It didn't occur to me that she would know the staff at the restaurant better than I did.

"Mademoiselle Rhodes," the manager greeted her, "welcome back. How lovely to see you again." He shook my hand with a sly smile on his face, and I was reminded that I was the new blood around here.

"Is that a new suit?" she asked me as I helped her into her chair.

"Yes." I stood back so she could see it before taking my seat. "Your father took me to a tailor to have it made."

"Looks very familiar. I think he has one just like it," she said with disappointment coloring her tone. Before she allowed herself to recede into displeasure about her father, she changed gears and I spent the evening listening to her regale me with stories about her work with the foundation.

"I went to Florida after Hurricane Andrew hit," she began. "I remember before I went, I had always felt like hurricanes were just intensely bad weather, and the devastation was exaggerated for the sake of television ratings."

I smiled, having had the same thoughts myself.

"But my God. When I got there, I was completely overcome. Everything was flattened, and all the street signs and landmarks were destroyed, so there was no way to figure out where you were or where you were going. There was nothing recognizable, and everyone wandered like zombies, lost, desperate and terrified."

"What took you down there?"

"I wanted to see firsthand what had happened, so when I presented to the board the idea of having a fund-raising gala, I would be able to speak from experience."

"But why bother putting yourself through that? Couldn't you have sent someone on your behalf?"

"If I sent someone else, I never would have known what it

was really like." She sipped her champagne and smiled at me. "I can't begin to describe to you the landscape. Everything was rubble. It was like standing on top of a landfill, nothing but anonymous, unidentifiable rubble. And people were desperately trying to salvage pieces of themselves, pieces of their lives, but nothing was left." She was becoming choked up at the memories.

What struck me was that she really cared. She would agonize over the well-being of struggling families she met during goodwill trips to places like Sarajevo after the war, sub-Saharan Africa during the AIDS epidemic or a gypsy camp in northern Greece. She told me about a time she doubled over in physical pain when she heard news that a beloved shelter dog had been euthanized.

"I'm going to stop before I bawl right here at the table," she said, elegantly blotting the corners of her lips. "Tell me about you. How is it going with the law firm?"

"It's going fantastically well," I lied, remembering to always radiate an air of success. "Marcus hired a new attorney to join us, a Turkish guy called Sinan Khan. Great guy, real character. He's been in the business a long time, recently left a big firm, looking for something a little more boutique. He's got an impressive record, and he scares people, so Marcus snapped him up as quickly as he could."

"Sounds just like my father."

"Sinan's been working some of the bigger cases for me. I decided to take on a little less work than I normally would." I lied again to make it look like *I* was the one who made the decision to pull away. I didn't want her worrying that her father was taking control of me.

"Oh? Are you busy with other things?"

"Well, I hope so, Juliette. I'd like to be busy with you." I kissed her knuckles and hoped she would allow me to spend more time with her.

"Would you?" she teased as she leaned in to kiss me.

From that moment forward, we were inseparable. I went to the office most days of the week, but spent my time there planning dates and thinking of ways to impress Juliette. Professionally, I was becoming indifferent to the nature of my cases, the plight of my clients and their accusers, disengaged from the emotional aspects, but with Juliette, I was infatuated.

NOW

Claire has been living in my house for eight years, but I still can't fully acclimate to cohabitating with another human being with her own will and own needs. The last person I lived with was Juliette, and I got used to my solitude in the interim. Claire didn't need to move in with me. She had made plenty of money on her own, working for a prestigious interior design firm. She wanted to live with me. Yet I still stumble over her things, crash into her when she stands between me and my destination and I can never remember how she takes her coffee.

When we prepare and dress ourselves for an evening out, we holler between rooms; Claire in her boudoir between the master bedroom and the master bath, and me fixated on my own image in my dressing room mirror. Just as we are doing this evening.

"He's never been to a benefit with his father," I remind

her, "and you're constantly saying that I need to develop a relationship with him, so why not let him go in your place? It's not like you enjoy these things." I tie and untie my silk bow tie, never satisfied with its position.

Claire is already in a full face of makeup, hair held in place with clips and pins while she tools around with a curling iron. She wears a flesh-colored slimming leotard, intended to smooth out any undesirable bulges even though she has none, unless protruding hip bones and delineated vertebrae are no longer in style.

"It's his first week with us—he hasn't even unpacked yet. You think he wants to go to a formal affair?" Claire calls across the rooms.

"Why not? He'd love it, famous faces galore."

"So, I got all dolled up for nothing?" Claire leans out the door to look at me, probes her hair and pouts.

"I didn't ask you to put all that on." I walk into her boudoir and position myself behind her as she leans over the vanity and puts on lipstick, teasing me with her ass in the air.

"You never ask me to put things *on*," she coos, smiling at me in the mirror.

I hold her waist with my left hand and lean back to look for a way to remove her leotard. There are no clasps, no zippers or buttons for me to undo, so I slip a finger under the elastic on her hip and slide it between her legs. Bending her down farther with my other hand, I glide her legs apart with my knee and pull the crotch of her leotard to the side. I control her movements while I unzip my tuxedo pants.

I can feel Claire's eyes on me, but I'm staring only at myself in the reflection. No matter with whom I'm having sex, my mind always slips back to that night Marcus and I went to the strip club. Every girl, every soft, slim body I enter, inevitably turns into the stripper at the club who Marcus defiled. If I don't look at Claire's eyes, I can pretend that I'm not completely indifferent, that she is special and loved, but in reality, Claire could have been anyone. She's disposable. Expendable.

Every time we have sex, I feel as though I turn inhuman. I become a robot; not violent, not hurtful, but mechanical, disconnected. My hips thrust back and forth, and I can see myself in the mirror, but I feel nothing. The physical pleasure I'm supposed to experience is buried underneath the idea that I am controlling another human being. That's where I get the gratification from; it's not about connection or intimacy, because I don't care. I *can't* care.

Once I finish, I pull out of her and leave her standing there, red handprints rising on her ass. I tuck myself back into my pants, zip up and return my attention to my bow tie.

"I'll tell Jamie to get ready," I say, disregarding the intermission in our conversation. Claire readjusts the crotch of her leotard so she isn't exposed, pulls a silk robe off its hook and wraps it around herself. I walk out of her boudoir to the bedroom and buzz the intercom in Jamie's room.

"You busy tonight?" I pause and wait for Jamie's response.

"Um, no?" He asks me more than tells me. "Just homework, I guess."

"Good, take a quick shower and get a tux on. We're going out."

Claire stands in the doorway and looks on as Jamie tells me he's grown out of his tuxedo.

"Don't worry," I respond, "you can borrow one of mine. We're probably the same size."

A peculiar look spreads across Claire's face as she watches me slip my antique cuff links through my French-cuffed shirt. She's not quite looking at me, more through me, and I tell Jamie I'll be waiting for him downstairs in fifteen minutes.

"Claire will bring the tuxedo to your room," I say before hanging up the phone.

Her inquisitive look turns dark. She pulls the tuxedo from my hand to bring to Jamie, and I can just hear her mutter, "Who am I living with?" under her breath as she leaves the room.

I reach into a drawer and pull out several masks to choose from. Claire and I have attended several masquerade balls and costume parties over the years, and we never seem to throw any of the masks away. I study each one, some feminine, silky and feathered, others simple and sleek. I pull out two and move to the mirror to try them on. I've worn one of them before, but the other, the white one, I've been saving for a special occasion. The smooth white mask covers the top half of my face, and at the forehead, above the small eyeholes, two large golden horns protrude.

I slip the mask over my head and it settles perfectly on my face. I'm reminded of a minotaur as I look myself over. Before I walk down the stairs to meet Jamie, I say loudly to my reflection, "Yes, Claire, who *are* you living with?"

THEN

It wasn't a year from the day we met before we were married. Juliette and I flew down to the Turks and Caicos, just the two of us, knowing exactly what we were planning on doing but telling no one. She had hidden her engagement ring from public view before we got on the plane, but as we looked out over the turquoise water, she slipped it on her finger. We rented a house on the beach and spent a few days relaxing in the sun, completely wrapped up in one another.

I wanted to keep Juliette happy. I was already elated that she'd agreed to elope and I wasn't forced to attend a wedding where I would inevitably have to discuss my upbringing, and why my family wasn't in attendance. We lay on a daybed on our porch overlooking the sea, and as if she could read my mind, Juliette started in on a conversation about family.

"Do you think we should call my parents?" She looked up at me while I stroked her hair. "If your parents were alive, I'm sure they would want to be here, don't you think?"

I was jolted with conflict—I had sold my story to Juliette. The story about my art dealer father, my philanthropist mother and their tragic and untimely deaths. I had told the story so many times since leaving Vermont that it had become true to me. It was only with Juliette that I felt like I was lying, and it gnawed at me. We were about to get married, and if I was planning on spending the rest of my life with her, I felt compelled to tell her the truth.

"Yes, I do think they would want to be here. But…" I paused, concerned that she would be hurt and upset that I had lied, but sure that if such a time existed that would be perfect for a confession, it was right then. "But we've gone our separate ways, and I can't turn back now." I started my revelation.

"Your separate ways?" she asked, confused but not yet suspicious. "You mean after the car accident?" She turned uneasy.

I sighed deeply, slowly responding, "There was never a car accident. As far as I know, my parents are probably still alive."

"What?" She quickly sat up and turned to face me, pulling off her sunglasses. "You told me they died in that accident when you were still living in Europe. What do you mean they're *alive*?"

"I know." I hung my head, embarrassed and apprehensive. "I know what I told you. It's the same thing I tell everyone. But it's not really what happened."

"What really *happened*, Peter?" The anger was rising in her voice.

"Nothing happened, darling." I tried to hold her, but she leaned just out of reach. "We just went our separate ways." I couldn't fully bring myself to tell the truth. I felt terrified of being exposed, bringing my humiliating past to the surface and letting her know that I didn't belong among her venerated peers.

She didn't say a word, but her wide eyes and furrowed brow told me to keep talking.

"I didn't grow up in Europe," I confessed. "My father wasn't an art dealer." I threw my sunglasses on the daybed beside me and rubbed the ache out of my eyes. "I hate where I came from, and I never want to go back there. I started making up stories a long time ago, and I never told anyone the truth after I left."

She softened slightly, a look of sympathy rising in her eyes. "Where did you grow up?"

My stomach burned with adrenaline. "Vermont. In Burlington. My father took off, and my mother gave up custody when I was an infant. I was raised by my uncle and his wife." I felt light-headed as I continued, completely unaccustomed to saying these words aloud. "They were dead inside. No drive, no passion. They floated through life and I couldn't stand it." I couldn't look at Juliette as I admitted the truth. I had buried the truth so deeply, bringing it back up made me feel like I was violently heaving. "I was a burden to them. They barely scraped by raising their own four kids—they certainly didn't want to have to worry about me."

"I don't understand. You grew up in the States? Your parents are alive?"

"It's hard to explain." I shook my head, frustrated. "My mother... I didn't know her. She came by once in a while, but she didn't take responsibility for me. She dumped me with my uncle Tommy and his wife. They were *dead*, Juliette. I don't know how to make it clear to you. They were nothing at all, just bodies with no souls, no vitality, no life inside them. They didn't raise me or teach me or discipline me. I just existed alongside them. They gave me *nothing*. Not a chance, not an expectation, not a modicum of concern. Nothing."

She examined my face, looking at me hard, as if she were

trying to find a sign I was telling her the truth. "Are they still in Vermont?" she asked, the anger in her voice waning.

"I guess so. I don't know. I left before college, and I haven't spoken to them since."

"And you never had any contact with them? They never tried to find you?"

"No. As far as I know, they were just as happy to be rid of me as I was to be rid of them. My cousins, Tommy's kids, they always reminded me I wasn't one of them, and I didn't belong. I didn't look like them, I didn't act like them. I was smart, I wanted to succeed in life. When my eldest cousin, just two years older than me, finished high school, I took off that summer. I was seventeen years old, I had worked after school to earn some money, and when I could afford to get out of there, I got a one-way ticket to Chicago and never looked back."

"Jesus." She gently scooted up beside me and laid her hand on my lap. "No wonder you left."

"Yes." I sat up at attention, surprised she could understand me. "Yes, I had to get out. I needed life, I needed to be loved and respected and *seen*. I needed to be up in lights, on top of the world..." Just as suddenly as I felt understood, it flipped, and I felt like I was right back in Vermont. I felt vulnerable and desperate for the first time since leaving Burlington, and I hated it.

Juliette looked at me for what felt like years before speaking again. "It all makes sense," she said. "No wonder you went looking for *my* father. He's the opposite of what you grew up with."

"Yes." I glanced away, afraid of being exposed, of letting anyone see that I did in fact have vulnerabilities. "I will *never* allow that to happen to me. I will never be nothing the way they were. I can only accept the best, be the *most* successful, amass the highest achievements possible. Otherwise, I just won't be a part of it. I learned to hate it, Juliette."

"And it's no wonder my father went looking for *you*." She stared out toward the sea in front of us. The breeze blew her hair out of her face, and I could see a pained expression. "He wanted a son, an heir. Someone like-minded, who he could mold into his successor. Someone exactly like you, who thinks he's the be-all and end-all. I feel like you two have been searching for each other."

"I was jealous when you told me he was your father," I admitted. "I had always looked up to him in that way, and I wanted my father to be like him. All drive and ambition, never satisfied, all hunger for the best."

She turned to me suddenly, stern and almost scolding. "But please tell me that's not why you want to marry *me*."

I pulled her onto my chest and stroked her long hair to help ease the tension. "I want to marry you because I love you, Juliette." I'd never said the words to another human being before, and they felt foreign and sticky coming out of my mouth. "It has nothing to do with Marcus."

Those were the words she needed to hear, to be reassured that we were both going into the marriage for the right reasons. Before the conversation ended, I made sure to add a final caveat. "One more thing," I began, "no one knows the truth about where I came from, and it's going to stay that way. If you ever repeat anything I told you, there will be trouble."

I realized my comments were bordering on threatening, but Juliette understood me. I had only scratched the surface of the truth of my upbringing, and I hadn't yet shared with Juliette how I got out of there and into the world where she found me.

Two days later, we had a small ceremony on the beach in front of our rented house and cemented our mutual commitment.

★ ★ ★

In the time since I had stepped out of the public's attention, Stu Bogovian had hired a different attorney to represent him during the sentencing and subsequent appeals, but Marcus made sure it appeared my absence was for the sake of my wedding and honeymoon.

"You want to get all the way to the top, don't you, Peter? There are steps to be taken, and it's a very delicate dance you have to perform to get where you want to be." As if he were raising a son, he was using me to proliferate his own legacy. "You lost a very public and very high-profile case, and your client has been sentenced to the maximum. You needed to get that ego in check. Your law school reputation and the name you made for yourself at that white-bread firm were impeccable. We needed to dismantle that a bit."

I seethed listening to him. I felt like he was treating me like a lost little boy, scolding me and putting me down. "I don't need to be publicly humiliated just to be put in my place, Marcus. I'm extremely good at my job, and I would appreciate it if I could get back to work on the kinds of cases I should be working on."

"Don't worry, Peter." He laughed a hearty, guttural laugh and slapped my shoulder. "The rest of this is going to be fun for you. There's no more losing involved. You're making the right moves now. Getting married was a very good step. People trust a married man, especially one married to such a humanitarian as Juliette. Her shine will reflect on you, and you'll fall in with the right crowd." Marcus's demeanor shifted in that moment, and he turned his back to me, holding his hand to his mouth.

"What?" I demanded, fearing his caginess. "What am I supposed to do now?"

"There are two things." He turned to face me but didn't

take his hand away from his mouth. "First, I'm going to give you some cases, and you'll have to win. None of the big ones—leave that to me and Sinan. You just have to keep winning and do it powerfully and without remorse. That's the way I've gotten to where I am today, and where you want to be."

I wanted to protest. How could he withhold all the desirable cases from me? "And the second?" I asked with teeth clenched.

"The second step is more personal, more private. Something I need from you because I never did it myself."

"Stop stalling, Marcus."

"I never had a son, and now you're here filling that role. And if this empire is going to last beyond my death and yours, we'll need an heir. You'll need to become a father."

NOW

Jamie and I ride in silence up to the Metropolitan Museum of Art, and I can't think of a thing to say to him.

"How are you adjusting?" I attempt, just as Jamie opens his mouth to say, "Was Claire supposed to come?"

We both grumble awkward half laughs, and I wave Jamie to go on, so he asks his question again. "Um, tonight, to this party, wasn't Claire supposed to go instead of me?"

"The invitation was addressed to me, and I was permitted a guest, so frankly, it's up to me who I bring," I respond. "And Claire never seems comfortable at these things anyway."

"Oh." He adjusts his seat and tugs at his sleeves.

"You're not uncomfortable at these events, are you?"

"Where are we going again?" Jamie looks beyond me, out the window as we continue north on Madison Avenue.

"The Met. We are going to a masquerade ball, a benefit for your mother's foundation. Didn't she bring you to these before?"

Jamie's face blanches. "Yes, I've been to a couple of Rhodes Foundation benefits before."

"Well, soon you'll receive your own invitations, and you won't need to be escorted by the old man."

I practically lunge for the door handle as soon as we pull up to the museum to free myself from this awkward car ride. I grab the two masks off the seat, one a basic black Zorro-style mask, and the white satin one with the gold horns. I slip the white one over my face and hand the other to Jamie.

A narrow hunter green carpet has been draped down the front steps of the museum, creating an exclusive pathway for the benefit-goers. Jamie slides on his mask and fumbles with his borrowed cuff links, as if he's worried they'll fall out. I hurry in front of him, ascending the stairs, periodically checking my Rolex. I can't stand being late, and getting my son properly dressed took longer than expected. We arrive, finally, with just fifteen minutes left in the cocktail hour.

This is a philanthropic event filled with New York social-ites. All the men are wearing tuxedos, and the younger women have on more jewelry than clothing. The masks range from cheap Halloween versions to massive feathered-and-bejeweled affairs held up on golden rods. The stick-thin plastic women are hard to differentiate, and all share the same manufactured smile. Hardly a natural face or body exists in my present company, but I'm scanning the party for one gorgeous creature in particular.

I navigate the crowd, stopping in for greetings among various groups.

"Hello, Senator," I say, popping up behind an elderly gentleman who is not actually in politics and his much younger trophy wife. "And how is your daughter this evening?" I say, kissing her hand and smiling. He gives me a jovial slap on the shoulder and she looks at me through glazed, unfocused eyes.

The cocktail hour conversations all revolve around thinly veiled competition over whose child is the most accomplished—who has been accepted to which Ivy League school, who was offered a modeling contract with Ford.

Jamie follows me as I insert myself into small clusters of guests for quick shallow greetings. "Alysia," I coo, wrapping my arm around the bare shoulder of a gaunt middle-aged heiress known to be desperately waiting for her father to die. "How beautiful you look this evening."

She kisses both my cheeks and offers condolences for the loss of my ex-wife. I raise my finger to my lips and hush her before she can continue, pointing to Jamie by way of excuse. Jamie politely introduces himself, and she kisses both his cheeks, as well. Jamie wipes his face absentmindedly and we continue on our walk to the bar, so I can fetch something suitable to drink.

I steer Jamie around the Temple of Dendur, careful not to slip into one of the reflecting pools. Jamie clumsily shakes hands with dignitaries and powerful Wall Street executives, nervously patting down his hair and fiddling with his bow tie. I knew he would enjoy it here. He seems noticeably star-struck when I pull him aside and point out a recently retired thirty-year-old Giants receiver.

Exceptionally beautiful women traipse delicately from one small group to another, air-kissing each other, their enormous diamonds sparkling in the dim lights. But one natural beauty stands out. I am one of dozens of men stealing glances at her. She is wearing an emerald green dress with her long brown hair twisted into a braid falling down her bare back. With a long golden stick, she holds a teal-and-purple mask adorned with peacock feathers up to her face.

Charlotte Doyle is graciously greeting guests and thanking them for their support of the Rhodes Foundation. Charlotte was at the top of the board's list to replace Juliette as the face of the foundation when Juliette died. Her father's political and legal connections were not overlooked when the board selected Charlotte, and Harrison stood to gain significant ground with the democratic elite by associating with the Rhodes Foundation. A win-win situation.

Charlotte delicately places a long manicured finger on my shoulder as I order a drink from the bar, whispering something in my ear. Without turning, I firmly grab her hand. I pull her into me so that her breasts are pressed against my back, and I kiss her wrist. I know the whole room is watching, wishing they were in my position, and I know Harrison is watching, too. I intentionally avoided saying hello to him, knowing it would burn him if I greeted his stepdaughter first.

I am suddenly reminded of Jamie's presence when the boy coughs and gulps from his glass of champagne. I turn around and, still holding Charlotte's hand, greet her with a kiss on each cheek. She kisses the edge of my mask, and I know she's leaving a fat red lipstick stain. She pulls her massive feathered mask away, revealing her beautiful face, and extends her other hand to Jamie.

"Jamie," I say, not taking my eyes off her, "this is Charlie Doyle."

Jamie switches his glass to his left hand, wipes his wet palm on his pant leg and shakes Charlotte's hand. Although she traveled in the same circles as Juliette before she passed, Charlotte has never met Jamie before tonight.

"It's very nice to meet you, Jamie. I knew your mother. She adored you. I'm so sorry for your loss." Charlotte extracts herself from my hand and strokes Jamie's cheek. "You're very handsome, just like your father." I hate that she's touching him.

"Thanks," Jamie replies nervously. "Nice to meet you."

Jamie's eyes dart up to meet hers, then return quickly to the safety of staring at the floor. If I could see his face beneath his mask, I'm sure he would be blushing.

I yank Charlotte's hand away from my son's cheek, and leave Jamie standing alone. I'm holding her too closely and smelling her hair. My hand is too low on her back.

"Now that I have you here—" Charlie leans toward my ear to whisper "—I received a strange letter at the foundation yesterday that I wanted to ask you about."

"Strange?" I ask, not really paying attention.

"It was a condolence letter sent to the foundation, expressing sympathies for the loss of Juliette."

"That doesn't sound strange to me." I inhale the sweet scent of her hair, reminded of nights we spent together.

"The letter had a return address from Burlington, Vermont." She pulls back to look me in the face. "And it claimed to be from Juliette's mother-in-law." Her eyes are expectant and cold.

My face flushes beneath my mask. I force a clenched smile and dismiss her inquiry as if it were nothing.

"The letter included a clipping from the *New York Times* wedding announcement of your and Juliette's marriage. I thought your parents died in a car accident. Who is Linda Abelman?"

A fuzzy vignette of my mother stewing on Tommy's couch clouds my vision. I dig the tips of my fingers into Charlie's forearm, pulling her away from anyone whose ears may have been perked. I never should have allowed an announcement in the *New York Times*. I didn't think they would ever have the capacity to go looking for me, much less *find* me after I changed my name.

"My parents *did* die in an accident," I lie. "It's probably some scam artists looking for a handout." My throat feels thick with anger, and I need to find a way to keep Charlie's mouth shut without tipping her off that I know exactly who these people are. "Don't give it another thought," I say, desperate to smother my secret back into the darkness where it belongs.

I feel a rough slap on my shoulder and immediately know it couldn't be anyone but Harrison. He turns me around for a convivial hug, trying to perform for the crowd as if we were friends. He wears a red sequined mask, the elastic stretched almost to its breaking point.

"Evening, Peter," he says in an atypically restrained voice. I nod a hello. My hand remains firmly planted on Charlie's lower back, and I feel her being steered away from me as Harrison grips her shoulder.

"There's Judge Abernathy, Charlotte. Run and say hello, would you?" Harrison murmurs to his stepdaughter.

"You don't think it's something to worry about?" she whispers to me as Harrison looks on. I shake my head, separating myself from her. "You're probably right that it's scammers," she says, a little too loudly. "That would explain the other weird part. The return address is in Vermont," she repeats, "but the postmark was from Manhattan."

Charlotte squeezes my hand before she saunters off to drape herself on Judge Abernathy. My jaw reflexively clenches, and I feel a familiar heat building at the back of my head.

"What's the matter, Peter?" Harrison asks with a smile. "Having a strange night?"

If a letter from Linda Abelman really did appear at the Rhodes Foundation, then characterizing the sender as a scammer wouldn't be too far from the truth. My mother was always looking for a handout. She mused about faking accidents and suing huge corporations so she could live off the payouts. If she's managed to find me, I'm sure she'll come knocking at my door, looking to exploit my wealth and status. I will never allow that to happen.

Harrison is staring at me from behind his mask, hoping I will take the bait he's thrown at me. "Not in the slightest, Harrison. I'm having a lovely evening."

In the days before the internet, disappearing was easy. I changed my name and jumped on a train and left my former identity behind me in Burlington. No one ever called me George again. Harrison has unparalleled access to legal records from all over the country. Charlotte clearly told him about the letter, and if he decided to use it to go digging, then it's only a matter of time before he finds out what else I've been hiding.

THEN

As soon as we returned from our honeymoon in the Turks and Caicos, Juliette moved into my apartment in Tribeca. We were young and happy and completely in love. Everything was beginning to fall into place as I expected it would if I just worked hard enough to achieve it.

When I went to work in the mornings, Juliette would choose my tie and pocket square for me while I shaved, and often tucked a small note into my jacket pocket for me to find sometime during the day. Whereas I felt Marcus was turning my heart cold at work, it was still warm at home. I felt confident I could live both sides of that life—a ruthless attorney and a loving husband. It wouldn't last.

Juliette got straight back into her work with the Rhodes Foundation. Only a month after we got married, she flew to Colorado to meet with the families affected by the Columbine massacre. She called me every day while she was gone, devastated, recounting the horrors they experienced.

I listened and wondered how she could feel so deeply, when for me, accessing my emotions was starting to feel like digging down through rubble. I tried to comfort her with soothing words but found myself distracted with thoughts of work now that I was back on some smaller cases at Rhodes & Caine.

One day, I got off the phone with Juliette and went to sit with Marcus and Sinan in the conference room. My assistant, Anna, approached us and stood in the doorway, reciting the following day's schedule before she left for the evening. My chest expanded with pride and excitement to get moving on some new cases.

"Oh, and you're due at Rikers tomorrow morning at 8:30 a.m.," she reminded me as she walked out the door.

"Who am I seeing at Rikers?" I looked over the printout she had given me. "That wasn't on the schedule."

"Got a message on the machine with a request to see you ASAP." She held a piece of paper close to her face to read, "Prisoner number 071486."

"Is there a name to go with this prisoner?" Marcus asked her.

"You wouldn't believe me if I told you."

I cracked my knuckles in the back of the black car on my way to Rikers the following morning. Not knowing what I was about to get into but far too intrigued to turn down the invitation, I rode in heated silence to the prison gates.

Inside the interview room, even more fat and slovenly than he'd looked at trial months ago, Stu Bogovian stood to greet me.

"Caine," he said. "Never thought you'd see me again, huh?"

"*Ex*-Congressman Bogovian. To what do I owe the pleasure?" I ignored his outstretched hand.

"Sit, sit," he said, pointing at the low metal chair on the opposite side of the table.

I flopped my briefcase between us and sat at the edge of my seat. I wasn't planning on staying long.

"I've heard you're none too thrilled with DA Harrison Doyle. Pissed he worked the case against me. Pissed he won. That true?"

I kept my face stoic and didn't respond. I could hear the reverberations of my teeth gnashing inside my ears.

"Well, I stay pretty plugged in, even while I'm here, and I've got some intel that you may be interested in."

Again, my face betrayed no emotion; I simply blinked in his direction.

"My appeal is coming up. I don't know if you knew that. You've been out of the loop, getting married and whatnot. Congratulations, by the way."

"Why am I here, Stu?"

"You want to take down Harrison Doyle? I've got the ammunition you'll need."

"What makes you think I want to take down the DA?" I looked away from him and picked imaginary lint from my lapel.

"He's the reason you've got marks in your loss column, Caine. Everyone knows that. And he's been gloating all over town that he was the one who dethroned the golden boy."

"What in the world makes you think I care what he says? You're the one who should care that you were found guilty, not me. You're the one rotting in jail." My fists clenched and unclenched reflexively, infuriated at the image of being dethroned.

"Yeah, but I deserve it, right?" He smirked and rolled his fat eyeballs. "I'm going for my first appeal soon. What kind of pull you got with Judge Abernathy?"

"I'm not pulling any strings for you, I don't care *what* insider information you think you have."

"You're a real piece of work, you know that, Caine? You fucked up my case, I'm about to go to prison for God knows how long and you won't even accept a bribe to take down your fucking enemy?"

"Officer," I called to the guard at the door, "we're done here." I stood up and gathered my briefcase.

"Okay, okay, okay, sit down, sit down," Stu whispered loudly, patting the metal table.

"One minute, Stu, and I'm out of here." I stood with my fists clenched at my sides, waiting to hear what he thought he knew.

"Son of a bitch, Caine. I know people like you. I *am* people like you, so I'm going to do you a fucking favor even if you *don't* put in a word with the judge. Just because I know you can use this information on the outside better than I can on the inside."

"Thirty seconds."

"He's dirty. Corrupt and sick, and if you take him down, you could get my conviction tossed. I've talked to other lawyers since I fired you, and no one's got the balls to do it. They say Harrison is too big to take down, but I bet you've got the balls, don't you, you son of a bitch?"

"What's in it for you? You'd *never* share information with me just to bust a corrupt politician. What the hell do you care?"

"You discredit the big man with this shit I'm telling you? The cases he tried are gonna get thrown out. At *least* I'll get a new trial."

"You think you've got enough to take him down?" A light flickered at the back of my head, thinking that if I brought the information Stu claimed to have over to Marcus, he would be thrilled with me, and maybe he'd put me back on the cases he'd been promising.

"The shit I've got is dirty, it's scandalous, it's long-standing and I can't *begin* to tell you how much evidence there is." He jiggles with excitement inside his droopy prison-issue khakis.

"Stu, if that's the case, then why has no one done anything about this yet? Sounds like another pile of garbage coming out of you."

"I'll tell you why—it's all connected. The people who know? They only know because they were a *part* of it. They all benefited, so they wouldn't have a leg to stand on if they were to call him out, you see? But you, *you're* not in on it. You're clean, and you've got the reputation that everyone's gonna believe you. Good thing you got married there, smart move. Now you're gonna look all wholesome, too. Coming from me? No one's gonna wanna hear it. But from *you*? You could take the whole Manhattan legal system down."

I pulled out a legal pad and placed it on the table between us. "Tell me."

"You know Charlotte?" Bogovian lowered his head and whispered, "His stepdaughter. *She's* the bribe, you understand? She's the spy *and* the pot of gold when he needs to do some under-the-table convincing, you know what I mean?"

Bogovian laid out the details of Harrison's perversions and corruption, telling me everything. All the dirty jobs that he and Charlie were pulling. Now I had him in my back pocket.

Now it was just a matter of time.

NOW

The morning after the masquerade ball, Sinan and I are sitting in my office facing a giant flat-screen TV, waiting for Stu Bogovian's face to appear on-screen. He was released last night and is expected to make a statement this morning. I've got a laptop open on my knees, and I'm scrolling through archived wedding announcements in the *New York Times* to remind myself what details I gave about my upbringing.

My past is crawling out to haunt me, with Bogovian getting out and now this letter from my mother, and it's putting me extremely on edge. I need to keep a tight lid on everything happening around me, and I'm sitting in this chair feeling like I'm losing control. Sinan lights a cigarette and pulls a heavy crystal ashtray toward him.

"You recording this?" Sinan asks me, leaning back in a leather chair, not bothering to turn around and face me.

"For what? No, I'm not recording this. I don't even know

why we're watching. I don't need to see Stu Bogovian's greasy face again."

"We're watching because you haven't failed in a long, long time, and I think you should be reminded of what it's like—so you keep winning brilliantly." Sinan grins and hangs his head over the back of his chair to look at my reaction. I don't acknowledge him, but a burning sea of anger at the word *fail* roils in my stomach. I'll keep winning brilliantly because I *am* brilliant.

"Here it is, here it is," he proclaims excitedly, pulling his long legs off the coffee table and sitting at attention.

I peer through a fog of disdain at the television screen. Stu Bogovian, having gained what looks to be fifty more pounds in prison, steps up to a makeshift lectern surrounded by reporters from various local news outlets. He coughs and clears his throat while wiping his sweaty head with a white hankie.

"Hello, thank you for being here this morning. I am Stuart Bogovian, former New York congressman. I stand before you today, having paid my debt to society. I've served my time for the terrible actions I took many years ago. I would like to take this opportunity to apologize to the woman I hurt. I will not say her name now, as it would be distasteful to bring her back into the spotlight."

"Except by mentioning her *at all* he's bringing her back into the spotlight. What a wanker." Sinan sucks hard on his cigarette. His British accent is particularly shrill this morning.

"And he's saying *woman*, singular, like he only assaulted *one*." I shake my head and return half my attention to the *Times* archives.

"I learned a lot about myself and the world while I was incarcerated," Stu continues, "and what I came to realize is that we live in a flawed society filled with flawed individuals. And while we all struggle with our own flaws, one thing everyone deserves is a fair and just legal system. Unfortunately, we do not have that here in Manhattan."

My interest is now piqued, and I get up and walk to Sinan's side to better see the television. Sinan slides to the left of his seat and pats the fat roll-arm of the chair, inviting me to sit down. I shake my head and stare at the television. Is Bogovian going to drop the bomb he told me about when he had me to visit him at Rikers seventeen years ago?

"Harrison Doyle, your New York County district attorney, is a corrupt and dirty politician."

My shoulders tense up. I can't believe he's going to do it.

"Though you may imagine I have been stewing in bitterness and anger toward my defense attorney, I have not."

Sinan and I exchange approving looks.

Stu continues, "He performed his job, and in the end, justice was done. The guilty man—myself—was punished accordingly."

"Did you put him up to this?" Sinan suddenly hollers, staring hard at me. "Is that why you're so *over* this loss? This burned you for years, and now you don't care? Did you tell him to say this shit?"

"I haven't spoken to him since that morning at Rikers. I'm just as surprised as you are." I feel my breath catching in my throat as I wait to hear what Bogovian is going to say.

"I do, however, think that Harrison Doyle's witch-hunting tactics were the work of an unskilled and bitter old man," Stu was saying. "The relentless media circus that surrounded my case, especially after I was found guilty, was nothing more than a publicity stunt pulled by DA Doyle to draw attention away from his own shortcomings and misbehavior. He knows exactly what I am talking about. I am talking to you now, Harrison." Stu points at the camera. "You're going to get yours. It's coming to you. You know it, I know it, and Peter Caine knows it."

"*What?*" I sneer defensively. "What do *I* have to do with this?" Sinan and I are both taken aback with disbelief.

"What the hell is he talking about?" Sinan puts a fresh cigarette in his mouth.

"Your guess is as good as mine." I quickly switch the channel to NY1 to catch Bogovian's address one more time. "Like I said, I haven't seen Bogovian since Rikers. If he's planning to do something to Harry, I don't know anything about it."

I never told anyone what Bogovian told me at Rikers Island that day about Harrison and Charlie's dirty little games. I never needed to expose him; I just kept winning my cases against the DA's office, without having to bring out any subterfuge to defeat him.

But upon hearing the news that Bogovian still has an ax to grind, I slide back behind my desk and smile at the idea that Harrison is about to suffer very, very deeply, and my hands will stay clean.

THEN

Harrison Doyle had invited me for a round of golf at some exclusive Westchester golf club, and as I prepared myself to go, I asked Sinan to join me.

"I don't golf, Peter. I'm Turkish, you understand. This isn't something we do. Why do you have to bring a partner anyway?"

"I don't, but I've been invited by Harrison Doyle, and it seems appropriate to outnumber him." In reality, I felt that Sinan's presence would help me to behave as I normally would around Harrison and not allow Bogovian's revelations to change my demeanor. Harrison had told me over the phone that the matter he wanted to discuss with me was business, and I assumed he was going to talk to me about an upcoming case that he wanted to be settled out of court.

My car pulled up a long winding driveway to an impressive brick clubhouse. I was never interested in golf, but I found a lot of business took place on the course, so I made an effort to develop a decent game. Harrison was waiting for me when I pulled up, having arrived even earlier than I did.

"Peter," he said, nearly jogging to meet my car, "how are ya?"

"Hello, Harrison." I'd been repeating Marcus's words over and over in the car, reminding myself that I couldn't show that I cared about the loss or my humiliation. I kept my sunglasses on, so my eyes wouldn't betray me.

"We've got a third with us today, and the caddie master told us we can go whenever we're ready." I was busy pulling my golf bag from the trunk. "Wow, nice set of clubs you got there."

I ignored his compliment, irritated that he had invited a third person and Sinan refused to join me. "Who's the third?" I asked.

Just as the words came out of my mouth, he turned to the clubhouse and a door on the left side of the building opened. Ethan, his slovenly son, came ambling out from the men's room.

"Here he is!" Harrison pretended to be genuinely happy his son was joining us, but I could see in his face he found Ethan to be as much of a nuisance as I did.

I elected to take my own golf cart and allow the two Doyle men to ride together. We played the first two holes in relative silence, occasionally commenting on the weather and current events. I noticed Ethan seemed desperate to please his father, looking to him for acknowledgment and encouragement after every shot he took.

At the third tee box, while Ethan was lining up his drive, Harrison finally spoke candidly. "Tell me," he asked, eyes fixed on his son, "have you been hearing anything about me recently?"

"I don't generally listen when people talk about you, Harrison. Why? Worried about your reputation?" I watched Ethan slice his tee shot into the woods, drop another ball and line up again. Liar, just like his father.

"Anything about my family?"

"What in the world would you be asking *me* for?" I stepped away from him and began polishing the head of my club. "How do you imagine any information I may have would be helpful to you?" A small fire ignited in the back of my head as I remembered every detail that Stu Bogovian had told me about Harrison and his dirty secrets.

"I'm asking you, Peter, because I think you know something. Well, I think you *think* you know something, and I'd like to talk to you about it." He refused to look at me as he spoke. "Maybe we can talk about making a deal."

"Ha." I was immediately amused at the turn of events. I couldn't believe my luck, listening to him beginning to confirm the stories Bogovian had told me. "You think you have anything I *want*?"

"Great shot!" Harrison yelled to his son, presumably to overpower my laughter. "Yes." He lowered his voice to a whisper. "I absolutely have something you want."

I couldn't even respond. The laughter was rising in my throat and my smile was too big to contain. I made my way up to the tee as soon as Ethan settled back in the cart and smashed a drive right down the middle of the fairway.

Harrison's face fell from contrived confidence to outright fear; he seemed in disbelief at my reaction. "You're not interested?"

"Are you trying to keep your enemies close, Harrison?" I pulled off my glasses to show my eyes were condescendingly wide, and the curl of my lip seemed to infuriate him. "Do you think that if we forge a friendship, or if I 'owe you one,' you'll have the upper hand and I'll be forced to keep my information to myself?" I spoke far too loudly, but I didn't bother containing my excitement.

"Careful, Peter." Harrison was not amused.

"What is it that you think I want?" I cleared my throat and mitigated my excitement.

"High-level position in my administration." I looked into his face to see he was completely serious. "Total control over most of my ADAs—you choose your cases, you choose your work schedule. Access to *everything* you could ever want or need. Your reputation would be stellar, ideal. Going from criminal defense to criminal prosecution? You'd be hailed a hero." He listed the features of his offer as if any of them could possibly appeal to me.

Too tickled by the absurdity of the situation to respond, I walked away to sit in my golf cart while Harrison flopped his shot at least thirty yards shy of mine. The Doyles drove their cart ahead of mine, and I pulled myself together on the drive to the fairway. I knew my outburst was inappropriate, and I had to keep a handle on Harrison, especially if he knew I had dirt on him and his family. How could he know what I knew?

We finished up the next two holes, Harrison seeming to nearly burst waiting for me to respond to his offer. When Ethan was again up at the tee box and we could speak alone, I told Harrison how I felt about his proposal.

"Harry, under *no* circumstances will I ever come to work for you. Your misguided attempts to pull me under your wing are ludicrous and absolutely laughable. Whatever information I may have shouldn't concern you. You keep on living your life, and I'll keep on living mine." I felt a sense of placidity if only for a moment, before the tightening of my skull reminded me how much I hated this man and what he did to my reputation. In a position of power over him in that moment, I decided to exploit it.

"Ethan," I called to his son. I watched Harrison's face turn panicked. I walked up to Ethan, threw my arm over his shoulder and leaned in to whisper, "How's your sister? I hear she's just a lovely girl." I felt his muscles go rigid when I mentioned his stepsister, and I turned to glare directly into Harrison's terrified eyes.

"Don't even try me, Harry," I said, releasing his son. "I've got enough to take your whole family down."

NOW

I trudge up the stairs of my brownstone to the bedroom, exhausted from a long week of work and too much alcohol and the lingering confusion about Stu Bogovian's bizarre threat. Charlie's mention of my past is haunting me, and all I want is a shower and a scotch in peace, away from people and their prying eyes. So I am more than disappointed to find Claire in a heap on the floor of our bedroom. She's sitting in front of the fireplace, legs bent at awkward angles, with an open laptop at her side, a box of tissues and a crystal decanter filled with what looks to be vodka.

"Claire, what are you doing on the floor?"

Claire spins around. I startled her, and I can see she's been crying. "Peter! When did you get home?" She pulls the laptop to her chest and tucks her legs beneath her. She's clearly hiding something.

"I just walked in—what's the matter with you?"

"Ugh." She exhales heavily and turns back to face the fireplace. "I can't talk to you right now."

My exhaustion amplifies. So much for a break from other people. I drop my briefcase on the chaise longue by the boudoir door, take off my suit jacket and step onto the carpet behind her. I pull the computer out of her hands and place it on the bench at the foot of the bed and tap the space bar to light the screen. I open a minimized webpage to see what she's hiding.

New York Social Diary appears before me. The "Party Pictures" tab is open. I scroll down with my right index finger, growing annoyed.

Claire pulls her hair away from her face and watches the screen, as if waiting for me to land on the offending photo.

I reach a section entitled "Rhodes Foundation Masquerade Ball" where I see wide-angle shots of the floral decorations and the floating candles at the Met. I see pictures of sports heroes and New York politicians, photographs of celebrities holding tiny canapés, hamming it up for the camera.

I scroll down and see a long thick brown braid. I see an emerald green dress with an open back. I see an Armani tuxedo. I see myself wearing it. I look at the picture of Charlotte with her shoulder pulled up to her chin, not knowing the camera was there, holding my right hand with her left hand, while my left arm was wrapped around her lower back, my lips pressed against her exposed shoulder.

"This is what you've been looking at?" I expel an aggravated sigh in Claire's direction.

"What the hell do you have to say for yourself?" Claire pulls her robe tightly around her. "Are you going to explain this one away like you always do? Are you going to tell me this is *nothing*, and I'm overreacting—like you always do?" She blows her nose hard and throws the tissue into the fireplace.

I don't want to bother with this. "I didn't know there was a camera there," I reply dismissively.

"You didn't know there was a *camera*? You're not even going to address the fact that you're drooling down her back, you're just shocked that it was documented? God, Peter. Have some respect for yourself."

"You shouldn't bother yourself with this nonsense." I close the laptop.

I hear Claire's brain suddenly grasping the idea that this picture may not be the only incident of me drooling down Charlotte's back, and she jumps to her feet and backs into the wall. So dramatic.

"It's *her*? Still?" The words come out of her mouth in a low growl. "*She's* the one you've been seeing? Jesus, I knew you were fucking around, but Charlotte Doyle? Have you no decency at all?" Claire slides down the wall to the floor and snatches up her glass. I'm caught without argument, so I position myself behind the desk and flip through the mail the housekeeper stacked on the corner.

"You cheated on your wife, the *best* woman in the world, and you're still seeing the woman you cheated on her with," Claire hollers from her seat on the floor. "How could she still want you?" She plucks ice cubes from her crystal rocks glass and throws them one by one into the fire. "Juliette and Charlotte must both be brain damaged to fall for you! And that means that *I'm* brain damaged, too!"

"You're hysterical, Claire. Calm yourself," I respond without turning my attention away from my mail. She certainly knows how to put on a show.

Claire sucks in a deep calming breath, and in a steady voice says, "Peter, this isn't about me. This is about you, and why *you're* so messed up. Wealth and status." She shakes her head. "All you've ever wanted. And it doesn't matter who you have to hurt, just so long as you can keep up your precious appearance." After the last ice cube, Claire throws her entire glass into the fireplace. It shatters against the bricks and the pieces scatter among the logs.

"Claire." I gesture angrily toward the fireplace. "That was Baccarat."

"Who cares that it was fucking Baccarat?" she screams, her tearful face popping out from beneath a curtain of sweaty hair. "Buy another one! Buy a million more of them! It doesn't matter that the glass is broken, what matters is that you're hurting *me*, Peter! You're killing me! Fuck the glass, you prick!"

I wince at the word *prick*—I don't like it when she says that—but I keep my attention on the mail. She hasn't calmed herself at all. I glare at her for a moment, then simply look away.

Claire clutches her robe in her fists. "You're exactly like my father," she scoffs, trying to find a way to get to me. "You want to have your cake and eat it, too. You think I'm just going to sit here and take it?"

I produce an exaggerated sigh and flop my stack of mail on the desk. I'm not going to get her to shut up unless I engage in this nonsense. I stare at her with expectant eyebrows. "Your father?" I finally say.

"Just like my father. A playboy about town, cheating on my mother with Connecticut society ladies? Charming, revered, but scary and cruel behind closed doors? Sounds *exactly* like you."

"Your father was an irretrievable asshole." I dismiss her with a flick of my hand.

"I needed my father, Peter. I needed him because I was a child and I had no other options. But I don't *need* you. Don't you ever forget that. I have my own money and my own life. I'm not here for your wealth or your *status*." She smirks insolently in my direction. "I'm here for you. Tell me the truth,

I want to know what's been going on. I deserve to be told the truth."

I pull off my tie and begin unbuttoning my shirt. "That's true," I lie. "You deserve to know the truth." I step out of my suit pants and throw them onto the chaise with the rest of my discarded clothing. I busy myself emptying the pockets of my jacket and pants, folding my pocket square, returning various items to their rightful places.

Claire stands defiant—hands on hips like a superhero—ready to dismantle me if I refuse to talk. "Let's have it, Peter. What's been going on between you and Charlotte Doyle?"

"Nothing," I begin, knowing this one isn't going to end unless I give her *something*.

"Bull*shit* nothing! I'm not blind, you know, I can—"

"Let me finish," I growl and flash an angry look at Claire. Her mouth snaps closed in shock. "Nothing has been going on between me and Charlotte Doyle *for a while now*." I enunciate the last words condescendingly. She should be glad I'm telling her anything at all. "It started when I was married to Juliette and it's been on and off ever since." My flared temper settles down, and I return my attention to arranging the bedroom detritus.

"Does Harrison know?"

"Who cares, Claire? Who cares if Harrison knows? It's nobody's business."

"Is it *my* business? We've been living together for eight years! And you've been carrying on an affair with another woman? Was it Juliette's business?"

"Juliette knew about Charlie." I straighten the pillows and smooth the creases in the duvet.

"Jesus, stop calling her that. I *hate* that. Call her Charlotte. Her *real* name. You're telling me that Juliette knew you were sleeping with Charlotte while you were married?"

"You know that's why we got divorced, Claire. Why must we discuss this now?"

"We're discussing this now because apparently this issue isn't over!" Claire pulls another rocks glass from the shelf of the wet bar and fills it with ice cubes. She pours a full glass from the decanter, never taking her eyes off me.

I step toward the fireplace and sit down at the edge of the bricks. Wearing only underwear, I reach between the burning logs and begin plucking out the pieces of broken glass.

"I was seeing *Charlotte* on the side—Juliette knew about it. She turned a blind eye because she didn't want Jamie to grow up without his father. I don't see how any of this is relevant to you."

I pile the bits of broken glass in an ashtray I pull from my desk. Some have nearly liquefied and burn my fingers when I touch them. It feels good. It feels good to *feel* something. I keep pulling at the pieces of molten crystal, rubbing my burned skin on the edge of the rug. Claire wants me to feel pain because of my affair, so I burn my fingers to feel the pain.

"How could you do that to her? To both of them?" Claire looks down at me with disgust.

"What makes you think they were such angels? You have these fantasies about Charlotte Doyle and my ex-wife, and you don't even know them."

"I know what it's like to be cheated on, Peter. I know what it's like to watch a man mistreat a woman. I saw what it did to my mother. I hate knowing it happened to them."

"What do you mean 'to them'? You're making it sound like I cheated on both of them. I cheated on Juliette with Charlie. I never cheated on Charlie."

"You cheated on Charlotte with *me*, you idiot," Claire cries, shaking with rage and adrenaline.

"You have no idea what you're talking about, Claire. You're

not listening to me. I told you, Charlie and I weren't in a relationship, so I couldn't have cheated on her. If anything, I cheated on *you*. And Charlie's no angel, either. Believe me."

"No angel? Compared to who? You? A criminal defense attorney who specializes in finding the absolute *worst* human beings on the face of the planet, who have committed the *most* atrocious acts, and spinning the truth, charming the jury, playing the system so that these disgusting excuses for citizens can walk free? Yeah, Peter. I'm sure *Charlotte* is the one who's no angel." The silk sash from Claire's bathrobe slides onto the floor as she marches back and forth.

"You don't like it? Leave." I don't even lift my head to address her. I squeeze a piece of melted glass between my thumb and forefinger, leaving the grooves of my thumbprint. I look down to see it isn't the impression of my thumb, but a layer of burned-off skin.

"Are you still seeing her?"

I stare down at my fingers. Blackened and burned, with sweat glistening in the creases of my palm. "Not really."

"I'm not going to stay here if you continue on with this. I'm going to that bachelorette party in the Hamptons tomorrow, and when I'm back on Monday, it better be over. Do you understand?" She balls her fists and grits her teeth, forcefully stating her final assertion: "Call it off. I mean it."

I stand up, gently taking Claire's drink to soothe my burned fingers with the condensation from the glass. She extends a rigid hand to keep me an arm's length away.

I look into her eyes. "It's off. She's not a threat to *you* anyway. She's not trying to take me away from you. She's using me." I turn away from her and walk through her boudoir toward the bathroom. I turn on the shower and discard my underwear on the floor. "Has been for years."

THEN

Just months into our marriage, the elegant confidence and effortless grace that drew me to Juliette when we first started seeing each other was beginning to crack at the edges. She started to seem distrusting of our relationship and worried constantly. She called a little too frequently while I was at work, asked a few too many questions. I understood that she was probably just having trouble getting used to playing second fiddle when she had been my primary focus up until then.

One evening, I took her to the Big Apple Circus, and we sat in the front row, watching the clowns and animals perform. I thought it was a romantic and creative idea for a date; I had been spending more time at work and wanted to show Juliette some effort and attention.

"Are you not enjoying yourself?" I asked when she seemed to be looking anywhere but inside the ring.

"Oh, no, I'm having a wonderful time," she politely lied.

"I'm just so sad for the elephants." She looked into the ring at the huge creatures and dabbed her eyes with a hankie.

"Oh, God, of course. Let's get out of here," I said. She had told me about her abiding love for animals and the pain she felt when she saw them mistreated. I hurried her out of the tent and across the street to P.J. Clarke's. We sat down at a booth with a red-checkered tablecloth, but her tears didn't stop.

"Are you sure that's all that's wrong?" I tried to comfort her with red wine and cheeseburgers. She picked listlessly at the fries but still smiled warmly through her tears.

"It *is* the elephants, yes. I hate to see them like that—it's unnatural. But it was the families that made me cry. Seeing mothers and fathers with their babies, all smiling and laughing, and it made me wish for things to be different."

"You want to start a family?" I winced, nervous that she would say yes, and I would have both Juliette *and* Marcus looking for me to become a father.

"Of course I want to start our own family, but I was talking about mine. I wish that my father and mother could get along, and I wish that my father was back to the man he once was."

I immediately felt defensive and wanted to tell her that Marcus was my hero, and I didn't want to be stuck in the cross fire between them. But as she continued her thought, she showed that I didn't need to protect him.

"I know how much you love my father, and I won't interfere. I just wish that things could be different, that's all." She bit into her cheeseburger, and I knew the conversation was over. Knowing how she felt about her father and how she felt about our work, I made sure to keep my life with her separated from anything having to do with Rhodes & Caine.

The following day, while I was sitting at my desk working on a case, my intercom buzzed. Anna informed me that Juliette was at the front desk.

"*What?* My wife? What is she doing *here*?" I was suddenly panicked; my two worlds were colliding, and I wasn't prepared. She was supposed to stay away from the things that happened at the office, she was supposed to stay away from the person I was at work. And now she was making her way down the hall to my office. I was powerless to stop her.

"Hi, babe," she said, opening my door and walking in like she owned the place.

"Uh, hi—" I sputtered awkwardly. "What are you doing here?"

"I was in the neighborhood, and I wanted to pop in and say hi." She started looking around my office, at the decor, the furniture, the books on my bookshelves. "I've never been in here, you know."

"Uh, yeah. Yeah, I know." I shoved my desk chair back and came around to where she was standing. I didn't take her jacket, offer her anything to drink or kiss her hello. I shifted my weight from foot to foot, my agitation and discomfort increasing. She shouldn't have been there.

"Wow," she said sarcastically as she surveyed the details of the office. "Is this a new briefcase?" She held up a brand-new Hermès case Marcus had given me just days before.

"Yes, your father gave that to me. Thought it would look more suitable in court." I gathered the briefcase from her hands and tucked it back onto the couch where she found it.

"Something wrong with the one I bought you?" she asked as she pulled open my closet door and peered at the contents.

"Nothing, nothing at all. It's just Marcus gave me this one, and—"

"Since when do you wear glasses?" She cut me off before I could finish my sentence, holding a pair of horn-rimmed spectacles.

"They're just frames, not prescription. Marcus thought it

would make me look more refined." I tug them out of her hand and place them inside my desk drawer. "What brings you here?" I asked, trying to appear calm while completely flustered and uncomfortable. "Are you staying?"

"Certainly doesn't seem like you *want* me to." She held up a cylindrical package. "Just going to bring this bottle of gin to my father, and then I'll get out of your hair." She huffed a disappointed breath and pushed open my door.

I didn't follow her out. I wanted to behave like her husband, but I couldn't. I felt she had violated some unwritten rule that was supposed to keep her separated from my work. She came in and pulled back the curtain on the person I was becoming at work. At home with her, I was a loving husband. But at work and in court, I was a hard-hearted criminal defense attorney. These two worlds shouldn't have collided.

Ever since I told Juliette some semblance of the truth about my family while we were in the Turks and Caicos, I'd been feeling more and more anxious and exposed while I was with her. I was afraid of my secrets existing in someone else's head, and someone else having the ability to let them out. I always trusted that I would take my past to my grave, but now I had let the truth escape the confines of my mind, and I was becoming fearful that Juliette was going to misuse the information. Her appearance at my office door just served to increase my fears.

The thoughts that were creeping into my head distracted me for the rest of the afternoon. Heat traveled up the back of my neck, and a tightness—a rigid compression—started to squeeze at the base of my skull. I paced my office, slowly sipping bottled water and taking deep breaths, calming myself.

She knew too much, and I hated it. She knew I didn't have a glamorous and tragic upbringing in Europe among the cultured and educated. What she didn't know, and I hoped no one would ever find out, was that I had lied my way into the elite world where Juliette found me. I left George Abelman back in Burlington and became Peter Caine while aboard a train to Chicago. It was Peter Caine who got accepted into Northwestern. And then Peter Caine who went to Columbia Law and passed the bar in New York State.

I took a deep breath. I had to eventually go home and face Juliette, and I felt ill equipped to do so, like I no longer remembered how to talk to her. I didn't buy apology flowers on my way home, I just walked into the loft empty-handed and waited for Juliette to start the conversation.

"Are you okay?" She was kind, worried. "You weren't yourself when I saw you at your office."

"No," I began, but stopped short when I realized I couldn't tell her that I *was* myself at the office. Just not a side of me she had met yet. "You shouldn't have come."

"I know." She kissed my cheek and cocked her head apologetically. "I'm sorry, I shouldn't have bothered you."

Her response should have softened me. Her kindness should have made me see her as untarnished again, but it was too late. She wasn't rejecting me, she was *accepting* me, because for her, love was easy to access. Until that day, I had loved Juliette with every fiber of my being. But at that moment, she became compromised. I had told her too much, and I couldn't live comfortably knowing someone out there knew that I was lying and that I didn't belong in the life I so desperately needed to lead.

"What brought you there anyway? Taking your father a bottle of gin? That's not like you." I wanted to deflect and accuse *her* of not being *herself*.

"I had been thinking about the way I felt last night at the circus. I was upset, and I know he's never going to change, but I thought it would make *me* feel better if I offered an olive branch."

"Did it work?"

"Well, I guess it made me realize that I'm kicking a dead horse, and I should just back off because the man I once knew is gone. So, in a way, yes. I don't feel upset with him. I feel some sense of peace."

"Good. So, you won't be visiting the office anymore."

"No, I won't bother you again."

I wanted to believe her, and some part of me did. But I eyed her with suspicion now, knowing that she was aware of the person I used to be. The higher up I got in the world, the further I would break away from my past, and Juliette was beginning to feel like the tether that could keep me attached to my former life. I wouldn't allow that.

NOW

I tap my foot impatiently under the table, waiting to be joined by Harrison Doyle. I'm pretending to flip through emails and messages on my phone, so distracted I don't notice the waiter approaching the table to refill my water glass. Harrison hurries through the revolving doors to my table, collapses in the leather armchair with a huff and immediately downs the glass of ice water sitting at his place.

"Pete, sorry I'm late." Harrison speaks between gulps.

"Slow down," I scold, "it's not a trough." I lean back and glare at him. I only have so much patience for Harrison, but now I'm forced to see him and determine what he knows about where I came from. If Charlie really did receive a letter from my mother, and that's all she and Harrison have to go on, then I don't have to worry. But if either of them went digging, and they actually know the whole truth, then they could take me down. They could ruin everything.

"So, what's for dinner?" Harrison booms. "Lobster? I saw some monsters in the tank on my way in. Seems there's a prehistoric beast up there, nine-pounder. Been living in there for years."

I force myself to behave as I normally would, so I don't give Harrison the impression that anything is bothering me. I usually ignore him, so I'm keeping my mouth shut and concentrating on my menu.

"We drinkin'?" Harrison asks, watching the waiter place an Oban in front of me. I hold up my glass of scotch while perusing the menu and take a long sip.

"Uh, scotch for me, too," Harrison roars at the waiter, who is pushed back by the volume of his voice.

"Oban?" the waiter asks.

"Whatever he's having." Harrison points at me, and the waiter turns to fetch Harrison his glass. "I can't drink like you can anymore, Peter. Had a bit too much that night at the Four Seasons. Hungover for days."

I'm not sure I believe he was drunk at all that night at the Four Seasons.

"Well, I guess you've made it clear now that you're definitely not coming to the district attorney's office, huh?" Harrison shellacs an unmoving smile onto his face. "Nothing left for me to offer you, huh?"

Is he serious, or is he mocking me? The waiter reappears with Harrison's scotch and asks if we're ready to order. I politely gesture to Harrison to order first.

"Sir?" the waiter asks, already fed up with our table.

"Porterhouse, medium well," Harrison proclaims, satisfied with his decision.

"And for you, sir?"

"What's your biggest lobster?" I ask innocently.

"We have a couple of four-pounders today, sir."

"No, no, your *biggest*. I saw a creature up there at least twice that size." I wave at the tank by the hostess stand.

Harrison looks amused that I am trying to order the pre-historic beast.

"Oh, you mean Bruno. He's more of a mascot than a menu item, sir." The waiter laughs off my request and hoists his pencil for a legitimate order.

"That's it. Bruno. I'll have him, boiled." I close my menu and hand it to the waiter.

"Sir, that's a nine-and-a-half-pound lobster," the waiter pleads.

"And I am a paying customer—" I squint at his name tag "—*Adam*. Are we going to have a problem?"

"No, sir. Boiled lobster, and the porterhouse for you, sir." He nods at Harrison, drops his head solemnly and approaches the lobster tank. I can hear the hostess squeak in distress when Adam pulls Bruno from the tank and places him on a round rubberized tray. He slowly returns to our table and presents the massive creature, and I nod and wave him away. As Bruno is carried to the kitchen, several patrons and a bartender protest loudly, trying to keep their beloved mascot unharmed.

"You're gonna eat a nine-pound lobster?" Harrison probes, eyes wide. "The big ones are chewy and tough, you know."

"What are we doing here today, Harry? Having dinner, yes? Well, I want lobster for dinner. What is it that you wanted to discuss with me?" I pick at the wrapper from my straw and look anywhere except at Harrison.

He drops his jovial air and turns serious. "We need to talk about what Stu Bogovian said in his half-assed press conference the other day."

"Do we?" I still refuse to look at him.

"I would characterize his comments as threatening, wouldn't you?" Harrison tentatively sips his scotch.

"Not really. I would characterize them as a man desperately trying to return to a spotlight that forgot him years ago." My pulse slows as I begin to believe that this dinner is about Bogovian and has nothing to do with Vermont.

"You and I were both mentioned by name in that little speech he gave, and I think we need to look into damage control."

"His comments have absolutely no effect on me, and frankly, if you publicly address any of it, you're going to look weak, and that's not going to get you any votes."

"Weakness is not my fear here."

"Weakness isn't your fear?" I bounce my head in disbelief. "Okay, what is?"

Harrison leans over the table, pulling the tablecloth in his fists. "Votes, like you said. I've already got enough on my plate trying to get the crybaby left and the independents over here, and if my name is in this scumbag's mouth, I've got problems, understand?" he whispers violently. Frothy drops of white spittle gather at the corners of his lips.

"Harry, this guy is an absolute nobody. You address his ludicrous threat in public, and you're gonna make everyone remember what he said. Let it die a natural death. No one was even watching that nonsense." I drain my scotch, settling down.

"What did Bogovian mean when he said that you knew?" Harrison is no longer plying me with saccharine kindness. He's switched over to his professional persona.

"What?" Now I fear I've dismissed him too soon. "What the hell do I know, Harry? I haven't seen him since his sentencing almost twenty years ago. Forget this guy, you're wasting your time with him."

"Stu Bogovian doesn't like me very much." Harrison's voice is stoic and detached. "I tried to help you guys out, you know. Before his trial when I was first elected DA, I offered him a deal." Harrison twirls the straw in his water glass. "I thought, 'no way Peter Caine is going to take this loser to trial,' so I figured I'd give you guys a nice deal, plead him to a lesser charge, win-win."

I'm listening intently but stealing frequent glances out the window, trying to make it look like I don't care what he's telling me.

"He didn't take the deal. He was *sure* you'd get him off, what with your flawless record and just partnering with the best defense attorney in New York." Harrison licks his lips and glares at me, knowing full well I would be angry that he's talking about a humiliating loss. "People don't turn me down, you see. I make very attractive deals for people. So, I talked to Judge Abernathy and ensured Bogovian didn't get any reduction in his sentence or any special treatment. It's never a good idea to turn *me* down."

"Why are you telling me this? This happened nearly twenty years ago. Why would I possibly care?" This isn't about Bogovian and I know it.

"What is it you think you know about me, Peter?" he asks me, his voice turning volatile, his bushy eyebrows furrowing.

"I know much more than you would like me to." The waiter brings me another scotch and I practically snatch it out of his hand.

"If that's true, then why haven't you spoken up?"

"I haven't had a reason to tell, Harrison. Don't give me one."

"Be careful, Peter. Don't forget how much power I have in this town." He returns to a state of infuriating calm. "I hadn't thought about what Bogovian may have told you. I knew how angry he was when you lost that trial. But since he's gotten out and made those ludicrous comments, I went snooping around."

"Again, why in the world do you think I care?"

"His prison records indicate you went to see him before his appeal. Hmm. I wonder what he may have told you while you were there. He had already fired you, yet he asked you to come see him in prison? Strange. Must have had some very juicy information to share with you. Too bad it's not protected under attorney-client privilege, since he'd already fired you."

"What are you getting at, Harrison?"

"You let this shit with Bogovian get out of hand, and you can kiss your career goodbye."

"Is that a challenge? You should watch how much you drink, *friend*. Might go letting your secrets out without meaning to," I say, reminding him that he offered me his stepdaughter.

"I know exactly what you think you know. That's why I've always been so nice to you. I have given you enough chances to get into my good graces, and I am tired of this supplicant bullshit. Keep your fucking mouth shut, or you'll find out *exactly* what I'm capable of." He shakes a thick finger in my face.

When Adam appears with our entrées, the restaurant patrons and staff all watch as their cherished Bruno is placed, bright red, split in two and drowned in clarified butter, in front of me. As the onlookers gawk, I push the lobster away, throw my napkin on top of the prized crustacean and signal for the check.

"You've got nothing on me, Harry."

"Don't I?" He leans across the table and snarls, "It's amazing what you can find on the internet these days, isn't it, George?"

THEN

Our one-year wedding anniversary loomed on the horizon, and I knew the push to start a family would be getting stronger as time passed. With Marcus encouraging me to cement the professional reputation he wanted from me, I started spending all my time at work. I often slept and showered at the office, working tirelessly to get to the point where I could have the cases I had started the partnership to take on.

Where Juliette was supportive and understanding at first, by the end of that first year she'd lost patience. She told me that Marcus had been a devoted husband and father until he let the job take over his entire being and she was convinced the same would happen to me.

"I'm worried," she told me one afternoon as she dragged me around an art gallery. "I'm feeling you disconnecting from me, and I don't know how to reel you back in."

"Stop taking me to places like this, for one." I couldn't

stand looking at the photographs of starving children from third-world countries. Their desperate eyes staring blankly at me, looking for a handout.

"Buy a photograph, Peter. It's a charity event, and the money goes to the kids you're seeing. Jesus, when did you become so cold?" she admonished me.

"Is that how you're going to *reel me in*?" I sneered. "Forcing me to spend my money on garbage like this?" I waved my hand at a photo of a child lying next to the carcass of an emaciated gazelle.

"Don't do that, Peter." Her tone turned from scolding to concerned. "Don't dismiss me and the things that matter to me. This is not who you are. You're acting like my father."

"That's because I *am* like your father, Juliette. It's probably what drew you to me to begin with." I pointed to a red sticker on the bottom of the picture, indicating it was already sold, smirked at her and walked outside.

"Yes," she said, following me out, "maybe so. But the man he *used* to be is who I see in you. Caring, interested, kind. He lost those parts of himself years ago." The wind whipped around the corner of the wide Chelsea street, and Juliette hugged herself to stay warm. "You're wearing the same suits he wears now, Peter. You've got a new haircut. You're wearing glasses that you don't even need. It's like you're becoming a new person."

Exasperated, I hailed a taxi. "I'm going back to the office," I said as I held the door open. "I'm the same as I've always been. Maybe I dress better now, but that's all."

Before the cab drove off, I promised Juliette that nothing had changed, knowing full well that my feelings for her were compromised. I was preoccupied constantly with the notion that she was the only person in my new life who knew anything about that dungeon of nothing I came from, and I was realizing what a mistake it was to tell her the truth about my lies. I could no longer look at her without seeing myself trapped in a world I needed to escape.

Despite how I felt about her and what I was beginning to see about our relationship, she hadn't lost faith in me. Later the following week after work one night, I walked into my apartment to find candles lit, a bottle of champagne sitting in a crystal ice bucket on the dining room table and Juliette waiting patiently for me to arrive.

"Hi, honey," she said, "I'm glad you're not home too late." She used her sultry, bedroom voice.

I checked my watch to see it was 9:15 p.m., already late enough. "What's all this?" I asked her, waving my hand at the display she had set up, completely out of place in my former bachelor pad.

"I have a surprise for you," she said. She slid out of the leather dining chair and glided toward me.

"I'm exhausted, Juliette. I don't have the energy for surprises. What's going on?" Frustrated already, I pulled off my tie and threw it along with my coat and briefcase onto the table with the candles and champagne, ruining her romantic spectacle.

"We're going to have a baby," she said, leaning in for the kiss and embrace I should have provided.

I felt immediately wrenched in two. Instead of automatically celebrating the news, I stood in stunned silence, evaluating the repercussions. On the one hand, Marcus would be thrilled; he wanted a biological heir, and now one was on the way. Yet at the same time and in the same mind, I was dismayed. I never wanted children. I never spoke about wanting children or indicated to Juliette that I was interested in becoming a father. The model I had for a father was nothing but a disappointment and source of shame for me; I didn't want to risk being a less than perfect exemplar for a child. It just didn't fit with the life I wanted for myself.

"Peter." Juliette wrenched me back into the moment with her pleading voice. "Didn't you hear what I said? I'm pregnant." She held my cheek in her hand and gently turned me to face her.

"Yes, I heard you," I said, unable to save the moment. "How long do we have?"

"How *long* do we have? You mean, when am I due? Late September. *Our* baby is due in late September, I'm eight weeks pregnant."

Her frustration apparent in her upturned scowl, I tried to salvage whatever I could. "I'm sorry, Juliette, I'm just in shock, I think. I didn't see this coming." I walked to the champagne and poured myself a full glass, though not in celebration. I should have known what was coming when I noticed only one champagne flute next to the bucket.

"Well, it's coming, Peter. So, you better wrap your mind around it." She stalked into the other room and slammed the door behind her.

I should have followed her in to comfort her as she cried, but I didn't. I didn't want to be a father. I grew up without a father, with an uncle who couldn't have cared any less, and I had no aspirations for fatherhood. Would this child grow up and ask questions about my past? Would he want to see photographs and hear stories about his grandparents? Stories I would be unwilling to tell?

I drank the champagne alone, steeped in conflict and a fear that I was about to lose control.

NOW

I jog across Sixth Avenue, dodging tourists stopped in the middle of the road to take pictures of Radio City Music Hall. After just making the light, I slow to a walk and slide through the revolving doors at the front of the massive building.

"Peter Caine to see Rick Friedberg," I say to the security guard, pulling my driver's license from my wallet. Rick Friedberg, the attorney handling Juliette's estate and the custody paperwork for Jamie, was a law school classmate of mine. While I was interested in gaining wealth and social status from my work, Rick went in the opposite direction and used his elite education and superior abilities for virtuous work in public defense. Rick and I couldn't have taken more divergent career paths, but we've remained in contact nonetheless.

Rick's morality and wholesomeness in a field that often generates the opposite was what captured Juliette's attention, and it was their shared sense of decency that produced a close and lasting friendship. Rick had transitioned into family law after leaving public defense, and Juliette went to him to manage her estate when she was first diagnosed with terminal cancer.

I check my watch in the elevator, ten minutes early for my appointment. I am never late. I walk past the front desk and nod at the receptionist. "I know I'm early."

"Yes, Mr. Caine. I'll let Mr. Friedberg know you're here," the receptionist responds.

I am meeting with Rick to finalize the custody paperwork for Jamie. The other night was the first night I had spent alone with him in his entire life, and today I am gaining sole custody. While we were together, we watched a movie, ate leftovers and shared a bottle of wine. I didn't have much to say to him, because I don't know him very well, but I feel like I made a sufficient effort. He went to his room after the movie was over, presumably to go to sleep, and I was relieved to be left alone.

As I replay the events from the other night, I feel my phone vibrating in my pocket. I see Harrison's number appear on-screen and furiously slam the button to send him to voice mail. Thoughts of Jamie fall out of my mind and are replaced with thoughts of Charlie and Harrison and how much they actually know.

Rick appears from around the corner and interrupts my troubling thoughts. "Good morning, Peter." He holds out his hand for me to shake. He stands just my height, maybe a quarter inch taller. I automatically rise up on my toes to greet him.

"Rick, good to see you."

He leads me away from the waiting area toward a small conference room with a large marble table surrounded by six tan leather office chairs. With a flip of a switch, the glass walls turn opaque and the overhead lights flicker to life.

"Sit, Peter. Can I get you anything? Coffee? Water?"

"A water, Rick. Please." I study the stack of legal pads, sticky notes, monogrammed pencils and highlighters displayed in a leather tray at the middle of the table. I take a small handful of gold paper clips and sprinkle them on the table in front of me. Rick places a Poland Spring bottle and a glass next to my paper clips.

"How have you been? I understand Jamie has moved in already?" Rick adjusts his seat and interlaces his fingers on the conference table.

"I've been very well, Ricky, very well." I don't look up from my paper clips. "Yes, Jamie is living with me now."

When Marcus passed away, I was again left without a father figure, and although I had established myself by that point, there was still a missing sense of stability that I craved. I was able to gain that stability through professional success and wealth, but now that I'm thrown back into a tumultuous past with Bogovian's release, and the mysterious resurgence of my parents, I'm again beginning to feel apprehensive and uneasy. The timing of Juliette's death and gaining custody of Jamie couldn't be more ideal; now I have something solid to focus on.

"Great, I'm glad to hear that. Poor kid's been through a lot. There's not much left to complete the custody paperwork." Rick gets right to business. I have a feeling he preferred talking to me when Juliette was still around. "Most of it was taken care of before, but a few things need to be covered now that Juliette has passed away. And we should discuss updating your will now that you have full custody, and what you want to do about Claire and the adoption paperwork."

"Adoption paperwork?" My attention is pulled away from the stack of paper clips I folded together. "We never discussed that."

"If you and Claire want to coparent officially, she will have to legally adopt Jamie. You can do whatever makes you happy in an informal capacity, but should anything happen to *you*, if you lose custody for whatever reason or pass away, then she could be his legal guardian after that."

"Lose custody? Is that a possibility? Is someone contesting this agreement?"

"No, not right now. But I like to take precautions. Safeguard for the future."

"Jesus, who the hell adopts a teenager?" I twist the unfolded paper clips together, forming a long jagged stick. "Give me the adoption papers. It's not like I'm going to *die* in the next few years, and then he's eighteen, and this whole mess is moot."

"Well, there's something else." Rick is avoiding eye contact with me, and I can't begin to imagine what else he may be talking about.

"What? Don't keep me in suspense. What else?" I poke my paper-clip stick into the table to punctuate my point.

"I have an envelope that Juliette left for me before she died." Rick holds a large envelope to his chest like an heirloom pendant.

"What's in it?" I ask.

"I don't know what's in here. She sealed it before she gave it to me. She said I should have these documents in the event something happens to you." He taps the edge of the envelope on the conference table.

"If something *happens* to me? Like what?"

"I imagine something like if someone contests your custody of Jamie."

"Oh. So, these papers are beneficial to me." Maybe Juliette wrote a letter, indicating she only wants *me* to have custody.

"Maybe. Maybe that's what these documents say. But

they're sealed. And Juliette instructed me to keep them sealed until I need to unseal them."

"And how will you know when the time has come to unseal them?"

"She said if something happens to you. I will unseal them in the event that something happens to you." With that, Rick tucks the envelope back into his briefcase and returns his attention to the adoption papers he wants Claire to look over. He amasses a set of documents and folds them into a large manila envelope. "Take these to Claire, have her lawyer look them over or have her call me, make whatever decision works for you and your family. How is Claire, by the way? I haven't seen her in ages."

"Claire's fine, been out of town in the Hamptons at some girls thing." I pour my water into the glass and don't give the sealed documents another thought. "She couldn't be more excited that Jamie is living with us."

"Claire will make a fine mother."

"Yeah. It's been her dream to be a mother since she was a kid. Her father was a real piece of work, and she thinks if she can do a better job with Jamie, then she's going to change the past or something. She's been pestering me for years to have kids. She'll be elated when I show her the adoption papers." I look around the room for something else to play with, having wound all the gold paper clips together into a thick rod that I am now using to scratch the surface of the marble table.

"I hope that she considers adopting Jamie. I would be happy to help her if she would like to discuss it further." Rick extends his pen to me. "Let's get this signed. I know you're busy."

I reject Rick's pen and pull my Montblanc from my jacket pocket. I quickly review the fine print and sign each page.

Rick hands me a copy, as well as the adoption papers for Claire. "Good to see you, Peter."

"All right, Ricky," I say, tucking the papers into my briefcase. "I suppose I'll see you when I see you. We'll have to plan a lunch." I am already out the door as I call my disingenuous invitation behind me.

As I wait for the elevator, I clench my fist and listen to the voice mail that Harrison left me before I went in to see Rick. With static in the background, I hear Harrison's heavy breathing before he begins to speak.

"Peter Caine, you son of a bitch." The volatility in his voice is extreme. "I knew you were a monster, but I didn't know you were capable of *this*. You didn't need to involve Charlotte, you motherfucker. I told you not to try me, Peter. I told you not to."

THEN

Marcus was as thrilled with the news that Juliette was pregnant as I thought he would be. He loudly proclaimed that he knew we were going to have a boy, and I hoped he was right. As a token of his affection, he put me on a high-profile murder case. Working constantly on my defense, I didn't see Juliette for what felt like months. Determined to keep up appearances and ensure I still looked like a happily married man, one night I arranged for a special dinner, like I used to do before we were married.

I reserved the same table at Cipriani that we went to once when we were dating. It was an especially memorable dinner— I had set up a scavenger hunt for her across the city, which ended at a window table at Cipriani where I waited with two Bellinis and an enormous Harry Winston engagement ring. Waiting for her again at that same table, I ordered two Bellinis as before. I didn't like being in midtown in the summer when the tourists were suffocating the sidewalks. But for the sheer showmanship of it all, I wanted to re-create that special day.

Waiters and bussers whom I had known for years but hadn't seen in months stopped by my table to welcome me back.

"Wonderful to see you, Mr. Caine," they said, and I nodded politely in return. As a service captain regaled me with some celebrity story, I saw Juliette appear in the doorway. She was decked in her usual splendor, but something had changed. Her shine was dulled. The maître d' kissed both her cheeks and led her to our table.

"Hello, Juliette," I said. I stood to greet her and kissed her in a way that people would perceive as passionate. The passion was not reciprocated, and she sat, exhausted, with a huff.

"It's boiling out there," she complained, using her napkin to gently dab the sweat away from her temples. As she composed herself, I pushed the Bellini her way, imagining whatever ailed her could be solved with a drink. She angrily pushed it back to me.

Confused, I tried again. "Have a drink. It'll cool you down." I knew she must be disappointed with me for being so absent, but I was making the effort and I wished she would appreciate it.

Instead, she quietly scolded me: "Peter, is it possible you've forgotten that I am pregnant?" She forcefully slid the drink back toward me.

I had. I had forgotten that she was beleaguered and exhausted from gestating a burgeoning fetus. Even with Marcus's praise, I had become so disconnected from Juliette and the baby, I didn't associate his enthusiasm for my progress with Juliette's pregnancy.

"Of course I didn't forget," I lied. "I didn't think a bit of champagne would be bad for the baby." As I tried to explain my gaffe and hide the truth that I had forgotten, she reminded me that I had missed each of her doctor's appointments. I slumped in my chair, disappointed. This was the first time I had unintentionally failed my wife.

Juliette ordered a water and gulped it down while holding her hand up for the waiter to stay. She reminded me as he refilled her glass that she was in fact nearly seven months pregnant, and I hadn't been around for any of it.

I found myself struggling to stay in the moment and listen to Juliette pouring her concerns onto the table. I drank my Bellini and then hers and signaled to the waiter to bring me an Oban, because champagne and peach nectar was proving insufficient to quell my restless mind.

"It's like you're turning into a ghost," she said, pulling my arm so that I was forced to look at her. "Peter, aren't you interested in your child at all?"

"I'm just preparing for fatherhood differently than you're preparing for motherhood. Can't you let me do what I need to do?" I felt defensive, attacked.

"How? By working more? You'll never learn to be a father by spending time with mine. He'll never teach you to be a husband, either. I feel like an idiot. I should have known he'd have this effect on you."

Her anger furrowed deeply into the lines of her face, and I finally noticed that my relationship with her father wasn't comfortable for her.

"Your father is my partner and my professional hero. He always has been, and you've known that. The business we are in is what has kept you afloat and able to pursue your charitable dreams, so don't start knocking him to *me*." Even the Oban wasn't doing the trick at this point.

"I know him better than you do, Peter. And I know what he is capable of. Just because you're enjoying it while he takes you on as his protégé more than his partner and molds you into a monster just like he is—" She cut herself off just as she was getting to the meat of the problem.

"What's your problem with your father, Juliette?"

"He's dead inside, Peter," she snapped. "There's nothing left of him but a suit and the masks he wears."

Only now that we were about to become parents did Juliette fully acknowledge her feelings about her own family. She didn't like what she saw in Marcus, and she didn't like what she was beginning to see in me. But to me, Marcus was Olympic-level in his parenting compared to the nightmare I grew up with, and I was much more inclined to emulate him.

Juliette seemed destitute, unable to manage the burdens of pregnancy on her own. When she clutched my hand, I found myself repulsed by her neediness, and I snatched my hand away.

Realizing I couldn't behave this way, I tried to pretend to listen, to pretend to care that she was suffering, but I found the feelings that used to come naturally were difficult to muster. I reached down into myself to try to find sympathy, but I came up empty. Something inside of me was fading away, and I knew Marcus had something to do with it.

NOW

I impatiently slap the down button for the elevator in Rick's office building as Harrison's voice mail replays over and over in my head: "You didn't need to involve Charlotte." I grip the railing in the elevator tightly, trying to process what Harrison was saying to me. He may be right.

I didn't need to involve Charlie. I could have gotten back at Harrison a thousand different ways.

I can hear the blood pulsing in my ears as I traverse the crowded lobby out onto Sixth Avenue, and I begin to think about what I've done. I never imagined it would be possible that I would take it too far.

Instead of going back to my office like I planned, I sit down on a bench beneath the flags at Rockefeller Center. I watch them flow with the currents in the wind, methodically drifting back and forth in unison. The rhythm is calming and it's sending me deeper into my thoughts. I pull the custody papers from my briefcase and stare at my signature.

I never wanted to become a father because I felt it would lead to too many variables that I couldn't control. I grew up in a situation where I had no control. My father was gone, my mother didn't want me, Tommy and his wife were burdened and unmotivated and there was nothing I could do to change my situation. I watched as the people around me allowed life and circumstance to take control of them, and they did nothing to fight against it.

I knew I was going to get away from that life as soon as I possibly could. I knew I was going to obtain the kind of success they could never imagine, and I was willing to work for it. I had to cut ties with Tommy and his family, and especially with my mother. I dropped out of high school and moved to Chicago when I had saved enough money from my job at the hardware store. I wasn't even reported missing, and I don't imagine anyone went looking for me. From the moment I stepped off that train, I was in total control of my life. My destiny, my future, it was finally in my hands. I had become Peter Caine.

I fabricated the story of my European upbringing because it contained the perfect mix of glamour and tragedy, but mostly because it was so hard to trace. It turned out that falsifying documents to get new identification and forging foreign transcripts were the easiest parts of becoming someone new. I was smart and studious enough to get through the rigors of Northwestern University, even if I faked my way in. I wouldn't allow myself anything less than success. I couldn't get a ninety-nine percent on an exam—it was one hundred or it was a failure. I became addicted to success. I took it to the extreme and I kept it there.

As I watch the flags above me carelessly flop and sway, I realize that I've gone too far. To escape the nothingness I felt growing up, I've gone too far into success, too far into *anything* so I didn't have to suffer with nothing.

I tuck the papers back into my briefcase and stand up to make my way downtown. I see images appearing before my eyes. Images of Charlie, alone in her house in her black lace panties. I see Juliette and Jamie, smiling at me from across a wide room. I see Marcus, smoking a cigarette, sitting next to a shackled man. I picture Claire scrolling through the internet photos of the Rhodes Foundation masquerade—for the first time, I try to imagine how she must have felt seeing me draped all over someone else.

I realize that I am lying to myself as much as I'm lying to everyone else. I'm not in control, and I see now that I never have been. I've just lied so much that I believe myself.

A rush of adrenaline and emotion suddenly envelops me, and I see flashes of Jamie's face when he was born, when he was growing up and the day I left them; when I left them with *nothing*. I realize I went so blindly away from my upbringing that I never saw I went full circle and returned to the nothingness I was trying to escape. I realize the custody papers could be the change I didn't know I was waiting for.

Jamie might be the only chance I have left. They're all gone, but I still have Jamie, and I still have a chance to give him something better than what I had.

Hurried masses of commuters slam into me from all angles as I pinball down the blocks as if drugged and lost. I pause at a streetlight on Forty-Sixth Street and look down at my hands. I see the wounds on my thumb and forefinger from the melted glass I plucked from the fireplace. Pedestrians shove me from behind when I don't jump off the curb as soon as the light changes and I'm jolted back into the present. I walk toward home instead of returning to the office, knowing Claire will be back from her trip. When I spoke to her before she left for the Hamptons, the last thing she told me to do was cut off my affair with Charlie. I told her I would, and now the affair is over.

My legs feel heavy as I trudge the blocks toward my house. I've walked these city streets a million times, and yet today the hostility in my fellow pedestrians is palpable. They seem to bump into me intentionally as I navigate the crowds, and their angry eyes are focused squarely on me. It looks as if every second person is scowling in my direction and I feel my chest beginning to tighten.

A group of people across Thirty-Fourth Street are wearing matching translucent rain ponchos, all with their hoods up, despite it being a sunny day. The light changes and I convene with the group in the middle of the road. They collect into a tight mass around me, their ponchos sticking to my suit, all of them staring at me and knocking into me from all sides. I feel trapped in a sea of stinging jellyfish, and I claw my way out of the scrum and gasp for air.

I turn to look at what the hell just happened. The last man in a rain poncho climbs onto the lowest step of a tour bus, and he turns to glare at me, and I could swear it's Marcus Rhodes.

I hurry east toward the wider blocks of Fifth Avenue, and dodge into the relative peace of Madison Square Park. I stop at the fountain on the south side to calm myself with the soothing sounds of water flowing.

Just as I lean against the surrounding fence, two enormous dogs with their leashes tangled escape from the adjacent dog park and run, snarled together and barking, jumping at each other's throats, right into my legs. Two frantic owners chase after their dogs and desperately try to pull them apart, and I'm forced to hold myself up against the fence, pushing the dogs away with my feet. As one of the owners snatches her dog's leash and pulls it free from the other, her enormous engagement ring catches the sun, and it's the exact same ring I gave to Juliette. I strain to see her face, but her wild hair, the same dirty blond as Juliette's, has obscured her features, and she hurries out of the park before I can tell if I know her.

My breath is shallow and short. I can't seem to get oxygen past my throat. I walk to the easternmost exit from the park, carefully studying each person sitting on the benches. Every other person is Juliette. Juliette when she was pregnant, when she woke up in the morning and her eyes were swollen and foggy, Juliette when we first met.

There is a Pomeranian sitting on an old woman's lap, and when the dog barks a piercing series of yaps, the old woman yanks her collar and cries, "Stop that, Charlie."

My deliberate walk turns into a run as I near my house. I need to get inside to hide myself from these things I'm seeing. I need to breathe. I need to see Claire and get these haunting images out of my eyes.

I rush up the steps of the brownstone and slam the door behind me. I hear the faucet in the kitchen sink and see a bucket of cleaning supplies sitting at the base of the stairs. My housekeeper must still be working. It's not often I'm home in the middle of the day to catch her while she cleans. I wipe the sweat from my forehead and walk into the kitchen to let her know I'm home, and the woman at the sink turns around to reveal it's Claire, not the housekeeper.

"You're home?" she says, turning quickly to check the clock. "It's the middle of the afternoon. What are you doing here?"

"Claire," I say, uneasy and conscious of every word I choose, "things are going to be different."

"Different? What do you mean?" She turns off the faucet and wipes her hands on a striped dish towel. "What's going on? You didn't call it off, did you?" Apparently, her time away with her friends hadn't rid her mind of my affair.

"It's over, it's all over, I promise you." I know I'll never cheat with Charlie again.

Claire looks at me with skepticism, but I can see she wants to believe me. Her hands drop to her sides in defeat, and her features soften. She knows I won't do it again.

"There's no one else now, Claire. No one."

THEN

Marcus had me working on a case defending a man accused of beating his pregnant wife so badly that she lost the baby. I wondered if he was trying to send me a message, or if he was using the opportunity to further harden my heart against compassion that would hit close to home. Regardless of his motives, I felt completely one-sided in the battle between home and work, and which side would get my attention, my efforts and my dedication. My work would win out every time. With my mind completely preoccupied by the outcome of my trial, I was unable to focus on anything else. Every high-profile case I had since Stu Bogovian was another chance for me to replace the memory of defeat and humiliation with a glorious triumph.

One morning before heading into court, I ate breakfast with Juliette, giving her as much of my time as I could tolerate.

"We need to move out of this apartment, you know." Juliette started in on me. "We can't have a baby in your bachelor pad."

"It's a 2,500-square-foot loft, we can easily put in at least two more bedrooms. One for the baby and one for a nanny," I said, sipping my morning coffee.

"I don't want to live down here. Tribeca is no place for a family, it's so sterile and stark." She looked around at the huge support columns inside the loft, the fire escape that I often used as a balcony during parties, and she clutched her belly. "I want something homier. A house. A *real* townhouse, not an apartment. I want a fireplace, and a garden, something peaceful. I don't want to look out the window and see bridges and traffic and hear horns blaring all day."

"Fine," I said. "I will look into it this afternoon when I'm back from court."

"There's a lot we need to talk about before the baby arrives, you know." She fiddled with her wedding ring; one of her telltale signals that she was about to broach an uncomfortable topic. "More than just our living arrangements." A sense of dread started to fill the room.

"What do you need to talk about?" I put down my newspaper and steeled myself.

"My parents are getting a divorce." She looked up at me from her seat, and I couldn't tell if she wanted sympathy or if she was simply stating fact.

"Okay," I began, worried that this was not the subject matter that was making her fidgety. "This isn't a surprise to you, is it?" Perhaps it wasn't the most compassionate response, but it was honest.

"No, it's not a surprise." She sighed, frustrated. "It's probably for the best, but I can't help feeling really down that my family is splitting up just as the baby is about to arrive."

"The baby won't know the difference. I wouldn't worry about that." I returned most of my attention to my newspaper.

"Well," she went on, fidgeting with her ring again, "I don't have much of a relationship with my father anymore, and my mother is as cozy as a grizzly bear..." She paused, hoping I would catch her drift before she had to articulate her point.

"And?" I said, hoping she wasn't going where I thought she was going.

"And, since our family is already so small and disconnected, I wondered if you would be willing to extend an olive branch—"

"Are you crazy?" I threw my newspaper onto the table and jumped to my feet. "Don't even finish that sentence, Juliette. I *never* should have breathed a word of that to you." The anger rose into my face and I was immediately transported back to my childhood living room, feeling completely invisible, completely inconsequential. I was infuriated that Juliette was the one who pushed me back to this place.

"But," she pleaded, "for the sake of the baby, so he can grow up with a family, please, Peter."

"As far as I'm concerned, I never told you anything, you don't know anything and whatever you *think* you know is a wild fabrication created entirely in your head. So don't you dare ever, *ever*, say a word about this again." I stormed into the bedroom, hands trembling with fear and rage. I could hear Juliette burst into tears in the great room.

I dressed quickly and stood facing the bathroom mirror, combing my hair over and over again. Juliette must be going crazy, I told myself. She's making up stories about my past because she wants to hurt me. She wants to take me down. Now that I'm so successful, and following in her father's footsteps, she's jealous and wants to ruin me.

I continued combing my hair, allowing these thoughts to

saturate my brain. I didn't grow up in Vermont. I grew up in Europe. Traveling from country to country, living a glamorous life with sophisticated parents. We were rich. I've never even been to Vermont. I allowed the thoughts to swim around to the deepest corners of my brain, methodically passing the comb from front to back, front to back, watching myself in the mirror. My breath steadied, and my pulse slowed. It must be the pregnancy, I thought, messing with Juliette's mind. Or her parents' divorce, making her think crazy things.

"I'm off to court now," I said, returning to the great room, calmed. "I have to concentrate and keep my mind clear. I can't have another episode like Bogovian." I spoke robotically, making it clear to Juliette that I would not entertain her insane suggestions.

"What happened to you, Peter? Where the hell is the man I married?"

I didn't answer her, despite the despair on her face. I walked to the door and called behind me, "I'll start looking for townhouses when I get back from court."

NOW

This morning feels suspiciously like every other morning; the three of us having breakfast sitting at the round table in the kitchen. Claire is especially sprightly, perhaps because I told her my affair was over. She buoyantly tells Jamie and me about her Hamptons getaway.

"It was the cutest little house. We had a lot of fun. It's hard to get your girlfriends all together when everyone has their own lives." She sips her coffee, then continues, "How did you boys get on without me?"

"We had a great time," I bellow, too loudly to be genuine. I clear my throat and try again. "It was very nice to spend some time together—like you were saying about your friends. It's hard to find the time, and I really enjoyed being with Jamie."

Both Claire and Jamie look at me with disbelief, like I couldn't possibly be serious.

"I mean it. I haven't sat down and watched a movie in a long time. I enjoyed it, Jamie. I hope you did, too."

"You watched a movie?" Claire prompts, "Which one?"

"Pulp Fiction," Jamie responds. "Downstairs in the theater you were telling me about. We had leftover Chinese. And drank a bottle of wine." Jamie seems to have enjoyed himself. I look to Claire, hopeful that his recounting of our evening together will convince her that I am turning over a new leaf.

"Not just *any* wine, either. An '86 Margaux." I smile proudly.

Claire nods, intrigued if not yet convinced. She keeps nodding slowly as she turns her attention back to the paper, and the conversation about my and Jamie's night together concludes.

"Harrison's above the fold again," Claire reports, seeing the enormous face of my adversary on the cover of the *New York Times*.

"Snatching the limelight, is he?" I'm immediately reminded of the horrible voice mail he left me the other day.

Claire's coffee cup suddenly clatters to the table as she grasps her face and cries, "Oh, my God. Peter, oh, my God!" She thrusts the paper at me, pointing frantically at the cover story. "Charlotte was killed!"

"Killed?" I exclaim, and my mouth goes dry. "What are you *talking* about?" I pull my feet off the chair opposite me and examine the photo on the front page, my heart slamming against my rib cage. There is a large picture of Harrison's face, next to a smaller photo of police and EMTs carrying a gurney with a body covered by a white sheet from the front of Charlotte's house on Twentieth Street.

"Who's Charlotte?" Jamie asks, setting his phone down on the breakfast table.

"Charlotte is Charlie." I cough, my lips sticking to my parched gums. "Harrison's stepdaughter. You met her at the masquerade we went to at the Met." I quickly gulp my water to soothe my arid mouth. "Remember? The hot one?" I take the *New York Times* in my hands and scan the article.

"The hot one?" Claire scoffs, throwing her hands up. "Peter, the woman is dead. Don't you care at all?"

"Of course I care. Let me read this and see what happened."

"The poor woman. And Elizabeth! A mother losing a daughter, so horrible." Claire wipes tears from her eyes with her napkin, a little too theatrical for my taste. "Poor Harrison. He's probably devastated. I can't imagine how they must feel."

"Oh, he's not devastated," I sneer, knowing just what kind of man Harrison is. "This is the most perfect timing for him. He needed something to get support from the liberal electorate." I drop the paper onto the table. It's easy for me to fall back on sarcasm and wit in times of emotional upheaval. "'Grieving father' is *exactly* the kind of stuff these hippies eat up. He just got the sympathy vote and now he's going to win the election. He probably had her killed, heartless son of a bitch."

"Really?" Jamie perks up, suddenly interested.

"Why not? Harrison Doyle is a grade-A scumbag. I should congratulate him for having a stepdaughter with the good sense to get herself killed two months before an election." Claire stares at me with furrowed brows. "What? It's not *me*. I'm not the one who would off my own daughter. Why are you looking at me like that?"

"Jesus, Peter," Claire scolds. "A woman is dead. And you're making jokes?" She turns her attention to Jamie. "Of course Harrison didn't hire someone to murder his stepdaughter for political gain." She shoots me a vicious glance.

I suddenly remember my conversation with Claire by the fireplace a few days ago; now is the time to show compassion. "Jamie, I'm just kidding. I'm sure Harrison had nothing to do with what happened to Charlie."

As we finish breakfast, Jamie goes up to his room to get ready for school, and Claire and I stay at the kitchen table, refilling our coffee cups. The air in the kitchen is stagnant and stuffy; it feels like I can't get a good breath.

"I don't want to talk about this in front of Jamie," Claire says. "He's too young to understand all the nuances and complexities of the situation."

"You mean the murder?"

"No, I mean who Charlotte really is. Or *was*, I guess. He doesn't know about the two of you, does he? Does he know that she was the one who broke up your marriage with Juliette?"

"How could he? I never told him, and I don't think Juliette would burden her son with that kind of information. He didn't seem to have any idea who she was when I introduced him to her at the benefit." I see Claire's fists clench when I mention Charlie and the benefit. Clearly this is a wound that will need a long time to heal.

"Well, don't you think he asked why you got divorced? Don't you think when he was old enough, he might wonder why you broke up?"

"I'm sure Juliette invented a suitable fairy tale." I stare at the picture of my former lover on the front page of the paper and think about that day Stu Bogovian called me to Rikers Island. Everything he told me that day must have led to this awful fate for her.

"Did you love her?" Claire cocks her head to the side, and I can't tell if she's asking me out of sympathy or if she's trapping me into a confession.

"Claire, come on." I lay the paper on the table but keep looking at the photo of Charlie's lifeless body hidden by the white sheet. "This is not normal. I can't sit at the table with you and discuss Charlie—who was just *murdered*—over coffee and croissants. You asked me to stop seeing her and I did. Not that I was *seeing* her anymore, but you know what I mean. I don't want to talk about this with you."

"When did you see her? When did you call it off?" Claire's suspicion reappears.

"I didn't *tell* her that it was over. Like I said to you, it's been done anyway, there was no reason for me to bring anything up with her. What you needed was for me to not start it up again, and I promised you that I wouldn't. I told you, things are going to be different now."

"You did love her—I can see it in your eyes. You've never looked that way when we talked about Juliette, not even when she died. You loved Charlotte, didn't you?" Her tone is not sympathetic.

"I love *you*, Claire. And that's the only thing that should matter to you. You have no one to share me with. Juliette is gone, and, well, Charlie is gone now, too." I push the newspaper onto the chair next to me. "There's no one else. It's just you."

Claire looks at me skeptically. I hope she believes my remorse is genuine.

"What did you mean the other night when you told me she was using you? You said that you didn't stay together long after you broke up with Juliette, and you said it was because Charlotte was using you. What did you mean?"

"I told you she was no angel, Claire. She was a phony, only out for herself."

"A phony? How?"

"She wasn't interested in *me*, she was interested in Juliette. She used me to get to Juliette because she wanted the foundation."

"The Rhodes Foundation?" Claire brings her coffee to her lips.

"Yeah." My mind clouds with images of Juliette. "Juliette built the Rhodes Foundation out of kindness, generosity and a genuine intent to help people with the money she raised. She was the darling of the philanthropic world. Nothing could ever compete with Rhodes and everyone knew it. Charlie wanted the foundation, and she would do whatever it took to get it."

"So, she started an affair with you? Juliette's husband." Claire scoffs. "That seems stupid."

"She went through me for information. She was looking for weak spots, anything she could capitalize on to compromise Juliette's standing at the foundation. She rode her coattails, took advantage." I think about it some more. "She was staging a hostile takeover." For the first time, I feel a creeping sense of guilt that I was complicit in the behaviors I'm describing. "Charlie felt enormous pressure to climb to a social level that would help her overcome her father's brutish and unrefined persona. People don't *like* Harrison Doyle. He figured he was too late to change, and he convinced his daughter to play the game and used her to pad his social stock."

"His own daughter? This all sounds so depraved."

"It's not depraved." I try to explain a world that Claire can't possibly understand. "It's the way it works. You're either born into it, or you have to claw your way up. Everyone wants to be at the top. Some people take dirtier paths to get there."

"I thought she was supposed to be so wonderful. She has such a different reputation."

"So, it worked." I shake my head and toss up my palms. "She's a snake, Claire. She had it all planned out. It wasn't about having an affair with me, it was about proving to Juliette that she could and *would* aggressively take from her whatever she wanted. Husband, foundation, whatever."

"And she managed to keep her methods under wraps?" Claire seems both disappointed and intrigued.

"As far as I know, her reputation was pristine. Everyone believes Charlie to be like a little sister to Juliette. Looked up to her, wanted to be just like her. But in my experience—what I saw—Charlie wanted to skin Juliette and wear her."

THEN

We put my loft on the market to have the money we needed to invest in a townhouse. Juliette suggested we move out and live temporarily in a hotel, so we weren't constantly disturbed while potential buyers came in to view the loft. We put our things in storage and headed to The Carlyle on the Upper East Side.

"Are you comfortable here?" I asked Juliette as we slowly unpacked our belongings into the ample closet space in the suite.

"I'm much happier uptown than I was in Tribeca, yes." She struggled with the zipper on her jewelry bag. Juliette had been so out of place downtown, she considered it practically a miracle that we moved to the Upper East Side when we did because our child was born soon after.

As Juliette and I were settling into life at the hotel, at work, my domestic violence trial concluded, and Marcus was thrilled with our victory; my client had been found not guilty on all charges. My chest puffed with pride as it did each time I took another step toward my rightful place at the top of my profession. I left court and returned to my office to find my desk had been rearranged.

I pulled open drawers, looking for my notebooks, pens and supplies to find a new leather folder holding a legal pad, and a gold Montblanc pen. A pristine new blotter sat on my desk, surrounded with Tiffany & Co. crystal ashtrays and cups to hold my office detritus. The ashtray was filled with gold paper clips. I opened my closet and saw a cashmere overcoat hanging where my trench coat used to be. A note written on Marcus's thick stationery stuck out from the lapel pocket. *Keep it up, and you'll keep going up*, it read.

I looked around my office; everything in it was chosen by Marcus. The chairs, the marble chessboard, everything. Each time I won a case, he would remove pieces of me and replace them with pieces of him. He called them gifts, prizes for a job well done, and I found myself in a place where I felt I couldn't be anything less than excessively grateful.

"Peter." Anna stepped into my office while softly knocking.

I looked up from all the new luxury around me. "Yes, Anna?"

"Juliette has been trying to get through to you. She's on her way to the hospital. She's in labor."

My breath caught in my throat. The inevitable day had finally arrived. Right on schedule. I walked over to Sinan's office to let him know I was leaving. I entered the room, this time taking notice that all the items in his office were those he had brought with him when he joined the firm. He had his tattered old briefcase, his Turkish rugs on the floor and his scented candles burning in the corner. The office clearly belonged to Sinan and no one else. Mine had morphed into a replica of Marcus's office.

"I'm off to the hospital," I said, taking a seat across from his desk. I was surprised to feel almost nothing other than a low-grade sense of discomfort in my stomach.

"She's in labor?" Sinan asked.

"Apparently so." I thought of movie scenes and television shows with happy husbands and wives rushing to the delivery room, clutching each other in anxious anticipation, and I just felt uneasy leaving the office while I had things left to do.

"It's going to be vile in there, you know." Sinan scowled, completely unsentimental. He was the perfect person to keep me occupied so I could miss the birth. "But I suppose the father is supposed to be present, eh?" He rolled his eyes, and I was immediately jealous that he wasn't the one who was about to become a father.

I drank one more cup of coffee while Sinan worked, delaying my exit as much as I could. I used the time as my last chance to wrap my mind around the idea that this child was coming and there was nothing I could do to stop him. I hoped he would take after Juliette. I knew that if she were the one raising him, his chances of developing traits from her side of the family were much higher than turning into some version of the person I left in Vermont. I allowed my mind to settle on that as the reason I would leave the child-rearing exclusively to my wife.

I walked into the maternity ward at Lenox Hill Hospital an hour later and sat uncomfortably in the waiting room. Several nurses and doctors approached me, inviting me into the delivery room.

"Your wife has been asking for you, sir," a bubbly nurse told me, extending her hand to help me from my seat.

"I think it's better for everyone if I stay out here and wait for her to be finished—in *there*," I said, completely turned off from the idea of witnessing the event. The nurse glared at me, horrified that I didn't want to participate in my son's birth.

I read newspapers in the waiting room until a nurse notified me that my son had been born, and both baby and mother were healthy. I finished the article I was reading and slowly entered her room, legs heavy.

"You didn't want to cut the cord?" Juliette asked me, arms outstretched, begging me to come to her. The air between us felt like it was some alien atmosphere, thick and impassable. I trudged through it, grimacing, scanning the room for evidence of birth.

"Where is the baby?" I asked as Juliette grasped my forearm.

"They took him to be cleaned and weighed and wrapped up tight." She looked at me quizzically. "Aren't you happy? We have a boy! Aren't you excited to meet him?"

"What did you name him?" I asked, not answering her question.

"Jamie," she said. "Jamie Rhodes Caine."

A boy, a biological heir to maintain the family name, I thought to myself, just as Marcus had wanted. "Marcus will be thrilled that you included Rhodes," I said.

Later in the afternoon, Juliette's parents came to see the baby. Katherine and Marcus played nicely together for Juliette's sake, Katherine seemingly delighted at the sight of her first grandchild. Marcus looked at him the way one would regard a golf trophy or sailfish; an accomplishment more than a human being. After her parents departed, separately, Juliette and I were left alone in the recovery room while Jamie slept in his bassinet.

"Aren't you happy?" she asked me again.

"Of course…of course I am. This is going to be very good

for us, very good for business, as well." I didn't realize this was absolutely the wrong thing to say.

"Business?" Juliette was too exhausted to fight and lay her head back in defeat. "Jamie is my child, the most precious thing in the world. He is not here for my father's professional gain. Or yours."

I assured her that wasn't how Marcus felt, and even though she knew I was lying, she held my hand and pretended we were what we appeared to be—happy. She quickly fell asleep in her bed, and I looked into Jamie's bassinet, trying to conjure up some emotion other than fear.

NOW

I arrive at my office on Church and Leonard, head filled with memories of Charlie. Only weeks have passed since Juliette died, and here I find myself again, thinking of the death of another former lover. As I walk by Sarah at the front desk, she quickly lowers her *Times* and shoves it into her top drawer. She attempts to gasp out a few words as I walk by, but nerves seem to choke her.

I notice several associates and two junior partners standing around a conference room, drinking coffee and discussing Charlie's murder. I walk in and take my time surveying the spread of breakfast items, eavesdropping. I need to hear how people are discussing Charlotte's murder; what kind of thoughts they have, what kinds of emotions they display. I listen intently to the women in the room. They're horrified at the vicious nature of the crime. The men, inclined to comfort their coworkers, downplay the brutality, assuring everyone they're safe in their own homes.

"Hey, you okay? You were friends with Charlotte Doyle, weren't you?" a young, verbose attorney asks me.

I don't turn around. I finish filling my cup with coffee and somberly nod.

"Sorry, man. That really sucks."

I hold up my coffee and give a tight-lipped smile.

He looks at me quizzically, and I realize I've misread the situation. Smiling was not the proper response. I cough into my hand, quickly furrow my brows and say, "Thanks." I walk out of the conference room and head to my office.

I sit down at my desk and concentrate on pushing my instinct to make light of the situation to the back of my mind. I pull my cell phone from my jacket pocket and scroll through my contacts looking for Harrison Doyle's office number. I punch the numbers from my cell phone screen into the office phone. Before the first ring, I slam down the receiver and drop my head to my hands in frustration.

How can I call this man to offer condolences after the last message he left me? I pull the bottle of scotch from my bookcase and pour a shot into my coffee. I never do this, but I need to steel my nerves, for the first time, conscious of how my comments will be perceived; concerned that I need to say the right thing in this moment, and afraid I don't know what the right thing is.

Next to the Oban, I see the stack of unopened letters and cards that Sinan had left here for me days earlier. They aren't business envelopes, and the addresses on the front are handwritten. Trying to distract myself, I look over the cards and wait for the scotch to take effect. With a gold letter opener, I tear open the first envelope.

Dear Peter, we are so sorry for your loss. Juliette was a dear friend...

They're condolence letters. I read through more of the

notes. They're filled with genuine sympathy and compassion. It's like stumbling onto a movie script; exactly the guidance I need to make this phone call to Harrison.

I pour another shot into my coffee and continue reading the letters. I find one in particular that I feel is the best to imitate, written by someone named Christine, who I can't remember. I read the letter over and over. I stand up and walk to the mirror by the front door of my office and recite the letter to my reflection. I practice different intonations, stress different words, until I find the rhythm that feels most natural.

I sit back down at my desk with the letter in front of me. I close my eyes and suck in a few deep breaths. Now I'm confident enough to dial Harrison's office number, and I put the phone on speaker. With each ring, I feel my confidence grow, knowing I'm going to say the right thing. As I listen to Harrison's voice-mail message, I prepare myself to speak.

"Harrison," I begin, "it's Peter Caine. I am so sorry for your loss. Charlie was a dear friend to me for many years, and I looked up to her—" I lose my place on the card "—her, uh… philanthropic leadership. She will be sorely missed."

Thrilled with my performance and somewhat shocked that I was lucky enough to get his voice mail, I feel galvanized and snatch up the phone back up to see if I can get Harrison's mobile voice mail, as well. Two attempts look even better than one. The phone rings and rings and when the voice mail chirps in my ear, I hold the card to my face and read aloud again, making sure to remember to replace "Juliette" with "Charlie."

I watch myself in the mirror as I speak the last few words from memory. "Charlie was a dear friend to me for many years, and I looked up to her philanthropic leadership. She will be sorely missed."

Suddenly, my heart jumps into my throat and my delight

quickly turns to panic as I realize I've left the exact same message on both machines. Harrison will surely recognize I'd rehearsed or worse, read from a script. "Um, again, I'm so sorry, and um…" I'm stumbling over my words and grasping at the racing thoughts in my mind for something else to say, to salvage my message and put across something that sounds like a genuine apology.

"Harry, old friend, it's a good thing I'm taking time off Rhodes & Caine, or else you might find *me* defending the bastard who did this." Satisfied, I triumphantly hang up the phone and flop back into my chair.

I think of the message Harrison left for me yesterday; I remember the words he said to me, the threats. Then I think of our dinner a few days ago. I had Harrison in my pocket for nearly twenty years, and after that dinner and the masquerade ball, I knew I was just as much in his.

Now we were deadlocked, I would only keep my mouth shut if he shut his.

THEN

Juliette and I returned to The Carlyle after Jamie was born, both scared and unprepared. Jamie was colicky and cried from the moment he woke up to the moment he went to sleep, and Juliette cried nearly as much. Marcus and Katherine finalized their divorce, and neither of them came to see us. At first, they phoned now and again, sent enormous arrangements of flowers, but after a couple of weeks, they barely answered the phone when Juliette called. She was feeling abandoned by her parents, rejected by her baby, and I wasn't equipped to help her. I bought her expensive gifts, but they brought her no joy. I made reservations at the best restaurants, but it just made her feel worse because she didn't have the energy to go out.

After a month living at The Carlyle, we bought a town-house in Gramercy Park that Juliette loved. It needed a full renovation, but it was the only thing that seemed to make her feel alive again. She was excited to be building a real home for our family. While she spent her time on the town-house and with the baby, a new girl started showing up at the Rhodes Foundation, Charlotte Doyle, the stepdaughter of DA Harrison Doyle.

One afternoon, I got a phone call at my office from Juliette. She asked me to meet with the new girl to discuss an upcoming benefit since Jamie was sick and she had to stay home with him. Always looking for reasons to avoid my domestic responsibilities, I jumped at the opportunity to spend more time away from home. That night was the first time I met Charlotte Doyle.

She was perched on a stool at a high cocktail table in the rooftop bar of the Peninsula Hotel. She was stunning. Where Juliette was lithe and elegant and lit from within, Charlotte Doyle was angular, dangerous, sexy. I was drawn to her immediately. She was charming and winsome, gushing about my wife and telling me how she had long looked up to her. It was clear Charlotte wanted very badly to fall in with New York society types and saw Juliette as a key to that door.

"I haven't seen her since I officially started working there, but I'll tell you, she is thick in the air at the Rhodes Foundation office."

I wasn't concentrating on what Charlotte was saying, instead transfixed by the way her red lipstick shone in contrast to her perfectly white teeth.

"I've been following her work for years. She is so elegant and effortless. I've never once heard a bad word about her."

Charlotte was fighting an uphill battle trying to gain acceptance in New York society, her mother coming from nowhere Long Island and her stepfather a boorish, classless district attorney. Although she was distractingly sexy, and one could learn how to properly ingratiate oneself into the upper classes,

Charlotte would never have the natural abilities Juliette had that propelled her to the stratospheric status she held.

"Charlotte," I said, "how can I help with the benefit planning?" I ordered us both another cocktail, secretly hoping the evening might turn from business to pleasure.

"I couldn't believe my luck when I found out I would be meeting with *you* tonight instead of Juliette," she began, transforming her manner from confident and direct to coy and flirtatious. "Now I can pick your brain about my hero and find out what she's really like. How she got to the top, what it would take for *me* to get there." She crushed an ice cube between her teeth. "And call me Charlie."

She seemed entranced and infatuated with Juliette and the Rhodes family. She asked me all sorts of questions about Juliette's journey to the apex of New York society. I told her the truth; it was in her blood.

"Well, Juliette's parents are both from old established New York families, so she was born into this life. She grew up surrounded by only the best. The best prep schools, summers in Europe, internships that her parents arranged. She had connections before she was even born."

"Surely that's not the *only* way someone can rise to the top of this exclusive world? Is it?" She oozed confidence and flirtation.

"If you're not born with it, you'll have to fight a harder and longer fight. You'll have to know all the right people, and they'll have to love you. You can't sneak your way in here, you have to earn it." I was careful not to give specific advice. I didn't want Charlie getting suspicious about how I knew the back way into the world she wanted to get into.

"Did you come from such an illustrious background, as well, Peter?"

"Well, not quite a Rhodes family upbringing." I signaled to the waiter. "But good enough, I suppose."

At the end of the evening, I left with her phone number in my pocket and walked back to The Carlyle, my head rife with duplicity.

What I didn't want to tell Charlie when she asked about my social standing was that I *didn't* belong. I was an interloper, a fake. I'd sneaked into this New York privileged life, just as she was planning to do. My story of growing up jumping between elite prep schools in Europe, keeping up with my father's exciting and glamorous art business, was the perfect mix of intriguing and believable while also being sufficiently obscure that it could not be verified. I found more often than not, people simply assumed I belonged among them. Northwestern and Columbia Law acted as visa stamps in my passport to the privileged world. When Marcus Rhodes took a personal interest in me, the deal was sealed.

Charlie's interrogation that night reminded me how fragile the whole facade could be, and now that I had such a strong foothold, keeping up appearances would be more important than ever. If anyone found out I was a liar and a fraud, I would be ruined. If Charlie were going to start poking around in my life, I would have to keep her under control.

I could say that it started out innocently enough. Charlie Doyle captivated me, seeming to fit the bill for both friend and foe, and I wanted to keep my enemies close. Being Harrison's stepdaughter just increased the intrigue. What did she really want with me, and what did she want with Juliette?

I told myself I was helping my wife by taking over some of her responsibilities at the Rhodes Foundation. I told myself I wasn't hurting anyone. Charlie was married at the time, after all—we weren't free to explore any burgeoning desires.

It wasn't until one night when Charlie confided in me that her marriage was heading for divorce that I could no longer convince myself I was guiltless. But before I had the opportunity to fully commit to infidelity, I got the call from Marcus that changed everything.

Juliette and Jamie were asleep in the bedroom at The Carlyle when my phone rang as I sat alone in the living room.

"Peter." Marcus's voice sounded distraught and pained. "We need to talk."

"What is it? Are you all right?" I hadn't heard him sound anything less than fervent and intense since I had met him.

"We're going to have a problem soon."

"What is it? Harrison? DA's office?"

"No, it's not about work." He stalled, and I didn't want to keep guessing.

"What's the problem?"

"It's cancer. Stage four." His voice deflated as the diagnosis escaped his lips.

"Cancer? What kind of cancer?" I was floored. I couldn't begin to imagine a man as powerful and controlling as Marcus besieged with something as catastrophic as stage-four cancer.

"It's everywhere now. It's a rare form that originated in my liver. But now it's lungs, too, and pancreas. It's a death sentence, Peter. I'm finished." His voice was defeated, filled with disappointment more than fear.

"Jesus. How much time?"

"They can't say for sure. But the head of oncology at Sloan Kettering said it's a matter of weeks."

I listened to the man I had admired for the entirety of my adult life shift from an unflinching master to a decrepit old man, and I couldn't help but cringe. He was supposed to be superhuman, and the mundane occurrence of terminal cancer made him seem weak, pliable and suddenly unworthy of my admiration. Another father figure, leaving me disappointed and alone.

Juliette and I discussed funeral planning the following morning. To my surprise, she wasn't devastated at the news of her father's diagnosis.

"Terminal cancer?" she repeated incredulously. Her face betrayed no emotion. If anything, she seemed flippant. "You realize it's insane he didn't tell me this news himself."

"He said it was a rare form of liver cancer, likely caused by long-term ingestion of toxins." I ignored the part about him telling me instead of her.

"I knew he would eventually kill himself. If that *job* didn't give him cancer..." She didn't finish her sentence, she just stared at me expectantly.

"It's not the job, Juliette." I was so tired of defending our work, I didn't even bother to continue.

Cancer, I thought. So weak and unbecoming. My hero was falling, and a strange sense of freedom washed over me, like I was regaining control of my own life. Just as I did when I left Vermont, I would once again be the only one setting rules for myself. And in my rule book, I was open to exploring whatever I wanted with Charlotte Doyle.

NOW

I hear Sinan's office door close loudly just as I disconnect after leaving Harrison my voice mails. I tuck my cell phone into my pocket in case he calls back and walk over to chat with Sinan.

"Good morning, my friend," he says, welcoming me into his office.

"Morning, Sinan." I sit down and pull a pile of paper clips from a crystal ashtray on Sinan's desk. I pull them straight and wrap the straightened clips around one another.

"What happened to you? You look like a drowned rat." Sinan gives me a look of disgust. He gently places his cigarette between his lips.

"Things have been a little strange recently," I reply somberly.

"What are you wearing, exactly? Are those Levi's?" Sinan doesn't acknowledge my response and presses the intercom button to page his assistant. "Jessica, some stranger wearing Peter's skin is sitting in my office," he teases. I ignore my friend's joke and concentrate on my paper clips. "You okay?" he asks. "You're usually much more tickled by my humor."

Completely entranced, I won't look up from my paper clips. I keep twisting more and more together just as I did at Rick's office the day before.

"Hey." Sinan lowers his voice, leans across his desk and places his heavy hand on top of mine. "All seriousness, you all right? You're not yourself. This about Charlotte Doyle?"

"Maybe. Maybe this is all about Charlotte Doyle."

Sinan quickly switches gears to talk about Charlie's murder. "Bogovian is the first person anyone will think of," he proclaims. "After threatening Harrison on television? What better way to get someone back than to kill his daughter?"

"Yeah, that's the obvious answer. But that's not what *I* think."

"What do you think?" Sinan leans back and lights another cigarette.

"What I told Claire and Jamie this morning—I bet Harrison has his dirty hands in this. Regardless of Stu's threats the other day, Charlie's death will be hugely beneficial for Harrison. If Stu Bogovian actually had her killed to get back at Harrison, it was a mistake. Her death is going to be magic for Harry come the election. If Stu wanted to punish him, he should have come up with something else."

"Interesting theory. But the Bogovian thing is on everyone's radar, so he'll be investigated immediately." Sinan takes a hard drag. "And I haven't heard a peep about the notion that her stepfather had her killed for political gain."

"Well, I didn't quite say *that*, Sinan, but anyone who knows that family will know that something fishy is happening in the Doyle household."

"It's still early, but the media is portraying Charlotte as an absolute darling. Even mentioned Juliette on *Morning Joe*."

Sinan impersonates the news reporter: "Charlotte Doyle, following in the footsteps of legendary philanthropist Juliette Rhodes, had been given the reins of the Rhodes Foundation after Juliette's untimely passing—I'm paraphrasing, but something to that effect."

"Mark my words, Sinan. You're going to see lots of dirty laundry coming from the Doyle family. Lots of it."

"You know something?" He raises a suspicious eyebrow at me.

"I know Charlotte and Harrison Doyle. That's what I know." I send a sly smile back to Sinan. "I just left him a message, well, *two*, actually. I didn't have a thing to say to the man, so I read from a condolence card someone sent me when Juliette died."

"Very clever, Peter." He stubs out his cigarette.

I get up from my seat and javelin the paper-clip stick into the garbage can. "I'm leaving now, Sinan. Don't take on anything big, okay? Keep yourself available just in case."

I avoid the elevator and head down the back staircase onto Leonard Street. The humidity is waning, and the crisp air feels refreshing as I walk north and east toward the house. I haven't walked home from the office in years—I usually elect to go out for drinks, to parties or engage in affairs before returning home, frequently to find Claire already asleep.

As I walk up Broadway, I survey my surroundings in a way that feels unfamiliar. I'm cautious and exploratory, seeing what has changed since I last paid attention. I walk east on Canal into Chinatown, a neighborhood I've always hated and avoid unless absolutely necessary. I breathe deeply through my nose, expecting the rank stench of decaying fish, but am instead greeted by fresh air and a lingering ginger scent. I look into storefront windows with rows of ducks suspended on shiny silver hooks, and a mechanical cat waving its right paw.

I continue north on Mulberry, passing through the ever-diminishing Little Italy. I stop in front of Lombardi's, breathing in memories from my past, and march on to Bowery.

Everything has changed since I last walked home this way. I have that uneasy feeling again, like everyone is staring at me. I feel as if I'm a tourist, out of place, walking through the narrow roads of some European town. The people I see on the street are looking at me funny; angrily. I see a woman whip around a corner as Bowery turns into Third Avenue, and I could've sworn it was Charlie. Unsettled, I pick up the pace to return home.

I find Claire sitting at the kitchen table. She has the *Post* and the *New York Times* on the chair next to her and is intently clicking through news sites on a laptop.

"Have you read this stuff?" she asks when she hears me behind her. "It's insane. This poor woman."

"You're still reading about Charlie?" I glance over Claire's shoulder to see various gossip sites open, as well as legitimate news sources. "You didn't go to work today?"

"I dropped off some fabric samples with a client, and I'm going to do some sketches, but I can't tear myself away from this. TMZ has crime scene photos up already, and the descriptions are horrifying. They say it was probably someone who knew her because of the brutality of the crime. She was stabbed nearly *thirty* times. Can you believe that?" Claire turns to me with incredulity. "How could you hate someone so badly?"

I don't like the way she says *you*. My mind wanders to who could hate her so badly. What could Charlotte have done that triggered a person to get rid of her with such violence? "Does it say anything about when she was killed?" I ask.

"They're not positive yet. The housekeeper was off for a few days, and apparently found Charlotte's body when she returned." Claire clicks through different tabs to find the housekeeper's account. "Here, look—it says here that the housekeeper, Sylvia Santos, came in with her keys yesterday morning, started cleaning downstairs and didn't go to Charlotte's bedroom because the door was closed, and she didn't want to disturb her. But then it got later and later, and she worried, so she knocked on the door. And the door wasn't fully shut, so she pushed it open and saw her body on the floor." Claire shakes her head while she reads the story.

"That's going to be a real problem for the prosecution." I straighten up and pour myself a glass of water from the fridge.

"What's going to be a problem?"

"The housekeeper. She cleaned the house before she found the body. Whatever physical evidence may have been present in the house has been compromised. That's a nice stroke of luck for the defense." I sit down across from Claire at the kitchen table.

"So, what are they going to do? Can they prosecute him if there is compromised evidence? You're always getting people off because of compromised evidence, aren't you?"

"Look, I don't know anything about the case, but if I were defending the guy, I would push really hard to show that whatever physical evidence may be found has clearly been compromised, and I would get it chucked. A housekeeper? In a ten-million-dollar mansion? She's no slouch. I'm sure she's trained to keep every room completely dust-, fingerprint- and dirt-free. Which means bleach, scrubbing, what have you. It destroys evidence, and this guy could walk from lack of evidence."

"You keep saying 'him.' It could have been a woman, you know." Claire crosses her arms defensively. "You're acting very *lawyerly* about this." She looks at me through squinted eyes. "Shouldn't you care just a little bit more about someone you've known for so long getting killed? You're not working this case, you know. Don't you care that she's dead?"

My cell phone rings before I can respond. I hold a finger up in Claire's direction and check the caller ID. Harrison Doyle. I answer immediately.

"Harry." I pause, not quite knowing what to say next. "Harry, how are ya?"

"How the hell you think I am?" Harrison responds angrily, quickly, clearly not enthused to be on the phone with me. "Got both your messages. Nice script." His voice sounds just like it did on the message he last left me.

"Never been good with condolences, Harry. But I mean it. I loved Charlie once, very much." I quickly peek at Claire, who is listening intently. She pulls her sweater tightly around her and looks away when she hears what I said. "This never should have happened."

"Of course it never should have happened!" Harrison hollers. I can practically hear him sweating from every pore, mopping his face with a sodden handkerchief. "And I would love to know what *your* client Stu Bogovian was talking about when he said that *he* knows and *you* know that I am going to get mine. What the fuck does *that* mean? Huh? You're gonna fry for this, Peter." Harrison chokes and sputters the last words through gritted teeth.

"Harrison, stop it. I had nothing to do with your stepdaughter's death. I know you're upset, I can't imagine how you must feel—" I repeat the thoughts Claire expressed that morning "—but be sure—be *certain*—that I had absolutely nothing to do with this. I am just as confused at Bogovian's threat as you are. I haven't spoken to him since sentencing, I—" I stop midstatement when I realize I'm talking to no one. Harrison hung up the phone. I pull the mobile away from my face and stare into the blank screen.

"He hung up on you?" Claire demands.

"I think we just got disconnected. He's all over the place, very upset."

"You loved her. I knew it." Claire amasses her papers and closes her laptop. She piles everything under one arm and gets right in my face. "You know what's just as intense and serious as love?"

I step back against the counter and shrug.

"Hate," Claire says, and disappears up the stairs.

THEN

When Charlie and I were able to see each other again, her fixation on my wife and all things Rhodes family seemed to have waned. She knew about Marcus's diagnosis—it seemed the whole world held its breath waiting for the news of his death—but she didn't ask questions. Her edge had softened, and a vulnerability I hadn't previously seen began shining through. We sat at an outdoor table at Da Silvano in the West Village. I was drinking Barolo served in an enormous bathtub of a glass and she was sipping a tiny espresso. Instead of focusing our conversations on how I could use my social standing to assist her, she had changed her tune since she filed for divorce from her husband.

"I feel like I'm losing my footing," she said. "It's lonely in that big house all by myself, and I don't like to be on my own." Charlie lived in a massive brownstone on Twentieth Street, just a block and a half from the mansion Juliette was renovating. The house was too big, and she told me that every creak and shudder sent a wave of adrenaline surging through her body. "I just get the feeling that someone is trying to get into my house. I'm scared." She looked around her as if to see if anyone were watching. "And I don't like to be scared."

"Have you changed the locks?" I asked. "You need to put in a new security system, and if you're afraid of your ex-husband coming to break in, get yourself a dog, too."

"Sean won't come back." She once again surveyed her surroundings. "It's not my ex-husband I'm afraid of."

"Who is it, then?"

Charlie didn't answer. Instead she wrapped her scarf tightly around herself.

"You don't have to tell me," I assured her. "But if you're afraid of someone breaking into your house, get a dog. A big one. Dogs are much more of a deterrent to burglars than a security system."

"He's not a burglar," she said, "and he isn't afraid of dogs."

She wouldn't tell me who it was she was scared of, but the look on her face told me she had a real reason to be afraid.

I dropped Charlie off at her house on my way uptown. I'd been beckoned to Marcus's bedside and was dreading seeing him in his weakened state. He was in the living room of his massive Upper East Side apartment, lying in a mechanical hospital bed, being cared for by around-the-clock hospice workers. The smell of death and decay in his home was almost more than I could stand.

"Marcus." I greeted him from the doorway of the room, not wanting to come in any farther.

"Peter." He struggled up to a seated position. "Come in, sit down on the sofa. My housekeeper will get you a drink." He motioned toward a short round woman hovering in the adjacent dining room, wringing her hands together in worry. "What can she get you? Gin?"

"I never drink gin, can't stand the stuff."

"Good, don't, it'll kill you like it's killing me. Come over here, sit down."

I delicately edged into the room, settling onto a paisley couch adjacent to his hospital bed. He had a two-pronged oxygen line in his nostrils and an IV dripping into his left arm; the picture of deterioration.

"There's nothing left to fight for." His voice was gravelly and defeated. "I've done everything I set out to do in life, and here I am, dying alone, with nothing but a brutal reputation to show for it."

I looked around at the splendor and riches in the room, shocked that Marcus could think he didn't have anything to show for his life. "What more could you possibly ask for?"

"Something…something more than this. This empty house, the destruction I've left behind. I'm not an old man, Peter, and look at me." He held up thin ragged arms, once powerful and muscled, now frail with blue veins and yellowing bruises crisscrossing the surface. "I'm sixty-eight years old, and I look like I'm a hundred."

I tried to remain expressionless, but I couldn't stop my lips from curling in revulsion. "I don't know if you noticed, but I'm not wearing robes, Marcus. I'm not here to listen to your confession."

"You'll sit and listen!" he yelled, and anger flashed in his eyes, the first sign of life I'd seen. "You have no idea what I've done, and how it affects a person. Didn't you ever wonder why I came after *you*? There were a million hotshot law students I could have handpicked to come work with me— did you even bother to wonder why I chose you, or did you just let your ego bask in the glory of being the chosen one?"

Surprised at his words, I realized I had never asked that question. I had never imagined that he would have picked anyone else, or that I was one of many candidates. "I don't think you had a choice. You wanted the best and you got the best," I reminded him.

"I picked you because you oozed desperation. I could see beneath the veil of lies you hid behind."

My chest tightened.

"You were looking for me just as much as I was looking for you," he continued. "You needed somewhere to fit in, and I needed someone to carry on my legacy. I had no son, just Juliette, but I worked too hard and sacrificed too much to allow the Rhodes empire to die with me." He expelled a thick, phlegmy sigh, and I couldn't tell if he was sorry or delusional. "Juliette hates what I do, she hates who I am, and I forgive her for that, but I needed *someone* to continue the business for the Rhodes name to live on. I wanted a son, and I got a son-in-law instead. That's enough. It's enough for me. And now we have Jamie, and he will continue your legacy and mine." He shook his head, wheezing, and signaled for a nurse to bring him some water.

"You don't actually believe this, do you? What do they have you on?" I lifted a prescription bottle from his bedside and saw he was taking Demerol, a powerful painkiller and sedative. "You're *drugged*, Marcus. You don't actually believe this nonsense." I tried to convince myself that he wasn't just preying on me, that he hadn't spent that last few years molding me into a young version of himself.

"Poor girl, my Juliette. She hates me." His voice began to fade, the words grating in his throat. "And God, Sinan was a perfect fit for us, huh? He came in the perfect package. I didn't even have to teach him. He's the embodiment of half the world's fear—gay, Muslim, brilliant." He sputtered a sip of water onto his pajamas and struggled to clean himself. "Keep it up, Peter. Keep my name in lights. Sinan… He's going to make it… You'll all be fine without me… Bring me a gin, would you?" His eyes turned vacant and couldn't focus on me any longer. "A gin…my favorite thing. It's always your favorite things that kill you."

The nurse who had brought him the water hurried in to ask me to leave. I rushed into the powder room by the front door and scrubbed my hands to get the stench of decay off me. I used a hankie to open his front door and push the elevator button, frantic to get out of there and into the fresh Manhattan air.

I scratched furiously at the back of my neck, the tiny hairs prickling in a cold sweat as I walked quickly down Park Avenue. I thought back to the years Marcus and I had spent together, and finally looked at the truth of what happened between us, now that my rose-colored glasses were off. Marcus didn't set me up to fail on my first trial with Rhodes & Caine to put my ego in check; he did it to prove he was in control. He set me up to lose the Bogovian case because he wanted to remind me that I was his pawn, and he was calling all the shots.

Marcus didn't look at me and see a cutthroat defense attorney. He saw a lost and malleable little boy he could steer in any direction he chose. He saw me desperate for acceptance and he took advantage.

NOW

I'm sitting at my desk in the bedroom looking over the media reports of Charlotte's murder when I hear Jamie's booming footsteps returning to my house from soccer practice. News reporters and investigators have attached themselves to the idea that Stu Bogovian is somehow responsible for Charlie's death. I'm annoyed but not surprised to find my name splashed all over the articles, having been mentioned in Stu's cryptic press conference, and various news outlets have pinned me as a coconspirator. They should know better than to think I would associate myself with Stu Bogovian again.

Just to torture myself, I pull up Charlotte's Facebook page. I slowly scroll through pictures of her; pictures when she was young at summer camp and on European vacations with college friends. I scroll through her timeline and look carefully at the Doyle family Christmas cards.

I have received these cards every year for a decade but never actually opened them or looked at the family photos. Harrison stands prominently in the middle of the photo from the 2014 card, larger than life, with his right arm around Elizabeth and his left arm around Charlotte. Standing off to the right is Ethan. Slovenly and resentful, he looks like a stranger to the rest of the Doyles. *Happy Holidays from our family to yours*, reads the script, signed Harrison, Elizabeth, Charlotte and Ethan. *And* Ethan. Together, yet separate.

I'm reminded of the frightened way Charlotte talked about her brother. The way Harrison dismissed him as nothing more than a financial drain and irritation. I think about the way rejection can stir up hate in a person.

I wander down the stairs with thoughts of Charlie in my head to find Jamie and Claire standing a little too close together, stirring a pot on the stove.

"Oh, hey, Dad," Jamie says, stepping away from Claire. "You okay?"

"Okay? Yeah, I'm fine. You okay?" I ask, noticing that he's called me Dad.

"Fine, yeah. Just asking 'cause your friend, you know. And then the news said, um, your old client…" Jamie comes around from behind the stove and leans a hip onto the counter, trying to finish his sentence. "You know, the guy who maybe killed her?"

"Bogovian? Have you been reading the news?" I laugh, amazed that my teenage son is so informed.

"I get news alerts from CNN on my phone, and I guess it's a slow news day today, but I keep getting stuff about you and that guy, Stu."

"You're getting alerts about me? Let me see this." I sit down at the kitchen table and pat the chair beside me, inviting Jamie to sit down.

"Well, I got a couple yesterday after you showed me the

article at breakfast." Jamie awkwardly sits next to me, holding his phone out for me to see. "And then more today, saying that Stu Bog-whatever probably did it. He said something weird after he got out of jail, right? He's supposed to say something again on TV tonight."

"What? Really?" In all my media investigations today, I haven't heard or seen anything about Stu Bogovian addressing the allegations.

"Yeah. And they found out earlier that he was in Las Vegas when they think Charlotte died. So maybe he *didn't* do it." Jamie eagerly scrolls through the alerts from the last thirty-six hours since the news of Charlotte's murder broke.

"Vegas, huh? And what about the alerts you said were about me?" I peer at my son's telephone screen, trying to still my discomfort at being so close to him.

"They said that Stu said something about you when he got out of jail, and then some CNN newscaster said that maybe it was you who did it *for* Stu, like he paid you or something, because he was in Vegas. You haven't heard about this?"

"I knew my name was being mentioned, but it's news to me that I'm being *implicated*. I guess I've been on the wrong sites." I curse myself for wasting time looking at Charlotte's Facebook page. "When did you get the alert about that reporter thinking I killed someone?"

"Um, recently. Hold on." Jamie looks at the time stamp for the news alert. "I got the notification at 6:17 p.m. So, not even an hour ago." Jamie stares at me.

I say nothing, and instead pull my own phone from my pocket and Google my name. Claire comes out from around the counter and stands behind Jamie's chair, placing a hand on his shoulder. I find my name mentioned frequently in connection with Stu Bogovian and both Harrison and Charlotte Doyle. As I click through the links, I feel eyes on me and look up.

"What?" I snap defensively.

"*What?* You're being accused of murder!" Claire hollers as she flings a dish towel over her shoulder.

"I haven't actually been accused of anything, Claire. A bunch of media schmucks are just kicking up dust and trying to get ratings. I didn't do anything. Calm yourself."

Jamie's expression turns worried. "You didn't do anything, right, Dad?"

"Of course not, Jamie, don't be ridiculous." I continue reading the news reports, squeamish that he's called me Dad twice now.

"How come they're saying maybe you did?" He's flushed, looking at me with the skeptical eyes of a typical distrusting teenager.

"Because it's fun to speculate. Until they have evidence, these reporters just throw theories at each other and try to get people riled up. Nothing is going to come of this. I didn't do anything, so there is nothing to worry about."

"Is *that thing* common knowledge?" Claire asks from her spot back by the stove.

"What thing?" I look up at her. "Is *what* thing common knowledge?"

"That *thing* you told me about Charlotte the other day after the masquerade?" Claire sticks to her nebulous wording so Jamie can't understand that she's asking if the world knows that Charlotte and I had an affair.

"Oh, *that* thing. No. No, I don't think people know about that."

Jamie eyes shoot back and forth between us, but he knows better than to ask us to divulge the secret.

"You better hope not." Claire angrily stirs the pot on the

stove, clearly still bitter from yesterday's revelation that I may have once loved Charlotte.

"The Stu guy is supposed to talk at 8:00 p.m. Do you want to turn on the TV?" Jamie asks, trying to diffuse the tension in the air.

"Yes, let's see what this moron has to say." I tuck my phone back into my pocket. Jamie opens the hutch doors that hide a large flat-screen TV and flicks through channels until he settles on CNN. He mutes the TV since it's not quite 8:00 p.m. and starts setting the table.

Claire is making spaghetti Bolognese and splashes tomatoes all over her apron and the countertop. She stares at the headlines on the screen. I gaze up to see, "Daughter of NY County DA murdered in cold blood." Photos of Charlie are flashing across the TV. Photos of her with Harrison and Elizabeth—Ethan noticeably absent, not presentable enough for television. Not presentable enough to boost the image that this was a beautiful, wholesome family, worth supporting in the upcoming election.

When a photo from the Rhodes Foundation masquerade appears on-screen, my stomach drops as I notice the hand Charlie is holding is mine. I quickly look at Jamie and Claire, to see both of them occupied with dinner.

Relieved and embarrassed, I return my thoughts to the brutality of Charlie's murder. Who could possibly have hated her so badly to stab her twenty-seven times? I begin to recall the conversations I had with Charlie when she thought I wasn't paying attention. Even while I was still married to Juliette, I remember her telling me stories with the same themes over and over again: Ethan. She was afraid of her stepbrother, Ethan.

Jamie brings two brass candlesticks to the table and lights the candles as Claire sets down a steaming platter of pasta in the middle of the table. She dims the kitchen lights and pushes the button on the stereo.

"We have time to listen to music while we eat before your old client speaks, don't we?" She isn't looking at anyone as she asks.

"Yes, of course," I respond, surprised and unsettled at the romantic nature of this dinner. We eat in silence, stealing frequent glances at the time on the cable box, watching as the minutes click away, getting closer to Stu Bogovian's address.

Marcus, Sinan and my assistant, Anna, are the only ones who know that I went to Rikers to speak with Bogovian after we lost at trial, and only Marcus knows what Bogovian and I discussed that day. Now Marcus is dead, so he can't reveal any secrets. Charlie is dead, and whatever she knew is dead along with her, but now Bogovian's about to open his fat mouth, and my stomach roils with nerves about what he's going to say.

Claire and Jamie will have to believe that I've been telling the truth. Whatever Bogovian says, it won't matter, because they trust me, and I'll convince Claire to allow herself to believe that I'm innocent. She wants so badly to be a family, she'll never let anything destroy that.

Jamie suddenly reaches a long arm to the top of the sideboard and grabs the remote control. He unmutes the television and turns off the stereo in one swift movement.

"Here," he exclaims. "Stu's on."

We're all brought to immediate attention, and my stomach leaps into my throat. The screen shows a makeshift podium with fuzzy microphones attached haphazardly, illuminated by camera lights, with a dark street in the background. A voice inside the studio can be heard saying they expect Stuart Bogovian, disgraced ex-congressman, to address the allegations against him momentarily. I pour myself another glass of wine to occupy my unsteady hands. Stu Bogovian slowly walks on-screen, dressed almost casually in ill-fitting suit pants and a pit-stained dress shirt. Without any introduction or pleasantries, Stu immediately delves into the accusations against him.

"I want it stated in no uncertain terms that I had absolutely nothing to do with the murder of Charlotte Doyle. My statements against her stepfather, Harrison Doyle, were taken very much the wrong way, and I was not making a threat on his daughter's life or the life of anyone else, for that matter. My words were simply referencing the upcoming election, which I believed Harrison Doyle would lose when the people of Manhattan learned of his corruption and behavior unbecoming of a representative of the judicial system."

I wince at the word *corruption* and steel myself for what's to come. Bogovian dramatically bows his head, takes an exaggerated deep breath and continues. "I cannot speak to the actions or whereabouts of my former attorney. When I said upon my release that Mr. Caine knew what was coming to Harrison Doyle, I meant simply that he was also aware of Harrison Doyle's deep and abiding dishonesty and immorality.

"I want it to be perfectly clear—I was not making a threat on anyone's life. I used vague and tenuous language at my press conference, but what I meant was that I believed Harrison would not be reelected. No one should have died. No one should have suffered what that poor woman suffered. Again, I speak only for myself. As you have seen on surveillance footage, I was in Las Vegas at the supposed time of the murder, so I couldn't possibly have done anything. Again, I speak *only for myself*—" Stu leans into the microphones and enunciates the words "—I have heard the speculation that my former attorney and I may have been in this together, and that I could very well have paid him to do my dirty work. No dirty work was done by me, and no one was paid or compensated in any way by me to commit this heinous crime. I can't speak for Mr. Caine. But *I* had nothing to do with this." Stu steps away from the press pool and then jumps back in to add, "Any further inquiries can be directed to my lawyer, Sheldon Greenbaum. Thank you for listening, and I hope this clarification exonerates me in the court of public opinion."

A cacophony of questions trails him back toward his apartment building. Stu walks away, head held high, having slickly shone the light directly onto me.

THEN

The first time I slept with Charlie, she invited me over to her house on Twentieth. She was officially separated from her husband, but I was still very much married. Again, Charlie and I planned a meeting to discuss Rhodes Foundation business. Neither she nor I would admit that we were meeting at her home for something other than business.

When I walked up the stoop, Charlie was already at the door. She appeared in stark contrast to the last time I had seen her at Da Silvano, when she was vulnerable and nervous. This night, she wore a low-cut dress and high heels. She walked me into the living room, where candles were lit and a bottle of Laphroaig sat next to two rocks glasses. It was a seductive scene, all set for me, and I wondered who was seducing whom.

We didn't bother to pretend that we were planning a benefit, instead just downed two glasses of scotch and began devouring each other. She had that carefree wild-girl thing about her. Sex was an adventure, as meaningless to her as it was to me. Just another means to an end.

Juliette must have known immediately. She was an incredibly intuitive person, and I had become so disconnected from her that I wasn't concerned with covering my tracks.

"How's it going with the benefit planning?" she asked me one night.

"I'm doing very little planning, to be honest. Your protégé seems to have it all under control." I knew she wouldn't believe me if I took credit for any actual work outside of my job.

"You seem different these days, distracted." She must have known but stopped short of actually confronting me about it.

"I'm working on a very difficult case with Sinan, and it's constantly on my mind. That's probably why I seem distracted."

"Mmm, well, don't work *too* hard." She humored me for a while, letting me pretend that I was busy being a dedicated lawyer, committed to my work.

Thoughts of fidelity and devotion danced in my head, remaining just out of reach like a mobile dangling above a baby's crib. I just didn't care. Weeks later when she confronted me again, her reaction wasn't so lenient.

"You haven't been home before midnight in weeks. You hardly see your son anymore. When was the last time you put your family as a priority?" she hissed at me, watching as I pulled on my shoes to walk out the door again.

"I'm working to pay the bills, Juliette. How do you think we can afford to live in this hotel while you work on the townhouse? Do you have any idea what it'll cost to send Jamie to private preschool? And the nannies?" I lied right to her face. We had plenty of money in the bank, enough to keep living at The Carlyle even if it took years to finish the house renovation.

"We don't need your money, Peter. We need *you*. Your time, your presence," she pleaded with me as I opened the door to leave.

I watched the disappointment spread across her face and turn the corners of her mouth down. Instead of saying anything, I left her standing in the doorway and walked to the elevator. I waited for my stomach to drop, my hands to sweat, my heart to race, but there was nothing. Where there used to be an overwhelming love for Juliette that drove me to do all I ever did for her now sat an empty space. I didn't hate her. I just didn't feel anything at all.

Charlie didn't have a traditional work schedule, so we would meet in the afternoons while I took an extended lunch break. The first few weeks were filled with negligees and scented candles, but it quickly changed to torrents of questions and delays moving into the bedroom. Questions about my wife, again.

"Does she ever dress like this?" Charlie asked, wearing something with feathers.

"I don't know what she wears. How could this possibly matter? And frankly, I don't care what *you* wear. You should be taking that thing off."

"What perfume does Juliette use? I'm looking for a new scent."

"I don't want to come over here in the middle of the afternoon to sleep with you and end up smelling my wife." It was a turnoff. Instead of answering the questions, I would often fake a phone call or email from Sinan. "I have to go. Sinan needs me back at the office. Next time I come here, I don't want to hear about my wife, or else I'm not coming here anymore."

I wasn't skipping out on work to develop a friendship with Charlie. If the sex wasn't going to happen, then I wasn't going to stick around. My job was already done; you only need to sleep with someone's daughter once to hurt him. Somehow, I never wondered what *she* was getting out of it.

Marcus had succumbed to his illness just eight weeks after he was diagnosed, as the doctors predicted. But as far as I was concerned, he was dead the moment he told me he had terminal cancer. Now with my mentor and partner gone, my training would finally be complete and I would be in control of my life—and the firm. Just a week after his death, Juliette took back the Rhodes Foundation responsibilities that she had entrusted me with, keeping up appearances that the Rhodes family was still as strong as ever, despite being temporarily derailed by the loss of its patriarch.

Charlotte Doyle, of course, attended Marcus's funeral. I expected to see her there, as it was a society event, but something about her was different this time. She didn't try to go through me for introductions to the important people at the funeral, and she didn't thrust herself into the middle of everything. She seemed vulnerable and shy, and I remembered that afternoon at Da Silvano when she told me she felt scared to be alone in her house. Afraid of someone trying to get in.

"You're not yourself," I said, pulling her aside as soon as I could get away from funeral-goers kissing my cheeks and trying to commiserate.

"I can't stay. I just wanted to be polite, you know, show my face." She looked terrified, but she wouldn't say why.

"Where are you going? What's the matter?"

"Please," she begged as tears began to form at the corners of her eyes. "Please come to my place as soon as you can get out of here." Before I could respond, she dashed out the door, holding a hankie to her face as if the emotion of the event had overwhelmed her.

NOW

With Claire at her office and Jamie at school, I sit alone in the house, ignoring the calls on my work phone, the emails and knocks on my front door from media looking for comments. My agitation grows after watching the morning newscasters continue to hypothesize about my supposed involvement in Charlotte's murder. Frustrated, I snatch up my phone and slam the buttons to call the most talented defense attorney I can think of other than myself.

"Khan," he answers on the second ring.

"Sinan, it's me. I need to talk to you."

"Yes, you do. You all right? Can you come to my office?"

"No. Come to the house. I'll wait." I hang up the phone before Sinan accepts or rejects my invitation.

I pace the parlor until I hear knocking at the front door. Squinting out the window, I see it's Sinan and go to open the heavy mahogany door. I peer behind him as he walks inside and see that, thankfully, the news van that's been parked out front is gone. I motion for Sinan to follow me to the kitchen, and we sit down at the round table.

"Aren't you going to offer me a drink?" Sinan looks down at the glass of scotch I'm holding. He hangs his jacket on a chair.

"I thought you Muslims didn't drink in the morning."

"Today's a little different." He stands and opens the refrigerator. "I've been getting calls for comment from the media, you know." He uncorks a bottle of white wine sitting in the door, pours a glass nearly to the top and sits back down at the table with me.

"What have you been saying?"

"I haven't been answering the phone, Peter. They're just clogging my machine with messages."

"Good, don't." I pull back the curtain and peer again out the kitchen window. I think I see someone across the street pointing to my house. "How much of a problem is this going to be?" I speak in hushed tones.

"That depends on you, love." Sinan smirks. "How much of a problem is it?"

"I didn't kill her, if that's what you're asking." I take a long pull of scotch and wipe my sweaty palms on my thighs.

"That's *exactly* what I'm asking." Sinan hides his feelings with an air of professionalism, and I can't quite tell if he believes my innocence.

"We need to figure out what the hell happened here, Sinan. My name should not be coming out of anyone's mouth in this context."

"You honestly care what happened to her?" Sinan shakes his head and stands up from the kitchen table. "Wait, before you answer that, I need you to tell me the truth. What's really going on with you?"

"What's really going *on* is that I have privileged information that could lead you to the truth about who did this. I know things that I'm not supposed to know, and I know them because Charlie told me in confidence. And Charlie told me in confidence because we were in bed together at the time."

"Jesus Christ. Close the fucking door." He slams the kitchen door shut and upends his wine. "You had an affair with Charlotte Doyle? When? When did you pull this genuinely senseless move?" His bright British accent turns dark.

"Claire's at work, and she knows about it anyway." I stay seated, knees bouncing in agitation. "It had been going on for years, on and off. Started back when I was with Juliette, she's kind of why we got divorced."

Sinan snatches up a brand-new legal pad from his briefcase and starts jotting down notes. "When did it end?"

"Couple weeks ago, maybe."

"A couple of *weeks* ago? Are you serious? You call off an affair with a woman who caused your divorce—" he counts out the infractions on his fingers "—you're acting extremely bizarrely recently, you've got a score to settle with her father and now you call me over to your house for some clandestine meeting telling me to go find out who did it? Sounds like *you* fucking did it."

"Why do you think I called you? I *know* what it sounds like. That's one of the main reasons I'm trying to find an alternative. Anyone who looks can see we had an affair—it wasn't a well-kept secret. I need to offer an alternative."

"What's your alternative? Bogovian? He already cleared himself. You heard the statement last night—he was in Vegas. There were eyes all over him there."

"I'm aware. That's not the privileged information I have from Charlie."

"Spit it out, man," Sinan says impatiently.

"Ethan Doyle."

"Who the fuck is Ethan Doyle?"

"The brother? Charlie's degenerate stepbrother? Come on, Sinan. You know who I'm talking about. That scummy greasy kid. You've met him before, I'm sure—he follows Harrison around like a lost puppy."

"All right, and what makes you think he brutally murdered his sister?"

"You don't believe me, do you? You really think *I* did it?"

"Of course I think you did it. But that's irrelevant. I'm your friend, and as of now, I'm your lawyer, so I'm going to do everything I can to help prove you innocent, regardless of whether you are or not."

"I didn't. Sinan, I swear to everything holy that I never hurt that woman. We had an affair. That's true, and believe me, I know it looks bad. But I did not kill her."

"What's your alibi, while we're on the subject of you not doing it?"

"I was home with Jamie."

"And Claire?"

"No, Claire was in the Hamptons with some friends."

"You're telling me the only person who can corroborate your story is Jamie? A minor who's *related* to you? Jesus, Peter. Not making my job easy, are you?"

"I know what we're up against, but I need you to listen to this Ethan thing. And I need you to believe me. I didn't kill Charlie."

"All right, for now, I believe you. Get me another fucking bottle of wine, would you? This is going to be a long day."

I stand and open another bottle from the massive wine fridge. "Ethan hated Charlie," I begin, handing him a full glass of chardonnay. "Charlie was *afraid* of him. She told me this on a number of occasions. She would check her windows at night, make sure he wasn't lurking outside. She said that he had hated her since childhood, but it was getting worse of late because he was stagnating in life and she was falling in with all the right people. He was jealous. Their parents preferred her."

"Jealous sibling stuff? You think that's sufficient?" Sinan jots down notes.

"This is not standard jealous sibling stuff. Charlie was legitimately afraid. She didn't want to be in the same room with him. If he went to an event with Harrison, Charlie wouldn't go. This went down pretty deep. There's definitely an electronic paper trail—I saw an email he wrote her. Threats, all sorts of creepy stuff."

"Okay, this could be something. How much investigating have you done on your own already?"

"Practically nothing. But I'm saying it was Ethan because I genuinely believe it. My first thought was Bogovian, but then it turned out he was in Vegas, with a million cameras to prove it. And knowing what Charlie said about Harrison's son, it's entirely plausible." I begin to see in Sinan's eyes that he's open to hearing me out.

"Did she have a life insurance policy?"

"How the hell do I know?"

"Well, life insurance or no, the brother stands to inherit twice as much if his sister is out of the picture, so either way, that's a possible motive." Sinan furiously scribbles in his notebook.

I nod excitedly, relieved that Sinan is willing to entertain my theory. "Send in the Franks."

"The Franks?" Sinan hesitates. "You want me to get the Franks on this already?"

Frank Tomlinson and Frank LaBianca are the two investigators we use at Rhodes & Caine to perform our own investigations. LaBianca is an ex-cop with a tendency to rough up suspects, and Tomlinson, a bodybuilder turned lawyer turned private eye, makes up for his partner's physical indiscretions with flawless paperwork and a tremendous track record for finding his man.

"Have the Franks look into Ethan, do some sniffing around. I know this kid isn't clean."

"And how do you plan on explaining it when the Franks begin their investigation, and Rhodes & Caine has *not* been hired to represent anyone? How do you explain that *you* have decided to launch your own investigation into the death of your former lover? A murder you're *nearly* accused of committing? Don't you imagine you will have to answer for this?"

"Of course I won't, Sinan. You will. Because *you* will be the one who sics the Franks on Ethan. And the Franks are going to be discreet until the cops come knocking on my door. Once I'm questioned, I will announce that I have retained *you* as counsel, and the Franks can make themselves known."

"Before we get ahead of ourselves—" Sinan slows down "—I need *all* the details of what's been going on with you. Start from the beginning."

"The beginning? The beginning of *what*?" My stomach lurches. "I just went too far, Sinan. I spent so much time and energy making sure I became *something* that I lost sight of whether that something was good or bad."

"And now you're feeling like what you've become is *bad*? Is that what you're telling me?"

"Maybe." My thoughts are faraway; I'm not bad, I'm not evil. I'm not even misguided. I'm the product of people who couldn't care. So, I cared enough for all of us. I wanted so badly to be someone that I was willing to do anything to reach the top and to stay there. Any iota of challenge to that was a threat more frightening than death. Kill me, but don't take this away from me. I never considered the consequences. There was collateral damage. Juliette was collateral damage. Claire and Jamie are collateral damage. I don't mean to, but I just can't help it.

"Look, I realized that I couldn't go on living the way I was." I bring myself back into the room. "I hurt everyone I knew. Juliette before she died, I treated her horribly. I wasn't a father to my only son. I didn't even remember Jamie's birthdays. If it weren't for Anna, he never would've heard from me. And Claire? I pretty much treated her like she didn't even exist."

"So, taking time off of work will give you the opportunity to right these wrongs?" Sinan looks back over the notes he's already written and then flips the page of his notebook for a fresh sheet. "You know, this is good stuff. We can use this."

"I'm not mounting a defense, you cynical asshole. I mean it. I'm not the guy I used to be. I can't be like that anymore."

"All right, but you *should* be mounting a defense." He puts down his pen and notebook and interlaces his fingers in his lap. "Listen, I've known you a long time. I've never seen you go soft before. I understand that your priorities are changing—what with getting custody of Jamie and all—you want to settle down. But, tell me. If Charlotte were killed before you had these realizations, who's to say that your former self didn't kill her?"

THEN

I dropped Juliette and Jamie back at The Carlyle after Marcus's wake and went to see what had happened to Charlie. There was no response when I buzzed her front door so I walked down the stoop and peered into the first-floor windows. I couldn't see anything, but just as I was about to walk away, I heard the front door buzzing, and I jogged up the stairs and let myself in.

Charlie was in her bedroom, eyes wild, with the covers pulled up under her chin. She had her computer and cell phone on her bed next to her and piles of mascara-stained tissues. She clutched at my shirt desperately and pulled me onto the bed with her, breathing erratically.

"What happened? Are you all right?" I asked her, suddenly aware that I may have put *myself* in danger by coming to her house.

"Look," she started, but the emotion was too much for

her and she couldn't eke out another word. She opened her email on her computer and showed me a message from her stepbrother, Ethan.

Get out of my family. You're not a real Doyle, and he's not even your real father. You don't belong in our family.

As I read the words, I pictured Ethan's face: slovenly, unkempt and, now that I thought about it, angry. I couldn't help but feel a twinge of excitement inside that something bad was happening to Harrison. His son, his flesh and blood, was threatening his beloved stepdaughter. I read the message again while Charlie sniffled and shook next to me.

"Why did he send you this? Did something happen between you two?"

"Who knows? *I* don't think anything happened, but who can tell what goes on in his mind?"

"Has he sent this kind of thing before?" I looked back over the words he'd written.

"Yes, this *isn't* the first one." Charlie confessed that Ethan had been sending her these messages since childhood, but usually on scraps of paper that he hid in her personal effects. "He hates me, and he's hated me for as long as I can remember. He never wanted me to be a part of their family. I'm scared, Peter. I know he's going to hurt me."

"Don't be afraid—you're safe here. You have locks on your doors, an alarm system. You're right near a precinct. If you're so worried, why don't you file for a restraining order?"

"I couldn't do that. It would be a matter of public record, and with Daddy being the DA, I couldn't make our family business public." She shook off my suggestion as if it were patently ridiculous.

"Daddy?" I winced.

She buried her face in a tissue. "I don't deserve this, Peter. I don't. He pins all his hate on me, just because he's lazy and useless."

I could see her fear was giving way to anger, her sobs replaced with clenched fists and deep ragged breaths. I knew in these emotional states women were likely to let their guards down, and I wanted to see what kinds of secrets she would divulge. I kept my mouth shut and let her proceed uninterrupted.

"Do you know how hard I've worked to make a name for myself?" She stared in front of her, yelling at the void, "How much I've had to sacrifice just to drown out his stupidity? I've *earned* my place!"

"You're rambling, Charlie. What are you talking about? What sacrifices?"

"You couldn't possibly have any idea how *hard* it is to overcome where you came from."

I could have told her I knew exactly how hard it was. I could have told her I'd spent more than half my life lying and burying secrets to get away from my past. I could have told her that I truly understood her. But I didn't say a word.

"Harrison is so obsessed with winning and getting ahead that he doesn't care what he has to do to get there."

Once she started calling him Harrison, I knew the floodgates were about to open.

"Everything I do, *everything*, is to help him gain traction. He doesn't want anyone to even know he *has* a son, because Ethan is such a mess, so *I* have to be this *perfect* daughter, and then Ethan hates me for it!" Her anger waned and returned to sadness as she crumpled into her sheets and sobbed.

"Why do you bother? What's in it for you?" My words could've been taken as comforting, but I was looking for Charlie to corroborate what Bogovian told me at Rikers Island. I wanted to hear from Charlie herself what she and Harrison were really up to.

She clutched her duvet to her face and blubbered, rocking back and forth repeating how she felt it was all so unfair. I couldn't leave well enough alone when I was so close to hearing the truth she was hiding, so I probed again. "What's in it for you, Charlie? Why do you keep doing it?"

She pulled the duvet away and rubbed her swollen eyes. "Because I want to help my father, Peter," she said, her voice exhausted and broken. "I would be nothing without him. But I can't take more of *this*." She pointed to the email on her computer. "He's going to kill me one day, Peter."

That night, she didn't tell me the details of what she and her father were up to but shared enough to prove to me that we were all in the same boat together. We were all hiding from something, hoping no one would ever look close enough to see the truth.

N O W

Sinan wants to go back to his office to meet with the Franks now that he and I have discussed my theories and I've answered his questions about my leave. But I'm not going with him.

"There have been news vans parked outside the door. I'm not going out there." I peek out the window again, but it looks like only regular pedestrians on the street. Bogovian has made Charlie's murder into an even bigger story, and with the election coming up in just a couple of months, I'm sure the vultures must be hiding somewhere, circling my house until they nail me.

"I emailed Tomlinson and told him it was urgent, but I'll give him a shout and let him know to come here. May be quicker, since their office is uptown anyway."

Satisfied that I won't be dealing with the outside world just yet, I pace uncomfortably around the house. When I come back downstairs, I find Sinan sitting in the formal dining room like I asked him to, reading over the notes he had taken earlier.

"We should stay at the back of the house in case anyone decides to stake out in front… They won't catch us in the windows."

"Fine, Peter. This paranoia is something you're going to have to wrangle if you want to appear innocent."

"I *am* innocent, Sinan. I don't need to do anything to *appear* that way."

"Right. Moving on. Tomlinson said they would be here in thirty minutes, and that was twenty minutes ago."

I sit down at the head of the table and put my feet up on an adjacent chair. Before I can take a deep breath, the buzzer to the back door blares in my ears. Sinan gets up to answer it.

The Franks walk into the dining room, notebooks in hands, and stand awkwardly by the edge of the table opposite me.

Tomlinson speaks first. "What's happening? This about the boss and the DA's daughter?"

Sinan clears his throat. "Yes, that's exactly what this is about. We need you to look into someone for us."

"Who is it?" Frank LaBianca blurts, looking over at me. "You want us to investigate the boss?" He chuckles at his own joke.

"No, Frank," Sinan begins. "We are asking you to dig up anything you can about the brother of the deceased. His name is Ethan Doyle. He is the son of District Attorney Harrison Doyle. I need everything—social media, financial profiles, psychiatric history, friends willing to roll over. Everything you can find. But…" Sinan pauses. Tomlinson lifts his pen from his notebook. "*But* I need you to do all of this without making yourselves known."

Tomlinson immediately tears the page out of his notebook

and rips it into tiny little pieces. He drops the pieces into a crystal ashtray that Sinan has been using and sets them on fire with his lighter.

LaBianca starts in with questions. "Who's this kid? You think he's involved in the murder? What do we know as far as witnesses, evidence, weapons?"

"I'm getting that information together," Sinan says. "Now that my client, your boss, has been implicated, it makes sense for me to start sniffing around. I'm sure the investigation is very thin as of now, there hasn't been too much time since the discovery of the body. But this is the DA's stepdaughter. You can bet your boots this is going to be a circus."

"Call my secure line when you have some more details into the investigation. Until then, we'll get digging into the brother," Tomlinson says, shaking Sinan's hand.

Sinan pulls a cell phone from the outside pocket of his briefcase, switches it on and punches in a phone number. "I'm calling my guy," he says to me, knowing I'm aware of his dirty little secrets. Sinan has been carrying on an affair with a married detective at One Police Plaza, and he owes Sinan a favor.

"It's me," he says as soon as a voice appears on the other end of the line. "I need you to get me the police report from Charlotte Doyle's murder. I need all the details you can find. Witnesses, murder weapon, everything. How soon can you get it?"

I hear a muffled reply on the other end.

"All right, then I'll meet you tomorrow at 7:30 p.m. at that place we went to that time."

Sinan stands out everywhere he goes, so discretion proves difficult for him. Tall, dark-skinned, covered in thick black hair, perfectly polished with a booming voice, heavy accent and ostentatious mannerisms, he can't quite blend in with the crowd. *That place* he refers to is the line outside a methadone clinic on Tenth Avenue. He had met the detective there once before to give him information about a suspect the detective was investigating. The other people in the line didn't care who they were, and passersby always averted their eyes. It was the perfect place for him to hide in plain sight.

"I'm going back to the office. I didn't see any news vans this morning but if there's anything there now, I'll let you know."

"Make sure no one sees you leaving the house."

"I'll go the back way. Deep breaths, Peter. Nothing has happened yet."

As if on cue, Claire walks in through the front door while Sinan leaves out the back. I hear the glass hallway door closing and watch as she hangs her jacket on the hook by the door.

"Hey," I call to her. "I need to talk to you."

"What the hell is going on, Peter? Some reporter just accosted me in front of my office."

"Who was it? What did you say?"

"I don't know who it was, nobody I recognized from TV. It was an NBC van, though. She asked me what I thought about you being accused of murdering Charlotte Doyle, and then when I said no comment, she yelled after me that I'm married to a murderer."

"We're not married."

She shakes her head in disbelief. "And I hope you're not a fucking murderer!"

"Claire, come in here with me. We really need to talk." The urgency in my voice doesn't seem to be prompting Claire to hurry up, and she stops in the kitchen to make herself tea. I bob my head impatiently and guide her into the dining room once her tea is ready.

"Okay, I'm listening."

"I went to Rick Friedberg's office the other day to pick up the custody paperwork for Jamie."

"Right, I remember you were going to do that."

"Well, I was going to wait until this stupidity with Bogovian blew over, but now it looks like we may need to act quickly, so I'll tell you now. Rick gave me a set of adoption papers to give to you, so you can officially adopt Jamie."

"Wait, *what*? Why do I need to adopt him? Is something going to happen to you?"

"I am his only legal guardian as of now, and if I'm arrested or if anything happens to me, Jamie is still a minor, and he will be placed in someone else's care. Now, I want that someone to be you, don't you?"

"Of course I do. Of course," she stammers, flustered. "But what's going to happen to you?"

"Nothing is going to happen to me. But the media seems to think I had something to do with Charlie's death. Again, I *didn't*. But we still need to take precautions should this go any further, okay?"

"Yes, of course. What do I need to do?" She pulls her chair tight against the table and reaches out to look at the adoption paperwork.

"You need to call Rick and have these documents signed, notarized and taken to the judge at family court as soon as you can. Rick will expedite the process."

"Does Jamie know this is happening?"

"No, I haven't spoken to him, but I will. I didn't mean for this to all happen so fast, but we have to hurry now in case they're coming for me, okay? I need you to call Rick *today*."

"I will, I will call him now. And, please, let *me* talk to Jamie about this. I have a closer relationship with him than you do, and I think it'll be easier to understand coming from me."

"Fine, if that's what you think is best." I'm relieved that I won't have to figure out how to explain this situation to my son. "I'll get the phone and Rick's number."

I leave the dining room and walk toward the kitchen to grab my cell phone and call Rick's office. As I walk back into the room, I see Claire getting up from her chair.

"Someone's here," she says nervously, pointing at the front door behind me.

I step back into the kitchen and poke my head out to steal a glance at whoever is ringing the doorbell.

"They can see you, Peter." Claire stands awkwardly in the doorway to the dining room in full view of the two men at the front door.

I straighten up and walk into the hallway when I realize I recognize the men outside. I unlock the front door and Claire comes up next to me, holding on to my arm.

"You're not under arrest, sir. Just want to ask you some questions," says a large detective with a gray moustache.

"I know the drill, Lou. I'm going to have Sinan meet me there before we get into anything." I pull out my cell phone and text Sinan that Lou and Rodrigo are at my door and taking me in for questioning.

THEN

Juliette was one of the more brilliant people in the world, and this is why I married her. This is also why I divorced her.

On the surface, things had returned to normal after Marcus's death. Jamie was well looked after by his nannies and caretakers, Juliette was back entrenched in her world-saving work, and I was reveling in money and professional prestige. Even with the house on Twenty-First Street coming along and the promise of a brighter future, Juliette remained dissatisfied. All the money wasn't making her happy, all the help with the baby wasn't making her happy and more than anything else, *I* wasn't making her happy. These concerns were very easy for me to ignore. Although she seemed hurt by my obvious infidelity, she didn't outright ask me to stop. She didn't whine, she didn't complain, she carried herself with grace and elegance as she always did—but I could see that she wasn't herself.

Her melancholy was becoming tedious, and I detected looks of concern on the faces of our associates and acquaintances, which I did not swallow easily. I pulled Juliette aside one day and asked her what she needed in order to remove herself from this emotional gutter and avoid plummeting our social stock.

"I'm glad you asked, Peter. I want you to come somewhere with me." She casually dropped a bomb and asked me to come with her to couple's counseling.

"Counseling? Are you suicidal or something?" I was appalled.

"Not that you bothered to notice, but since Jamie was born, I have been seeing a psychiatrist for postpartum depression."

"Is that what they're calling it?" I dismissed her diagnosis; psychiatry always seemed so exculpatory and self-indulgent. Paying someone to listen to you whine and coddle your emotions was the biggest waste of money I could imagine.

"My psychiatrist thinks that *you* could benefit from counseling, as well, you know. He's been asking for you to join our sessions."

It sounded awful. Of course I didn't want to go to therapy, but if this was what I needed to do to get the woman I married back onto my arm and rid the world of her miserable replacement, then fine. I would go. It was never a good look in the society world to have a depressed wife, like I couldn't take proper care of her.

Her psychiatrist was Dr. Steven Kimball. Seemingly a talented and educated man, he went to med school at Johns Hopkins and did his residency at Yale. He had a plush office on the Upper West Side across from the Museum of Natural History and appeared to know quite a bit about me the first time I begrudgingly sat on his Chesterfield leather sofa.

"Welcome, Peter," Dr. Kimball said. "I'm glad you've decided to join us and offer your support in your wife's recovery."

Juliette's despondent demeanor had morphed into a smug air of superiority while we sat in Dr. Kimball's office, and I found it incredibly annoying.

"Has she told you much about what we discuss in this office?" he asked, almost laughing at me. He shot Juliette a look.

"No, Dr. Kimball," Juliette responded for me. The two of them tried to toy with me as if they were in on some secret. "I haven't even told Peter that we've been working together. He has been very busy recently." She looked at me sideways, mocking me. "While I was too depressed to work, he assisted with my responsibilities at the foundation, working very closely with Charlotte Doyle, who seems to want to take over, and since my father passed away, he has had to run the whole law firm by himself. Poor baby."

I didn't want to play these games, and I felt my time was being wasted. If she knew I was having an affair, why not just confront me and get it over with? She clearly had a problem that her father and I had been partners, so why not just come out and say it?

"Enough with this. Why am I here?" I demanded. Dr. Kimball realized I wasn't willing to be treated like a child and regaled me with the goings-on of their previous sessions.

"I will give you a brief synopsis of our time together. Juliette and I have discussed confidentiality, and she is willing to share these details with you. Juliette didn't initially come to therapy because she was depressed. She came to talk and work out her feelings and only while in therapy did she discover the things that sent her into a depression."

What she pawned off to me as postpartum depression was now being touted as a crippling series of revelations that pulled the rug out from underneath her. Revelations about me.

"Although the hormonal changes of pregnancy and the postpartum period certainly played a role in your wife's depression, the greater issue has been her relationship with *you*." Apparently, Dr. Kimball had led my wife down a path of self-discovery that was based almost entirely in bashing me. I didn't respond to his commentary, instead listening quietly and without expression.

As Juliette sat on the sofa next to me, wringing her hands, Dr. Kimball laid out what he thought was going on. "Well, Peter, from what your wife and I have been gleaning in our time in counseling, I believe you've been exhibiting symptoms of antisocial personality disorder, commonly known as sociopathy, as well as some narcissistic traits."

"Mmm-hmm. According to my *wife*, of course." I nodded along, humoring him.

"Yes, most of these observations are drawn from what Juliette has shared with me in our sessions. But she has painted a very clear picture, and some of the behaviors she reported are not matters of opinion or conjecture. She is simply reporting the facts of how you behave."

"Sociopathy, you said?" Juliette flinched when I said the word out loud.

"Yes, sociopathy refers to maladaptive patterns of behavior that are characterized by callousness, a lack of remorse or guilt and a dampened ability to read or access human emotions." Dr. Kimball looked at me with pleading eyes as he described what sounded like a zombie.

"Inability to access human emotions? What species of emotion *can* I access?" I chuckled, feeling very much like the whole situation was a joke.

"Peter, your ability to care about things that most human beings care about has been damaged." He used a stern voice, presumably to try to get me to take him seriously.

"Damaged how? What has damaged my ability to be a person?" I was incredulous. This prepubescent upstart was telling me that I was less than a man.

"We believe the catalyst, or trigger, if you will, is the nature of your work. You've probably got some genetic predisposition, and the cruel and unsympathetic nature of criminal defense pushed you over the edge and initiated the sociopathic behaviors."

"So, Rhodes & Caine turned me inhuman? Can I sue for damages?" I turned to Juliette. "Your father would have been thrilled to know that our practice turned on my sociopath switch."

"It's not so much that something got turned on, as much as something got turned *off*. It's like you've lost a chip in a motherboard. The chip that allows you to experience and read the full range of human emotions."

"The same thing happened with my father," Juliette finally chimed in. "He wasn't always the man you knew, the ruthless, soulless version of himself. He had a heart once. He had a *huge* heart once." Juliette's face finally showed some emotion in relation to her father. She had seemed so unaffected by his death, and now it was clear to me that for Juliette, Marcus had died years before.

"Juliette has a unique ability to spot this behavior because she saw it in her father. You see, Peter?"

She cut him off. "The important thing to remember is that if the switch turned off, it can turn back on. It's not hopeless. My father was a lost cause because he never confronted the issue, but *you* can. *You* can get better."

With that comment, I realized she didn't bring me to her therapy sessions to break me down, throw wild diagnoses in my face or try to prove our problems were my fault. She brought me there to try to help me. Dr. Kimball told her that if I once had the chip that was now missing, I could get it back and I could be the loving husband I once was.

I felt the reptilian part of me beginning to take hold again, a creeping claw reaching up from the base of my skull and gripping my brain. It didn't take long, but once it settled in, it was nearly impossible to amputate. If I fed it even once, it would stay.

I filed for divorce two days later.

NOW

I walk east with the detectives toward the thirteenth precinct, only two short blocks from my house on Twenty-First Street. I know the two detectives from years working in New York City criminal defense. We are rarely working on the same side. After initial pleasantries, we walk in silence.

Once we arrive inside the overly air-conditioned building, they bring me into a small interrogation room with a Formica-topped table, two metal chairs bolted to the ground and obnoxious fluorescent lighting. Lou drags two wheeled office chairs into the room behind him and asks me if I want a cup of coffee. I don't respond. Instead, I sit in a metal chair with my hands clasped together on top of the table.

The officers are scrutinizing my appearance, looking for anything they can use against me.

"What happened to your hands?" Rodrigo asks. He notices the burns on my fingers, still healing from when I pulled the smashed glass from the fireplace.

I don't respond, simply look up at him and smile.

Lou and Rodrigo shuffle around the room, realizing I'm not going to say a word until Sinan arrives. Rodrigo peeks through the blinds. "Your boy is here," he says.

Sinan parades into the room in a pale gray suit, slim pants hemmed just above his anklebone with suede loafers and a navy trench coat. He sits down next to me and draws a notebook from his leather briefcase.

"Gentlemen," he addresses the detectives. "Good afternoon."

"Good afternoon, Mr. Khan," Lou speaks, squeezing himself into the metal chair across from me, leaving Rodrigo with the office chair. "We need to ask your client a few questions about his whereabouts the night of September 24." Lou flips the pages of a small notebook covered in his chicken scratch. "Saturday night, can you tell me where you were?"

I don't consult Sinan before replying, "Yes, I was at home. At my house on Twenty-First Street, where you just picked me up."

"Wait—back to my question from before," Rodrigo interrupts. "What happened to your hands?"

I hold up my fingers for the detectives to see. "I burned myself."

"How'd you do that?" Rodrigo continues.

"Pulling pieces of broken glass from the fireplace in my bedroom," I state, flatly.

"How'd you get glass in the fireplace?" Lou is taking notes.

"That's irrelevant, gentlemen," Sinan interjects. "Stick to your questions about the night of September 24."

The detectives look at each other, obviously disappointed that my attorney is with me. "You say you were home," Lou continues. "And who were you with?"

"I was with my son, Jamie."

"Your son?" Rodrigo asks, still standing in the corner of the room, having refused to sit in the other chair.

"Yes, my sixteen-year-old son, Jamie." I sit up straight and look directly into the eyes of the officer addressing me.

"Anyone else?" Lou continues.

"No, it was the just the two of us," I calmly reply.

"Where was your wife that night?"

"I don't have a wife. But if you're referring to Claire, my live-in girlfriend, she was in South Hampton." Sinan smiles broadly at my response.

"What was she doing there?" Rodrigo asks.

Sinan's smile disappears. "Detectives, please focus on what my *client* was doing. He can't comment on the exact activities of his girlfriend, or of anyone other than himself. Feel free to continue your questioning but limit your inquiries to my client's behaviors alone."

"What did you and your son do on the night of the twenty-fourth?" Lou diverts the questioning back to my activities the evening Charlotte Doyle was killed.

"We ate Chinese food, shared a bottle of wine and watched a movie in the basement theater at my house."

"Did you order the Chinese food?" Lou asks.

"I had ordered Chinese a few nights prior because I had gotten home late and missed dinner with my family. I ordered too much, as usual, and kept the leftovers in the fridge. Jamie and I heated up those leftovers. That's what we had for dinner." I remember exactly what we did that night, down to the last detail.

"Where did you order from?" Lou jots down notes.

"First Wok," I decisively respond.

"What did you have?"

I gaze up toward the ceiling and rattle off the list. "Beef

with broccoli, pork fried rice, vegetable lo mein and sweet-and-sour chicken."

"That's it?"

"And fortune cookies, of course." I leer at him. I've advised clients during interrogations many times before, and I'm completely comfortable ensuring I only divulge what's specifically asked of me.

"And what movie did you watch?"

"We watched *Pulp Fiction*."

"On Netflix? Cable? iTunes?"

"We watched the DVD. Platinum edition." I can clearly see that the detectives are trying to find a way to corroborate my story; wondering if they can find a timeline, a paper trail, some electronic confirmation that I ate Chinese food and watched *Pulp Fiction* with my son.

"Where did you buy the wine?"

"We brought out a special bottle from the wine cellar. An '86 Chateau Margaux." I smile, and Sinan cocks his head and grins alongside me.

Lou drops his notebook to the table and leans back in his chair, frustrated. He props his elbows on the armrests and clenches his entire body. "You watched a DVD," he starts. "You ate leftovers, and you've had the bottle of wine you drank sitting in your cellar for years. You know your son isn't of age to be sharing that wine with you."

"Is that why you called me in here? Endangering the welfare of a child? He drinks more than I do." I know they don't have anything on me.

"What time did all of this occur?"

"At dinnertime. I don't know, specifically."

"What exactly was the nature of your relationship with Charlotte Doyle?" Rodrigo pipes up from the corner of the interrogation room.

"Is my client under arrest?" Sinan interrupts, leaning a heavy forearm in front of me.

"Not yet," Lou responds.

"Then we are going to terminate this session, gentlemen." Sinan replaces his notebook into his briefcase.

"Don't you think it's odd that you're choosing to walk away from a completely innocent question about a girl you know? A girl who was recently found brutally murdered? Why would an innocent man refuse to answer my question?" Rodrigo plants his thick hands on the Formica table, attempting to intimidate us. "What was the nature of your relationship? When was the last time you saw Stu Bogovian?"

"My client has been more than cooperative, and this interview is over." Sinan stands and extends his hand, inviting me to leave the room. I smooth back my hair and stifle a smile. They shouldn't have shown me their cards so soon.

Sinan and I walk quickly and silently back to my house, where we find Claire sitting on the top step of the stoop, blowing into a mug of coffee.

"Peter!" she calls when she sees us approaching. "Thank God." We walk up the stairs, and Sinan bows and kisses her hand.

"Hello, Claire. How are you on this beautiful day?" Sinan says as I walk through the open doors.

"Hello, Sinan. Nice to see you. Peter, are you okay?" she calls after me, trying to pull her hand back from Sinan. He stays with her in the vestibule, handing her a jacket and convincing her to leave the house.

"Call Rick," I yell to Claire as Sinan ushers her out the door. "Get those papers filed today."

Seeing Lou and Rodrigo under these circumstances, where I stand accused, has begun to stir up old familiar feelings. I start to feel a heat crawling up my neck as I fiddle with a receipt I find sitting on the coffee table in front of me. Sinan sits beside me on the couch and sips at Claire's coffee. I crumple the receipt and move to throw it into the fireplace, but Sinan reaches a muscled forearm in front of me.

"Don't throw that away."

"Why?" I look down at the crumpled paper in my hand. "It's just a receipt, who cares?"

"Let's just hold on to anything time stamped, all right? Just in case." Sinan takes the paper from my hand, smooths it out and tucks it into his briefcase.

"What'd you do with Claire?"

"I sent her to her office. Told her that you and I need to talk for a little while. She seems very nervous. I suggest you call her and let her know everything is okay."

"I will. I'll text her." I pull out my phone to write to Claire, but Sinan pushes my hand down and shakes his head, indicating he needs my undivided attention.

"Everything you said in there was accurate?" he asks.

"Down to the fortune cookies, my friend."

"If I go downstairs and check your DVD player, will I find *Pulp Fiction* in there?" He curls up the ends of his sentences into a playful singsong.

"Platinum edition," I say, deadpan. "I was here the whole night, Sinan. Like I told you over breakfast wine this morning. It was the first time Jamie and I were alone together, and I remember every excruciating detail. We were both completely uncomfortable around each other. The hours felt like years, so I went to bed as soon as the movie was over. It's exhausting developing relationships with people."

"And if I sit Jamie down?"

"He will tell you exactly what I told you. And my housekeeper will be able to vouch for the wineglasses and chopsticks piled in the sink the following morning. And the ass indents in the front two seats in the theater downstairs. It's the truth, without editing or alteration."

"What happened that night?"

"Claire went to some bachelorette thing in South Hampton, so when Jamie got home, I asked him what he wanted to do for the evening. You know, this was my opportunity to play father, and I wanted to look good, I figured a teenager would like watching a movie, and that way I didn't have to *talk* to him, so I offered a movie in the basement theater." I crack my knuckles, trying to shove down the real thoughts I had that night. "I threw some Chinese leftovers in the microwave and I completely forgot how long the movie was and had to sit there with him for three hours. It was terrible. I think that was the first time we had been alone together his entire life." I realize the words I'm saying are callous and I should feel ashamed, but I'm being honest.

"What happened next?" Sinan ignores my struggle and continues to scribble in his notebook.

"At some point in the evening, I went to the wine cellar and got the '86 Margaux. I only picked that bottle because I have several of them, and it wouldn't make a difference to my collection if we drank one of them. He didn't seem to know the difference between that and a Coors Light. When the movie ended, Jamie helped clean up, he brought the wineglasses up to the kitchen and then we went our separate ways. I told him I was exhausted and needed to sleep, and he yawned at me and said the same. That was that. The next morning, he went out before I left my room, and we didn't cross paths. That was the end of it."

"And what is this pulling glass from the fireplace? Burning your hand?" Sinan looks at me quizzically.

"Claire smashed her glass into the fireplace when we were

arguing, and I was intrigued by the melted pieces, so I pulled them out and burned my fingertips," I respond, as if this were a completely rational behavior.

"All right. Well, now for the fun part." He places Claire's coffee cup on a cocktail napkin. I instinctively walk into the kitchen and sit down at the round table. Sinan hangs his trench coat and suit jacket on the hook where he found Claire's jean jacket and follows me to the table. He lays a yellow legal pad between us.

"When was the last time you saw Charlotte Doyle?"

I inhale a deep breath and blow loudly out of my mouth. "The Rhodes Foundation masquerade ball. Uh, a week ago or so. I can check the invitation."

"Please do. And what *was* the nature of your relationship at that time?" Sinan parrots the detective's question.

"Mostly just social friends. Used to have an on-again, off-again sexual thing. A relationship, I suppose. But Claire put two and two together after seeing a picture from the benefit and asked me to call it off." Although the questions are intrusive, I trust Sinan, so I'm able to stay calm.

"And did you?" Sinan scribbles on his legal pad.

"I mean, I stopped seeing her. I hadn't *really* been seeing her. We hadn't slept together in quite some time, but I suppose we were still flirting."

"How did she take the breakup?" The follow-up questions come naturally to Sinan.

"She didn't. I mean, I never officially broke it off. Didn't think I needed to. We both needed to participate to keep the affair alive, and if I simply stopped participating, then it would die a natural death."

"Please don't use those words if a prosecutor gets the chance to ask you that question," Sinan warns. "Was she married at any time you two were having an affair? Isn't there some weasel ex-husband in the mix here?" He sucks hard on his cigarette.

"There is an ex-husband, Sean. Worked in contract law, didn't know his ass from his elbow, but chased enough ambulances to amass a small fortune. Bought their house on Twentieth Street."

"And why hasn't his name come up in connection with this murder yet? Jilted ex is usually the first one in the interrogation room."

"Sean had an accident a few years back, pretty severely brain damaged. Get this—autoerotic asphyxiation in a hot tub in Miami. Two male hookers, blowing enough coke to make Escobar blush, found him with a bikini top around his neck, slumped over in the water."

"Mmm, sounds like my kind of party," Sinan teases. "How did *that* not make the headlines?"

"He was nobody, so it wouldn't have been a scandal. Charlie wasn't really someone then, either."

"So, the ex-husband is *out* as a suspect. The ex-con, Stu Bogovian, is *out* because he was confirmed in Vegas." Sinan writes down the names and puts big X marks next to them. "It seems from preliminary reports that the killer must have been known to her because there is no forced entry. So, either the killer had a set of keys, Charlotte left the door unlocked by mistake or she willingly opened the door to let the killer in."

"Yup, all that sounds about right." In my mind, all the evidence points to Ethan Doyle.

"And you're telling me the person for whom Charlotte opened the door was not you?"

"Absolutely not."

"Not the man with whom her affair was so steamy that it led to not one but *two* divorces, the man who she had been seeing on-again, off-again for over a decade, the man who never outright stated to her that the affair that was in fact *over*? The woman who was awkwardly obsessed with your wife and stepped into her shoes at the Rhodes Foundation well before it would have been considered appropriate, you're quite sure that woman didn't let *you* in?"

"Fuck you, Sinan."

"Well, all right, then. I suppose we'll just have to find out who she *did* let in." Sinan slams his hands down on the table and grins at me.

THEN

When Juliette and I got back to The Carlyle from the farce therapy session, she told me that infidelity was just a symptom of my disease and that she was willing to stay with me and help me get better. I called the concierge and asked for another room. They told me they had something available on the same floor, and I asked for the penthouse.

"Don't go, Peter. If you just take some time away from the office, away from that work you do, you'll find yourself again."

"I'm not *lost*, Juliette. I don't need to find myself. You and Dr. Kimball have manufactured a fantasy world for yourselves, and you're taking out your problems with your father on *me*."

"My father was just like you when you and I first met. He was kind and doting, and he cared about his family when I was a little girl. And I watched as that job sucked the life out of him. He became a monster and stopped seeing people as anything more than objects. It's exactly the same as what's happening to you."

"Amazing how you think our jobs have made us sociopaths, yet you have no problem reveling in the fruits of our labor." I shook my head and looked around the suite for what to pack.

"What do you mean? You've been absent for years now, I haven't reveled in anything."

"You're an ungrateful hypocrite is what *you* are. My job certainly wasn't an issue for you when it was buying you diamonds. How do you think you live in this hotel with nannies raising your child?"

"My father died because that *job* ate away at his insides until there was nothing left. I don't want to see that happen to you." Somehow, it seemed she still genuinely cared for me.

"Your father died because he was weak," I snapped, defensive and annoyed.

"Jamie needs you in his life. He needs his father. I grew up with a ghost, and you didn't even know your father. I won't have that for my son."

I was immediately infuriated that she had mentioned my upbringing, so I closed the conversation and moved out that night with nothing more than the overnight bag I had recently used when I slept at the office. I emailed Anna, telling her to buy a couple of suits and have them messengered to the hotel.

Our divorce was finalized within only a couple of months. I let Juliette have custody of Jamie and I moved into the house on Twenty-First Street as soon as the construction was complete. I had just won a high-profile child abuse case, and Sinan stopped by the new house on our way to celebrate the victory. He was appalled at its unfinished state, and without even asking my permission, he flipped open his phone and texted some sought-after interior designer.

A designer and design assistant arrived at my house the following week. The assistant was charming, beautiful, simpler and more naive than Juliette and less cunning than Charlie. Her name was Claire and she was twenty-one years old and full of promise and life. While her boss took measurements on the first two floors, I brought Claire upstairs to look at the bedrooms.

"Are you from New York?" I asked, steering the conversation away from decorating.

"Connecticut. Small town near the coast. But I've been living in the city since I moved here for college three years ago. Would you like to expand the existing closet? I think we could make a really special his-and-hers on either side here." She was dedicated to work and drove the topic back to design.

"I don't know that I would need a closet for a 'her.' I'm divorced. Just me and my work now." I dropped the hint, hoping she would pick it up.

"With all the light in here, a boudoir could easily double as a home office until you find a new relationship." She spoke professionally, clearly indicating that the new relationship would not be with her.

"I've been looking, but until now, I haven't seen anything I really like." I stood closer to her, pretending to look at her notes, and placed an arm against the wall behind her.

"Mr. Caine, I'm flattered, but I won't compromise my work ethic or jeopardize the opportunity I've been given here." She walked out from under my arm and joined her boss in the kitchen.

It took more than a year to finish the design and decorating of my house. Claire and I got to know each other professionally, but I stopped my flirtations when I saw she wasn't interested. When the job was finally complete, Claire bade me farewell and made no moves to indicate she would be willing to pursue anything romantic once our professional relationship ended. Not wanting to give up, I called her cell phone one afternoon and asked her to join me for a cup of coffee to discuss some changes to the kitchen cabinets.

"Claire, it's Peter Caine. I'm sorry to say you're not yet rid of me." I held a design magazine to my face—not knowing or caring about cabinet types or colors, I used the suggestions outlined in the magazine to tell Claire what I wanted. "I think we need to meet. My kitchen cabinets are not satisfactory. I'd like some of the cabinets replaced with, uh, exposed shelving. Salvaged wood."

"You want to tear out custom cabinetry and replace it with exposed shelving? That's going to be quite a waste of your money." I'm sure she knew I wasn't calling about cabinets.

"Maybe it's not worth it. Would you be willing to meet with me and discuss it?"

She was waiting at a small table by the window when I arrived at the café. It was getting cooler outside, and she had a huge scarf wrapped around her neck, pinned down beneath a fitted leather jacket. As dutiful as ever, she had her notebook from my townhouse project sitting on the table in front of her.

"I really think the Shaker cabinets you have now should stay. Exposed shelving on either side of a giant hutch will be out of place." When she reached for magazines to begin a business discussion, I held her wrist and admitted I hadn't called to discuss design.

"I thought I would give it another try, since you're not working for me anymore, and you wouldn't be compromising your professional integrity…" I left my thought unfinished and hoped for an affirmative response.

"Mr. Caine," she began, holding her notebook to her chest.

"Please, call me Peter." I kept my hand between us on the table, a gesture of strength and control.

"Peter, I'm hesitant to get involved with clients, whether they're former or current. I know our work together is finished, but I met you through my job, and I don't think it's professionally appropriate." She gently bounced her head and looked down as she spoke.

"Well, you see, if you had told me you weren't interested in me, I would have just backed off, but since you're telling me this is something I can talk you into, I'm going to keep talking." I watched her face for a reaction, and I could have sworn the slightest blush appeared on her cheeks.

NOW

Since Sinan left my house, I've been engrossed in my own thoughts about the detective's questions. I'm comfortable and confident that my performance in the interrogation room was perfect. I answered all of their questions accurately and didn't divulge anything further. Other than eventually having to explain my affair with Charlie, I'm not worried about anything the police have on me.

I come slowly down the stairs to find Jamie and Claire seated together at the kitchen table.

"Did you speak with Rick?" I ask Claire before she can say anything to me.

"I did, yes." She perks up from her position slouched over the table and smiles broadly. "I went to his office and signed the papers you gave me, and he said he would take care of the filing. As soon as we have approval from the judge, it'll be official. I was just telling Jamie about it."

"Well, Jamie? What do you think? Are you excited that Claire will officially become your stepmom?"

"Yeah, it's great." He sounds despondent and distracted.

"Jamie has some other stuff on his mind right now," Claire says. "Why don't you ask your father what he thinks?" She pats his arm and nods her head in my direction.

"Ask me what?" I'm not in a place to answer any more questions today.

Jamie doesn't immediately respond. Instead he fidgets with the pile of school books he has in front of him. When he fails to speak, Claire chimes in for him.

"Jamie wants to take some time off school because his classmates are tormenting him. Wait until your name is out of the papers."

Jamie heaves a frustrated sigh and slumps over his things.

"Is that true, Jamie? What happened?" This is what a father would say, isn't it?

"It's just my friends are jerks, you know?" Jamie's obviously upset. Usually meticulously put together and tidy, he appears sloppy and unkempt of late.

"Tell your dad what you told me." Claire pats Jamie's arm, and he sits up quickly in response.

"So, today I'm at school, right? And I'm standing in line for assembly, and I'm a little bit late, even though I'm never late, so I'm not standing with the people I'm usually with. So, this one kid goes, 'Hey, man, saw your pops on the news last night. Heavy shit.'" Jamie uses a slow, stupid voice to imitate the friend. "And then everyone starts listening in. Another kid asks me, 'You think he killed that lady?' and then they all start laughing. Someone said that their mom won't let me in their house anymore because my dad is a murderer and another kid gave me a pound and told me it was awesome that my dad killed someone."

He huffs out the sentences, exasperated and irritable. He's not looking at me but staring toward Claire as he says this. I realize that he always looks to her for approval when he speaks to me. The same way he used to look to Juliette when he was small.

"What did you say to them?" I ask, somewhat amused that his friends are accusing me of murder.

"I told them to shut up!" He slams his hands on top of his books and then pulls them into his lap and hangs his head when Claire shoots him a scolding glance. "Even the teachers were looking at me differently. The principal gave me a really bad stare, and I couldn't do anything because you're supposed to be quiet during assembly. People kept turning around to look at me, and they were whispering to each other and giggling."

I look to Claire, suspicious. How's she going to react now? And how is Jamie going to respond to her? A radar in my head is seizing, and I'm tuned into their every move.

Jamie draws in several deep breaths. "So, can I skip school until it blows over?"

"You're not running away from these guys, Jamie. But maybe you can stay home a day or two next week." I give in to what he wants so he can have a better view of me.

Jamie lets the traces of a smile appear on his face as he picks up his backpack and slings it over one shoulder. As he crosses the doorway into the hall, he turns, and the evidence of happiness has disappeared.

"One kid—" he pauses "—one kid said you probably killed my mother, too."

The moment Sinan gets back to the office after meeting with his connection, he calls me to report in. He received a copy of the police report, the evidence list and some photographs from the crime scene. He gives me a rundown of the pertinent pieces of information.

Charlotte Doyle's body was discovered on Monday, September 26 by her housekeeper, Sylvia Santos. He pulls up the crime scene photos and tells me the pools of blood around her body seem small for twenty-seven stab wounds. She was slumped on her left side, hair matted to her face, wounds concentrated on her chest and torso. She wore a lacy black bra, the strap on her right shoulder slipped down to her elbow.

Sinan reads on to report about the murder weapon, a Shun six-inch chef's knife, which was probably taken from a knife block in Charlotte's kitchen and was left at the scene. There were no fingerprints on the knife.

The front door and the service entrance showed no signs of forced entry. That singular fact was likely going to be the most important. Whoever opened that door knew the person on the other side or thought she did. The evidence showed no signs of struggle anywhere else in the house, and the housekeeper reported the house seemed completely normal when she arrived. She didn't encounter blood anywhere. She didn't think anything was amiss, and if anyone knew the normal state of that house, it was Sylvia Santos.

I reviewed the information in my head as Sinan paused to look through the rest of the documents. Charlotte was murdered inside her bedroom. The clothes Sylvia reported seeing her wearing the day of the murder were in the hamper in her dressing room. No blood was found on her clothes, meaning she undressed before she was killed. The housekeeper believed that none of Charlotte's clothes were missing, as far as she could tell. She was responsible for laundry and dry cleaning, so she considered herself very familiar with Charlotte's wardrobe.

The only thing the stab wounds told the detectives was

that the murderer was right-handed, strong and probably taller than Charlotte, because of the angle at which she was stabbed. The blood spatter analysis and coroner's reports suggested that the crime was committed by someone who knew and passionately hated the victim, as the sheer force of the stabbing broke several of her ribs. That fact combined with no evidence of forced entry reiterated that Charlotte knew her murderer.

"I'm just looking over everything one more time, Peter, but none of these facts point to you specifically." I can hear him shuffling between sheets. "Hold on a sec, there's something odd here." His voice becomes tense, and I hear him shuffling between pages.

"What? What's odd?" And just like that, a lump begins to form in my throat.

"Something was found inside of a bedroom garbage can that hadn't been emptied since Sylvia took the garbage out before she left on her trip…" He trails off.

"What is it?" I'm starting to feel light-headed.

"The detectives found and bagged something they thought could be relevant." He expels a long sigh. "It's bizarre, but it's familiar. Come into my office tomorrow morning and look at the report. I want you to see this."

I arrive to see Sinan sitting in one of the large, leather roll-arm chairs in the corner of his office by the television.

"I've looked a bit deeper into some of the reports," Sinan begins, voice low and steady. "From the first officer on the scene, the coroner's report and the CSI report, as well. The coroner's report has results pending for tox screens and such but paints a pretty clear picture of what happened." He draws in a deep, pensive breath. "Again, I can't say there's too much in there that implicates you."

"There isn't 'too much'? What does that mean?" I bark defensively. "That's not what you said on the phone yesterday."

"The report indicates that the killer was right-handed, strong and taller than the victim, like I told you. You happen to be taller than the victim, strong and right-handed."

"Completely circumstantial, obviously." I dismiss this information. "*You* could have done it if this is all the evidence they have."

"I'm surprised you haven't noticed in all these years that I am, in fact, left-handed." Sinan holds up the pen he's using with his left hand.

Ignoring him, I press further. "What else did you find? Most of the scene was compromised because of the cleaning lady, right?"

"The crime scene is limited to the bedroom, which the maid cleaned before she left for a short vacation. So, any fingerprints or evidence from *before* the murder would have been cleaned, or at least would be compromised. Anything from *during or after* the murder would be intact in the bedroom." He continues, "She was found in a bra and no panties. CSI determined she had been wearing underwear at the time she was killed, based on the pattern of the blood spatter and the streaked blood on her legs caused when her underwear was pulled off postmortem. So, it looks like the killer made off with her panties."

"A souvenir? Sounds like a sex offender or a serial killer."

"That's the trail. The panties are going to make or break this case. Find the panties, find the guilty man."

"I don't have any of her panties, so they have nothing on me." I am gaining comfort with every piece of information that has nothing to do with me.

"The shower drain had traces of one blood type," Sinan goes on. "Looks to be only Charlotte's blood."

"So, he washed himself off after killing her?"

"Precisely. That's what it looks like."

A thunderous knock on the door interrupts our conversation before Sinan can reveal what he hid from me yesterday. He stands and opens the door for the Franks.

Tomlinson and LaBianca sit in the two small chairs opposite Sinan's desk, and Sinan reoccupies his desk chair. I remain seated in the corner by the television.

"Well, you were right," Tomlinson begins, "this kid definitely hated his sister."

I point at Tomlinson and wag my finger. "See?"

"We have one police report from 2013—Charlotte Doyle called the cops on Ethan because he wouldn't leave her house and was drunk and belligerent. The report shows that she refused to request an order of protection." Tomlinson reads over his notes. "And she declined to press charges, so he wasn't arrested, simply removed from the premises."

"This is Charlotte's house on Twentieth Street?" Sinan clarifies.

"Yes, that's correct. And Ethan has a sketchy criminal record. Looks like he had his record cleaned up by his dad, but even the DA can't make *everything* go away. He had two drug charges, both cocaine possession, and several incidents with hookers. One of the hookers claimed he was abusive, but withdrew her complaint and was later deported. I'm willing to bet all the money in my pockets that she didn't withdraw the complaint of her own volition, if you know what I mean. Also there is a stalking incident with an ex-girlfriend. Again, his record has been cleaned up, so he doesn't really look like a criminal, but the reports still exist. His father also fought to seal his juvenile record, but we have a guy who can get around that, and it shows arrests for animal abuse—he cut off the family cat's tail—and again, stalking in some kind of Peeping Tom incident."

"Sounds like a sexual predator to me," I pipe up. "You know animal abuse is one of the most common childhood traits among serial killers?"

"He does sound like a predator, boss." LaBianca turns to face me. "And listen to this—his Facebook page was removed because he posted threatening statuses. It's not looking too good for this guy."

"Jesus," I say. "Why hasn't anyone investigated him yet?"

"Alibi, boss. The kid's got an alibi," LaBianca says. "He was at a club opening in the Meatpacking District. Friends with the owner. Stayed there all night."

"Wait a minute," Sinan interjects. "A club opening is not going to start in the evening, it's going to start at eleven or midnight. The wankers show up at nine and ten, but not the owners, not the promoters or the VIP guests. If he's supposed to be a big shot or a scenester, he's not going to show up on time."

Tomlinson flips through his notes to see what kind of time stamps they have. "Clubs are filled with cameras—I'm sure there's footage of his arrival. When we can make ourselves known as investigators in this case, I can get the footage from the club."

"Do that. Get to the club and find out what the hell is going on. The coroner's report puts the time of death between 10:00 p.m. and midnight. Find out when that prat got to the club."

LaBianca and Tomlinson nod excitedly.

"What else?" I ask.

"Nothing better than what we already told you, boss."

"Okay, don't cut any corners," Sinan wraps up. "Be careful on this one, and only use legitimate verifiable sources. I don't want anything that was collected illegally. Technically impeccable, you understand?" Sinan opens the door, and La-Bianca quickly hurries out. Tomlinson holds out his hand for Sinan to shake and follows his partner into the hallway.

"Oh, one more thing." Frank Tomlinson steps one foot back into the office. "No life insurance policy. So, only the scumbag brother would financially benefit now that he doesn't have to split his inheritance." Tomlinson waves and walks down the hallway.

"I knew it was Ethan, Sinan. I knew it was." I begin pacing the office. "*That's* why Harrison has disappeared from public view. He's probably finding a way to cover all this up. He'll never live it down if his son murdered his stepdaughter."

Harrison has been noticeably absent; he's spoken to the press only once since his phone call with me the day the story broke. At the press conference, he asked for privacy and ensured the public that he would still be running for reelection but would put his campaign duties on hold until he got the person who did this to his child. He didn't address Stu Bogovian's comments, and he didn't make any further statements. It was a brilliant career move to disappear. The sympathy of the electorate will grow if he never gives himself the opportunity to say the wrong thing in public.

"Well, I'm not quite so sure." Sinan reaches to the stack of papers in front of him and pulls the photo he found of the strange object in the evidence bag. He gently lays it on the end of his desk. "Recognize this?"

I scrutinize the picture, not quite able to make out what the object inside the evidence bag could be. I shrug my shoulders and hand the photo back. Sinan pulls out a second page, the evidence list with the item highlighted. I read over the words and my heart shoots into my throat. *Twisted paper clips.*

I look back up at Sinan, confused. Sinan stands, reaches

into his desk drawer and pulls out a twisted paper-clip stick, the one I threw into his trash can earlier this week. He slowly returns to his chair, softly placing the object next to my other hand.

"I don't know anyone else who makes these things. You've been fucking up my paper clips since I joined the firm. Can you explain to me how one of your paper-clip sticks could have ended up in Charlotte Doyle's bedroom on the night she was murdered?"

THEN

Claire didn't outright agree to go out with me when I invited her for coffee that afternoon, but she also didn't outright turn me down. I hadn't been in an official relationship since Juliette and I divorced more than a year prior. Claire was the first woman who seemed interesting enough to pursue, and with her dedication to her own career, I assumed she wouldn't demand too much of my time if we were to eventually develop anything serious.

"Claire." I had called her work phone. "I can't remember your personal number, so I'm sorry to bother you at work, as this is not a professional call."

"Yes, Peter?" she said, a hint of excitement in her voice.

"I've been invited to a movie premiere that a client of mine produced, and I thought you might enjoy it. Would you like to accompany me?" I thought a glamorous and exclusive event would be just the enticing she needed.

She paused a moment before responding. "That sounds like a really special invitation, Peter, but shouldn't you be bringing someone closer to you?"

"It's tomorrow evening, at 7:00 p.m. I can come and pick you up," I say, ignoring her question.

She let out a deep, pensive breath. Apparently unsure if she wanted to go out with me. "Tomorrow?" She still wasn't convinced.

"Yes, tomorrow at 7:00 p.m." I was beginning to get impatient and annoyed. Although I was enjoying the cat-and-mouse game, I didn't want to be dangled on a string and give Claire the upper hand.

"Okay. I'll come with you, and thank you for thinking of me. Is it black tie?"

"Um, I believe the invitation said cocktail attire." I scrambled to come up with a response. "And where can I pick you up?"

Claire told me her address, and when I hung up, I immediately called to book a limousine. I needed to come up with some excuse as to why the fake movie premiere would be canceled.

The following evening, I idled in front of her crappy apartment building for nearly ten minutes before she exited her lobby door. She looked stunning. I got out of the limo and held her hand to help her inside. I almost regretted that I wouldn't be bringing her to a movie premiere.

"Good evening, Peter," she greeted me formally, despite the intimate nature of our date. "Thank you for picking me up."

"You're very welcome. You look beautiful. And I'm so sorry to tell you that our plans tonight have changed." I pasted a look of disappointment on my face.

"Changed?" She eyed me suspiciously and kept her hand on the handle of the door.

"Yes, unfortunately the premiere has been postponed due to some unforeseen circumstances, but I didn't find out until late this afternoon. I didn't want you to have gotten ready for nothing, so I thought I would take you to dinner instead. How's that? Not quite a movie premiere, but hopefully you'll still enjoy the show." I beamed with confidence and asked the driver to bring us to Restaurant Daniel.

Claire clutched her bag nervously until we arrived at Daniel. I wanted to impress her, so I booked the Skybox, a small room above the kitchen that used to be Daniel Boulud's office. We could dine overlooking the goings-on of the kitchen—it was a very exclusive reservation. She hadn't said a word in the car once I told her our plans had changed. When we got up the small ladder and settled into the banquette, she seemed to calm down a little bit.

"I'm sorry to have disappointed you. I know you were looking forward to the premiere."

"It's fine, I'm not disappointed. In fact, this dinner will give us an opportunity to get to know each other better. I imagine a premiere would be filled with distractions."

I ordered for both of us, champagne, tasting menus, the works, hoping to impress her. I had trouble reading Claire; her opinion of me seemed yet unformed, and I wanted it to be a good one.

I asked her about her work with the design firm, feeling rusty with my first-date banter. She was so young, seemingly at ease on dates, and my confidence grew that I was making my desired impression.

"You know." She narrowed her eyes at me. "I nearly jumped out of the limo when you told me you fabricated a movie premiere."

I was aghast, caught completely off guard. "Fabricated?" She was right, I had invented the premiere, but that didn't mean I was ready to be accused of lying. "I did no such thing."

"You don't have to try to impress me with that kind of thing. I'm not here tonight to go out on a date at some fancy place with a wealthy attorney," she said, flinging a small baguette at my plate. "You seem like an interesting guy, and I'm curious."

I breathed easy. She wasn't accusing me of lying. "Well, if you don't want movie premieres and fancy dinners, I will take you to the ball pit at Burger King. I'm capable of enjoying less exclusive excitements, as well." She wasn't after my money or status. I was intrigued.

We eased into a relationship from there, moving from dating casually to using nauseating terms like *exclusive* and *boyfriend*. I fell back into the idea that Marcus put into my head after I married Juliette; it looks good when a man with a questionable reputation is ensconced in a stable relationship.

I made it very clear to Claire that I wasn't interested in getting married again. I felt that was too severe a sentence for anything I'd ever done, and she seemed to understand me. When we broached the subject of children, I told her again I was unwilling, and then she asked to meet Jamie. The idea of separate worlds colliding was dreadful, so I made excuses and put up roadblocks for almost five years to keep Claire and Jamie separated. In fact, I successfully pushed their initial meeting until Jamie was nearly thirteen years old.

I plied her with childhood stories about European adventures and kept her sympathetic with the tragedy of my parents' deaths. I feigned an inability to truly process what had happened to my parents that fateful day in Positano when their car was crushed into a cliff face by a speeding van on dangerous winding roads. I choked up, turned inward and refused to talk about it in detail. I began to use the heartbreak of my parents' deaths as a means of keeping Claire away from Juliette and Jamie. I told her that I was so traumatized by the accident, still so unsure of my ability to be a father to Jamie as I had lost my father so young, that I was terrified to develop a relationship with him, for fear of losing it.

She bought it all. I knew better than to share any of the truth of Vermont, Chicago and the man I was before Peter Caine. I had already made that disastrous mistake once before. But I knew I couldn't keep them apart forever. Eventually, I would have to allow them to meet.

NOW

Bewildered, I sit with my mouth agape. I look back and forth between the picture of the evidence bag and the stick I had javelined into Sinan's garbage can. I've been winding straightened paper clips together absentmindedly since high school. I remember getting in trouble for wasting whole boxes of clips like this. Anyone who knows me knows about this distraction that occupies my hands.

"But I wasn't there..." I softly speak. "I swear it. I haven't been to Charlie's house in months."

"Tell me, tell me how the *hell* this stick—this stick that probably has your skin cells trapped in its crevices—ended up at her house *after* the maid emptied the bin the day she was killed?" Sinan demands, glaring at me.

"She must have found it somewhere and thrown it away that day." I pace the office, switching from panicky to cautious and defensive. "Just because it went into the trash that

A.F. BRADY

day doesn't mean that she only *got* it that day. Maybe she had it for months. Maybe I made it at her house, or I dropped one there by mistake ages ago. I don't know how the hell it got there, but I *wasn't* in that house the night Charlie was murdered."

I return to the leather seat in the corner of the office. "The paper clips won't be a problem, Sinan. Think about it. Chances are they're going to find my fingerprints somewhere in her house. I'm probably all over that place, cleaning lady or no cleaning lady. Either way, I'm falling on my sword and admitting the affair, there's no way around that. The affair opens the door to her house. Of course I'm in there."

"I'm not worried about arguing your presence, I'm worried about arguing your presence in the bin *after* Sylvia Santos emptied that bin. How did you get in there *that day*?"

"It's called reasonable doubt, Sinan. Give them a reason to doubt it. We were seeing each other for ages, then I broke it off, and she was purging me from her house. Going through her stuff, found some old evidence of me and made sure to chuck it. One jilted ex-girlfriend on the jury is all we need."

With my unverifiable alibi, the mystery of the paper clips and the lack of physical evidence, we surmise that the case against me will be mostly circumstantial. The affair will be the biggest obstacle to overcome; significant others are always at the forefront of murder investigations. The preliminary investigation into Ethan is promising, but if Charlotte had been afraid of him, and he had been hateful and abusive toward her in the past, we'll have a hard time proving that she would be willing to open the door to let her brother in.

Sinan resumes wondering aloud how we can obtain further information into Ethan, to start mounting a case against him as part of my defense. Knowing I will eventually have to answer for my affair with Charlotte and my presence in her house, we want to ensure that Ethan is viewed as an un-mistakable monster.

"We are going to have some trouble with the brutality. This is true hatred shown here." Sinan flips through the pictures. "And they'll argue that you have reason to hate her."

"Reason or no, Ethan has *proven* he hates her. We need to get those emails that Charlie showed me. If the Franks can get that information, then the press can get it, too, and this whole thing is going to play out in the court of public opinion more than anywhere else."

"You're absolutely right, and it certainly wouldn't hurt to improve the public's opinion of *you*."

"What do you want me to do?" I'm prepared to put on a show if needed; if potential jurors have heard of me, we want them to have heard only good things.

"Can you propose?" Sinan suggests.

"Propose? Are you serious? You want me to get married?"

"Engagement has an air of hope about it, and it shows your commitment to Claire, which is a nail in the coffin of your affair."

"That will absolutely look contrived. If I go out and buy a ring now, propose to Claire amid all this bad publicity? Looks like a Hail Mary. Can't do it."

"What about therapy? Can you see a shrink? Go together with Claire, say it's part of your transition into parenting together."

I think immediately of Dr. Kimball. "I guess I can do that, sure."

"You know anyone good? I could find out some names."

"No, I've got someone." If I see Dr. Kimball, it'll look like a continuation of previous therapy and not an attempt to prove myself responsible and caring.

Sinan puts down all his papers and lights another cigarette.

"What's important to me is how we *make* you look, not how you *really* look."

"Sinan, the way I see it is thus… I'm not getting indicted because there's no evidence to indict me—"

Sinan holds up his free hand to stop me and blows a huge plume of smoke from his mouth. "You've got motive *and* opportunity. What makes you think they *won't* indict you?"

I don't immediately realize that Sinan has started playing an old game. "Wait—by motive, you mean what?"

"If I were prosecuting this case, I would argue that you have motive to silence your ex-lover because you're trying to become a family man now. You recently gained custody of your child, and you don't want anyone throwing a wrench in that particular operation."

This is a game the two of us play when preparing for trial. We play devil's advocate, finding the possible cracks in our theories or strong counterarguments—this way we can find any hole that needs filling and prepare for whatever the prosecutor may throw at us.

"Claire knows I had an affair with Charlie, she isn't leaving me. That's bogus."

"Doesn't matter what she knows or doesn't know. It's the argument. You have motive. And hatred. Maybe Charlotte was the one who told Claire. Maybe Charlotte demanded you leave Claire. You're the clandestine affair—motive." He stubs out his cigarette with a flourish.

"Opportunity? How do you see that?"

"You have a completely unverifiable alibi. You were at home alone with your son, there is no paper trail whatsoever to corroborate this and you live one block away from Charlotte Doyle. Whether Jamie makes a statement or not is practically irrelevant. The statement of a minor is always weak, and he's *related* to you. It's not going to hold up, and you know that. What else?" Sinan is getting louder, excited, ready to attack anything I throw at him.

"They don't have a timeline," I remind him. "I don't know when we sat down to watch the movie, and there's nothing that can show what time that was. Could have been 10 p.m. for all I know."

Sinan suddenly halts his excitement and points a long finger at me. "You're right." His eyes are wild, and he quickly snatches up a pen and writes *no timeline* in heavy black ink. "They can't have any idea what time all of this happened. Your dinner, the movie… There's no way to verify what time that started. *That's* exactly the kind of hole we can squeeze through."

"There's no way to know," I repeat, comforted that timelines are regarded as massive pieces of evidence in court cases. As much as Sinan and I can't prove I was home, the prosecution can't prove I wasn't.

"The murderer probably still has her panties, and that's what I'd like to find. You can't stab someone twenty-seven times and have no blood on you, so I would like to find the murderer's clothes, as well. I have the Franks sniffing around like fat bloodhounds, and hopefully they find something useful." Sinan grabs the crime scene photos and flips through them in the light from the window. "When the tox screen comes back, we'll see if she was drugged, because that's going to make a difference, too. If the rape kit shows evidence of sexual assault…" He pauses. "We will cross that bridge when we get to it."

"For now, we can explain away whatever motive they may say I have, we can inject some doubt into my opportunity and we can shine a very bright light on a very creepy man and outline, in detail, how Ethan has more motive than I ever could, and a criminal record to boot. This is almost a throw-away. There's no evidence. No case. Until someone finds the killer's clothes or Charlie's panties, it's all arguing. And you could argue any man under the table." I wink at him.

"Mmm, a man under the table," he jokes. "Tell me the truth, old friend." Sinan leans down to my ear and whispers loudly, "Did you kill her? Certainly looks like you did." He nudges the paper-clip stick toward me.

I stand to look at Sinan as my confidence grows. "Like you said, it doesn't matter how I *really* look, it matters how you *make* me look."

THEN

Claire and I were living together and practically acting as a married couple. We were happy enough, both working on our careers more than our relationship, but as we approached our five-year anniversary, Claire started to push me toward a greater focus on us.

"I'm feeling like a clandestine lover." She started in on me right when I walked through the door one evening. "You're always at work, and you don't take me to any of the places you go after work. I'm beginning to feel like no one even knows I exist."

"Who do you think I'm spending time with, Claire? I'm at work with Sinan and Anna. I hardly even see any of the junior partners or paralegals. You want to come to Rikers with me? Meet my clients? There's a little thing called attorney-client privilege, Claire. I'm not compartmentalizing you—it's just the nature of my life."

"Compartmentalizing! That's exactly what it is." I had given her the perfect word, and she would use it against me. "You're keeping all the parts of your life separated."

"I have two parts of my life—work and you. What more do you want from me?"

"I want to meet your son." She stood defiant in the hallway, looking to have practiced the line before she delivered it to me.

"Jamie? Why do you want to meet Jamie? He's hardly a part of my life."

"And I want to meet Juliette, as well."

"Juliette and Jamie are a part of my former life, Claire. What even made you think of it?"

She held up a multicolored card and bobbed her eyebrows. "We've been invited to a party, and we are going."

I snatched the card from her hand to see it was an invitation to Jamie's thirteenth birthday party. "I am *not* going to this, Claire, and neither are *you*." I immediately tore the card in half and threw the pieces to the ground.

"Look." She held the envelope from the invitation up to me as she followed me into the kitchen. "The card was addressed to you *and* me. So, you can ditch your son's thirteenth birthday if you want, but I'm going."

I was horrified by the idea of Claire attending a party with my ex-wife and ex-son without me there. "What's it going to take for you to drop this?" I hoped I would be able to bribe her away from this appalling plan.

"Dinner."

"Okay, I'll take you out to dinner tonight. Wherever you want to go." A sense of relief washed over me.

"No, Peter. Dinner with Juliette and Jamie. You've had me locked in your castle for five long years now, and I'm not going another year without meeting them. We're seeing them."

I could see in her eyes that she wouldn't take no for an answer. The only way I could foresee staying in control of the situation would be for me to make all the plans and arrangements and to be present for every second of the godforsaken event.

The next day I had Anna get a reservation at Smith & Wollensky. I needed a place that was loud and fast, where I knew everyone and everyone knew me. The more distractions, the better. As soon as the reservation was secured, I had her call Juliette.

"Don't ask questions, don't say anything, just get Juliette on the phone and tell her that I made reservations at Smith & Wollensky for Thursday night at 8:00 p.m., and she and Jamie shouldn't be late."

"Is it to celebrate his birthday?" Anna asked gently.

"Say whatever you want, just tell them not to be late." I felt backed into a corner, and I wanted to attack. I wasn't prepared to let my old life and my new one intermingle. I didn't want Juliette's opinion of me—or worse, her knowledge of my secrets—to interfere with my relationship with Claire. I had finally secured my place as New York's top defense attorney and I didn't want to worry any longer about my past being exposed.

When we divorced and Jamie was just in first grade, Juliette called me every month to give me updates and would usually ask me to talk to him. After a year or two, I avoided so many phone calls, they dwindled down to just a few times a year and I asked Anna to send them all to voice mail. To me, that part of my life was over, and I no longer felt I had to play the role of husband or father. The more I removed myself from their lives, the more comfortable I felt in my own life.

On the day we were scheduled to have the dinner, anxiety churned in my stomach. I still couldn't believe Claire had manipulated me into doing this. When 7:30 p.m. rolled around, I hurried her into a taxi, ready to get it over with.

"I don't want to be a topic of dinner discussion, understand? You can meet these people and talk about whatever else you want, but keep the details of our lives between us," I growled in the back of the cab, unable to bring myself to look at her.

We arrived at Smith & Wollensky twenty minutes later and were escorted swiftly to our table. I made a huge scene of calling hellos to everyone I recognized. I figured the more eyes on me, the better; I would be better suited to perform with a bigger audience. I asked for a table for six, so I wouldn't have to be seated too close to anyone. I ordered an Oban the moment we sat down and told the waiter to stay close.

Claire kept one eye on me, and one eye on the door, waiting with heavy anticipation. When they arrived, Juliette glided toward our table with a wide smile on her face. I looked around her for Jamie and was nearly knocked over with surprise when a man wearing Jamie's face slid in beside Juliette. He stood taller than she did, only thirteen, looking like a youthful version of me.

Before I fully grasped what was happening in front of me, Claire and Juliette were wrapped in a warm embrace, plastering one another with compliments. Jamie stood awkwardly by, shaking Claire's hand and smiling politely when introduced, and I noticed no one was looking at me. My unease was temporarily stilled, I began to feel ignored and the discomfort of embarrassment started to fill me.

"Happy birthday, Jamie," I bellowed to force them to attend to me. "Hello," I said, leaning over to Juliette and Jamie, not quite looking at either one of them.

"Hello, Peter," Juliette said, and Jamie nodded and smiled.

I allowed my ears to focus on the din in the restaurant around me and detached my senses from the table. I held the menu in front of my face, even though I knew precisely what I was going to order. I kept a minute amount of attention on the conversation at the table, just to ensure no one was talking about me.

"I'm so glad we're finally doing this," Juliette squealed, and her voice pierced my eardrums. "It's been such a long time coming. I'm so happy to finally put a face to the voice."

Voice? I thought. When did Juliette ever hear Claire's voice? My heartbeat filled my ears, and as if from inside a tunnel, I heard Claire say, "I know. It's so much better to be seeing you in person than talking to you on the phone." They'd been talking on the phone? A fuzziness clouded my vision. Both the women look over to me and I heard Claire say, "We've become friends, Peter, and now I get to meet Jamie, who I've heard so much about."

My apprehension tore through me, and I realized I had no control over the situation and what information they may have shared about me. I knew I couldn't react with all the eyes in the restaurant on my table, so I silently prayed that Juliette hadn't told Claire the truth about where I came from. They'd been talking for years, they'd become friends. Good God, Juliette could have told her everything.

I could hardly breathe by the time we finally got into a taxi after dinner and away from public view.

"I was so surprised to see how upset you got at dinner, Peter. You usually don't care that much about anything." Claire was triumphant and condescending, having succeeded at pulling the wool over my eyes. "I guess that's the kind of thing that can happen when you ignore everything that's going on around you."

Her patronizing voice grated on my nerves, but I was desperate to keep my panic under control. She was right, I didn't usually care. But she was meddling in places she didn't belong, and she was interfering in parts of my life that I kept separate for a reason.

"Are you trying to teach me a lesson, *Claire*?" I asked through gritted teeth.

"Oh, not at all, darling, no one could ever teach *you* anything." Her phony smile didn't suit her, and I was not amused.

"You should mind your own business, you know. Keep yourself occupied with the things that concern you, and don't go dragging my past back into my present." I looked out the taxi window, hopeful that the mile-long drive home would speed by.

"Don't you want to know how Juliette and I ended up having a relationship?"

"Ha, whatever you think is going on, you certainly don't have a *relationship*, so I wouldn't call it that." I thought belittling their connection would help to discredit anything Juliette may have said.

"We've been talking almost once a month for two years now. The phone calls you two used to have, where she would update you on how Jamie is doing? She's been having those calls with me."

Her defiance was infuriating, and I began to realize that having a girlfriend and benefiting from the image may not be worth the trouble. I didn't respond, hoping she'd take my silence as a sign to stop talking.

"I know you had no interest in talking to Juliette, but when she called the house phone and I happened to answer, we got to talking." Claire didn't need me to respond. Stuck in traffic on Lexington Avenue, I was trapped, and forced to listen to her explanation. "She had been calling to tell you that Jamie was having trouble without a father in his life. He started acting out at school, getting in trouble. The kids would tease him when parents day came around and you never showed up."

I maintained my silence, sure that whatever I said would back me further into the corner.

"My father was never around growing up, so I knew just what Jamie was going through. Juliette told me that Marcus was a ghost, so we supported each other. We came up with ways to keep Jamie out of trouble and told him stories about you to keep him happy, make him feel complete."

"I gave Juliette full custody years ago. She *knew* I wasn't going to be involved. I didn't lie to her. You think you're making things better by lying to the kid?" I shook my head. "You're just getting his hopes up for nothing."

That night stuck in my memory as a turning point when I realized that no one could be trusted. Even Anna, my long-time assistant who always followed rules without question, even she was out to get me; no one else could have given my home number to Juliette.

Claire had already been complaining that she was insufficiently involved in my life, and after pulling that stunt, I pushed her even further away. I realized that having a stable image at home *was* worth it, but it didn't mean I had to put in any effort—it just meant it had to *look* like I was putting in an effort.

So, I played the game. As party invitations flooded in like they usually did, I took Claire with me. If she felt like she was being included and she knew everything that was going on, then I would save myself the nightmare of having to actually involve her in anything at all. As Marcus taught me, it only mattered how things appeared.

Her relationship with Juliette and Jamie continued over the following years, but once I was aware, I was sure to check in and monitor their conversations. I still refused to involve myself because, as I had made perfectly clear, I had no desire to be a father. I still didn't see Jamie, and I let Claire and Anna take care of whatever gifts needed to be sent his way. I didn't foresee any time that our paths would inevitably cross; given that he was still a teenager, he wouldn't be attending the same events I attended. Or so I thought.

I received an invitation from the governor of New York to attend the engagement party of his daughter. It was a major society event, filled with Manhattan elite and political fat cats. It would have been social suicide to turn down the invitation, and despite my discomfort at the idea of my disparate worlds colliding, I told Claire we were going.

"You know Juliette will be invited to this," Claire said, still probing in her closet for something suitable to wear.

"I'm sure that she will, but it's going to be a huge event, and there's no reason I have to say more than hello."

"Except that she'll bring Jamie as her date, and you don't want to *ignore* your son. Certainly not in *public* anyway." Claire's attitude toward my parenting was unforgiving.

"Jamie is too young to go to something like this. I'm sure she won't bring him."

"He's nearly sixteen, Peter. He looks and behaves like a grown-up, he would fit right in at an event like this." She gave me that look she always gave me when she told me about him; the pathetic judgmental look that said I should have known all of this.

"So be it, Claire. If he's there, he's there, and I will say hello to him, as well." I had tolerated my ex-life and my current life crashing into one another once before, and I was sure I could tolerate it again, especially being prepared for it in advance. But I never could have guessed just how many worlds would collide that night at the engagement party.

NOW

The morning of Charlotte's funeral, I wake up to find Claire isn't next to me. We had talked before bed about telling Jamie that Charlie and I had a relationship before he inevitably saw it on television. I check the clock and am shocked to see it's nearly 10:00 a.m. I haven't slept as late or as peacefully in years. I drag through my morning routine, showering and dressing as if for a workday, and come down to the kitchen, where Claire and Jamie are sharing a breakfast sandwich. A part of me hopes that Claire has already told Jamie everything, and I can avoid the awkward conversation.

"Good morning," Claire says, mouth full of bagel. "I can't believe you slept so late."

"Morning," I say, eyeing the foil packages on the kitchen table.

"Oh, Jamie brought us breakfast," Claire says, pointing at the bacon, egg and cheese sandwiches.

Jamie holds up a package for me. "Want one? They're really good."

Not wanting to offend my son, especially considering the conversation we need to have, I take the sandwich from him and sit down at the round table.

"Jamie," Claire begins, jumping right into it, "your father and I need to talk to you about something." She looks at me expectantly, wanting me to take the lead.

"Oh, man, again? What is it now? Is this about the lady who got killed?" Jamie looks back and forth between us.

"Yes, Jamie. This is about Charlie."

"What is going on? You guys are making me nervous." Jamie puts down his sandwich.

"Before your friends get wind of it, we wanted you to be prepared that it's probably going to come out in the press that Charlie and I were once romantically involved."

"Okay, Peter." Claire speaks with her espresso cup to her lips, blocking the expression on her face. "It was more like an affair, Jamie." She looks at me and shakes her head, disappointed that I muddled the truth. "This is probably going to become public knowledge as the investigation into her murder continues, and we wanted to make sure that you heard it from us first."

"That's it?" He shrugs her off and scoots his chair away from the table.

"Well, Jamie," I continue, "it's kind of a big deal and—"

"I already know. And it's *not* a big deal. Why are we even talking about this?" Jamie's frustration is immediately apparent, and he suddenly looks uncomfortable in his own skin.

"You know?" Claire seems incredulous. "How do you know?"

"Because I'm not stupid, Claire. If you think people don't know, then *you're* stupid." His normally gentle demeanor downshifts. He stands up and backs into a corner of the kitchen as far away from us as he can. His defenses are up, like a threatened animal.

"Jamie, it's important that we talk about this. You obviously have some feelings about it." I hold out my hand, offering back the seat Jamie has just abandoned.

"I don't want to talk about it."

"Can you at least tell me what you think you know? Maybe I can help you to understand the truth."

"I know that you had an affair and that's why you and Mom got divorced, and I know that when we went to that masquerade, you didn't even talk to anyone because you were all over her. Okay? So, I know enough, and I don't want to talk about this anymore." He hugs himself in self-protection and keeps his eyes on his sneakers.

"Jamie, sweetie, why didn't you tell us that you knew about this?" Claire tries to soothe him.

"Because what *difference* does it make? It doesn't matter if I know or I didn't know. It wouldn't have changed anything. You still would've gotten a divorce, you still wouldn't have cared about me or anyone else." He addresses me in response to Claire's question.

"You were a kid when we got divorced, Jamie. It was much more than just the affair that led to me and your mom breaking up."

"Fine, whatever. I know. Can we *please* stop talking about this?" Jamie looks like a wounded animal, trapped in a snare, ready to attack anything that dares near him.

"We don't have to talk about it anymore," I concede.

"Can I *please* be excused?"

"Yes, of course you can go. I'm so sorry we upset you." Claire clutches her napkin to her chest. We hear Jamie clamber up the stairs to his room and slam his door shut.

"Well, *that* was a disaster," I say. "I've never seen that kid get pissed before. Didn't know he had it in him."

"What do you expect?" Claire flaps her napkin at me. "He knew his father was cheating. And he saw you with her at that benefit you took him to. Can you *imagine* how he must feel?"

I stare at Claire in disbelief. I can't wrap my mind around what I did wrong this time. I've already admitted the affair, fallen on my sword. I tried to apologize and make amends, and yet I am still paying for my mistakes. I try to imagine how Jamie must feel but my mind turns corners to dead ends. I can't step into my son's shoes. I have no idea.

Claire looks racked with overwhelming compassion and pity. She must know exactly how Jamie feels: hurt, angry, lost and terrified. She spent her childhood experiencing little else. I don't understand.

Jamie spends the afternoon avoiding confrontation in his room. Claire stays off on her own, as well, running errands earlier and now cleaning a house that is already clean. Satisfied to be alone, I stay glued to the television. With my phone in one hand and my computer open on the table in front of me, I watch as many news outlets as I can, trying to gather intelligence on the events of Charlotte's wake, funeral and burial. I am disappointed to find Charlie has faded from the headlines. HLN is the only network featuring a segment on the funeral.

They're broadcasting footage of a visibly bereaved Harrison stepping out of a limousine in front of his home between the burial and wake. The newscaster comments that his poll numbers have risen since the murder, and he stands to maintain his position as district attorney despite the allegations Stu Bogovian raised about Harrison's immorality and incompetence. She mentions Bogovian by name, and my ears perk up.

"Harrison Doyle, seen here exiting the car after the burial of his stepdaughter, who was murdered less than two weeks ago, has been accused of being an unfit district attorney, prone to dishonest practices within the DA's office and often impeding the course of justice in cases that he does not favor. After the accusations former Congressman Stuart Bogovian unleashed in a press conference, HLN launched an exclusive investigation. What we found, after the break."

I quickly pull up the HLN website on my laptop and try to find anything about Stu Bogovian or Harrison Doyle.

"Claire," I holler up the stairs. "Claire, come down here and watch this." I strain to hear a response. When there is none, I send her a text message: "I know you're upset, but something big is about to come up on TV, please come down and watch with me." A moment later, Claire appears in the living room and sits down beside me. She rubs her eyes, looking at the commercials on-screen.

"What's happening?" she asks.

"Apparently HLN has been looking into Bogovian's allegations against Harrison. Remember his first press conference when he said that Harrison was corrupt and immoral?" Claire nods. "Well, someone at HLN thought it was enough of a story to go digging." I take an enormous breath and steel myself in preparation for what I assume must be Bogovian exposing Harrison's soft underbelly with the information he gave me at Rikers.

The newscaster reappears on-screen and repeats the story hook. The frame closes and another opens on a different reporter sitting on a sunny balcony, interviewing Stu Bogovian.

"Mr. Bogovian, you stated prior to the murder of Charlotte Doyle that her stepfather, Harrison Doyle, was a corrupt and unfit district attorney. You also stated that he was going to get what's coming to him. Since Charlotte was killed, you somewhat clarified your previous statement, insisting it was not a threat to DA Doyle in any way. Can you further explain your position?"

Stu Bogovian has a microphone pinned to his lapel and clearly spent time prepping for the interview. "Well, Carol, first off I'd like to thank you for the opportunity to clarify my statements. Considering what happened to Charlotte, my remarks were highlighted in such a way as to make them appear threatening. That was never my intention. I spent quite a few years in prison, serving my time for a horrible crime I committed against a woman in my office. While in prison, you meet people." Stu readjusts his seat and takes a sip from a drink in a sweaty glass. "I happened to be in a place that was filled with inmates pretty similar to myself. Many of them had been in positions of power and authority here in New York City before things went downhill for them. After some years developing trust with one another, some of us came to realize that we all had similar experiences dealing with a certain Manhattan district attorney."

"You're speaking of DA Doyle now?" Carol the reporter interjects.

"Yes, ma'am. Harrison Doyle was known to me while I was still working in congress, prior to my arrest and conviction. You might even say we were friends. Now, I don't want to appear insensitive or speak ill of the dead, but there was a strange relationship going on between DA Doyle and his stepdaughter, Charlotte."

My chest tightens, and my temples begin to throb. If Stu Bogovian publicly outs Harrison and Charlie, then *I* no longer have any insider information against Harrison that would force him to keep a lid on anything he may know about me. I watch and silently hope Bogovian doesn't divulge all the details.

"Strange, how?" Carol leans forward and raises a fist to her chin.

"Well, in his business dealings, he would find himself backed into a corner and tended to use his daughter as a kickback or payoff to get what he wanted." Stu can't help but smile. He is giddy to be able to smear Harrison Doyle on national television.

Carol feigns disbelief. "When you say kickback, you mean as a bribe? He would bribe people with his stepdaughter? How do you mean?"

"He would outright give his permission to sleep with his stepdaughter. In some cases, even offering her up on a silver platter. I remember she was at an event with him, and he called her over after some conversation with a defense attorney and twirled her around like a prize hog."

Claire looks at me with disgust, and I have to shield my face with my hand to obscure the panic rising in my throat.

"Do you know any of the men who received this offer?" Carol continues.

"Certainly. A couple of fellas in jail with me told the exact same story. You're looking at one of them right now."

"And what were the circumstances around his offer to you, Mr. Bogovian?" Carol asks.

"When I was indicted, Charlotte was just a young thing. Just out of college, I bet. During one of the early interrogations—without my lawyer present, mind you—the DA told me that if I pleaded guilty to a lesser charge, I would have his blessing, and he would arrange for me to sleep with his stepdaughter."

"You realize these are devastating accusations. Mr. Doyle allegedly offered to facilitate sex with his daughter in exchange for your cooperation in his case against you. That's a huge allegation, Mr. Bogovian."

Stu again sips from his drink. "When Harrison needed a

defendant to plead out or when someone got wind of the illegal tactics he used in his investigations, he would clean it up with a bottle of scotch and a beautiful young woman."

As Carol concludes the interview and the program goes to commercial, Claire and I stare at the screen, stunned. I'm hearing Stu say these words for a second time, but watching it on TV, knowing the gravity of the fallout that will come, I feel paralyzed.

"There's no way that's true. No way. She would never sleep with that little troll," Claire gasps.

"Well, he didn't plead to a lesser charge, so I guess he turned Harry down," I tell her, as I don't know exactly what happened.

"How could her father put her up to such things?" Claire is appalled.

"Like I said, she was no angel. She and her father would do pretty much anything it took for social and political gain. I told you she was using me to get ahead. I don't see why she wouldn't be using other people, as well." I nibble at my lips in thought.

"That's disgusting. I just can't believe that."

"Claire, she was in on it. She stood to gain if her father did. And she was willing to go forward with that kind of thing," I say, slowly beginning to realize why Charlie came after me to begin with.

"You think it's *true*? It can't be true." Claire is incapable of understanding such depraved behavior.

"Harrison offered his blessing to me, Claire," I gently admit.

"You don't think he was just saying that he *knew* you two had been together, and he was just letting you know he wasn't upset about it?"

"No, Claire. He didn't know that Charlotte and I had been

seeing each other." I realize as I hear the words coming out of my mouth that I'm wrong. Of course Harrison knew I was having an affair with his daughter. She didn't come for me, he *sent* her to me. He sent her to get information out of me, to try to find my soft underbelly. When I didn't crack, she went after Juliette. Oh, God. They'd been in on it all along.

Our conversation stops when the program returns from commercial break, and we turn our attention back to the television.

"And you say this is common knowledge, Mr. O'Shea?" Carol asks a new interviewee.

"Common within a certain group, yes." Aiden O'Shea is a renowned criminal defense attorney, known for badgering the judges and complaining about unfair treatment. "He's like her pimp. Forgive me, I know the woman was killed, but Harrison Doyle frequently hung his daughter in front of attorneys like a rabbit in front of the greyhounds. But I'll tell you, I never heard *her* complain."

"What did Harrison Doyle stand to gain if his trick worked, and the attorneys took the bait?" Carol holds a fuzzy microphone in Aiden O'Shea's face.

"You ever seen a record like he's got?" Aiden balks. "Look, taxpayers are always going to be happy when a defendant pleads out because they don't have to pay for a trial. When a taxpayer is happy, he votes for whoever made him happy." Aiden holds out his fingers in a countdown. "When a defendant takes a deal, he usually has to plead to some lesser charge, and a plea deal goes into the win column for the DA. It's a win-win-win. Taxpayers win, Harrison gets to stat-pack and bank on reelection, and the defendant gets to sleep with a beautiful woman before being hauled off to prison. It's almost flawless." Aiden O'Shea's sloppy frat-boy attitude rubs me the wrong way.

"Why is this the first time this is coming to light? If this were a regular practice for Mr. Doyle and his daughter, as you've alleged, why hasn't this information been exposed?"

"Because they're all in on it, Carol. The people who know are the people who took the offers. Everyone is guilty, and no one could come forward without putting themselves in jeopardy, too."

I rake my hands through my hair, back and forth, back and forth, trying to catch the breath that's stagnating in my throat. Whatever Charlie knew didn't die with her. Harrison's been in on it all along.

THEN

Claire had been exactly right, and as we boarded the yacht for the engagement party of the governor's daughter, I saw Juliette standing with Jamie. I didn't like the idea of a party on a boat, with no exit strategy should I want to leave before the boat returned to dock. Still, I imagined there would be so many people, I could exit whatever situation I found myself in that may become unpleasant, namely having to interact with my son.

I steered Claire around the boat in the opposite direction of where I had seen Juliette, greeting everyone I knew with gracious hellos. The crowd was thick, and the yacht pulled out into the harbor at exactly 7:00 p.m., as stated on the invitation. Partygoers gathered at the railings, oohing and aahing at the beauty of the Hudson River as we started moving southward.

With everyone distracted, I had a chance to look around and see whom else I recognized to get my bearings before continuing around the boat. While most eyes were looking across the water to New Jersey, I caught one pair looking squarely at me. My breath caught raggedly in my throat as Charlie Doyle lifted her champagne glass and winked at me. I instinctively pushed Claire to the edge of the boat to look over the side, so she was distracted and wouldn't see Charlie.

God, why hadn't I thought of that? Of course Charlie would be there; the whole Doyle family would be, I was sure. Harrison could always be counted on to mangle my evenings.

The dread was rising in my mind as I realized Claire, Juliette and Charlie were all on the same boat together, and I couldn't escape. My watch told me we had pulled out from the dock only seven minutes before, and already I was getting sweaty and uneasy.

"Isn't it beautiful?" Claire said to me, gazing across the water as the sun began descending.

"Yes," I said, not able to concentrate on the vista. Instead I focused on ensuring Claire, Juliette and Charlie didn't come into contact with one another.

"Good evening, Claire." I heard a familiar voice behind us, and the tension burned in my stomach.

"Juliette," Claire responded, pulling out of my grip, away from the railing to embrace my ex-wife. "What a great party, huh? I've never done the tour of Manhattan on a yacht before."

As they had done at Smith & Wollensky years before, they ignored me as they exchanged pleasantries. Jamie, who seemed to have morphed into my twin, had developed a confident air about him and broke the silence between us.

"Evening, Peter," he said and held out his hand for me to shake.

Peter? I couldn't recall a time he had addressed me as anything at all, but I was shocked to hear him call me by my first name. I shook his hand, again taken aback by his strength and maturity. In my head, kids not yet sixteen were small, trite and unaware. But this one was practically a man; even his voice was just like mine.

"Jamie." I looked around the boat to see if anyone had noticed me interacting with my son. Here I was, presented with the perfect opportunity to show the influential elite what a cordial relationship my girlfriend and I had with my ex-wife and my son. I could see then that Jamie, now that he was practically an adult, could be a brilliant addition to my image. He could be exactly the person I needed to be seen with for people to view me as a caring, good-hearted individual. I had been looking at it all wrong; he wasn't a nuisance anymore. Now he could practically take care of himself, and he was social gold.

"Jamie, I'm so glad you're here," I said, taking him under my arm and steering him away from his mother and Claire.

I pulled Jamie around the yacht, now looking to locate the faces I'd been trying to avoid when I boarded. I almost slapped myself for having missed the opportunity to capitalize on the existence of my son; I didn't have to have a wife, I didn't have to have a girlfriend, now I just had to be a father, and considering my son was already grown, my duties would be purely social and self-serving. I vowed to ensure I could spend more time with him in the future.

"Harrison Doyle," I said when I saw the DA standing next to a table of hors d'oeuvres, "*this* is my son, Jamie." I smiled scornfully, elated to be able to show off a son so wildly superior to Harrison's own progeny.

"Hi there, son," Harrison said, wiping his greasy paws on a napkin before shaking Jamie's hand. "Wow, you've certainly grown into quite the young man. How old are you now?"

"I'll be sixteen in a few months," Jamie replied, his voice deep and mature.

"Ah, I would introduce you to my son, Ethan, but he's much older." Harrison kept Jamie's hand in his grasp and made a display of peering over his head. "Where is that kid, now?"

"Ethan is here?" I balked.

"Yes, I know he doesn't often come to things like this, but his mother insisted. I brought Charlotte because she should be mingling with all these folks, and Elizabeth insisted that Ethan not be left out." He scanned the crowd, looking for his wife and child.

"Huh," I sneered, "I was under the impression that Charlie and Ethan didn't have much of a…relationship." I chose the word carefully.

"Oh, nooo," he reassured, "those two kids get along great. I'll introduce you two once I find him, okay, sport?" he said to Jamie.

"Nice meeting you, sir." Jamie extracted his hand from the forceful shake and continued along with me.

"Are you enjoying yourself, Jamie?" I realized I had no idea how to talk to him, so I relied on imitating typical fathers in television shows.

"Yeah, this is a really nice boat," he said. I looked up as he was speaking and caught a glimpse of Claire and Juliette still conversing on the other side of the yacht, both delicately holding glasses of champagne. I stopped listening to Jamie and stared at the two women, trying to determine the nature of their conversation. They seemed perfectly happy, and I was about to turn my attention away when I saw Charlie appear and insert herself between Claire and Juliette. I felt the heat in the base of my skull and cracked my neck to relieve it.

"I heard some guy say there will be fireworks once the sun

goes down," Jamie was saying to me, but I couldn't listen. I watched Juliette courteously make the introductions between Charlie and Claire. My vision got blurry as I watched three women who should have forever remained separate bring their champagne glasses together in a toast. I couldn't imagine what they could possibly be celebrating.

As Charlie slipped away from them, I encouraged Jamie to return to his mother. I walked the other way to intercept Charlie to find out whether or not they had mentioned my name. Once I located Charlie, I grabbed her wrist and pulled her out of the line of sight of the other women.

"I see you're making new friends," I scolded.

"I was looking for *you*, Peter. He's here." Charlie, whose ability to mask her true feelings rivaled even mine, couldn't hide that she was becoming terrified. "My brother." She looked around to ensure he wasn't within earshot. "Ethan is on this boat."

"It's a big boat, Charlie. Just avoid him." I wasn't interested in playing protector that evening.

Turned off and much more interested in continuing to exploit my newfound relationship with Jamie, I patted Charlie's side in reassurance and walked off in search of my son. He stood with Juliette and Claire, so I implanted myself in the middle of their group, wrapping one arm around each woman. The perfect picture of a modern family.

When the fireworks display began to burst overhead, we all gazed up in silence, awed at the sound and the spectacle. With the whole crowd distracted, it was almost impossible to notice Ethan sidling up next to Charlotte, squeezing her arm and whispering something into her ear. The noise of the fireworks drowned out what must have been a terrified sound, as I saw Charlie reach up to cover her mouth, her eyes wide and tearful.

NOW

Now that Bogovian pulled the curtain on Harrison and Charlie's corruption routine, I am filled with fear that Harry is the only one holding any cards. I don't know how much he was able to find out, but he knows my real name is George, and he knows I don't belong here.

"It's going to get worse now, isn't it?" Claire rubs her tired eyes.

"Yes, Claire. It's going to get a *lot* worse." I instinctively peek out the front windows to see if there are any news vans outside the house.

Claire steels herself. "You said that Harrison *did* offer Charlotte to you. In exchange for what? And when did that happen?"

"He offered Charlie as a last-ditch effort to get me to come work for him at the DA's office. This was a few weeks ago." I look down and cover my mouth, hoping the fact that this happened so recently wouldn't incite a fight with Claire.

"You think *that's* why he wanted you to come to his side so badly? Because he knew he couldn't bribe you? So, he needed you in his pocket in some other way?" She pulls my hand away from my mouth. "Look at me."

"No...that's not exactly it." I'm getting cagey. I've spent half my life lying and hiding the truth from people, and suddenly I feel I'm a novice, and I have no idea how to properly evade a question.

"Answer me, Peter! Why does Harrison want you in his pocket?"

"Because I knew. I knew twenty years ago that Harrison and Charlie had their sick arrangement. When Harrison got wind that I knew something, he tried to bribe me with a position at the DA's office. He even offered me *his* job."

"So, he wanted you to be associated with his administration, so you would be involved in the corruption, too? And you wouldn't be able to expose him without screwing yourself, wow. Now I get it."

"That's right."

"Wait, then why did he try again to bribe you a few weeks ago? If he knew he couldn't get you?"

"He was drunk, and he let it slip." But he wasn't drunk at all, was he? He was giving me a false sense of security, making me think I had more control than I did. Explaining it to Claire, it's all beginning to make sense to me.

"This is too much, Peter." She begins frantically shaking her head. "This woman is dead, there are scandals popping up, *you're* somehow involved in all of this, it's too much!" She's starting to yell. "What am I supposed to do? I don't know *what* to believe anymore."

"Shh." I try to soothe her. "I know this is confusing, but please, I think I understand what's happening now."

"What?" she yells. "What's happening?"

"I think I'm being framed."

Just as I'm calming Claire, Jamie barges into the kitchen and says urgently, "Um, you guys?" He grabs the remote and turns on the volume of the TV. "I just got an alert on my phone—" There's a breaking-news marquee at the bottom of the screen on CNN. It reads, Former Congressman Accuses DA of Sexual Bribery.

"Yeah," I tell him, "we just watched the whole scandal unfold on HLN." I try to explain everything that Claire and I just watched and try to help them understand the corruption that went on behind closed doors within the New York County justice system.

"Harrison will never recover from these accusations, so he's trying to make it look like someone else did something worse. And the someone else…is *me*."

"Hold on, you think Harrison's framing you?" Jamie asks. "Are the cops investigating you?"

"Well, yes and no. There's no formal investigation that I'm aware of right now, but the police brought me in for questioning."

"What? Really?" Jamie perks up, interested. "What did they ask you?"

"They asked me all sorts of questions about what you and I did the night of Charlie's murder. They asked me what happened to my fingers." I open my hand and show my son the burns healing on the thumb and forefinger of my right hand.

Jamie leans in to inspect my injuries. "What *did* happen to your fingers?"

"I burned them on some melted glass in our bedroom fireplace." I look at Claire, who recoils and sips her drink.

"Wait, you said the cops asked about me?" Jamie wears a look of concern.

"They asked what I did that night, and I told them exactly

what you and I did. Down to the fortune cookies." I smile at my son, remembering awkwardly pulling apart the cookies and reading the absurd fortunes.

"They're not going to question *me*, are they?" Jamie asks.

"Probably not. But remember—" I lean forward and shake my finger at Jamie, then at Claire "—you don't have to say a word. No matter what they tell you, you don't have to answer any of their questions. And you *always* ask for your lawyer. Always."

The morning after Stu Bogovian lured the press into another layer of Harrison's degeneracy, I call Frank Tomlinson to ensure he is up to date on the newest accusations. Tomlinson reports that not only does he know about it, but the entirety of the English-speaking world is already playing judge and jury.

"We have a new theory to work with here, boss," Tomlinson reports.

"What's that?"

"It's just a theory and we haven't got all the meat to prove it, but I think we're on the right track after what we found out from the lawyers on TV last night. So, it seems to me the girl got tired of playing Daddy's little game. Maybe she didn't want to perform anymore, wasn't seeing the same benefits anymore now that she was all hoity-toity running your ex-wife's foundation, rubbing elbows with the blue bloods. She was expected to act the part of classy philanthropist. So maybe she told Daddy she'd had enough, right?"

"And?" My mind is racing back to the comments I made to Claire and Jamie the morning we found out Charlie had been murdered. *Harrison probably had her killed.*

"And maybe Daddy decided that she was no good to him anymore. She was a liability now. Knew too much. Maybe he had to shut her up." Tomlinson huffs out a deep breath, satisfied with himself.

"I'm thinking the same thing. Harrison knew he was running out of time, Charlie was going to turn on him. So, he killed her to silence her." It all makes perfect sense.

"Bingo, boss. That's the theory."

"How can you put some meat on this theory? What are you looking into now?"

"Ethan's alibi. LaBianca is at the club where the scumbag kid was supposed to be that night, and he's getting the security footage. If Khan's timeline is correct, and we are looking at a ten-to-midnight window and we don't see him on the tapes, that's enough to cast a very big shadow on his alibi." Tomlinson hangs up without a formal goodbye.

I feel the electricity in my veins that I used to feel when the defense of a client started to come together. I'm stumbling onto something huge, and I no longer think I'm deflecting from my own incriminating behaviors; instead I believe the case against me will soon be a distant memory for the cops and the DA's office. I pick up the phone again, this time to call Sinan.

"Have you talked to the Franks? They've got some pretty interesting theories brewing over there."

"Have they? Well, that's good to hear. And I'll save your breath and tell you before you ask, yes, I did see the ludicrous Harrison Doyle story last night. They're bloodthirsty bastards over there, eh? Can't leave a man in peace the day of his daughter's funeral?" Sinan sounds like he's been mainlining espresso all morning.

"Don't you want to hear the Franks' theory?"

"Of course I do. But you can tell me in person because you're coming to the office."

"What's the problem?"

"New shit has presented itself." Sinan hangs up.

Less than half an hour later, I blast through Sinan's office door without even a knock.

"There's a witness," Sinan begins, without a greeting. "The police canvassed only a six-block radius and didn't originally find anyone who saw or heard anything suspicious the night of the murder." He has one cigarette in his hand and another one burning down in an ashtray on the coffee table. He gestures for me to sit down. "That's why we didn't have any information in the original reports. But a woman came to the Thirteenth and said she saw someone around 10:30 p.m. loitering in front of Charlotte's house."

I inhale a deep breath, lean forward in my chair and stub out Sinan's forgotten cigarette.

"She was walking her dog across the street in front of the park," Sinan continues, "and she said while her dog was taking a shit, she slowed down and noticed the man because she felt like he seemed out of place."

"Did she give a description?" I ask, wringing my hands together.

"Yes. Average height, average build. Wearing a dark suit with a light-colored dress shirt. Real fucking specific."

"Hair? Face? Eyes?"

"Dark hair, well-groomed. Then just average height and average build and a dark suit."

"Who is this witness? Credible?"

"She's an English teacher, midthirties. Wears reading glasses. Not so much as a parking ticket. She turned down a lineup, said she didn't see the face, couldn't tell for sure."

"You realize I am neither average height nor build. Average American man is five-ten, and I'm nearly six-two. *Not* average. The average American man is a slob. A two-hundred-pound slob. I weigh 175 and you'd never call *this* build average." I stand up and examine myself in Sinan's mirror.

"Yes, you're a glorious specimen, nothing average about you. Her description doesn't mean shit, clearly. *Average* is one of those words with no definition. But it's another one of these fucking nuisance pieces of 'evidence'—" Sinan air-quotes the word "—that we now have to come up with a defense against."

"You said you saw the story on HLN, right?"

"No, I don't watch that putrid network. I saw the story on CNN. But, yes, your point is not lost." Sinan is spectacularly over-caffeinated and can't sit still or stop talking.

"I spoke with Tomlinson and he said they were getting the footage from the club opening the night of the murder."

"How many suits do you own?" Sinan is stuck in his own train of thought and hardly acknowledges that I've said anything at all.

"I have no idea. Fifteen, twenty, maybe? Probably more."

"And how many of them would you say were 'dark' as described by an English teacher with dodgy eyes, late at night, on a street where the lamps were above her head and not on the man she saw?"

"All of them? At least ninety percent anyway, in the scenario you described." I'm struggling to follow Sinan's drift.

"And would you call yourself particularly stylish?" Sinan's penetrating British accent is starting to annoy me.

"I would say I know how to dress myself, yes. Why? Did this woman say the average man of average build was well dressed?"

"Yes. As a matter of fact, she *specifically* stated that the suit fit impeccably, and she imagined it may even be custom-made. She said it's what caught her eye, usually the people she sees loitering about are not well dressed, and this suit made her feel like this gentleman stood out." He lights another ciga-rette while stubbing out the first one.

"Most of my suits are bespoke—does that make me a killer?"

"No, it's just another nuisance." Sinan picks up his legal pad and a thin silver pen. "And have you any suits currently at the dry cleaner's?"

"I may, I don't know. Claire and my housekeeper gener-ally handle these things."

"Find out. Find out if any of your suits were not in your possession on Saturday the twenty-fourth of September."

I turn my attention to the television in Sinan's office; muted, tuned into CNN. As the advertisements close and the news reports return, I see a familiar face standing at a podium encircled by microphones.

"Sinan." My voice breaks. "Look." The remote nearly slips out of my hands as my palms turn clammy and my muscles get weak with fear. "What the hell does *he* have to say?"

Surrounded by press, with cameras flashing wildly around him, Harrison stands tall, looking like a whole new person. I know him to be insecure, puerile and classless, but now he stands like a noble politician, wearing an expression that could be considered both solemn and robust. His public per-sona has taken over. Sinan stands behind my chair, foot tap-ping, watching intently.

Harrison addresses the crowd of reporters. "A disgraced ex-congressman from New York, who was recently paroled from prison where he served a twenty-year sentence for first degree sex abuse, has accused me and my late daughter of sexual bribery." He bows his head and takes a deep, pensive breath. "It is with great sadness that I find myself here, clear-ing the name of my beautiful daughter, who would never par-ticipate in such ugliness as the former congressman alleged.

Charlotte was compassionate, humane and pure-hearted, and to drag her through the mud after she was brutally murdered, on the day we laid her to rest—" Harrison takes a dramatic pause and covers his mouth with his fist as if to stifle an oncoming sob "—is deplorable. I will not rest until the person who did this to her is behind bars. It has been suggested that criminal defense attorney Peter Caine is involved, and you can be certain that he will be investigated to the fullest extent of the law."

My jaw drops, and the breath catches in my throat.

Harrison continues, "Stuart Bogovian is a criminal who has threatened me personally and sullied the good name of the entire Doyle family and is now going to find himself on the receiving end of a defamation lawsuit. I am returning to work now that my daughter is at peace, and I sincerely hope this is the last I hear of these outrageous accusations." Amid a flurry of questions, Harrison excuses himself, hankie at the corner of his lying mouth, and walks offscreen.

THEN

My newfound appreciation for Jamie's existence would increase enormously when I discovered that it had the added benefit of getting Claire off my back. While she had been struggling for years to encourage me to develop a relationship with him, now she was left with nothing to complain about. In the weeks following the yacht party, I thought of ways that I could gain from Jamie's presence in my life.

"That was Juliette on the phone," Claire said, approaching me as I sat at my desk in the bedroom.

"Look," I said, frustrated, "enough with you two. I know I said I was open to exploring a relationship with Jamie, but I'm not interested in you and Juliette becoming best friends."

"You don't have to worry about that." She pouted as she sat down on a bench across from me. "Don't you want to know what Juliette said on the phone?"

"Not really." I didn't focus on her, despite her moping for attention.

"She's sick," Claire said. "So, you don't have to worry about us becoming friends."

"I'm not worried about you getting the flu, Claire. It's May."

"She has cancer, Peter."

I couldn't tell if she was serious or just baiting me to pay attention. "Okay, I'm listening. What's this, now?"

"Juliette called the house phone. She was looking to talk to you, not me, but I know you don't want to talk to her, so I asked her what was wrong." Claire took a deep breath and continued, "She said that she's been sick for a while but didn't tell us because she didn't think it would matter, but now that you've shown an interest in Jamie, and now that she's sicker, she thought it was time to let you know."

"You said cancer?"

"Yes, she has the same thing your partner Marcus had. Tera's disease, the liver cancer. But she said that it's spread to her lymph nodes and lungs—" Claire suddenly choked up "—so it's just a matter of time now." She sniffled and coughed, clearly emotional but trying to stifle herself.

I thought back to Marcus's illness, surprised that the same cancer would befall his daughter. Marcus smoked cigarettes nearly all his life, drank gin with reckless abandon and could hardly be remembered for taking care of himself. Juliette was exactly the opposite. She never touched a cigarette, drank only socially and when she did, limited herself to one or two glasses of wine or champagne. She kept in peak physical condition, and when I knew her, was always up to date on checkups and doctor's appointments. It almost seemed unfair that two people with such different lifestyles would both be felled by such an illness.

"How long has she had this, do you know?"

Claire blubbered and reached to me for comfort. "She was diagnosed at the beginning of the year, and she was already in bad shape then, but there was hope that with treatment she could beat it."

"She looked just fine at the engagement party." I patted Claire's shoulder, wondering how such a thing could escape me.

"She didn't do the treatments. When they told her how aggressive they would be and how she would be bedridden, she decided she wouldn't live out her last months in that condition. She did homeopathic stuff, herbs and yoga, I'm not sure exactly. But she kept away from traditional medicine."

"Last months?" The news was so inconsistent with what I knew of Juliette that I had trouble processing it. "I don't believe it. She looked completely fine."

"She told me that she's always weak and exhausted, but she wants to keep up a good show for Jamie, so he doesn't get scared."

"Jamie knows?"

"Of course Jamie knows!" Claire's frustration burst out of her along with more tears.

"What am I supposed to do, Claire? I didn't make her sick. I'm surprised by this news. What do you want from me?" I was in no mood to be attacked for my reaction, so I got up off the couch and walked into the kitchen.

"What are you supposed to do?" she hollered after me, getting up to follow. "You're supposed to be a father, remember? You're the one who said you wanted to have a relationship with him."

"Not like this, Claire. I just want to see him now and again, maybe bring him places with me sometimes." I buried my face in the fridge so I wouldn't have to look at her.

"I've always wanted children, and you told me that it would never happen with you. And I sacrificed that dream because I love you and I want to be with you."

"Oh, *God*, Claire, you can't possibly be thinking *that*." Dread started to scratch at my throat as I waited for Claire to say what I thought she wanted.

"You have to be his father, Peter. You're the only one he's got. I'll help you, we can do it together."

"Get that thought right out of your head, because there is no way I am getting custody of that kid, you understand? I gave up my custody outright in the divorce, and he can go ahead and be a free agent for all I care. I'm his father in DNA alone." I slammed the fridge shut. "I knew I never should have gotten involved in all this."

"Who do you expect will take custody? He's fifteen years old," she began.

"Nearly sixteen!" I interrupted. "He will be sixteen soon and that's legally an adult in many states. He could just emancipate himself."

"Not in New York, it's not. He's going to be your responsibility until he is eighteen years old." The panicked tearfulness in her voice subsided, and a bizarre calm fell over her.

"I gave up my legal rights to Jamie when I got divorced. Didn't you hear me? I will make an effort, but I am not getting custody of him. Understand?"

"If you don't, then I will."

"You'll *what*? Adopt him? You're crazy." I ridiculed her preposterous idea.

"Am I? I've always wanted to be a mother, and now there's a kid I know who needs one."

NOW

My head is feeling too full of theories and possibilities of what happened to Charlie Doyle, and I need to clear my mind. Claire's wild-eyed pacing through the kitchen leads me to believe that she, too, is struggling to manage the overwhelming happenings of the past few days. I've asked Claire to come out to dinner with me, to take a break from the terrifying realities of our situation and try to breathe. I call Gramercy Tavern for a last-minute reservation.

Claire and I get dressed together wordlessly, now and again peeking around the corners and shooting grins at each other. It's been months since we've been out alone together, and we both feel it necessary to overdress for the occasion. I can't find the gold Tiffany cuff links Juliette gave me, so I settle for an antique pair Marcus bought me after we started the firm. Claire steps out of her boudoir in an elegant navy blue dress, fiddling with her earrings nervously, as if we are going on our first date.

"I have butterflies in my stomach. I haven't felt like this in a long time." Claire pulls me in for a delicate hug and shyly nuzzles my neck. "It's our first time out as parents, you realize that? Jamie is my son now, too."

"Yeah, you're right. I didn't look at it that way." I kiss the backs of Claire's hands and lead her out of the room and down the stairs. I'm trying to do the right thing, to remember the way I once was and to bring that man back up to the surface.

We walk out the front door and down the stoop to the corner of Twenty-First and Lexington. I steer Claire toward Park Avenue, and then turn south to Twentieth Street to avoid passing by Charlie's house.

The hostess at Gramercy Tavern smiles warmly as we enter and ushers us to our seats at a prime central table. I nod politely at a bartender I recognize, and when the waiter appears, I order two vodka martinis.

"I always knew it could be like this, you know." Claire reaches her hand across the table and places it on top of mine.

"So you've said," I respond.

"Things are changing so fast. I feel like we're in a tornado." Claire seems flustered. Even though we stepped out of the house for a change of scenery, her head seems to be rife with concerns. "It's your job, you know. That job sucks the life out of you." Claire shakes her head.

"I don't know that it's *just* the job." I feel a headache creeping up as I hear Juliette's words coming out of Claire's mouth. I scan the room for eavesdroppers and lower my voice. "A lot of things have changed in a really short time, Claire. My ex-wife died, I got custody of my son. Up until that point, I never saw Jamie as a vulnerable person. He was always just taken care of, I didn't need to think about him." I take a long sip of my martini. "I didn't need to value him. But when he cried at the funeral, and I saw him feel something...I guess he became valuable to me."

Claire crosses her arms and the air around us becomes thick with suspicion. "It's so strange to me that Juliette is gone."

"What do you mean?" I ask, unsure of her change in demeanor.

"She was incredibly healthy and vibrant, and so young, and then suddenly she ups and dies of the same rare cancer that killed her father? Seems strange, don't you think?"

"No, I wouldn't say it seems strange." Again, I look around, feeling like the eyes of the restaurant are on me. "I would say it seems genetic." I sip my drink and dismiss Claire's allusions of conspiracy.

"I did some research on Tera's disease." Claire looks to me for a reaction.

"Yes?" I'm annoyed with her probe.

"I learned some interesting information." Her eyes are on the tablecloth in front of her, periodically bouncing up to look me in the face.

"Oh, yeah?" There's a very slight sweat beginning to form at the back of my neck.

"It's not quite proper cancer, is it? More like a poisoning that becomes cancer, right?"

"Is that what you learned? That's like saying lung cancer from smoking is just cigarette poisoning. You don't know what you're talking about, Claire."

"Don't get defensive. I don't want to touch a nerve. I just found it very interesting that the articles I read about Tera's disease made no mention of a genetic component, and two people in your life both died from it. I just wonder if there's another side to the story, that's all."

"We have enough to worry about right now without you

poking your nose in places it doesn't belong. This is supposed to be a nice dinner out, not an interrogation. Drop it."

Our conversation is interrupted when a waiter approaches to take our order. Claire orders the Arctic char, and I opt for the pork loin. We ask for a bottle of Chianti to go with it, and I feel I'm going to need another martini, as well.

"Okay, fine, I'll drop it. What's going to happen with the other things we need to worry about?" she asks softly, fidgeting with her bread knife.

"First off, you should prepare yourself because my relationship with Charlie will be coming out soon. Harrison will probably drop that info to the press if the cops haven't already." Again, I look around to see if anyone can hear our conversation.

"Why would he wait so long? Doesn't that make it look like he doesn't have a case?"

"It's calculated timing. Publicity. Charlie was just buried, so symbolically, she's at peace, and now it's appropriate for him to launch an all-out assault. Remember, it's an election year. He's got very little time to make himself look moral and capable. Bogovian's press conference put him two steps behind, so he really needs to ramp it up."

"How come no one is going after that guy anymore? Last week every news outlet was saying it was him. And I haven't heard a peep about him since he went on television that night."

"It's a combination of factors." I begin explaining patiently, much more comfortable now that we've moved away from talking about Marcus's and Juliette's illnesses. "One, he was in Vegas at the time, and there are security tapes to prove it. Two, his motive was pretty thin, just getting back at Harrison for putting him away? If that's motive, then anyone the New York County DA's office has put away has motive.

And three, the murder was committed particularly brutally, which indicates a crime of passion, and that usually means the killer knew the victim. Stu Bogovian and Charlie didn't know each other. Seems like a stretch to include him in the investigation. Harrison is going to be under a lot of pressure to get a suspect, and to get him arrested and indicted quickly."

The waiter stands tableside and opens the wine while Claire and I awkwardly pause our conversation. Claire slurps the last dregs of her martini and hands the empty glass to the waiter. As he leaves, Claire turns her eyes to me.

"Why will they go after you? If Stu Bogovian, a *criminal*, isn't really a suspect, how come you are?" Her voice cracks.

"Like I told you before, I think Harrison is framing me for Charlie's murder." I swallow hard. "I'm connected to a lot of the players in this scandal. Harrison can argue that I would have motive. Motive to silence an ex-lover, especially after gaining custody of Jamie and starting a family again. He'll argue that I had opportunity—I live only a block and a half away, she would have opened the door for me because she knows me, and my fingerprints and DNA will probably be found inside her house because I have been inside her house."

Claire cringes and pulls her napkin to her face to hide her scowl.

"Harrison has it out for me and always has," I continue. "This is his grand opportunity to publicly destroy me. I have been refusing to work for him, and he is going to sell the story that I am still burned by the bad press after Bogovian's sentencing. And then this nonsense with the Bogovian press conference where he practically threatened Harrison and then retracts the threat and points the finger at me." I inhale a deep pensive breath and cross my arms over my chest. Only now that I've said it out loud to Claire am I really understanding the possibility that Harrison had his daughter killed and is framing me. I never addressed the message he left for me; the message telling me I shouldn't have involved Charlie. It seems so clear now that he was planting evidence.

Claire leans across the small table. "Why would he do that?"

"Probably because he's still sour that he was convicted. And frankly, he should have been convicted. Thank God I lost that case. He was a serial sexual predator, Claire. He deserved to rot in prison," I whisper.

"I've never heard you say that about anyone before." A warm smile spreads across her face. "How are you going to get out of this?" She's coming around, she's beginning to believe me.

"Their case is purely circumstantial." I flippantly jut out my chin. "It's about argument. They will argue my fingerprints are in her house because I killed her. We will argue they are there because we were having an affair. They will argue I had motive to silence her. We will argue that you knew about the affair, so I wouldn't have to silence anyone."

Claire's countenance seems to gray and harden whenever I mention my affair with Charlie. I don't continue with my explanation, hoping she doesn't descend into a place of anger. Apprehension rising, we finish our meals in anxious silence.

I pull out Claire's chair, eager to salvage the date we spent talking about legal matters and defense tactics. On the short walk home, I am too distracted to realize I'm walking east on Twentieth until I see the crime scene tape blocking off the front of Charlie's brownstone. We stop and wordlessly stare at the house, looking bigger and lonelier than it had ever appeared before. What happened inside that house is eventually going to come to light, and a dull pain forms behind my eyes as I think about it.

I feel Claire's shoulders tighten underneath my hand. I turn to look at her and I see a menacing scowl on her face as she stares up at the bedroom windows of Charlie's house.

THEN

I had allowed my personal life to take up space in my head, and I knew the only way to push it out would be to return to focusing exclusively on work. I buried myself in unnecessary research, examining emancipation laws and digging through child custody cases for ideas of how to avoid gaining custody of my son. I was headlong into my search when I heard a gentle knocking at my office door.

"Come in," I hollered without looking up.

I lifted my eyes just enough to see a pair of women's shoes walking into my office, but not the sensible ones Anna would wear. These were designer shoes, slipped onto the beautiful feet of my dying ex-wife.

"Hi, Peter. I know you told me never to come here again, but I needed to talk to you. May I sit down?"

"Yes, yes, of course," I couldn't believe her deterioration. While she still dressed as if she were young and vivacious, the woman underneath her clothes seemed old and frail.

"I'm not well, Peter. I imagine Claire told you?"

"Yes, she said you… She said that you've been unwell." It suddenly became real to me that Juliette was truly dying, and despite my protests that she looked fine on the yacht, the truth was, she hadn't looked fine at all.

"That's why I am here to talk to you. My doctor isn't confident that I'll make it through the summer, and I need to make sure that there are plans in place for when I'm gone."

"What can I do? Do you need some water? Anna!" I barked out the door before Juliette could even respond. "Bring some water!"

"You haven't been a part of our lives for almost ten years now," she began, her voice strained and small, "and I've done all I can do to respect your desire for distance. I tried to keep you involved because I wanted Jamie to have a father, but I saw that you weren't interested. It was very hard for him, I want you to know. He asked about you constantly while growing up, and I admit, I didn't always tell him the truth. I can't bear the thought of telling him the truth now that I won't be here for him." She clutched her chest and coughed just as Anna walked in with a water.

"Here," I said, opening the bottle and pouring it into a glass. "Drink this."

"I can't have him know the truth about you. About what happened to you. I want to protect him from everything, I want to keep him safe when I'm gone. I told him about the person you were when we first met. He loves to listen to those stories." She got a faraway look in her eyes. "The truth is, I've been dying inside for so many years and only now is it finally killing me. Disregard kills people, Peter, and I won't have you do it to our son. Please." She turned to me and held my arm with both her hands. "Please, don't ignore him any longer. Please, be the man you're supposed to be."

I felt her cold fingers pressing into my skin, and I wanted to see the possibility of living up to her expectations.

"I've been talking to Claire every now and again for a couple of years," she admitted, shyly. "I had called the office to talk to you about some problems Jamie was having at school, but Anna brushed me off. When I told her what was happening, I practically begged her to give me your home number, and eventually she did."

"I figured."

"Claire acted as a conduit between past and present, and I think she wanted to know about Jamie as much as we wanted to know about you. I felt at the end of my rope. I knew I couldn't go to your house or come here. It's been so hard being a mother alone. I felt like Claire was filling in for you and talking to her made me feel like you were somehow still involved with our family." She held a handkerchief to her face, weak and exhausted by the weight of her emotions. "Claire was supportive of me... I have no one else to support me." Steady tears began to stream down her face. "My mother is so cold and distant, like she's always been. She has no interest in helping me raise Jamie, and I feel like none of my friends can be there for me in the way I need. I'm expected to be perfect all the time and depression doesn't fit in well with perfection." She inhaled deeply and continued, "Jamie is such a good boy, and I know you'll love him. He's so much like you. He looks and sounds just like you—sometimes it scares me." She smiled. "And he has all your charm and wit. I know you'll get along so well, and he's so mature, you'll hardly parent at all."

"I'll hardly *what*?" I must have misheard her.

"Parent. I said you'll hardly parent at all. I want Jamie to live with you. I want him to be with his father when I'm gone." She finally admitted what she came to tell me.

"You want me to take Jamie?"

"I want *you* to have custody of him, yes. He's nearly sixteen, he'll be off to college in two years, it's hardly a long time. But, please, a boy needs a father."

"You just got finished telling me how I'm not a good father, how I was never there, now you want me to bring him to live with me?"

"Because I know the kind of man you can be, I know the kind of man you were. I'm *dying*, Peter. There's no turning back now, there are no more chances left."

"But I hardly know the kid, I don't know how to be a father..." I protested.

"Like I said, I've been talking to Claire, and when I told her what was happening with me, that I'm sick, I asked her how she felt about the idea of Jamie coming to live with you."

The compassion I was feeling started to wane when Juliette admitted that she and Claire had been planning my future behind my back.

"And Claire couldn't have been more open. She told me she had always wanted children, and she wanted them with you, but you refused. You have a chance now. You have a chance to make everything right after all that's gone wrong. You can give Claire what she needs, you can give Jamie what he needs, and for me? You can let me die in peace knowing my son will be taken care of."

The idea of acting the hero flashed across my mind, and as Juliette coughed into a handkerchief, I began to consider her plea.

NOW

I took a taxi to the office this morning, slumped low in the back seat to avoid the prying eyes of any media vultures who may be after me. There were no vans in my neighborhood last night, but this morning I fear they'll return. The Franks are on their way to Sinan's office with the footage from the nightclub where Ethan supposedly spent the evening when Charlie was killed. I arrived only moments ago, and I'm composing myself in the corner of the office when Jessica buzzes to say the Franks have arrived.

They thunder into the office, sit down and start pulling documents and notebooks from their bags.

"Well? Spit it out! I'm going gray!" Sinan hollers.

"He was there," Frank Tomlinson reports. "He is seen, very obviously, walking into the club with two women and another man, and the time stamp read 11:14 p.m." Tomlinson slaps down a small stack of stills he extracted from the security footage of the club. "A man who is definitely Ethan Doyle walked into the club and didn't walk out until 4:53 a.m. His credit card was run at 4:36 a.m."

"There's more," LaBianca pipes up. "I got a girl over at Capital One, owes me a favor. She doesn't have access to his financial records or credit card statements, but she's on the fraud alert team, and we got a lucky hit. Seems the kid doesn't take taxis too often. Must be a limo-with-a-chauffeur kind of guy, so when he paid for a cab with his Capital One card, they flagged it. Night of September 24, he paid for a taxi at 10:43 p.m. There's no origin or destination, but it does list the medallion number. We got a call in to the Taxi and Limousine Commission, trying to get the travel log for that night."

"You think a man who just murdered his sister would take a cab, presumably covered in blood?" Sinan asks, incredulous.

"This is New York City, boss," LaBianca says. "Everybody around here is so jaded, you see someone covered in blood, you just assume it's a costume party."

I wave away Frank's ridiculous assertions. "We need to get the inside of that cab investigated. If he took that cab from Charlie's house back to his place, we need to know. There would be blood, or *something* there, for sure. And we need to get someone in that house to find out what the fuck happened to his clothes from that night."

"I'm on it, sir," Tomlinson says.

"Legally, Frank," Sinan warns.

"Oh. That's different. Then you'll have to do it the old-fashioned way."

"The cops?" Sinan asks.

"Yeah, boss. I'll call the old precinct and tell the guys I need them to look into Ethan."

"He lives with the Manhattan district attorney. You think you're getting cops in there, you're crazy. *Beg* the court for a subpoena, and you're still not getting in there. Until he's arrested, we can't get in that house." Sinan's words are cutting and discouraged.

"Okay, but the least we can do is get into that taxi," La-Bianca points out.

"Do it. Get the travel logs, talk to the driver about what he may have seen that night, and if you find anything in that back seat, call the boys at the old precinct."

I order a car before leaving the office, fearing the press will be camped outside the building. The car picks me up from the back entrance, and on the drive home, as I gaze at pedestrians, I think about the mystery man standing outside Charlie's house that night. Average except for his suit. I think about this witness, and how she could possibly tell that his suit was special, but the man himself was nothing short of ordinary.

I think about Ethan; he was at the club at 11:14 p.m, with three other people. And if this witness saw the ordinary man in his special suit at 10:30 p.m., it's a stretch to imagine he could have committed a brutal murder and still managed to show up on the security footage at the club forty-five minutes after being seen at Charlie's house. A timeline was considered a solid, unchangeable piece of evidence, and a timeline with video and credit card time stamps just made it more reliable.

I wonder how I can possibly prove that Ethan Doyle put on a special suit, traveled to his sister's house, where he loitered outside for a moment—maybe debating what he was about to do, maybe savoring the moment—went inside and viciously stabbed Charlie to death. Ethan who hated his sister. Ethan who has a criminal past that includes hurting women and animals, stalking and harassing his sister.

I ask myself how I can show that Ethan is surely worse than I have ever been; more psychotic, more soulless and heartless than I was, even at my worst. Against what I think will be almost insurmountable obstruction from Harrison and his team of corrupt politicians, I wonder how I can prove that I didn't kill my former lover. When Bogovian first implicated me in the press, it was such a long shot no one seemed to care. But now I'm being mentioned every day, and Harrison is after me. It's not a long shot; I'm staring down the barrel of a gun, and I need to find a way to control the damage.

As I near my front door, seeing no signs of cops or media, I gaze at the windows of other homes around me. I look up to the apartment buildings down the avenue and see the flickering blue light of televisions reflecting against the walls of these rooms, and it hits me; I know exactly how to prove I didn't kill her. Do exactly what everyone else has been doing. Hold a goddamn press conference.

Sinan stands behind me, next to Claire and Jamie. All three wear subdued expressions and appropriate attire. Sinan contacted his connections at various news outlets and indicated that I wanted to make a public statement in the aftermath of all the goings-on around Charlotte Doyle's murder and Stu Bogovian's accusations nearly two weeks ago. The media was elated to hear I wanted to speak, and Sinan nearly found himself in the middle of a bidding war between networks, with CNN ultimately winning out.

I clear my throat to begin, and the reporters fall silent in anticipation of my statement.

"Good afternoon. As you know, my former client Stuart Bogovian recently mentioned my name in connection with a threat he made to District Attorney Harrison Doyle and again when clearing his name from any wrongdoings regarding the murder of Charlotte Doyle. I will be brief." I speak clearly and eloquently. "Make no mistake, I had absolutely nothing to do with Charlotte's murder, and I am truly saddened and deeply disturbed by what happened to her. DA Doyle also indicated that I am the subject of a murder investigation, and I can tell you that at this time, I am not being investigated. I have called this press conference to speak only those words I have spoken, but it is your job, and I believe your right, to know what you need to know, so I have reserved some time to answer whatever other questions you may have."

Before I even take another breath, a surge of questions bubbles from the crowd, and I'm having trouble discerning a singular sentence.

"Is it true you were having an affair with Charlotte Doyle?" a particularly shrill reporter demands.

"Yes and no. Charlotte and I had carried on a private involvement for a long time, but we weren't active recently."

"What do you mean you 'weren't active'?"

"Well, we had something of an on-again, off-again flirtation, and recently we were off-again." By opening myself up to questions, answering as honestly as I can, I will save myself the death sentence of the journalists' morbid speculation.

"Do you still work with Stu Bogovian?" calls another reporter.

"No. I haven't seen or spoken to Stu Bogovian since his sentencing hearing nearly twenty years ago. He hired a different attorney to manage his appeal and parole."

"Why would he mention you by name when he threatened Harrison Doyle?"

"I can't attest to that. Next question."

"Did Harrison Doyle ever make you an offer to have sex with his daughter?" the same journalist asks.

"Can you be more specific?"

"Did New York County District Attorney Harrison Doyle ever offer you a sexual encounter with his stepdaughter, Charlotte, in exchange for something he wanted from you?"

"Yes," I respond.

The reporters explode with follow-up questions, so many being shot at me at once that I am completely unable to differentiate once voice from another.

"Whoa, calm down." I temper the crowd with my hands. "I can't hear any of your questions. One at a time, please."

"Did you follow through?" someone screams.

"Follow through with what?"

"When Harrison Doyle offered sex with his stepdaughter, did you take him up on it? How did that work?"

"His offer was declined."

"What did he ask for in exchange?" the first shrill journalist asks.

"He asked me to come to work for the district attorney's office."

"When did this happen?"

"About three weeks ago."

"Did you kill Charlotte Doyle?" a small voice from the back tries to project.

"No. Again, I want to be completely clear. I did not bring any physical harm to Charlotte Doyle."

"If you didn't kill her, then who did?" The same small voice.

I take a deep breath and prepare to start a war. "I believe Ethan Doyle killed Charlotte."

The throng of reporters falls silent and stares at me in disbelief. I stand at the podium and watch as my words slip into the ears and brains of the journalists. I see the gears of their minds click together and realize that Ethan is, in fact, a viable suspect. As though the needle suddenly came back in contact with a record, the silence is broken with a torrent of questions. I can't hold back my smile and delightedly watch as the journalists clamber for my attention. I don't call on any one of them; instead I bask in their wild attempts to garner my focus.

The cries of the journalists eventually die down and they realize approaching the questions in a civilized manner will get the most information. The most senior CNN reporter takes the lead and begins the structured and methodical questioning.

"Why do you believe that Ethan Doyle is the murderer?"

"It has been known to me for many years that Ethan and Charlotte had a contentious relationship and that Ethan in fact hated his stepsister." I know by divulging all the information I've acquired from the Franks and from my own investigating that the press will run with it, the police will be forced to investigate and Harrison can no longer hide in the shadows.

"Where was he on the night of the murder?"

I carefully plant the seeds of doubt. "You'll have to ask him that."

"Do you think Harrison Doyle put him up to it?"

"I think that's *exactly* what happened." I wink at the reporter who asks.

"Can you paint us a picture, sir?" the CNN reporter asks.

"Well, speaking with inside information, I would say that Ethan was waiting for an opportunity to enter his father's good graces. He had been secondary to his stepsister all his life and was something of a disappointment to the Doyle family." I pause to take a sip of water. "And when Charlotte no longer wanted to be the carrot her father dangled in front of his rabbits, she became a liability to him. Charlotte was the holder of all of Harrison's secrets. She had to be silenced."

I have constructed a perfect story for the press. I wrap all my comments with a very thin veil of supposition, making it sound like I *know* this is what happened, not just that I *think* it could have happened this way. I don't lie—I don't need to. I am simply stating a position and defending myself.

A beautiful female journalist speaks for the first time. "How do you know she didn't want to be dangled in front of the rabbits? Did she tell you that?"

"Charlotte was striving to attain a certain degree of social acceptance within a very established and exclusive community. She had recently achieved that, and it seems to me she was no longer interested in participating in nefarious activities that could challenge or disrupt her newfound social status. Being the prize was no longer socially beneficial to her." I lay out an easily believable motive, especially while the journalists were still tingling from Stu Bogovian's reveal of Harrison and Charlotte's sexual bribery.

Versed in selling stories, I know exactly what words to use, what words to avoid and how to keep myself on the right side of the law while I'm doing it. I do not mention the idea that Harrison is intentionally framing me for the murder, because I know the vultures will look at that hypothesis as paranoid and desperate and it will compromise my Ethan theory. I answer two more follow-up questions before I'm able to manufacture an exit.

"I will have to wrap this up, I'm afraid. If there are any legal matters, please direct your questions to my attorney, Sinan Khan." I step aside and gesture to Sinan, who nods to the reporters. "Otherwise, be well, and I'm sure we will see each other again soon."

Journalists call out their protests against my departure as I step away from the podium, take Claire's hand, usher Jamie in front of us and walk away from the reporters. Sinan watches us go and approaches the lectern to field any remaining questions the journalists may have.

I pull Claire close to me as we walk north, having laid the

groundwork for a substantial case against Ethan Doyle and subtly displacing suspicion away from myself. As we reach the corner of the house, I send Jamie along home and pull Claire toward a taxi.

"Where are we going?" she asks, tugging gently in the direction of the house.

"We're going to therapy, Claire."

THEN

In the days after Juliette came to my office to discuss Jamie's custody, she spent all her remaining energy tying up loose ends and ensuring the practical aspects of her death were managed. She asked me to accompany her on one such trip, where she feared her emotions would overwhelm her, and requested my support.

"You want *me* to be there with you?"

"I don't want Jamie involved. It's just not the place for him. And I need support, please come do this for me," she croaked at the other end of the phone.

"It's today?" I asked, checking my watch.

"It's in an hour. I have a car coming to me in thirty minutes, I can pick you up on my way over."

"Okay, I'll come with you," I agreed, though I had absolutely no desire to go to the Rhodes Foundation with Juliette, especially knowing Charlie would be there. The board members were honoring Juliette and the work she had done to build and expand the foundation. Despite having been at the helm of the foundation since its inception, Juliette didn't feel she was close enough with any of the members to trust them in her weakened condition. The fact that she called on me reminded me of her kindness and ability to forgive.

Just as she did when she came to my office the week before, Juliette was dressed impeccably when she picked me up in a black car. I sat next to her in the back seat, and we rode in relative silence to the foundation offices.

As we pulled up in front of the building, the driver helped Juliette from the car, and she walked tall and confidently into the lobby. I began to get the feeling that Juliette didn't ask me to escort her to this event for support.

A large poster with Juliette's picture was erected outside of the first-floor party room that the board rented out. Juliette scoffed and shook her head as she walked past the poster and entered through the double doors.

I looked inside to see the room had been set up to host a lunch reception, with many round tables covered in cream-colored tablecloths arranged around the floor facing a small stage. There stood a wooden podium and another large photograph of Juliette. Most attendees were already inside the room, mingling with one another, some already seated around tables.

Juliette graciously greeted everyone she passed, and I hovered in the doorway, not wanting to make my presence known. She turned back to look for me, and I lifted a hand to show her that I was there but unwilling to participate. She nodded in understanding and proceeded around the room.

I watched as various board members and friends took to the podium to fawn over Juliette's accomplishments and visions and extend their promises to continue her legacy in her absence. I noticed that no one spoke of her disease, no one mentioned the word *cancer* and no one said her absence was, in fact, her death. It seemed the members of polite society were treating this event as they would a retirement party.

I looked from table to table, part of me trying to find and part of me hoping I wouldn't find Charlie. She hadn't spoken onstage, and when I watched Juliette say hello and thank everyone upon her arrival, Charlie was clearly not among the guests.

I was distracted as I scanned the crowd and lifted myself onto my toes when everyone stood and began to applaud. I expected to see Juliette ascending the steps to make a statement, but instead, it seemed this was the final applause, marking the conclusion of the event. I still hadn't spotted Charlie.

As the clapping slowed and guests finished their drinks, I peered through the crowd to ensure Juliette didn't need my help getting up from her seat. Just then, a figure walked into my field of view in an unmissable bright green jacket—Charlie Doyle. Smugly showing up at the end of the event, just enough time to show her face and perhaps be caught by a photographer, she waited toward the back of the room for Juliette to pass by on her way out. I managed to tuck myself between the door and the poster, obscuring my presence, but still able to watch as Juliette slowly made her exit.

She didn't need me to hold her up, physically or in any other capacity. Juliette walked with more strength and pride than I had ever seen and fearlessly approached Charlotte Doyle. While Charlie was pretending Juliette couldn't possibly have a reason to dislike her, Juliette no longer had anything to lose. She marched right up to Charlie, suddenly looking threatening, and firmly shook her hand.

Charlie opened her mouth to speak, but Juliette immediately held up her hand in protest Charlie's face fell from aloof to intimidated, and she instinctively took a step backward. Juliette looked over Charlie's shoulder and caught my eye, despite my hiding place, and she smiled at me. She knew Charlie would be there. She didn't bring me there for support. She brought me there to watch her.

"You win," Juliette said to Charlie as Charlie tugged her hand away. "But don't think you're going to get away with it."

NOW

In the taxi on our way uptown to therapy, I explain to Claire what we were doing.

"I know this man from many years ago. I went to see him with Juliette a couple of times, and she continued to see him for many years. She trusted him, and he's already somewhat familiar with me. I don't want to start from scratch and explain every detail of my life to someone. So, we're going to Dr. Kimball because Juliette has already explained my whole life to him."

"Remind me why we're going to therapy *at all*?" Claire asks, clutching the handle on the plastic partition as the cab makes a sharp left turn.

"Sinan and I were discussing ways to improve my situation should we find ourselves in defense mode. He thought therapy might be a good idea."

"You're not supposed to go because someone tells you to, you know. That goes against the whole principle of therapy."

I disregard Claire's comment. Therapy goes against *my* principles. It seems so indulgent, to pay someone to listen to me whine when I should be out there fixing whatever issues I'm facing.

We walk inside to find the waiting room empty and Dr. Kimball standing in the doorway to his office.

"Hello again," he calls as he waves us inside. Dr. Steven Kimball offers me a firm handshake and gently introduces himself to Claire. We take our seats on the same Chesterfield leather sofa I sat on with Juliette, and Dr. Kimball begins to speak.

"Welcome. I'm glad you've decided to come in. As you and I discussed on the phone—" he gestures toward me "—today is a consultation, as opposed to a full therapy session. I am not currently taking on new patients, but given that I have already seen you, Peter, and I worked with Juliette for many years, I did want to make sure that I was able to see you both and help you in whatever direction you need to go from here." He leans forward, places his elbows on his knees and cocks his head at Claire.

"Oh, I'm not even sure where to start." Claire puts a hand to her chest and slides back into the sofa.

"Well, I imagine there have been some changes at home, with Juliette's passing and the allegations in the press. Maybe you can tell me a little bit about what's been going on for you?"

I catch myself rolling my eyes and immediately pull out my glasses to obscure my distaste for this whole event. "Actually, I need you to help Claire to understand what's going on with me. You see, something recently happened to me, and I feel like that switch you told me about years ago—that switch has turned back on."

"The switch has turned on?" he says, leaning back and bracing the arms of his chair.

"Yes, and I need you to explain to Claire what we're talking about."

"You would like me to explain the nature of your behavior? The clinical stuff? Why?" Dr. Kimball furrows his brow.

"I have been implicated in the murder of someone I once knew, and it is important to me, to Claire and to my defense, that Claire can have an understanding of what this disease is that you say I had, and also that it's possible for it to change. To switch off or on or whatever. Just, please help her understand."

Claire pats my knee and takes over. "It would be helpful for me if you can explain it in layman's terms, please, because I've never been in therapy before."

"This is for your benefit?" he questions her. Dr. Kimball seems almost unwilling to discuss the diagnosis he was so happy to lay upon me many years ago.

"Yes. If I'm questioned by the police, or if he ends up getting arrested, it's important for me to be aware of the nature of his...*peculiarities*." Claire takes her time carefully choosing her words.

After a deep incredulous breath, Dr. Kimball says, "I am not at liberty to discuss any of the details or even the broad strokes of your ex-wife's treatment. I will simply explain the nature of the beast." He waves his hand at me. "Peter showed significant and persistent signs of sociopathic behavior. Because he was never my client, I couldn't formally diagnose him with anything, but anyone with a pair of eyes could tell you that he was living a life devoid of human emotion. No sympathy, no empathy, no guilt, no concept of how his behaviors could impact other people, frankly no regard for other people at all." His tone is teetering toward pissed off. "He is manipulative, charismatic and he gets what he wants. He will not tolerate failure and disregards anything that doesn't directly benefit him."

"But you said this thing can change, right? It can stop?" Claire asks, hope in her voice.

"I don't know. If Peter crossed the border into full-fledged psychopathy, then I would bet the farm that it couldn't stop. So, Claire, to answer your question, it *is* possible for someone to change, but it usually takes *years* of therapy and introspection. I've *never* heard of the catalyst of change being a murder accusation..." He scoffs, no longer putting on an air of professionalism nor pretending he doesn't hate me. "I don't see how that could kill the monster inside."

"Kill the what?" Claire asks, looking at me.

"You, sir—" he leans forward and bores a hole in my face with his penetrating eyes "—have a *monster* inside of you. The only question is, can you keep it contained? That is up to you and you alone."

"Dr. Kimball," I begin, "you gave me the impression that I was afflicted with an issue that worked on a hair trigger. If something pulled that trigger, then I would turn good again, and you and Juliette both told me that I could do that. And I am now here to tell you that I have experienced that triggering moment."

"I would have a very hard time imagining what could create the dramatic change you describe. I would say you were already too far gone."

"Be that as it may—" I find Dr. Kimball's doubt infuriating "—this is *indeed* what happened, and I would like for you to please explain to Claire that it's a possibility. She may be asked to testify as a character witness."

"I can't, Peter." He throws up his hands. "I don't believe you."

THEN

I walked into Rick Friedberg's waiting room, planning on meeting Juliette there. I spent time thinking about the idea of taking custody of Jamie after Juliette passed. It seemed like a nuisance at first, but as I thought about it, I realized that his needs would be attended to by Claire and the housekeeper for the most part. It would only be for two more years; Jamie was almost sixteen.

Juliette appeared at the door of the waiting room, looking as if she'd aged fifty years. Gaunt and frail, there were lines in her face I'd never noticed before, and as I got close to her, I could see that makeup was all that was allowing her to look alive. I offered my arm to help her to a couch.

"Thank you, Peter," she croaked. Before she could sit, we saw Rick hustling down the hallway.

"Hi, Juliette." He took her other elbow and escorted her toward his office. "Hi, Peter," he said to me as he pulled open the door. We helped Juliette settle into her seat in front of

Rick's desk and filled a glass with water for her. I sat in the chair next to hers, and Rick began pulling papers from his desk drawer.

"Let's get this done quickly so you can get out of here," he said. "Unless you have any changes you'd like to make to your will, I have a copy here for you."

"What do I need a copy for? I'm dying, it's not like I'm going to read it aloud to anyone. That's the executor's job." Even in her delicate state, she still joked and kept the air light.

"Fine." Rick smiled. "I'll keep it in your file. Other than that, we have custody paperwork to discuss. Is there anything else?"

"I shouldn't be here for any other discussions, Rick. I am here to talk about the custody agreement and my responsibilities moving forward. Other than that, Juliette's estate is not my business or my concern."

"That's correct, Peter. Thank you for acknowledging that. Juliette, do you have anything else you'd like to discuss? I can make time at the end of this meeting just for you and me to talk."

"Maybe just for a moment." She reached into her handbag and pulled out an envelope. "I'd like to give this to you in the event… Well, I'll speak with you about it afterward." She handed him the envelope, and Rick immediately scurried it away into Juliette's file.

"Peter, what questions do you have for me about custody?" he asked me.

"Beyond bearing parental responsibility for the minor child, what additional typical responsibilities come with custody?"

"Legally speaking? You have to take care of your kid, Peter. Just keep him fed and clothed and send him to school and you shouldn't run into any legal problems."

"Essentially, he just lives in my house? Like a younger roommate?"

"Are you serious?" Rick glares at me.

"I haven't played father in ten years, Rick. I'm just ensuring I'm aware of exactly what's coming my way."

"Then yes, for all intents and purposes, he's just a young roommate. Keep him alive and show him some moral guidance, if you can." I didn't like the way Rick implied I may not be able to be moral.

"Jamie just needs to be shown love and acceptance," Juliette says. "He hasn't known much beyond the two of us, and he is tough but scared. Make sure he feels you want him there, and that's all you need to do." I felt something like a pang of sadness as Juliette's voice creaked slowly from her mouth.

"We will need to meet again after the…after, um." Rick stalled, unable to bring himself to say the word aloud. "Well, *afterward*, to tie up any loose ends."

"Do I need to sign anything now?" I asked.

"Yes, you both do, actually. Why don't we do it this way? There's a conference room right next door. I'll give you the papers, and you can sign while I spend a minute discussing whatever Juliette wants to talk to me about. Then you can help her downstairs and into a taxi, okay?"

I excused myself to the other room and blocked out thoughts of parental responsibility as I signed the pages of the custody agreement. Thoughts of presenting Jamie as my offspring wafted in and out of my head. Maybe he would go to an Ivy League school, and I could tell people that he takes after his father. Juliette had spent her best years making sure Jamie grew up to be a wonderful man, and I was now able to reap all the benefits.

Rick escorted Juliette into the conference room and helped her sit next to me. He took the pages of the agreement that I had already signed and held them open for Juliette to countersign. She held the pen in her gnarled fingers like a child would hold a crayon. Missing the signature line and barely able to produce a legible mark, she sighed, frustrated, and dropped the pen.

"I'm having a lot of trouble with dexterity. I can't do this very well." Juliette looked exasperated and embarrassed, and Rick didn't seem to know how to solve the issue.

"I can get another copy of that page and try again, okay? And then we'll just take it slow." He scooted his chair back and quickly darted out of the conference room.

"Why don't I do it for you?" I asked her. "I can just sign all these pages and get it over with, so you don't have to struggle."

Her sad eyes brightened for just a moment, and she nodded. I took the pen and flipped through the pages of the custody agreement, signing Juliette's name on her signature line. When Rick reappeared with a new page, I took it from him and signed both our names.

"Oh, Peter, no, you can't sign for Juliette." He leaned over the table and flipped through to the other pages. "Did you sign all of these? I can't let you do that. She needs to sign her own signature. It doesn't matter if it's sloppy or illegible, I need to watch her sign."

"Rick, leave her alone. It's signed, okay? Let that be the end of it."

"I can't, Peter. I can't allow for you to sign for her unless she has a power of attorney form signed and notarized allowing someone else to—"

"It's okay, Rick," Juliette croaked, "I don't need a power of attorney form. I am of sound mind, just not very sound fingers. It's okay. We used to sign each other's documents all the time."

"Okay? Enough now. The papers are signed." I closed the packet, satisfied that everything was complete. Despite Rick's discomfort and protests, we stood up to walk out the door. I supported Juliette with one arm and opened the doors as we walked out into the summer sun. She wore a warm sweater and scarf, despite the heat, and I realized the months had dwindled down to weeks.

I hailed a taxi and tucked her safely inside. Juliette held her twisted hand out to me, and I squeezed it gently before closing the door. It was the last time I would ever see her.

NOW

"We got the cab," Tomlinson says, slapping a stack of sheets onto Sinan's desk. "Got the logs and snooped inside the back seat while it was in the garage. No sign of anything back there. Mind you, the woman was killed nearly two weeks ago, and the cab has been in circulation ever since. But still, nothing. Blood has a tendency to seep, and there was nothing in the seats or on the handles. Brought a black light."

"The taxi back seat was a long shot anyway," I interrupt. "What about the travel logs? Do you know where Ethan was picked up and dropped off?"

"Yes, he was picked up at the corner of his father's apartment building on Central Park West and Eighty-Eighth Street. Turned on the meter at 10:11 p.m."

"*And?* What's this shit with the half story? Where the fuck did he get dropped off?" Sinan is losing patience quickly.

"The drop-off was in Alphabet City. Ninth and Avenue B at 10:43 p.m."

"What's on Ninth and B?" I ask from my regular seat in the fat leather roll-arm chair in the corner.

"The girls he went to the club with. Couple of NYU students he met at some bar, invited them along to the opening, went to meet them at their place. Then the other guy they went with picked them up in a car to go to the club in the Meatpacking District."

"How did you get those details?"

"Doorman," Tomlinson replies. "He couldn't have been *happier* to check the security camera and show us all the time stamps."

"Fucking heroes," LaBianca adds, shaking his head. "Saw you on the news, boss. Trying to get the cops to investigate the dirtbag kid, huh? Throw it out there in the press and now they've gotta follow up. Smart move."

"Franks," Sinan interrupts, "anything else?" He is uncharacteristically curt and impatient.

"Not as of now. We're going to keep our noses to the grindstone, though. Anything else specifically you need to know sooner rather than later?" Tomlinson asks.

"Did you get the height and weight and handedness info?" I ask.

"Oh, yeah, we got DMV records for height, and LaBianca got a couple of pictures of Ethan." Tomlinson flips open his notepad and searches for the data. "Here we go. Driver's license indicates he's five-eleven, it doesn't list weight, but he's estimated between one-ninety and two hundred, and he is right-handed." Tomlinson closes his notebook.

"So, average height, average build, right-handed, enough money for fancy suits, hates his sister and..." I trail off before finishing my thought. I look hopefully at Sinan, who blows a long puff of air my way.

"And accounted for at the time of the murder. He left his

father's house, got into a cab, paid with a card, went to Alphabet City and then was seen entering a club where he stayed until the very small hours of the morning," Sinan deadpans. "Couldn't have been him the witness saw outside of Charlotte's house."

"That doesn't mean he didn't kill her," I insist. "The witness never said she saw the guy go in or come out of the house. She just saw a guy *near* the front of her house. And medical examiners can be totally off with their estimated time of death. You know that."

"Okay, gentlemen. Thank you for your work. I will be in touch." Sinan opens the door and doesn't bother to shake Tomlinson's outstretched hand. He is agitated and restless. The investigators walk out the door, and Sinan plunks himself down next to me in the other leather chair.

"This silence is absolutely wrecking me." Sinan lights a cigarette and fidgets with his lighter. "It's nearly 3:00 p.m.— how is it that Harrison hasn't addressed your statement from yesterday? I haven't seen anything else in the news." Sinan picks up the remote and begins furiously clicking between stations. "You see? There's nothing else happening on the news. Where is this slimy bastard?"

"Sinan, calm down. It's exactly what he did when she was first killed. He disappeared. He's thick and foolish. He's liable to say all the wrong things. He's going for stealth, I'm telling you." I wave the smoke away from my face. "You're not going to hear anything from him until someone is arrested. Mark my words."

Now that we are alone again, Sinan speaks in confidence. "Did you look into the suits?"

"The suits?"

"I asked you to find out whether or not you had any suits at the dry cleaner's at the time of the murder."

"Right. No, I haven't done that yet. Why are you so worked up? Now's the time to breathe." I pat my friend on the shoulder.

"It's hard to breathe easy when we've invited the world to speculate on this investigation, the other suspect has a time-stamped alibi and we can't explain away the one thing that puts *you* at the scene." Sinan leans forward and taps both his feet. His cigarette ash falls to the carpet next to him.

"The paper clips? Stop worrying about the paper clips. I'm sure they'll have my DNA in her house, as well as all over the paper clips. That's one sentence of argument—'my client has made and deposited many of these paper-clip sticks at the home of the deceased, and its presence in the trash can is irrelevant to the case,' blah, blah, blah. Come on, Sinan. You're better than that." I understand his fears that we don't have much to work with. What we need is for Harrison to reappear. We've given him the rope to hang himself, but if he remains in obscurity, the rope will simply dangle, idle and useless.

"There's an electronic paper trail of hateful emails dating back a long time and some incriminating Facebook posts, but there's nothing that points to Ethan beyond his hatred of his sister. Hating her and killing her are two different things." Sinan begins to look at me differently. Like he's waiting for me to tell him something.

"So, what's our next move, Sinan? I'm not going to stand here with a target on my back and wait for Harrison to pull the trigger. I didn't kill her."

Sinan steeples his long fingers over his face. "I don't know what our next move is, Peter. You were questioned by the police days ago and still there's no arrest. Your Ethan theory should have garnered a screaming response from the DA but there has been nothing but silence since your press conference. This isn't normal. Looks like everyone else is on the same page, and *we* are in a different book."

"What could they possibly know that we don't know?"

He drops his congenial tone and points a steady finger at me. "They know who did it, Peter." He frantically shakes his head. "I have to think. I'm going to keep digging. I'll come by your house tonight if I find anything."

Sinan arrives, sweaty and disheveled. I've never seen him this way before. Sinan is known for his style and composure, and in all our years working together, I've never seen him in a condition less than impeccable.

He doesn't perform his customary bow, he doesn't even say good evening; instead he walks quickly through the door that I hold open and staggers into the kitchen.

"What's the matter? I've never seen you like this. Are they out there?" I lean toward the window to see an unmarked van across the street. "Is that them?"

"I think it's press, but to be honest it *could* be the cops. No one made any moves like they saw me." Sinan unloads the files and notebooks that he brought with him onto the kitchen table.

"Is this about the tox screen?"

"It's more than just the tox screen. First of all, it showed no substances of any kind in her system. No booze, no Tylenol, nothing."

"But that doesn't set us back at all," I say, worry rising in my voice. "If she had a stomach full of Xanax, what does that prove?"

"That fact points the finger at fewer and fewer people. Now it seems Charlotte *must* have knowingly let someone into her house." Sinan sounds exhausted.

"What's to say someone didn't have keys?" I grasp desperately at the fraying edges of our case.

"I'm getting to that." Sinan shuffles his papers.

"Okay, what else?"

Sinan flinches and lays out the reasons for his concern. "Time stamps. Security footage from the club, credit card swipes in a taxi and at the club, travel logs and metered fares to corroborate. Ethan has a time-stamped alibi and was either on the Upper West Side, in a taxi, in Alphabet City or in the Meatpacking District at the time of the murder."

"You realize that you can go through Gramercy to get from the Upper West Side down to Alphabet City, right?"

"Sure, but can you hop a cab on Eighty-Eighth and Central Park West at 10:11 p.m., stop in Gramercy to murder your sister and *still* get to Alphabet City by 10:43 p.m.? Unlikely."

"Unless you had keys," I push.

"Right, the keys. Well, it turns out Charlotte had a very special kind of key. There are regular keys that have Do Not Duplicate stamped on them, and then there is this Rolls-Royce of keys that she had with magnets and rivets and divots and what have you. There is a special card and a unique code that's needed to make copies of these keys." Sinan pulls a photo of the key from his stack of papers. "So, the Franks tracked down the locksmith who makes the key and asked how many were ever made. The answer is *two*. After she divorced the half-drowned cokehead ex, she changed the locks, and only she and Sylvia Santos have copies."

"Okay, so we circle back to the idea that she opened the door for someone she knew. Could still be her brother."

"His timeline doesn't fit. And you can't mess with a timeline."

"It was a long shot, I guess."

"It wasn't a long shot, Peter. It was the *only* shot. The only places Ethan went that night were a club, a taxi and home. If he stopped by his sister's house to murder her, he magically did it without creating any physical evidence of his presence in her house, and he trailed nothing back to the taxi or the club."

"As you just said, if he and Harrison were in on it together, then he would be working with Harrison's legal expertise and with the benefit of all his connections. Don't you think Harrison would know exactly how to clean a crime scene after all the evidence he's seen in his career? He's practically an expert murderer with all the information he's learned in a lifetime prosecuting criminals. This doesn't refute the idea that he and Ethan were in on it together, like I've been saying from the beginning."

"If prosecuting criminals makes you an expert murderer, then defending them does, too. You may be getting other people onto hooks here, but you're not getting yourself off."

"Maybe Harrison didn't trust Ethan to do his dirty work. So maybe it was someone *else* she knew."

"That's what *I* think," Sinan confesses. He pauses and drags in a ragged breath. "What was that paper-clip stick doing in the bin?"

"You're back on *that* now? You're back to thinking *I* did this?"

"I can't think of anything else, and I think we need to switch gears and start focusing on damage control."

"Sinan, I told you at the start of this, I had nothing to do with killing Charlie Doyle. I am being framed by Harrison."

"I have to see your closet," Sinan demands.

"My closet? What's my closet have to do with anything?" Sinan offers me no explanation. "Okay, come on."

Sinan gathers his papers under his arm and follows as I lead him up the stairs and into the bedroom. We walk past the bed, and I open the door to my dressing room.

"Come on in. What do you need to see?"

Sinan doesn't respond. Instead he starts pulling back suits and shirts and looking at the contents of my closet. I take the cue and back up to sit in a large armchair in the middle of the dressing room. Sinan examines several suits and checks their labels and sizes. When he gets to a tuxedo, he pulls it off the rack and hangs it on a single forward-facing hook.

He sniffs around inside drawers and shelves, looks down at the shoes on the shoe racks, all polished and shining, and sorts through the pocket squares and ties. Then he finds what he's looking for—a leather box with small compartments for jewelry and watches. He pokes through the contents with his pen. I crane my neck to see what he pulls out and places on the counter next to the tuxedo.

"We have a problem, love." Sinan sighs.

"What?" I say, jumping up to see what he's looking at. "What's the problem?"

Sinan pulls a xeroxed copy of an evidence photo from his pile of papers and lays it next to the item he drew from the jewelry box. The picture shows a single gold cuff link, a Tiffany knot. Sinan has just taken its partner from the leather box.

"Now, how do you imagine this happened? I didn't have this piece of evidence at the beginning because my detective left it out of the original report by mistake. Again, how do you imagine one of *your* cuff links, a gift from your ex-wife, if I'm not mistaken, was found in your murdered lover's bedroom?"

"This doesn't mean anything. It's the same as the paper clips. I've been in Charlie's bedroom," I explain, panicked. "There have been plenty of opportunities for my accessories to get lost in there. You've got to believe me."

"I want to believe you. I *want* to believe you weren't involved. I'm laboring *tirelessly* to explain away the evidence, the obvious clues, but it just isn't adding up. Please, Peter.

Tell me what you've done so we can change our tactics and salvage our case. Please."

"Sinan, I didn't do anything. Keep working tirelessly, keep doing it. There's another explanation. I didn't kill her!" I pull back the curtains and I see another van creeping slowly down my street. The dread is almost choking me, and I need Sinan to believe I had nothing to do with this.

"Remember that piece of paper I stopped you throwing in the fire after the police questioned you?" Sinan's words are devoid of any emotion now.

"Yes, yes I remember."

"Well, it was a dry-cleaning receipt. With your name on it."

"Okay, so what?"

"The receipt shows you had two items cleaned."

"Yeah, so?"

"Two tuxedos." Sinan probes the tuxedo hanging from the hook. "Imagine my surprise to walk into your closet and find only one."

I choke on my response and lean into the rack with my suits. I push them aside, looking to see if Sinan is right. He is.

"You know what *I* consider to be an above-average suit?" he asks. "A tuxedo."

"I have another tuxedo, Sinan. It's probably back at the dry cleaner's again. Jesus, you're beginning to make me think I *did* do this!"

"When you're ready to tell me the truth, I'll be waiting." Sinan grabs his documents and walks out of the closet, down the stairs and out the back door into the brisk October air.

THEN

I was at the office when the call came in. Anna answered the phone and didn't patch the call through. Instead she solemnly knocked on my door and told me the news herself. With her hands over her face as if they'd been best friends, Anna reported that Juliette had succumbed to the effects of Tera's disease and had passed away that morning. It was September. She had made it through the summer, but she was just shy of seeing Jamie's sixteenth birthday. I called Claire to let her know the news.

"Claire," I said when she picked up, but she was already crying, so I knew she had heard.

"I know, Peter. I know—Jamie called me and told me."

"Jamie called you?" I said, surprised.

"Yes, the last time I spoke to Juliette, I asked to talk to Jamie and I asked him to call me when it happened."

"Well, since you know how to talk to him, you should arrange for a dinner or something for the three of us. We have to discuss some logistics now that Juliette is gone."

"Are you all right, Peter?" She blew her nose loudly into the phone.

"I'm going to take care of things, Claire." I pulled my face from the receiver. "Everything will be fine."

"Have you got the custody all worked out? I don't want that poor boy to be alone for even one second."

"Yes, Claire, it's all taken care of, like I said. I signed everything at Rick's office with Juliette. Everything is in order."

"And Juliette didn't have any issues? There are no limitations or anything?"

"No, I have full legal custody. She was very sick when we were signing. She couldn't even hold the pen, so I had to sign her name for her, but she was on board with the whole thing."

I knew from my meeting at Rick's office that Juliette had her funeral plans already laid out and her final wishes were to be cremated. She left her worldly possessions to Jamie and he stood to inherit quite a bit for a teenager when he turned eighteen. There was very little for me to do, other than meet with Jamie to talk about his wishes and then complete the final custody paperwork with Rick. As I mused about the way my life with a son would look, Sinan walked into my office.

"Sorry to hear about Juliette, love. Anna just let me know. You okay?"

"Yes, I'm just fine. I've worked out the details already, and I suppose we'll have Jamie move in sometime after the funeral."

"That cancer really took her quickly, huh?" he said.

"It certainly appeared that way, but we don't really know how long she had it. Apparently she refused traditional treatment. No radiation, chemo, surgery. She went the holistic route, Claire tells me."

"Still seems so odd to me that both Juliette and Marcus died of the same disease."

"Seems strange to me, too, but I guess that's how genetics works."

"Yeah," he said, doubtful. "Genetics…or something."

"What do you mean 'or something'?"

"You spoke with Marcus's doctors when he was sick, didn't you?" Sinan seemed suspicious, but he wouldn't let me in on what was in his head.

"I did, yes. Or they spoke to me more than anything else, why?"

"And they said that it was genetic?"

"No, I had no reason to ask if it was genetic. Marcus was the only one I knew who had that disease, so I didn't need to ask questions about genetics."

"Well, it's not. I'm surprised that someone like you, someone who's got such a nose for inconsistencies, such attention to detail, didn't go and research this disease."

"I had no reason to, and frankly, neither did you." I became uncomfortable in my seat and tired of Sinan's allusions.

"Didn't you tell me years ago that you felt trapped in your marriage? You felt that you had to stay married to Juliette so long as Marcus was around?"

"I did say that, but it's hardly relevant to anything. I never wanted to get married, which is precisely why I'm not married anymore."

"Right." Sinan smirked. He wasn't quite accusing me of anything, but I didn't like his tone. "And you got divorced quite soon after his death, yes?"

"Either say what you came to say or leave me alone. I have a lot of work to do."

"I just think it's strange, that's all. A strange coincidence that Marcus died, and you capitalized on his death with divorce, and then Juliette died, and you're suddenly happy to get custody of Jamie. And they both died of an extremely rare disease that *doesn't* actually run in families."

"Are you accusing me of something?" I stood up and lowered both fists onto the desk.

"No." He held up his hands in surrender. "It's just that Tera's disease can come as result of poisoning." He left me with a sly smile on his face, backed out of my office and closed the door.

NOW

I'm lying in bed with Claire, waiting for the other shoe to drop. I haven't been able to concentrate on anything since Sinan lost faith in me yesterday. Harrison remains unseen, making everyone nervous. Whereas I had believed Harrison's silence was warranted and intelligent after Stu Bogovian's initial perplexing threat, it isn't like Harrison to allow someone to attack him without retaliation. Now I fear his silence is just the calm before the storm.

It seems Claire and Jamie are the only ones left who believe me. But fear hangs heavily on my mind. Claire stirs and stretches next to me as she wakes up from her nap. She rolls onto her side and throws her arm over my chest.

"How long have you been up?" she asks, licking at her chapped lips.

"A while, just thinking." A feeling similar to indigestion starts to brew in my stomach. It isn't physical so much as emotional and I sense it traveling up my insides and into my face. It's remorse.

"What is it? Are you all right?" Claire sits up and wipes at my face.

"There's a lot of work to do," I say, "to get everything straightened out. I have a lot of work to do, to make up for what I've done to Jamie and to you all these years."

"You're starting already. You've got custody now, and we filed those adoption papers that Rick gave us—"

"Rick," I interrupt her. "Oh, my *God*, Rick." I suddenly remember my meeting with Rick Friedberg. "I have to call Rick. He has something for me."

"What is it?" Claire asks.

"It's going to help us. He has an envelope, and I think it has something inside that's going to help me get out of this mess." A wave of relief hits me as I imagine what Juliette could have left for Rick to help exonerate me. Something she knew about the Doyles. Something she knew about *something*, and it was going to be just the break we needed to get me safely out of harm's way.

I scroll quickly through my contacts for Rick's number and hit the call button.

"Are you sure?" Claire sits up.

"Yes." I kiss her knuckles, listening to endless rings. "I just know it. Everything is going to be okay now."

Rick's voice mail picks up and I leave him a message to call me immediately. I hang up and call him again. No answer.

We walk down to the kitchen, where Claire starts to prepare for another dinner at home. I look out the front windows to see the media vans are gone. Relieved, I sit at the round table and click on the television while Claire pounds veal cutlets. I click past football games and sitcom reruns, looking for news channels, hoping to find some information to fill the void that Harrison left with his silence. I find nothing. The nothingness opens a space in my brain for the worst kinds of ideas to blossom. I try Rick's cell phone one more time, but he's still not answering.

I watch as Claire dredges the cutlets in flour, egg wash and bread crumbs. I smile inwardly, pondering how I can make it up to her that I've been unfaithful. I try to picture Charlie, just to punish myself. I squeeze my eyes shut and imagine her in a black lacy bra. I can't remember when I lost that cuff link at her house and try to think of the last time I made a twisted paper-clip stick in her presence. Having spent so many years of my life uncaring, unaware and unimpressed, it's difficult for me to bring up memories of things I considered forgettable.

Claire approaches and pulls me back into the present moment. She strokes my cheek with her finger, and my mind stills. Whatever happened before today doesn't matter any longer. I vow to bury my former self, with all my secrets and all my lies, as soon as the Charlie mess is cleaned up.

I spent the morning trying to get through to Rick with no luck. I don't go to the office or talk to Sinan, even though we'd left things conflicted and unsettled. I have the utmost faith that Sinan will come around and accept my innocence after he gets some sleep and pulls himself together.

I sit at my desk in my bedroom and pick up the phone to call Rick again. He answers just before I hang up and sounds like he's underwater.

"Rick, you there? I've been trying to reach you." My heart pounds in my chest.

"Yeah, sorry, I'm out of town and the service here isn't great. What's up? Everything okay?"

"No, things are not really okay. I'm sure you've got television wherever you are?"

"I just left town last night. I know what's been going on in New York with the Charlotte Doyle mess. What can I do for you?"

"Rick, I need the letter Juliette left with you. She said to you that if something were to happen to me, that you need to open the envelope. Right? I need it, Rick. I need that letter." I strain to hear Rick at the other end of the phone. Sounds like he's in a monsoon somewhere. I can't hear anything more than noise from his end, so I repeat the request. "Rick, please. I think this constitutes a situation where you need to open that letter. Please."

He continues his infuriating pause before responding, "Yes. I suppose this situation warrants sharing that letter with you. But as I said, I am not in New York. I won't be back in the city until late next week."

"My situation could very well change *dramatically* before then, Rick. I need the letter *now.*"

I hear static and crashing waves as Rick pauses to think. "Here's what I'm going to do. I am going to have my partner open the file and determine the nature of the content. I will be on the phone while she does this, so I can quickly assess whether or not you should have access to whatever Juliette left for me. If I determine that you should see whatever is in there, I will have my assistant messenger a copy to you."

"And if you don't deem it appropriate for me to see?"

"Then I will send you an email to that effect and we won't discuss it again. Agreed?"

"Yes, Rick. Please understand, you could have something very important for me. I need that letter, and I need it now."

"I understand, and that's why I'm doing this. Good luck to you."

I hang up the phone and make my way down the stairs, sucking in a long hard breath, hoping that Juliette left something I can use in my defense. Finally feeling like there may be a light at the end of this disastrous tunnel, I sit down at the table with Claire and try to breathe. Before I can tell her what Rick said, Jamie appears in the doorway.

"Hi, Jamie," she says, smiling in his direction, "what are you doing home so early?"

"There were some cops that came to see me at school today," he reports, disheveled, and drops his bag on the floor.

"What?" I am ripped from this new tranquil mind-set and thrown headfirst back into old feelings of rage. "Did they have a warrant?"

"No, I don't think so. I was outside of school, I went to the bagel place across the street to get breakfast and they stopped me when I was heading back for class. They said I didn't have to go to class and talking to them was more important." Jamie holds up his hands in confusion.

"Jesus, Jamie, didn't I tell you? Dammit! Don't you know your *rights*? You never have to speak with a police officer, absolutely *never*! Even if they have a hundred warrants, Jamie!"

"I'm sorry, Dad, I didn't know." Jamie backs away from me. "They said they were detectives and I had to talk to them because I could prove that you're innocent. I didn't think you'd be mad. I thought I was helping." His wide eyes are distressed.

"Oh, Jamie," Claire says as she draws him in for a hug, "you sweet boy."

"Dad, did I blow the case? I'm so sorry, I thought it was going to help!"

"What did you tell them, Jamie?" My eyes flash like lightning, and the anger rises in my throat.

"They asked me if I wanted to talk to Sinan, and I said no, and—"

"They *asked* if you wanted your lawyer present and you refused?" My voice turns low and steady. The panic and fury subside into a terrifying calm.

"Yeah, because I *know* what we did that night. I know exactly what we did. I remember because I had this paper due for English for this book that I didn't read, and I remember looking up the synopsis online, and then you called me and asked if I was hungry, remember?" Jamie says desperately.

Eyes burning, I stare mercilessly at him.

"So, I told them I came down and we heated up Chinese food, because we don't know how to cook, and then we watched *Pulp Fiction* in the basement theater. That's all I said!"

"What else did they ask you, Jamie?" I speak each word as if it is its own crisp sentence.

"Uh, they asked what did we eat and I told them, and they asked which movie and I told them, and then they asked if I drank wine, and I said only when my mom would let me on special occasions, because I'm not twenty-one, you know, and then they asked what we did after the movie, and I said we went to bed. Dad, I didn't do anything wrong, please don't be mad."

"You told the detectives that you only drink wine on special occasions?" I walk slowly to the dishwasher next to the small sink by the pantry.

"Yeah. I mean the cops were asking me about drinking. I'm not twenty-one, I'm not supposed to drink. But I know we drank wine *that* night and I know I can't *lie* about that night, so I told them it was a special thing. Why? Is that bad?"

"Well, Jamie. You lied to the police." I pull from the dishwasher the three wineglasses from dinner the night before and arrange them neatly on the countertop. I point at the three glasses that were set at the round table in the kitchen. "You have wine at dinner almost every night, and sometimes even with lunch or for an afternoon treat out in the garden with your *mother*." The word *mother* slithers out of my mouth, accompanied by a chilling snarl. "And yet, you told the police you don't drink unless it's a special occasion."

"But how could they know that? They've never been in here, have they?" Jamie stammers.

"Jamie, did they ask you what time all this happened?" I speak softly and cock my head to the side.

"I said we ate at 7:00 p.m. I mean, I didn't look at the clock, but that's when we always eat, so that's what I told them. And then we went downstairs and watched the movie."

"How long would you say *Pulp Fiction* is, Jamie?"

"I don't know, three hours or something?"

"So, you told the detectives that we ate at 7:00 p.m., and then you said that we went downstairs to watch a movie that was approximately three hours long and then you told them we parted ways to go to our respective rooms and pack it in for the night, is that right?" I ask. I see my defense crumbling before my eyes.

"Yeah, you see? I didn't say anything wrong." Jamie holds up his hands in apology.

"Jamie, you gave them a timeline. You just told the detectives that not a single human being can account for my whereabouts after approximately 10:30 p.m. And as the medical examiner determined, Charlie was killed sometime between 10:00 p.m. and midnight."

THEN

Claire made a reservation for three like I asked her to and called Jamie to invite him out with us. I wanted to make sure that we were able to spend at least a little bit of time together before the funeral, so everyone who saw us all there would have the impression that we were close. Claire had told me 7:30 p.m., but when I arrived at Mezzaluna to find the two of them already seated, on the same side of the table no less, I was immediately uneasy. As I walked toward the table, I saw Claire pass a small object from her hand to Jamie's and urge him to quickly put it away in his pocket. He stood to greet me, tucking it away.

"What's that?" I asked, pointing to his jeans.

"That's nothing," Claire scolded, "just something I wanted Jamie to have, now that he's coming to join our family. Don't worry about it." She made it sound like it was innocuous, so I let it go.

"Jamie," I began my rehearsed statement to my son, "I'm so sorry that Juliette is gone. But this tragic event affords us the opportunity to really develop the relationship that we've been missing for all these years. So, welcome to the family." I remained standing, hoping to be able to practice a hug, but the table was awkwardly between us, and Jamie was unable to scoot out. He leaned over and gave me a half handshake, half hug that looked and felt incredibly graceless.

"Thank you." We all sat down, and I immediately lifted a menu to my face to create a separation between us. I could hear Claire and Jamie whispering, and the discomfort in the air got thick around me. I tried to shrug it off and concentrate on what I wanted to eat, but I couldn't help but feel like something was amiss in their relationship. I dropped my menu and focused in on them, so they would be forced to include me.

"Jamie," I began, "when would it suit you to move into my house?"

"Um, when would be good for you? Is there a room there? I've never been to your house," Jamie mumbled.

"I will get a room ready for you," Claire assured him, "and you should come as soon as you're ready, okay?" She looked so excited to have Jamie coming to live with us, like his presence would be the change she had been longing for.

"Thanks, Claire." Jamie looked almost the same way, as if they were two teenagers in on a private joke.

"You seem to be taking the death of your mother quite well, that's good. It's important not to fall apart when these things happen." I picked up the menu again and ordered several pizzas to share. I had finished what I came to say and was not interested in staying a moment longer than I needed to.

"Are you going to speak at the funeral?" Claire asked. I perked up my ears to listen, not having considered the idea that he may be delivering the eulogy.

"Yes. The lawyers said that in Mom's will she asked that I say something at the funeral."

"Are you prepared for that? It's a lot of responsibility." I cringed at the idea that Jamie would be left to his own devices, to write a eulogy that publicly chastised my absence or granted credit for his upbringing solely to his mother. "Do you need help deciding what to say?" I thought that if I were to have a say in his speech, I could edit out anything that I found unappealing.

"Thanks, but I have it mostly written already. I have a friend whose dad died, and he told me the kind of thing I should be writing, so we worked on it together."

"Remember to be nice. No one likes a eulogy with a lot of complaints," I warned.

"Right." Jamie looked away from me, and the conversation was over. We waited in awkward silence for the pizza to arrive, and I couldn't help feeling ganged up on with the two of them on the same side of the table and me alone on the other. Being younger than I was, Claire was more connected to Jamie and his generation, so instead of dwelling on feelings of exclusion, I figured I would use their connection to let Claire take over the parenting duties.

"How did you do on that statistics exam, by the way?" Claire asked once we were all distracted by the food.

"Oh, yeah, I forgot to tell you, I got an A minus. There was so much information, but the sports analogy you came up with, that was so helpful. I was taking the test, thinking about RBIs and ERAs, and it made it much easier. Thanks for the advice."

I tuned into their conversation for a moment, despite the tedium of its content: Statistics exam? Sports analogies? When were Claire and Jamie able to spend time together and study for a statistics exam?

"So, does that mean you'll be enrolled in the more advanced class this semester?" Claire asked with anticipation.

"It does, yeah."

She gave Jamie a high five followed by a congratulatory hug, and I dropped my slice of pizza.

"You two been spending some time together, have you?" I asked, eyebrows raised.

They both looked to each other like guilty children before responding, "Yeah," in unison.

"And when did this happy event take place?" Again, I was beginning to feel the telltale signs that something was amiss between the two of them, and I was not happy about it.

"When Mom and Claire started hanging out, I was there sometimes. Claire came to some of my games last year. It's no big deal."

"You told me you simply spoke with my ex-wife on the phone, Claire."

Claire cleared her throat to speak. "Juliette knew you would be upset if we told you that the three of us had been spending time together. She thought it best that we keep it to ourselves. We didn't want to disrespect her wishes." She flashed a sly smile.

"I'm not upset," I lied. "I'm glad to hear you've become so close." I picked up my pizza and looked away, indicating to them both that the conversation was over and their subterfuge was not appreciated.

"A family spends time together, Peter," Claire said, expressionless.

"And *my* family doesn't lie to each other and do things behind each other's backs," I said forcefully, looking into their unblinking eyes.

"Well, then I guess there's a *lot* we'll need to talk about." Claire smirked at me knowingly.

NOW

Instead of barging in as usual, I knock gently on Sinan's door. I hear him approach and pull the door open. He looks rested, back to himself. His hair is coiffed perfectly, and he performs his routine bow with extra flourish. He presses a fresh cigarette between his lips and ushers me inside.

"I'm glad you're here," he says.

"This might be my last time here, Sinan," I inform him. "Whatever happens, I'm not going to come back to Rhodes & Caine."

"No more Marcus Rhodes, no more Peter Caine." He sighs. "How shall I maintain the glory of years past?"

"I'm sure you'll find a way." I speak gently and kindly. "I will do what needs to be done to get your name where it belongs."

Sinan doesn't respond, instead just smiles respectfully. The relationship is forever changed. I look around, taking in my surroundings like a dying man. I feel a sadness swell inside.

Sinan watches me contemplatively. "I need to tell you something important."

"What is it?" I ask, almost too defeated to care.

"They've issued a warrant for your arrest in the murder of Charlotte Doyle." Sinan lays out the truth in a genteel manner only he could achieve. "There's no telling when it will be served, but it has been issued. My connection at One Police Plaza told me. Harrison Doyle himself petitioned the court early this morning." He reaches his hand to me and delicately pats my shoulder. We sit in a heavy silence, separately pondering what's to come. Sinan with an air of confidence as usual, and me shrouded in defeat. I suck in a deep breath and get to my feet.

"I didn't kill Charlie, Sinan." My voice is small but strong.

"And that's what I intend to prove. I will be there if they bring you in, or we can talk about voluntary surrender." Sinan stands to walk me to the door.

"There's only one thing that could save me now," I say. "I'm waiting for Rick to send me something."

"Rick Friedberg?" Sinan asks, intrigued.

"Yeah, he's out of town and it's difficult to reach him, but he's supposed to send me something Juliette left before she died. Told him to unseal the envelope in the event that something happens to me."

"'Something happens'? Did she say anything more? Something happens like you're accused of murder?" His face illuminates with hope that maybe this will be a break in my defense. He starts rifling through a pile of mail on his desk.

"She just said if something happens to me."

"I got something this morning, I didn't think anything of it, but it's from Rick Friedberg's office. I had no idea it was about you." Sinan pulls the large envelope from the tray on his desk and tears it open with a letter opener.

"What is it?" My breath is caught in my throat and my palms are sweating.

"It's a letter." He's scanning the page quickly, and I can't read the words. "A letter from Juliette, dated just before she died." He quickly reads over the words. Then, with wide eyes and a slack jaw, he hands the paper to me. "It's a confession," he says.

"A *what*? Confession of what?" I snatch the paper away from Sinan and try to read the words as quickly as I can.

"It's a murder confession," he says, dazed.

"Huh? Juliette was dead before Charlie was killed. That makes no sense. It couldn't have been Juliette. Oh, my *God*, it's *Juliette* who's framing me? *She* had Charlie killed?" I can't read fast enough to see what she's said in her letter.

"She's not confessing to *Charlie's* murder." Sinan steps away and stumbles against his desk. "She's confessing to *Marcus's*."

I slow down and look at each word she's written. Tera's disease. Liver poisoning. Bottles of gin. Juliette wrote in her note that she had been slowly poisoning Marcus for years, imagining the world would be better off without him and knowing he was the one who ruined me. She started after Jamie was born, making sure Marcus couldn't have an effect on him. "She killed him?"

"And she killed herself, Peter," Sinan says, pointing to the piece of paper.

Stunned, I keep reading to see that she finishes the letter by confessing that she couldn't live with what she'd done, so she poisoned herself, too. She left no apology, only explanation, and signed her name at the end.

"Why the hell would she leave this with Rick and say to open it in case *I* was in trouble? This has nothing to do with me." I am so racked with exhaustion and confusion that this letter isn't making any sense.

"Because it looks like *you* killed them, Peter. That's exactly what I thought. She left it in case you were accused of *their* murders. She's protecting you," Sinan says, expelling a smoky sigh. His hope extinguishes as quickly as it appeared. "Lovely of her, but this doesn't do anything for us in the case of Charlotte Doyle's murder."

"I'm not crazy, Sinan. I'm not a psychopath. I didn't kill *anyone*. This proves it—this letter shows that I *can't* kill someone, I wouldn't do it! People are dying around me, but I'm not killing them!" The panic is rising inside of me as I see the last hopes I held in Juliette's letter fading away.

Sinan is calm and breathes deeply to help me slow down. He takes the letter from my hand and looks me squarely in the face.

I gaze back at him with tranquil defeated eyes. I'm crushed under the weight of the mounting evidence against me.

He squeezes my shoulder and gently pushes me out the door. "You call me the minute they come for you," he says as I slip out into the hall.

I walk slowly home, looking over my shoulder at every crosswalk, afraid the press or the cops will jump me in the street. I inhale deeply as I pass Balthazar, trying to capture the smell of the bread. The autumn weather, without humidity or density, illuminates the city with high definition. Everything looks crisper, sharper and more detailed. I feel the blood coursing through my veins and pulsing in my burned fingertips.

Sinan's words finally permeate, and I prepare myself to break the news to my family. This is the storm I knew was approaching. I have seen Harrison toil behind the scenes in decades past, gathering information and biding his time until he was bursting with evidence insurmountable to the unprotected accused. I abhor the idea that I will now find myself in the role of defendant.

Vulnerable and powerless, I ascend the steps of my brownstone. Jamie is ensconced in his room. Claire is curled up under a blanket in the living room, flipping through design magazines. I take her by the hand and lead her to the round table in the kitchen, the de facto situation room. She can see immediately that something isn't right.

"Sit down, I need to talk to you."

"Oh, my God, it's happening, isn't it?" Her hands fly to her face as the tears begin to stream.

"A warrant for my arrest has been issued." I take her hands in mine. "It doesn't necessarily mean anything. Sinan has a flawless record, and I'm innocent. We will find our way out of this." I stroke her hand and speak softly.

"We have to tell Jamie," she sobs.

"We will. I wanted to tell you first, so you could have a minute to process and then we can tell Jamie together, okay?"

Claire nods, too choked up to speak.

"Breathe, Claire. It's going to be okay. Everything is going to work out. Breathe." My voice is soothing and gentle.

"When will they come for you? Will they come here?" Claire blows her nose and struggles to return to her normal voice.

"Depends on Harrison. He could make this a spectacle, or he could keep a lid on it for the sake of his image. So close to the election, I imagine he'll be discreet. Can't afford to rub anyone the wrong way."

"So, it will happen before the election, you think?"

"They issued the warrant today, Claire. It's going to happen before the weekend. It may happen tonight."

Claire drops her head and shoots out a wounded cry. I scoot my chair against hers and rock her back and forth.

"The sooner it happens, the sooner we can get it over with, Claire. It's going to be okay." I hold her until her sobs quiet and she regains composure.

"Would it look better if you turned yourself in?"

"Voluntary surrender? I thought about it. I have nothing to hide, and I won't resist when they come for me."

"Let's tell Jamie now—I feel like we're lying to him, having this conversation just the two of us."

"Okay, if that's what you want, that's fine." I call Jamie and invite him down to talk. I sit back down next to Claire, hold her hands and wait for Jamie to appear in the doorway.

We hear his loud teenage footsteps and compose ourselves. He walks into the kitchen, the air thick with tension, and sits down with a frightened look on his face.

"What happened?" he asks, skipping any formalities.

"A judge has issued a warrant for my arrest," I report stoically.

"Shit." Jamie's jaw falls, and he immediately turns to Claire for comfort. "When are they coming?"

"I can't say for sure, but probably soon. Cops usually come in the wee hours of the morning. They call it the time of least resistance. Less likelihood of a struggle."

"Are you gonna run?" Jamie asks, scrambling for words.

"No, Jamie. I'm going to fight in court like a civilized human being." My voice returns to authoritative and firm.

"So, this may be our last night together for a little while," Claire says. "I'm going to make something special for us. My mom used to make chicken and rice when we were little, and it always made me feel comforted and warm. I think that's what we need now." Claire stands up from the table and rifles in the pantry for the ingredients she needs.

Jamie and I sit at the table together. Just as we've gotten used to being in each other's presence, we have to wrap our minds around losing it. Words are insufficient, so we sit in silence and watch as Claire prepares the simple meal.

Jamie sets the table while I survey my family, and we sit and eat in relative silence, periodically looking up at one another. No one can find the right words to say. Each one of us nervously eyes the clock, watching the seconds tick by, knowing we have few hours left together.

As the sky starts to brighten at the edges, Claire's eyes become heavy, and she struggles to stay awake. "Boys, I'm going to bed. I hope they don't come for you before I wake up, but if anything happens, you wake me immediately, okay?"

"I'm just going to stay up and talk with Jamie for a while, man to man. We'll have a couple of beers, and then I'm putting us both to bed."

I look at Jamie across the table and extend my beer for a toast. "This isn't your fault, you know. I was hard on you when you told me about the cops. I just want you to know your rights. You never have to talk to cops. Always call your lawyer."

"Thanks, Dad. So, what's really going to happen to you?" Jamie asks. "I know you didn't want to say anything to frighten Claire." He takes a long pull from his beer bottle.

"Well, they're going to come arrest me."

"And then what happens?"

I shrug my shoulders. "Then they search. They're not going to find anything, because there's nothing here, and then Sinan and I start the fight."

"They're not going to find anything?" Jamie presses.

"No, there's nothing in this house that has anything to do with Charlie Doyle."

"You sure about that?" Jamie sets down his beer and the room turns cold.

"What do you mean?"

"Are you *quite* sure there's nothing in this house that will implicate you?" I don't recognize his tone, but it throws me off my train of thought.

"Implicate *me*?"

"Well, I imagine they'll find one cuff link in your closet. A gold one, from Tiffany's." He glares at me with inhuman terrifying eyes and his lips curl at the corners.

My heart skips a beat as I look into a face I've never seen before. "What cuff link?"

"One of the cuff links my mother bought you, that you lent me to wear to her benefit when you were dancing with that whore. The other one is probably in an evidence bag by now."

My breathing gets shallow.

"I imagine you're missing a tuxedo, aren't you? Something that could be described as a 'special suit'?" Jamie speaks through gritted teeth and tightens his grip on his beer.

I try to scoot my chair away from the table but find my legs are rubbery.

"Where did you even get the idea that Ethan Doyle was involved? I thought you were some brilliant lawyer? Ethan had nothing to do with this, *Peter*."

I'm getting dizzy, watching the pieces of evidence from the police report spin in front of me like fireflies.

"That congressman really screwed you, huh?" Jamie laughs and takes another long sip of beer. "I wasn't exactly sure how to frame you, and then he and Harrison practically did it for me."

I scramble for words, motionless. "It was you?" I squeak.

"And then you screwed yourself even worse. You burned your fingers? Who picks melted glass out of a fireplace? Looks like you're trying to burn off your fingerprints. Good luck explaining that away. And the adoption papers?" He laughs a sick cackle. "You're going to jail, I'm your only heir and Claire has legal custody now. Good thinking, Peter."

"It was you?" I say again, unable to grasp the reality that's crashing down upon me.

"Was it me? Was it me who went to see that whore? Who gave her what she deserved?" Jamie slurps another sip of beer and continues, "Was it me who convinced her to open the door by pretending to be *you*? I put on your stupid horned mask from that party with her slutty lip marks in the corner. She didn't even think twice. I buzzed the door and imitated your *asshole* voice. I told her to take off her clothes and answer the door. She didn't even hesitate, like the prostitute she was, and when I told her to close her eyes when she opened the door? No protest. I wore your cologne and she had no idea."

I sit paralyzed, entranced by Jamie's words.

"You were in bed. You couldn't *wait* to get away from me after dinner and a movie. Just three and a half hours of your time was too much to give to your only son. I knew you would never come out of your room. You didn't want to see me, you *never* wanted to see me. Just *Charlie*. You didn't even want to see Mom, only *Charlie*."

"Jamie, I—"

"Shut up, Peter. Don't you want to know? Don't you want to know what happened? She just lay there. She didn't say a fucking word. She just lay there and accepted her fate. It must have taken her five minutes with her eyes open to realize I wasn't you. So, I told her. I told her what she did to me, what she did to my mother. Mom never got over what you two did to her, you know that?" He throws the rest of the beer down his throat and slams the empty bottle against the table.

"She suffered every single day. You broke her. You took the brightest star in the galaxy and you smashed her into the ground. *You're* the reason she's dead. She killed herself,

Peter. The same way she killed her father. Poisoning. Slow deliberate poisoning. You and your slut led her to suicide. She never would have died if it weren't for the two of *you*." His green eyes turn dark, and he looms over the table. "You think you're going to get away with it? You think they'll find you innocent?"

"Jamie, I didn't do anything," I protest.

"They're not going to believe that when they find *Charlie's* underwear behind a brick in your fireplace." Jamie's face contorts into an awful scowl. "When they go looking for that broken glass you told them they'd find? They'll see a loose brick. A perfect hiding place for a trophy."

"Jesus, Jamie." My mouth goes dry and I struggle to hold myself together.

"I *hate* you, Peter."

"Don't do this, please."

"It's already done, *Peter*. You orchestrated your own demise. I couldn't have *written* it better myself. First Stu Bogovian signs your death certificate, and then *you're* the one who pisses off the district attorney so badly that he won't rest until you're crucified," Jamie cries, a sickly smile plastered to his face. He reaches across the table and picks up my beer. "I'm not the one who was so fucking narcissistic that I had to hold a press conference. You put the nail in your own coffin." Jamie takes a long swig of my beer and stares deeply into my face.

"I haven't done anything wrong, please."

"Well, all your lawyers and all your arguments can't save you now. Sit back, accept your fate. I'm the only one who knows where you were that night, and I'm never going to tell. And Claire? She likes me better than you, Peter. Who do you think gave me that stupid paper-clip thing you made? That night at Mezzaluna? She's just going to usher me away to safety, so we don't have to suffer anymore. And you know it."

He cracks his knuckles and stares at me. "Careful what you say now. Don't piss me off. Maybe I'll tell them you poisoned Marcus and Mom, too. I'm the only one who knows what she did. She left a note for me, Peter, explaining the whole thing. You broke her, and she never recovered."

"I have the note, too, Jamie," I tentatively speak.

"That's what *you* think. But I know, and you know, and even her *lawyer* Rick knows that you forge Mom's signature. I'll just tell them that *you* wrote that fake confession, Peter. You wrote it, and you signed Mom's signature like you always did." He switched to a shaky, desperate voice, emulating what he would say to the police.

I look at Jamie in a way I never have before and realize that I've never known this person. The stories Juliette told me—she must have doctored them the same way she doctored the stories she told Jamie about me. He isn't a perfect young man, unscathed by his father's abandonment, unaffected by his genetic lottery, no. He isn't a lucky one who escaped the monster within.

My life catches in my throat as I try to search for redemptive words. My mistakes hang like a fog around me and I realize I'm too late. Reality descends, and my neck prickles with cold sweat while the sun peeks through the kitchen window.

I hear a slamming at the front door.

When the officers scream, "Police," a wide smile spreads across Jamie's face.

I stand to run to the door, hoping against all odds that the police have been surveilling the house and heard what Jamie just said to me. I stop dead in my tracks when I see Claire standing in the doorway, leaning against the frame, awake and fully dressed.

"Well, Peter," she says, holding something in her hand.

"Claire." I stumble backward and grab onto a chair for support.

"I can't believe what I've just heard," she cries in singsong, holding her hand to her chest. "You've just confessed to the murder of Charlotte Doyle? In the wee hours of the morning, you admitted to your only son that you killed your ex-lover? That she was becoming a liability to you now that you've 'turned your life around'? Wow, Peter. That's very big of you, finally admitting the truth."

"Claire, I didn't kill Charlie." I can't breathe. The disbelief is choking me.

"Sure you did." She pulls a piece of paper from the envelope in her hand. "You know who would kill his ex-lover? A sociopath. And you know what this says here?" She runs her fingers along a page. "Says here that a psychiatrist told your ex-wife you're a sociopath, and you're dangerous, and she should be really careful leaving Jamie alone with you." Claire mocks me with a fake look of concern. "Shouldn't have brought me to therapy, Peter. Kimball was all too happy to write this letter. Sounds like you'll have some trouble keeping custody after all this. Good thing I signed those adoption papers."

The police slam on the front door, repeatedly stating their purpose and calling my name.

"You knew about this?" I ask Claire.

"*Knew* about it?" she says, shooting Jamie a triumphant smirk. "Yeah, you could say I knew about it."

"Claire told you we were close, Peter. You just didn't listen." Jamie has resumed his seat and leans back to watch as I pay for my sins. "Or should I call you George?"

"That is your *real* name, isn't it?" Claire asks. "George Abelman? From Burlington, Vermont? Yeah, there's a letter from your 'mother' sitting at the Rhodes Foundation. People know you're not who you say you are. Fake name, fake life... Sounds like a murderer to me."

"I didn't hurt anyone. Why are you doing this?"

"You didn't *hurt* anyone? You cheated on me! Just like my father cheated on my mother. You treated me like garbage." Claire throws the papers onto the kitchen table and takes a seat beside Jamie. "You treated your *son* like garbage. This is what you do to people. So now, this is what's being done to you. You're going to pay for what you've done, like my father never did."

"I almost didn't go through with it at one point. Thought maybe you'd really changed," Jamie says, and then he shrugs. "But I already had the tuxedo, I had the cuff links, the plan was in place."

"I don't understand." I can see the lights from the police cars reflecting against the kitchen walls.

"Of course you do. You deserve this," Claire snarls. "You spent your life tirelessly defending the indefensible and letting innocent people get destroyed. Well, now it's your turn."

"The police are here, Dad." Jamie's voice cracks and breaks as he puts on a mask to perform for the cops at the door.

"Oh, Peter." Claire forces a tear from her eye, and the two of them huddle together, ever the perfect family picture. She throws one last glare my way before stumbling to the front door and ushering the police inside.

Lou and Rodrigo walk slowly into the kitchen, Lou wielding the arrest warrant and Rodrigo opening up his cuffs.

"Gotta take you in, Mr. Caine. Hands behind your back, please." Rodrigo cuffs me as a uniformed officer reads my Miranda rights.

The early-morning sun is crashing through the kitchen windows and making it hard for me to see. Everything is a mess of light and dust. As I am walked from the kitchen to the front door, I watch the possibility of a different life fall down the stairs in front of me. I descend into the under-standing that this is the fate I deserve, and I have no one to blame but myself.

Everyone you think you know becomes someone else if you just look close enough.

Even you.

★ ★ ★ ★ ★

ACKNOWLEDGMENTS

Thank you to Marian, Liz, Natalie, Erika, Emer, Shara, Linette, Randy, Clio, Lily, Lucy and the rest of the talented and tireless teams at Park Row Books, Harlequin, HarperCollins and HQ. Thank you for your guidance, your efforts and your skills. It has been a wild and wonderful ride going on this adventure with all of you.

Infinite thanks to my brother for shaping this book through your professional opinion, expertise and advice. Peter, Marcus, Harrison and Rick never could have come to fruition without you. Thank you for answering calls and texts at stupid hours and for a lifetime of support and encouragement. Thank you for being a voice of reason and a shelter from the storms. And of course, for the Metallica concert.

Thank you to my parents for your excitement, your reinforcement and your beaming pride.

To my family in New York, Greece, Sweden and Ireland, thank you for your advocacy and support. I feel like I'm backed by an international army of ambassadors because of you.

Thank you to my husband, the light that guides me home. Thank you for taking a million additional roles so I would have the time and space to focus on this book. I adore you.

And endlessly, thank you to M, the glue that holds it all together.